The JUNIOR CLASSICS

VOLUME ONE • FAIRY TALES AND FABLES

L. Leslie Brooke

"Somebody has been sitting in my chair, and has sat the bottom out of it!"

[See page 7]

The JUNIOR CLASSICS

Edited by MABEL WILLIAMS *and* MARCIA DALPHIN.

With Introduction by WILLIAM ALLAN NEILSON, *Former President of Smith College; Introduction to First Edition by* CHARLES W. ELIOT, *Former President of Harvard University*

Popular Edition

ILLUSTRATED

VOLUME
ONE

FAIRY TALES
AND FABLES

P. F. COLLIER & SON CORPORATION

Introduction

By *WILLIAM ALLAN NEILSON, LL.D., Litt.D.*

Former President of Smith College

T HE editors of this collection of literature for young people have had much experience and have acquired an intimate knowledge of the needs and tastes of their special public. The greater part of the selections are the classics of their kind, stories and poems which have enchanted children for many generations, in some cases for many centuries. To these have been added carefully chosen examples of those writers of our own time who have been most successful in the difficult and delicate art of writing for children. Still other selections belong to the great simple things which because they deal with certain permanent and fundamental elements in our common nature are the exclusive possession of no age, but appeal to young and old alike.

It is no mere accident that by far the greater part of this literature is fiction. The world of children is a world of imagination. Their contact with fact has not been long enough nor intimate enough to give them that critical sense of the actual and possible that restricts the horizons of their elders. Their world is so full of the unexplained and the mysterious that they have not yet acquired the habit of testing every story by experience. Thus naturally and without effort they surrender themselves to the flow of the narrative as long as it holds their interest by suspense or wonder or surprise. Those older people who enjoy romantic writing often do so because it affords an escape and a relief from the unpleasant or harassing things that beset them in their everyday life. But children need no such escape. The shades of the prison house have not yet closed upon them and the world of imagination is their own domain. It is good that they should roam in it as widely and as late as possible, since what we call the real world will seize them all too soon.

There are theorists who are troubled about the imaginativeness of children and who fear the effect of fairy tales upon their characters. They make a stupid confusion between fiction and falsehood. They punish their children for romancing because they think they are lying, not realizing that the tests of truth in the world of the grown-up are not applicable in the child's natural world of make-believe.

So far from the exercise of the imagination constituting a moral danger, it is perhaps the most important discipline leading to right relations among people. For most unkindness and injustice and cruelty and intolerance are the result of an inability to put one's self in the other man's place. These are the vices that poison our society and ruin our peace, and their roots are in the weakness of our imaginations. Thus it is fundamental for ethical as well as aesthetic development that the imagination should be given wide scope in youth and kept free and flexible as long as possible.

The stories from real life, from history, biography, and adventure, deal for the most part with the heroic virtues. This, too, is a wise choice; for the normal child gives his admiration generously to courage and strength and self-sacrifice. Nothing is more important in the growth of a child than the direction of his admirations. All children are imitative, and they tend to imitate what impresses them. The spectacle of power is always impressive; and these tales of pioneers and explorers, with their feats of daring and endurance, do much to form the ideals of young people, ideals which often determine the level on which they will live their lives.

But all this is to put too much stress on the moral side. The fact that should be uppermost when we read these things with our children is that they are delightful; the important thing is that we should enjoy them together. A mere glance over the contents of these volumes will reveal an extraordinary range and variety, scores of old favorites of which they never grow tired. For one of the superiorities of children over adults is that they have so much greater a capacity for rereading, that their appetites are not easily jaded. In these books they have a treasure that will last a whole childhood.

No detailed attempt is made to classify the contents according to the age of the readers, though, roughly speaking, the easier things come first. For children are very varied in their rate of development, and what one child enjoys at six another does not reach till ten. Nor is it important that to be enjoyable a tale or a poem has to be entirely understood. The reader's power grows by contact with words and ideas that may be not merely unfamiliar but only partly intelligible. What matters is that he be given material of such quality that greater familiarity means greater enjoyment.

Great pains have been taken with the illustrations in these volumes. Many artists have been drawn upon: some are the old favorites with whom we cannot dispense, others are contemporaries who have shown power to enter with sympathy into the spirit of the text. Their work, whether in color or in black-and-white, helps to give gaiety and life to the volumes, and to make to their young readers the scenes and characters more vivid and arresting.

I congratulate the boy or girl whose childhood is enriched by intimacy with the contents of these volumes.

Introduction to First Edition

By DR. CHARLES W. ELIOT

Former President of Harvard University

THE purpose of *The Junior Classics* is to provide, in ten volumes containing about four thousand pages, a classified collection of tales, stories, and poems, both ancient and modern, suitable for boys and girls of from six to sixteen years of age. Thoughtful parents and teachers, who realize the evils of indiscriminate reading on the part of children, will appreciate the educational value of such a collection. A child's taste in reading is formed, as a rule, in the first ten or twelve years of its life, and experience has shown that the childish mind will prefer good literature to any other, if access to it is made easy, and will develop far better on literature of proved merit than on trivial or transitory material.

The boy or girl who becomes familiar with the charming tales and poems in this collection will have gained a knowledge of literature and history that will be of high value in other school and home work. Here are the real elements of imaginative narration, poetry, and ethics, which should enter into the education of every English-speaking child.

This collection, carefully used by parents and teachers with due reference to individual tastes and needs, will make many children enjoy good literature. It will inspire them with a love of good reading, which is the best possible result of any elementary education. The child himself should be encouraged to make his own selections from this large and varied collection, the child's enjoyment being the object in view. A real and lasting interest in literature or in scholarship is only to be developed through the individual's enjoyment of his mental occupations.

The most important change which has been made in American schools and colleges within my memory is the substitution of leading for driving, of inspiration for drill, of personal interest and love of work for compulsion and fear. The schools are learning to use methods and materials which interest and attract the children themselves. *The Junior Classics* will put into the home the means of using this happy method.

Committing to memory beautiful pieces of literature, either prose or poetry, for recitation before a friendly audience, acting charades or plays, and reading aloud with vivacity and sympathetic emotion, are good means of instruction at home or at school. This collection contains numerous admirable pieces of literature for such use. In teaching English and English literature we should place more reliance upon processes and acts which awaken emotion, stimulate interest, prove to be enjoyable for the actors, and result in giving children the power of entertaining people, of blessing others with noble pleasures which the children create and share.

From the home training during childhood there should result in the child a taste for interesting and improving reading which will direct and inspire its subsequent intellectual life. The training which results in this taste for good reading, however unsystematic or eccentric it may have been, has achieved one principal aim of education; and any school or home training which does not result in implanting this permanent taste has failed in a very important respect. Guided and animated by this impulse to acquire knowledge and exercise the imagination through good reading, the adult will continue to educate himself through life.

The story of the human race through all its slow development should be gradually conveyed to the child's mind from the time he begins to read, or to listen to his mother reading; and with description of facts and actual events should be mingled charming and uplifting products of the imagination. To try to feed the minds of children upon facts alone is undesirable and unwise. The immense product of the imagination in art and literature is a concrete fact with which every educated human being should be made somewhat familiar, that product being a very real part of every individual's actual environment.

While the majority of the tales and poems are intended for children who have begun to do their own reading, there will be found in every volume selections fit for reading aloud to younger children. Throughout the collection the authors tell the stories in their own words; so that the salt which gave them savor is preserved.

The Junior Classics constitute a set of books whose contents will delight children and at the same time satisfy the legitimate ethical requirements of those who have the children's best interests at heart.

Charles W. Eliot

CONTENTS

TALES FROM ENGLAND

xi

CONTENTS

CONTENTS

xiii

CONTENTS

CONTENTS

(The sources of the stories in this volume will be found listed on page 357.)

THE EDITORS OF
THE JUNIOR CLASSICS

———

MABEL WILLIAMS

Mabel Williams is a librarian, Superintendent of Work with Schools, in The New York Public Library. Her work has brought her in contact with many boys and girls of varying ages and interests. She knows the books they enjoy and through this first-hand knowledge has been able to make selections for The Junior Classics. She is nationally known in the library and educational world, for she lectures in different parts of the country to professional and to lay groups on literature for the young.

MARCIA DALPHIN

Marcia Dalphin is the Librarian of the Rye Free Reading Room, the public library of Rye, New York. She was formerly engaged in library work with children in New York City. In her present position as head of a library located in a suburban community, she has the opportunity of working directly with boys and girls and has continued to take a special interest in the reading of young children and in the literature for them. She has contributed many articles on children's books to the literary reviews.

L. Leslie Brooke

She sent them out to seek their fortune.

[See page 1]

Tales From England

THE THREE LITTLE PIGS

Illustrations by L. LESLIE BROOKE

ONCE upon a time there was an old Sow with three little
Pigs, and as she had not enough to keep them, she sent
them out to seek their fortune.

The first that went off met a Man with a bundle of straw, and
said to him, "Please, Man, give me that straw to build me a house";
which the Man did, and the little Pig built a house with it. Presently
came along a Wolf, and knocked at the door, and said, "Little Pig,
little Pig, let me come in."

To which the Pig answered, "No, no, by the hair of my chinny
chin chin."

"Then I'll huff and I'll puff, and I'll blow your house in!" said
the Wolf. So he huffed and he puffed, and he blew his house in,
and ate up the little Pig.

The second Pig met a Man with a bundle of furze, and said,
"Please, Man, give me that furze to build a house"; which the Man
did, and the Pig built his house. Then along came the Wolf and
said, "Little Pig, little Pig, let me come in."

"No, no, by the hair of my chinny chin chin."

"Then I'll puff and I'll huff, and I'll blow your house in!" So he
huffed and he puffed, and he puffed and he huffed, and at last he
blew the house down, and ate up the second little Pig.

The third little Pig met a Man with a load of bricks, and said,
"Please, Man, give me those bricks to build a house with"; so the
Man gave him the bricks, and he built his house with them. So the
Wolf came, as he did to the other little Pigs, and said, "Little Pig,
little Pig, let me come in."

"No, no, by the hair of my chinny chin chin."

"Then I'll huff and I'll puff, and I'll blow your house in."

Well, he huffed and he puffed, and he huffed and he puffed, and he puffed and he huffed; but he could *not* get the house down. When he found that he could not, with all his huffing and puffing, blow the house down, he said, "Little Pig, I know where there is a nice field of turnips."

"Where?" said the little Pig.

"Oh, in Mr. Smith's home field; and if you will be ready tomorrow morning, I will call for you, and we will go together and get some for dinner."

"Very well," said the Little Pig, "I will be ready. What time do you mean to go?"

"Oh, at six o'clock."

Well, the little Pig got up at five, and got the turnips and was home again before six. When the Wolf came he said, "Little Pig, are you ready?"

"Ready!" said the little Pig. "I have been and come back again, and got a nice potful for dinner."

The Wolf felt very angry at this, but thought that he would be *up to* the little Pig somehow or other; so he said, "Little Pig, I know where there is a nice apple tree."

"Where?" said the Pig.

"Down at Merry-Garden," replied the Wolf; "and if you will not deceive me, I will come for you, at five o'clock tomorrow, and we will go together and get some apples."

Well, the little Pig woke at four the next morning, and bustled up, and went off for the apples, hoping to get back before the Wolf came; but he had farther to go, and had to climb the tree, so that just as he was coming down from it, he saw the Wolf coming, which, as you may suppose, frightened him very much. When the Wolf came up he said:

"Little Pig, what! are you here before me? Are they nice apples?"

"Yes, very," said the little Pig; "I will throw you down one." And he threw it so far that, while the Wolf was gone to pick it up, the little Pig jumped down and ran home.

The next day the Wolf came again, and said to the little Pig, "Little Pig, there is a Fair in the Town this afternoon: will you go?"

"Oh, yes," said the Pig, "I will go; what time shall you be ready?"
"At three," said the Wolf.

So the little Pig went off before the time, as usual, and got to the Fair, and bought a butter churn, and was on his way home with it when he saw the Wolf coming. Then he could not tell what to do. So he got into the churn to hide, and in doing so turned it round, and it began to roll, and rolled down the hill with the Pig inside it, which frightened the Wolf so much that he ran home without going to the Fair.

He went to the little Pig's house, and told him how frightened he had been by a great round thing which came down the hill past him.

Then the little Pig said, "Hah! I frightened you, did I? I had been to the Fair and bought a butter churn, and when I saw you I got into it, and rolled down the hill."

Then the Wolf was very angry indeed, and declared he *would* eat up the little Pig, and that he would get down the chimney after him.

When the little Pig saw what he was about, he hung on the pot full of water, and made up a blazing fire, and, just as the Wolf was coming down, took off the cover of the pot, and in fell the Wolf. And the little Pig put on the cover again in an instant, boiled him up, and ate him for supper, and lived happy ever after.

THE THREE BEARS

Illustrations by L. LESLIE BROOKE

ONCE upon a time there were Three Bears, who lived together in a house of their own, in a wood. One of them was
a Little, Small, Wee Bear; and one was a Middle-sized Bear, and the
other was a Great, Huge Bear. They had each a pot for their
porridge: a little pot for the Little, Small, Wee Bear; and a middle-
sized pot for the Middle Bear, and a great pot for the Great, Huge
Bear. And they had each a chair to sit in: a little chair for the Little,
Small, Wee Bear; and a middle-sized chair for the Middle Bear, and
a great chair for the Great, Huge Bear. And they had each a bed to
sleep in: a little bed for the Little, Small, Wee Bear; and a middle-
sized bed for the Middle Bear, and a great bed for the Great,
Huge Bear.

One day, after they had made the porridge for their breakfast,
and poured it into their porridge-pots, they walked out into the
wood while the porridge was cooling, that they might not burn their
mouths by beginning too soon to eat it. And while they were walking, a little Girl called Goldenlocks came to the house. First she
looked in at the window, and then she peeped in at the keyhole; and
seeing nobody in the house, she turned the handle of the door. The
door was not fastened, because the Bears were good Bears, who did
nobody any harm, and never suspected that anybody would harm
them.

So Goldenlocks opened the door, and went in; and well pleased
she was when she saw the porridge on the table. If she had been a
thoughtful little Girl, she would have waited till the Bears came
home, and then, perhaps, they would have asked her to breakfast;
for they were good Bears—a little rough or so, as the manner of
Bears is, but for all that very good-natured and hospitable.

But the porridge looked tempting, and she set about helping
herself.

So first she tasted the porridge of the Great, Huge Bear, and that was too hot for her. And then she tasted the porridge of the Middle Bear, and that was too cold for her. And then she went to the porridge of the Little, Small, Wee Bear, and tasted that; and that was neither too hot nor too cold, but just right, and she liked it so well that she ate it all up.

Then Goldenlocks sat down in the chair of the Great, Huge Bear,

Till the bottom of the chair came out.

and that was too hard for her. And then she sat down in the chair of the Middle Bear, and that was too soft for her. And then she sat down in the chair of the Little, Small, Wee Bear, and that was neither too hard nor too soft, but just right. So she seated herself in it, and there she sat till the bottom of the chair came out, and down she came plump upon the ground.

Then Goldenlocks went upstairs into the bedchamber in which the three Bears slept. And first she lay down upon the bed of the

Great, Huge Bear, but that was too high at the head for her. And next she lay down upon the bed of the Middle Bear, and that was too high at the foot for her. And then she lay down upon the bed of the Little, Small, Wee Bear; and that was neither too high at the head nor at the foot, but just right. So she covered herself up comfortably, and lay there till she fell fast asleep.

By this time the Three Bears thought their porridge would be cool enough; so they came home to breakfast. Now Goldenlocks had left the spoon of the Great, Huge Bear standing in his porridge.

"SOMEBODY HAS BEEN AT MY PORRIDGE!"

said the Great, Huge Bear, in his great, rough, gruff voice. And when the Middle Bear looked at hers, she saw that the spoon was standing in it, too.

"SOMEBODY HAS BEEN AT MY PORRIDGE!"

said the Middle Bear, in her middle voice. Then the Little, Small, Wee Bear looked at his, and there was the spoon in the porridge-pot, but the porridge was all gone.

"SOMEBODY HAS BEEN AT MY PORRIDGE, AND HAS EATEN IT ALL UP!"

said the Little, Small, Wee Bear, in his little, small, wee voice.

Upon this the Three Bears, seeing that someone had entered their house, and eaten up the Little, Small, Wee Bear's breakfast, began to look about them. Now Goldenlocks had not put the hard cushion straight when she rose from the chair of the Great, Huge Bear.

"SOMEBODY HAS BEEN SITTING IN MY CHAIR!"

said the Great, Huge Bear, in his great, rough, gruff voice.

And Goldenlocks had squatted down the soft cushion of the Middle Bear.

"SOMEBODY HAS BEEN SITTING IN MY CHAIR!"

said the Middle Bear, in her middle voice.

And you know what Goldenlocks had done to the third chair.

"SOMEBODY HAS BEEN SITTING IN MY CHAIR, AND HAS
SAT THE BOTTOM OUT OF IT!"

said the Little, Small, Wee Bear, in his little, small, wee voice.

Then the Three Bears thought it necessary that they should make
further search; so they went upstairs into their bedchamber. Now
Goldenlocks had pulled the pillow of the Great, Huge Bear out of
its place.

Thought it necessary to make further search.

"SOMEBODY HAS BEEN LYING IN MY BED!"

said the Great, Huge Bear, in his great, rough, gruff voice.

And Goldenlocks had pulled the bolster of the Middle Bear out
of its place.

"SOMEBODY HAS BEEN LYING IN MY BED!"

said the Middle Bear, in her middle voice.

And when the Little, Small, Wee Bear came to look at his bed,
there was the bolster in its place; and the pillow in its place upon
the bolster; and upon the pillow was the head of Goldenlocks—
which was not in its place, for she had no business there.

"SOMEBODY HAS BEEN LYING IN MY BED—AND HERE SHE IS!"

said the Little, Small, Wee Bear, in his little, small, wee voice.

Goldenlocks had heard in her sleep the great rough, gruff voice of the Great, Huge Bear, and the middle voice of the Middle Bear, but it was only as if she had heard someone speaking in a dream. But when she heard the little, small, wee voice of the Little, Small,

"Somebody has been lying in my bed—and here she is!"

Wee Bear, it was so sharp, and so shrill, that it awakened her at once. Up she started; and when she saw the Three Bears on one side of the bed, she tumbled herself out at the other, and ran to the window. Now the window was open, because the Bears, like good, tidy Bears, as they were, always opened their bedchamber window when they got up in the morning. Out Goldenlocks jumped, and ran away as fast as she could run—never looking behind her; and what happened to her afterwards I cannot tell. But the Three Bears never saw anything more of her.

THE OLD WOMAN AND HER PIG

By JOSEPH JACOBS

Illustration by JOHN D. BATTEN

AN old woman was sweeping her house, and she found a little crooked sixpence. "What," said she, "shall I do with this little sixpence? I will go to market, and buy a little pig."

As she was coming home, she came to a stile: but the piggy wouldn't go over the stile. She went a little farther, and she met a dog. So she said to him! "Dog! dog! bite pig; piggy won't go over the stile; and I shan't get home tonight." But the dog wouldn't.

She went a little farther, and she met a stick. So she said: "Stick! stick! beat dog! dog won't bite pig; piggy won't get over the stile; and I shan't get home tonight." But the stick wouldn't.

She went a little farther, and she met a fire. So she said: "Fire! fire! burn stick; stick won't beat dog; dog won't bite pig; piggy won't get over the stile; and I shan't get home tonight." But the fire wouldn't. She went a little farther, and she met some water. So she said: "Water! water! quench fire, fire won't burn stick; stick won't beat dog; dog won't bite pig; piggy won't get over the stile; and I shan't get home tonight." But the water wouldn't.

She went a little farther, and she met an ox. So she said: "Ox! ox! drink water; water won't quench fire; fire won't burn stick; stick won't beat dog; dog won't bite pig; piggy won't get over the stile; and I shan't get home tonight." But the ox wouldn't.

She went a little farther, and she met a butcher. So she said: "Butcher! butcher! kill ox; ox won't drink water; water won't quench fire; fire won't burn stick; stick won't beat dog; dog won't bite pig; piggy won't get over the stile; and I shan't get home tonight." But the butcher wouldn't.

She went a little farther, and she met a rope. So she said: "Rope! rope! hang butcher; butcher won't kill ox; ox won't drink water; water won't quench fire; fire won't burn stick; stick won't beat dog; dog won't bite pig; piggy won't get over the stile; and I shan't get home tonight." But the rope wouldn't

She went a little farther, and she met a rat. So she said: "Rat! rat! gnaw rope; rope won't hang butcher; butcher won't kill ox; ox won't drink water; water won't quench fire; fire won't burn stick; stick won't beat dog; dog won't bite pig; piggy won't get over the stile; and I shan't get home tonight." But the rat wouldn't.

She went a little farther, and she met a cat. So she said: "Cat! cat! kill rat; rat won't gnaw rope; rope won't hang butcher; butcher won't kill ox; ox won't drink water; water won't quench fire; fire won't burn stick; stick won't beat dog; dog won't bite pig; piggy won't get over the stile; and I shan't get home tonight." But the cat said to her, "If you will go to yonder cow, and fetch me a saucer of milk, I will kill the rat." So away went the old woman to the cow.

But the cow said to her: "If you will go to yonder haystack, and fetch me a handful of hay, I'll give you the milk." So away went the old woman to the haystack; and she brought the hay to the cow.

As soon as the cow had eaten the hay, she gave the old woman the milk; and away she went with it in a saucer to the cat.

As soon as the cat had lapped up the milk, the cat began to kill the rat; the rat began to gnaw the rope; the rope began to hang the butcher; the butcher began to kill the ox; the ox began to drink the water; the water began to quench the fire; the fire began to burn the stick; the stick began to beat the dog; the dog began to bite the pig; the little pig in a fright jumped over the stile; and so the old woman got home that night.

TOM TIT TOT

By JOSEPH JACOBS

Illustrations by JOHN D. BATTEN

ONCE upon a time there was a woman, and she baked five pies. And when they came out of the oven, they were that over-baked the crusts were too hard to eat. So she says to her daughter: "Darter," says she, "put you them there pies on the shelf, and leave 'em there a little, and they'll come again."—She meant, you know, the crust would get soft.

But the girl, she says to herself: "Well, if they'll come again, I'll eat 'em now." And she set to work and ate 'em all, first and last.

Well, come supper-time the woman said: "Go you and get one o' them there pies. I dare say they've come again now."

The girl went and she looked, and there was nothing but the dishes. So back she came and says she: "Noo, they ain't come again."

"Not one of 'em?" says the mother.

"Not one of 'em," says she.

"Well, come again or not come again," said the woman. "I'll have one for supper."

"But you can't, if they ain't come," said the girl.

"But I can," says she. "Go you, and bring the best of 'em."

"Best or worst," says the girl, "I've ate 'em all, and you can't have one till that's come again."

Well, the woman she was done, and she took her spinning to the door to spin, and as she span she sang:

> "My darter ha' ate five, five pies today.
> My darter ha' ate five, five pies today."

The king was coming down the street, and he heard her sing, but what she sang he couldn't hear, so he stopped and said:

"What was that you were singing, my good woman?"

The woman was ashamed to let him hear what her daughter had been doing, so she sang, instead of that:

"My darter ha' spun five, five skeins today.
My darter ha' spun five, five skeins today."

"Stars o' mine!" said the king. "I never heard tell of anyone that could do that."

Then he said: "Look you here, I want a wife, and I'll marry your daughter. But look you here," says he, "eleven months out of the year she shall have all she likes to eat, and all the gowns she likes to get, and all the company she likes to keep; but the last month of the year she'll have to spin five skeins every day, and if she don't I shall kill her."

"All right," says the woman; for she thought what a grand marriage that was. And as for the five skeins, when the time came, there'd be plenty of ways of getting out of it, and likeliest, he'd have forgotten all about it.

Well, so they were married. And for eleven months the girl had all she liked to eat, and all the gowns she liked to get, and all the company she liked to keep.

But when the time was getting over, she began to think about the skeins and to wonder if he had 'em in mind. But not one word did he say about 'em, and she thought he'd wholly forgotten 'em.

However, the last day of the last month he takes her to a room she'd never set eyes on before. There was nothing in it but a spinning-wheel and a stool. And says he: "Now, my dear, here you'll be shut in tomorrow with some victuals and some flax, and if you haven't spun five skeins by the night, your head'll go off."

And away he went about his business.

Well, she was that frightened, she'd always been such a gatless girl, that she didn't so much as know how to spin, and what was she to do tomorrow with no one to come nigh her to help her? She sat down on a stool in the kitchen, and law! how she did cry!

However, all of a sudden, she heard a sort of a knocking low down on the door. She upped and oped it, and what should she see but a small little black thing with a long tail! That looked up at her right curious, and that said:

"What are you a-crying for?"

"What's that to you?" says she.

"Never you mind," that said, "but tell me what you're a-crying for."

"That won't do me no good if I do," says she.

"You don't know that," that said, and twirled that's tail round.

"Well," says she, "that won't do no harm, if that don't do no good," and she upped and told about the pies, and the skeins, and everything.

"This is what I'll do," says the little black thing; "I'll come to your window every morning and take the flax and bring it spun at night."

"I'll give you three guesses."

"What's your pay?" says she.

That looked out of the corner of that's eyes, and that said: "I'll give you three guesses every night to guess my name, and if you haven't guessed it before the month's up you shall be mine."

Well, she thought she'd be sure to guess that's name before the month was up. "All right," says she, "I agree."

"All right," that says, and law! how that twirled that's tail.

Well, the next day, her husband took her into the room and there was the flax and the day's food.

"Now, there's the flax," says he, "and if that ain't spun up this night, off goes your head." And then he went out and locked the door.

He'd hardly gone, when there was a knocking against the window.

She upped and she oped it, and there sure enough was the little old thing sitting on the ledge.

"Where's the flax?" says he.

"Here it be," says she. And she gave it to him.

Well, come the evening a knocking came again to the window. She upped and she oped it, and there was the little old thing with five skeins of flax on his arm.

"Here it be," says he, and he gave it to her.

"Now, what's my name?" says he.

"What, is that Bill?" says she.

"Noo, that ain't," says he, and he twirled his tail.

"Is that Ned?" says she.

"Noo, that ain't," says he, and he twirled his tail.

"Well, is that Mark?" says she.

"Noo, that ain't," says he, and he twirled his tail harder, and away he flew.

Well, when her husband came in, there were the five skeins ready for him. "I see I shan't have to kill you tonight, my dear," says he; "you'll have your food and your flax in the morning," says he, and away he goes.

Well, every day the flax and the food were brought, and every day that there little black impet used to come mornings and evenings. And all the day the girl sate trying to think of names to say to it when it came at night. But she never hit on the right one. And as it got toward the end of the month, the impet began to look so maliceful, and that twirled that's tail faster and faster each time she gave a guess.

At last it came to the last day but one. The impet came at night along with the five skeins, and that said:

"What, ain't you got my name yet?"

"Is that Nicodemus?" says she.

"Noo, 't ain't," that says.

"Is that Sammle?" says she.

"Noo, 't ain't," that says.

"A-well, is that Methusalem?" says she.

"Noo, 't ain't that neither," that says.

Then that looks at her with that's eyes like a coal o' fire, and that says:

"Woman, there's only tomorrow night, and then you'll be mine!" And away it flew.

Well, she felt that horrid. However, she heard the king coming along the passage. In he came, and when he sees the five skeins, he says, says he:

"Well, my dear," says he. "I don't see but what you'll have your skeins ready tomorrow night as well, and as I reckon I shan't have to kill you, I'll have supper in here tonight." So they brought supper, and another stool for him, and down the two sate.

Well, he hadn't eaten but a mouthful or so, when he stops and begins to laugh.

"What is it?" says she.

"A-why," says he, "I was out a-hunting today, and I got away to a place in the wood I'd never seen before. And there was an old chalk-pit. And I heard a kind of a sort of humming. So I got off my hobby, and I went right quiet to the pit, and I looked down. Well, what should there be but the funniest little black thing you ever set eyes on. And what was that doing, but that had a little spinning-wheel, and that was spinning wonderful fast, and twirling that's tail. And as that span that sang:

> " 'Nimmy nimmy not
> My name's Tom Tit Tot.' "

Well, when the girl heard this, she felt as if she could have jumped out of her skin for joy, but she didn't say a word.

Next day that there little thing looked so maliceful when he came for the flax. And when night came she heard that knocking against the window panes. She oped the window, and that come right in on the ledge. That was grinning from ear to ear, and Oo! that's tail was twirling round so fast.

"What's my name?" that says, as that gave her the skeins.

"Is that Solomon?" she says, pretending to be afeard.

"Noo, 't ain't," that says, and that came farther into the room.

"Well, is that Zebedee?" says she again.

"Noo, 't ain't," says the impet. And then that laughed and twirled that's tail till you couldn't hardly see it.

"Take time, woman," that says; "next guess, and you're mine." And that stretched out that's black hands at her.

Well, she backed a step or two, and she looked at it, and then she laughed out, and says she, pointing her finger at it:

"Nimmy nimmy not
Your name's Tom Tit Tot."

Well, when that heard her, that gave an awful shriek and away that flew into the dark, and she never saw it any more.

MR. MIACCA

Illustration by JOHN D. BATTEN

TOMMY GRIMES was sometimes a good boy, and sometimes a bad boy; and when he was a bad boy, he was a very bad boy. Now his mother used to say to him: "Tommy, Tommy, be a good boy, and don't go out of the street, or else Mr. Miacca will take you." But still when he was a bad boy he would go out of the street; and one day, sure enough, he had scarcely got round the corner, when Mr. Miacca did catch him and popped him into a bag upside down, and took him off to his house.

When Mr. Miacca got Tommy inside, he pulled him out of the bag and sat him down, and felt his arms and legs. "You're rather tough," says he; "but you're all I've got for supper, and you'll not taste bad boiled. But body o' me, I've forgot the herbs, and it's bitter you'll taste without herbs. Sally! Here, I say, Sally!" and he called Mrs. Miacca. So Mrs. Miacca came out of another room and said:

"What d'ye want, my dear?"

"Oh, here's a little boy for supper," said Mr. Miacca, "and I've forgot the herbs. Mind him, will ye, while I go for them."

"All right, my love," says Mrs. Miacca, and off he goes.

Then Tommy Grimes said to Mrs. Miacca: "Does Mr. Miacca always have little boys for supper?"

"Mostly, my dear," said Mrs. Miacca, "if little boys are bad enough, and get in his way."

"And don't you have anything else but boy-meat? No pudding?" asked Tommy.

"Ah, I loves pudding," says Mrs. Miacca. "But it's not often the likes of me gets pudding."

"Why, my mother is making a pudding this very day," said Tommy Grimes, "and I am sure she'd give you some, if I ask her. Shall I run and get some?"

17

"Now, that's a thoughtful boy," said Mrs. Miacca, "only don't be long and be sure to be back for supper."

So off Tommy pelted, and right glad he was to get off so cheap; and for many a long day he was as good as good could be, and never went round the corner of the street. But he couldn't always be good; and one day he went round the corner, and as luck would have it, he hadn't scarcely got round it when Mr. Miacca grabbed him up, popped him in his bag, and took him home.

When he got him there, Mr. Miacca dropped him out; and when he saw him, he said: "Ah, you're the youngster that served me and my missus such a shabby trick, leaving us without any supper. Well, you shan't do it again. I'll watch over you myself. Here, get under the sofa, and I'll set on it and watch the pot boil for you."

So poor Tommy Grimes had to creep under the sofa, and Mr. Miacca sat on it and waited for the pot to boil. And they waited and they waited, but still the pot didn't boil, till at last Mr. Miacca got tired of waiting, and he said: "Here, you under there, I'm not going to wait any longer; put out your leg, and I'll stop your giving us the slip."

So Tommy put out a leg and Mr. Miacca got a chopper, and chopped it off, and pops it in the pot.

Suddenly he calls out: "Sally, my dear, Sally!" and nobody answered. So he went into the next room to look out for Mrs. Miacca, and while he was there, Tommy crept out from under the sofa and ran out of the door. For it was a leg of the sofa that he had put out.

So Tommy Grimes ran home, and he never went round the corner again till he was old enough to go alone.

JACK AND THE BEANSTALK

By JOSEPH JACOBS

T HERE was once upon a time a poor widow who had an only son named Jack, and a cow named Milky-white. And all they had to live on was the milk the cow gave every morning, which they carried to the market and sold. But one morning Milky-white gave no milk, and they didn't know what to do.

"What shall we do, what shall we do?" said the widow, wringing her hands.

"Cheer up, mother, I'll go and get work somewhere," said Jack.

"We've tried that before, and nobody would take you," said his mother; "we must sell Milky-white and with the money start shop, or something."

"All right, mother," says Jack; "it's market-day today, and I'll soon sell Milky-white, and then we'll see what we can do."

So he took the cow's halter in his hand, and off he started. He hadn't gone far when he met a funny-looking old man, who said to him: "Good morning, Jack."

"Good morning to you," said Jack, and wondered how he knew his name.

"Well, Jack, and where are you off to?" said the man.

"I'm going to market to sell our cow here."

"Oh, you look the proper sort of chap to sell cows," said the man; "I wonder if you know how many beans make five."

"Two in each hand and one in your mouth," says Jack, as sharp as a needle.

"Right you are," says the man, "and here they are, the very beans themselves," he went on, pulling out of his pocket a number of strange-looking beans. "As you are so sharp," says he, "I don't mind doing a swop with you—your cow for these beans."

"Go along," says Jack; "wouldn't you like it!"

"Ah! you don't know what these beans are," said the man; "if you plant them over-night, by morning they grow right up to the sky."

"Really?" said Jack. "You don't say so!"

"Yes, that is so, and if it doesn't turn out to be true you can have your cow back."

"Right," says Jack, and hands him over Milky-white's halter and pockets the beans.

Back goes Jack home, and as he hadn't gone very far it wasn't dusk by the time he got to his door.

"Back already, Jack?" said his mother. "I see you haven't got Milky-white, so you've sold her. How much did you get for her?"

"You'll never guess, mother," says Jack.

"No, you don't say so. Good boy! Five pounds, ten, fifteen, no, it can't be twenty."

"I told you you couldn't guess. What do you say to these beans; they're magical, plant them over-night and——"

"What!" says Jack's mother. "Have you been such a fool, such a dolt, such an idiot, as to give away my Milky-white, the best milker in the parish, and prime beef to boot, for a set of paltry beans? Take that! Take that! Take that! And as for your precious beans here they go out of the window. And now off with you to bed. Not a sup shall you drink, and not a bit shall you swallow this very night."

So Jack went upstairs to his little room in the attic, and sad and sorry he was, to be sure, as much for his mother's sake, as for the loss of his supper.

At last he dropped off to sleep.

When he woke up, the room looked so funny. The sun was shining into part of it, and yet all the rest was quite dark and shady. So Jack jumped up and dressed himself and went to the window. And what do you think he saw? Why, the beans his mother had thrown out of the window into the garden had sprung up into a big beanstalk which went up and up and up till it reached the sky. So the man spoke truth after all.

The beanstalk grew up quite close past Jack's window, so all he had to do was to open it and give a jump on to the beanstalk which ran up just like a big ladder. So Jack climbed, and he climbed and he climbed and he climbed and he climbed and he climbed and he climbed till at last he reached the sky. And when he got there he found a long broad road going as straight as a dart. So he walked along and he walked along and he walked along till he came to a great big tall house. On the doorstep was a great big tall woman.

"Good morning, mum," says Jack, quite polite-like. "Could you be so kind as to give me some breakfast?" For he hadn't had anything to eat, you know, the night before and was as hungry as a hunter.

"It's breakfast you want, is it?" says the great big tall woman. "It's breakfast you'll be if you don't move off from here. My man is an ogre and there's nothing he likes better than boys broiled on toast. You'd better be moving on or he'll soon be coming."

"Oh! please, mum, do give me something to eat, mum. I've had nothing to eat since yesterday morning, really and truly, mum," says Jack. "I may as well be broiled as die of hunger."

Well, the ogre's wife was not half so bad after all. So she took Jack into the kitchen, and gave him a junk of bread and cheese and a jug of milk. But Jack hadn't half finished these when thump! thump! thump! the whole house began to tremble with the noise of someone coming.

"Goodness, gracious me! It's my old man," said the ogre's wife. "What on earth shall I do? Come along quick and jump in here." And she bundled Jack into the oven just as the ogre came in.

He was a big one, to be sure. At his belt he had three calves strung up by the heels, and he unhooked them and threw them down on the table and said: "Here, wife, broil me a couple of these for breakfast. Ah! what's this I smell?

> "Fee-fi-fo-fum,
> I smell the blood of an Englishman,
> Be he alive, or be he dead,
> I'll have his bones to grind by bread."

"Nonsense, dear," said his wife, "you're dreaming. Or perhaps you smell the scraps of that little boy you liked so much for yesterday's dinner. Here, you go and have a wash and tidy up, and by the time you come back your breakfast'll be ready for you."

So off the ogre went, and Jack was just going to jump out of the oven and run away when the woman told him not. "Wait till he's asleep," says she; "he always has a doze after breakfast."

Well, the ogre had his breakfast, and after that he goes to a big chest and takes out of it a couple of bags of gold, and down he sits and counts till at last his head began to nod and he began to snore till the whole house shook again.

Then Jack crept out on tiptoe from his oven, and as he was passing the ogre he took one of the bags of gold under his arm, and off he pelters till he came to the beanstalk, and then he threw down the bag of gold, which, of course, fell into his mother's garden, and then he climbed down and climbed down till at last he got home and told his mother and showed her the gold and said: "Well, mother, wasn't I right about the beans? They are really magical, you see."

So they lived on the bag of gold for some time, but at last they came to the end of it, and Jack made up his mind to try his luck once more up at the top of the beanstalk. So one fine morning he rose up early, and got on to the beanstalk, and he climbed and he climbed and he climbed and he climbed and he climbed and he climbed till at last he came out on to the road again and up to the great big tall house he had been to before. There, sure enough, was the great big tall woman a-standing on the doorstep.

"Good morning, mum," says Jack, as bold as brass, "could you be so good as to give me something to eat?"

"Go away, my boy," said the big tall woman, "or else my man will eat you up for breakfast. But aren't you the youngster who came here once before? Do you know, that very day, my man missed one of his bags of gold."

"That's strange, mum," said Jack. "I dare say I could tell you something about that, but I'm so hungry I can't speak till I've had something to eat."

Well, the big tall woman was so curious that she took him in and gave him something to eat. But he had scarcely begun munching it as slowly as he could when thump! thump! thump! they heard the giant's footstep, and his wife hid Jack away in the oven.

All happened as it did before. In came the ogre as he did before, said: "Fee-fi-fo-fum," and had his breakfast off three broiled oxen. Then he said: "Wife, bring me the hen that lays the golden eggs." So she brought it, and the ogre said: "Lay," and it laid an egg all of gold. And then the ogre began to nod his head, and to snore till the house shook.

Then Jack crept out of the oven on tiptoe and caught hold of the golden hen, and was off before you could say "Jack Robinson." But this time the hen gave a cackle which woke the ogre, and just as Jack got out of the house he heard him calling: "Wife, wife, what have you done with my golden hen?"

And the wife said: "Why, my dear?"

But that was all Jack heard, for he rushed off to the beanstalk and climbed down like a house on fire. And when he got home he showed his mother the wonderful hen, and said "Lay" to it; and it laid a golden egg every time he said "Lay."

Well, Jack was not content, and it wasn't very long before he determined to have another try at his luck up there at the top of the beanstalk. So one fine morning, he rose up early, and got on to the beanstalk, and he climbed and he climbed and he climbed and he climbed till he got to the top. But this time he knew better than to go straight to the ogre's house. And when he got near it, he waited behind a bush till he saw the ogre's wife come out with a pail to get some water, and then he crept into the house and got into the copper. He hadn't been there long when he heard thump! thump! thump as before, and in come the ogre and his wife.

"Fee-fi-fo-fum, I smell the blood of an Englishman," cried out the ogre. "I smell him, wife, I smell him."

"Do you, my dearie?" says the ogre's wife. 'Then, if it's that little rogue that stole your gold and the hen that laid the golden eggs he's sure to have got into the oven." And they both rushed to the oven. But Jack wasn't there, luckily, and the ogre's wife said: "There you are again with your fee-fi-fo-fum. Why, of course it's the boy you caught last night that I've just broiled for your breakfast. How forgetful I am, and how careless you are not to know the difference between live and dead after all these years."

So the ogre sat down to the breakfast and ate it, but every now and then he would mutter: "Well, I could have sworn——" and he'd get up and search the larder and the cupboards and everything, only, luckily, he didn't think of the copper.

After breakfast was over, the ogre called out: "Wife, wife, bring me my golden harp." So she brought it and put it on the table before him. Then he said: "Sing!" and the golden harp sang most beautifully. And it went on singing till the ogre fell asleep, and commenced to snore like thunder.

Then Jack lifted up the copper-lid very quietly and got down like a mouse and crept on hands and knees till he came to the table, when up he crawled, caught hold of the golden harp and dashed with it toward the door. But the harp called out quite loud: "Master! Master!" and the ogre woke up just in time to see Jack running off with his harp.

Jack ran as fast as he could, and the ogre came rushing after, and would soon have caught him only Jack had a start and dodged him a bit and knew where he was going. When he got to the beanstalk the ogre was not more than twenty yards away when suddenly he saw Jack disappear like, and when he came to the end of the road he saw Jack underneath climbing down for dear life. Well, the ogre didn't like trusting himself to such a ladder, and he stood and waited, so Jack got another start. But just then the harp cried out: "Master! Master!" and the ogre swung himself down on to the beanstalk, which shook with his weight. Down climbs Jack, and after him climbed the ogre. By this time Jack had climbed down and climbed down and climbed down till he was very nearly home. So he called out: "Mother! Mother! bring me an ax, bring me an ax." And his mother came rushing out with the ax in her hand, but when she came to the beanstalk she stood stock still with fright for there she saw the ogre with his legs just through the clouds.

But Jack jumped down and got hold of the ax and gave a chop at the beanstalk which cut it half in two. The ogre felt the beanstalk shake and quiver so he stopped to see what was the matter. Then

Jack gave another chop with the ax, and the beanstalk was cut in two and began to topple over. Then the ogre fell down and broke his crown, and the beanstalk came toppling after.

Then Jack showed his mother his golden harp, and what with showing that and selling the golden eggs Jack and his mother became very rich, and he married a great princess, and they lived happy ever after.

MR. VINEGAR

By JOSEPH JACOBS

MR. and Mrs. Vinegar lived in a vinegar bottle. Now, one day, when Mr. Vinegar was from home, Mrs. Vinegar, who was a very good housewife, was busily sweeping her house, when an unlucky thump of the broom brought the whole house clitter-clatter, clitter-clatter, about her ears. In an agony of grief she rushed forth to meet her husband. On seeing him she exclaimed, "Oh, Mr. Vinegar, Mr. Vinegar, we are ruined, we are ruined: I have knocked the house down, and it is all to pieces!"

Mr. Vinegar then said: "My dear, let us see what can be done. Here is the door; I will take it on my back, and we will go forth to seek our fortune."

They walked all that day, and at nightfall entered a thick forest. They were both very, very tired, and Mr. Vinegar said: "My love, I will climb up into a tree, drag up the door, and you shall follow."

He accordingly did so, and they both stretched their weary limbs on the door, and fell fast asleep. In the middle of the night, Mr. Vinegar was disturbed by the sound of voices underneath, and to his horror and dismay found that it was a band of thieves met to divide their booty.

"Here, Jack," said one, "here's five pounds for you; here, Bill, here's ten pounds for you; here, Bob, here's three pounds for you." Mr. Vinegar could listen no longer; his terror was so great that he trembled and trembled, and shook down the door on their heads.

Away scampered the thieves, but Mr. Vinegar dared not quit his retreat till broad daylight. He then scrambled out of the tree, and went to lift up the door. What did he see but a number of golden guineas.

"Come down, Mrs. Vinegar," he cried; "come down, I say; our fortune's made, our fortune's made! Come down, I say."

Mrs. Vinegar got down as fast as she could, and when she saw the money, she jumped for joy. "Now, my dear," said she, "I'll tell you what you shall do. There is a fair at the neighboring town; you shall take these forty guineas and buy a cow. I can make butter and cheese, which you shall sell at market, and we shall then be able to live very comfortably."

Mr. Vinegar joyfully agrees, takes the money, and off he goes to the fair. When he arrived, he walked up and down, and at length saw a beautiful red cow. It was an excellent milker, and perfect in every way. "Oh!" thought Mr. Vinegar, "if I had but that cow, I should be the happiest man alive." So he offered the forty guineas for the cow, and the owner said that, as he was a friend, he'd oblige him. So the bargain was made, and he got the cow and he drove it backward and forward to show it.

By-and-by he saw a man playing the bagpipes—Tweedle-dum, tweedle-dee. The children followed him about, and he appeared to be pocketing money on all sides. "Well," thought Mr. Vinegar, "if I had but that beautiful instrument I should be the happiest man alive—my fortune would be made."

So he went up to the man. "Friend," says he, "what a beautiful instrument that is, and what a deal of money you must make."

"Why, yes," said the man, "I make a great deal of money, to be sure, and it is a wonderful instrument."

"Oh!" cried Mr. Vinegar, "how I should like to possess it!"

"Well," said the man, "as you are a friend, I don't much mind parting with it; you shall have it for that red cow."

"Done!" said the delighted Mr. Vinegar. So the beautiful red cow was given for the bagpipes. He walked up and down with his purchase; but it was in vain he tried to play a tune, and instead of pocketing pence, the boys followed him hooting, laughing, and pelting.

Poor Mr. Vinegar, his fingers grew very cold, and, just as he was leaving the town, he met a man with a fine thick pair of gloves. "Oh, my fingers are so very cold," said Mr. Vinegar to himself. "Now if I had but those beautiful gloves I should be the happiest man alive."

He went up to the man, and said to him: "Friend, you seem to have a capital pair of gloves there."

"Yes, truly," cried the man; "and my hands are as warm as possible this cold November day."

'Well," said Mr. Vinegar, "I should like to have them."

"What will you give?" said the man. "As you are a friend, I don't much mind letting you have them for those bagpipes."

"Done!" cried Mr. Vinegar. He put on the gloves, and felt perfectly happy as he trudged homeward.

At last he grew very tired, when he saw a man coming toward him with a good stout stick in his hand.

"Oh," said Mr. Vinegar, "that I had but that stick! I should then be the happiest man alive." He said to the man: "Friend, what a rare good stick you have got!"

"Yes," said the man; "I have used it for many a long mile, and a good friend it has been; but if you have a fancy for it, as you are a friend, I don't mind giving it to you for that pair of gloves."

Mr. Vinegar's hands were so warm, and his legs so tired, that he gladly made the exchange. As he drew near to the wood where he had left his wife, he heard a parrot on a tree calling out his name: "Mr. Vinegar, you foolish man, you blockhead, you simpleton; you went to the fair, and laid out all your money in buying a cow. Not content with that, you changed it for bagpipes, on which you could not play, and which were not worth one tenth of the money. You fool, you—you had no sooner got the bagpipes than you changed them for the gloves, which were not worth one quarter of the money; and when you had got the gloves, you changed them for a poor miserable stick; and now for your forty guineas, cow, bagpipes, and gloves, you have nothing to show but that poor miserable stick, which you might have cut in any hedge."

On this the bird laughed and laughed, and Mr. Vinegar, falling into a violent rage, threw the stick at its head. The stick lodged in the tree, and he returned to his wife without money, cow, bagpipes, gloves, or stick, and she instantly gave him such a sound cudgeling that she almost broke every bone in his skin.

TEENY-TINY

By JOSEPH JACOBS

Illustration by JOHN D. BATTEN

ONCE upon a time there was a teeny-tiny woman who lived in a teeny-tiny house in a teeny-tiny village. Now, one day this teeny-tiny woman put on her teeny-tiny bonnet, and went out of her teeny-tiny house to take a teeny-tiny walk. And when this teeny-tiny woman had gone a teeny-tiny way, she came to a teeny-tiny gate; so the teeny-tiny woman opened the teeny-tiny gate, and went into a teeny-tiny churchyard. And when this teeny-tiny woman had got into the teeny-tiny churchyard, she saw a teeny-tiny bone on a teeny-tiny grave, and the teeny-tiny woman said to her teeny-tiny self, "This teeny-tiny bone will make me some teeny-tiny soup for my teeny-tiny supper." So the teeny-tiny woman put the teeny-tiny bone into her teeny-tiny pocket, and went home to her teeny-tiny house.

Now when the teeny-tiny woman got home to her teeny-tiny house, she was a teeny-tiny bit tired; so she went up her teeny-tiny stairs to her teeny-tiny bed, and put the teeny-tiny bone into a teeny-tiny cupboard. And when this teeny-tiny woman had been to sleep a teeny-tiny time, she was awakened by a teeny-tiny voice from the teeny-tiny cupboard, which said:

"Give me my bone!"

And this teeny-tiny woman was a teeny-tiny frightened, so she hid her teeny-tiny head under the teeny-tiny clothes and went to sleep again. And when she had been to sleep again a teeny-tiny time, the teeny-tiny voice again cried out from the teeny-tiny cupboard a teeny-tiny louder:

"Give me my bone!"

This made the teeny-tiny woman a teeny-tiny more frightened, so she hid her teeny-tiny head a teeny-tiny further under the teeny-tiny clothes. And when the teeny-tiny woman had been to sleep again a teeny-tiny time, the teeny-tiny voice from the teeny-tiny cupboard said again a teeny-tiny louder:

"Give me my bone!"

And this teeny-tiny woman was a teeny-tiny bit more frightened, but she put her teeny-tiny head out of the teeny-tiny clothes, and said in her loudest teeny-tiny voice, "TAKE IT!"

THE HISTORY OF TOM THUMB

By JOSEPH JACOBS

Illustrations by L. LESLIE BROOKE

IN the days of the great Prince Arthur, there lived a mighty magician, called Merlin, the most learned and skillful enchanter the world has ever seen.

This famous magician, who could take any form he pleased, was traveling about as a poor beggar, and being very tired, he stopped at the cottage of a plowman to rest himself, and asked for some food.

The countryman **bade** him welcome, and his wife, who was a very good-hearted woman, soon brought him some milk in a wooden bowl, and some coarse brown bread on a platter.

Merlin was much pleased with the kindness of the plowman and his wife; but he could not help noticing that though everything was neat and comfortable in the cottage, they both seemed to be very unhappy. He therefore asked them why they were so melancholy, and learned that they were miserable because they had no children.

The poor woman said, with tears in her eyes: "I should be the happiest creature in the world if I had a son; although he was no bigger than my husband's thumb, I would be satisfied."

Merlin was so much amused with the idea of a boy no bigger than a man's thumb, that he determined to grant the poor woman's wish.

Accordingly, in a short time after, the plowman's wife had a son, who, wonderful to relate! was not a bit bigger than his father's thumb.

The queen of the fairies, wishing to see the little fellow, came in at the window while the mother was sitting up in the bed admiring him. The queen kissed the child, and, giving it the name of Tom Thumb, sent for some of the fairies, who dressed her little godson according to her orders:

"An oak-leaf hat he had for his crown;
His shirt of web by spiders spun;
With jacket wove of thistle's down;
His trowsers were of feathers done.

His stockings, of apple-rind, they tie
With eyelash from his mother's eye:
His shoes were made of mouse's skin,
Tann'd with the downy hair within."

Tom never grew any larger than his father's thumb, which was only of ordinary size; but as he got older he became very cunning and full of tricks. When he was old enough to play with the boys, and had lost all his own cherry stones, he used to creep into the bags of his playfellows, fill his pockets, and, getting out without their noticing him, would again join in the game.

One day, however, as he was coming out of a bag of cherry stones, where he had been stealing as usual, the boy to whom it belonged

L. Leslie Brooke

The cow took Tom Thumb and the thistle at a mouthful.

[See page 33]

chanced to see him. "Ah, ah! my little Tommy," said the boy, "so I have caught you stealing my cherry stones at last, and you shall be rewarded for your thievish tricks." On saying this, he drew the string tight round his neck, and gave the bag such a hearty shake, that poor little Tom's legs, thighs, and body were sadly bruised. He roared out with pain, and begged to be let out, promising never to steal again.

A short time afterwards his mother was making a batter-pudding, and Tom, being very anxious to see how it was made, climbed up to the edge of the bowl; but his foot slipped, and he plumped over head and ears into the batter, without his mother noticing him, who stirred him into the pudding-bag, and put him in the pot to boil.

The batter filled Tom's mouth, and prevented him from crying; but, on feeling the hot water, he kicked and struggled so much in the pot, that his mother thought that the pudding was bewitched, and, pulling it out of the pot, she threw it outside the door. A poor tinker, who was passing by, lifted up the pudding, and putting it into his budget, he then walked off. As Tom had now got his mouth cleared of the batter, he then began to cry aloud, which so frightened the tinker that he flung down the pudding and ran away. The pudding being broke to pieces by the fall, Tom crept out covered all over with the batter, and walked home. His mother, who was very sorry to see her darling in such a woeful state, put him into a teacup, and soon washed off the batter; after which she kissed him, and laid him in bed.

Soon after the adventure of the pudding, Tom's mother went to milk her cow in the meadow, and she took him along with her. As the wind was very high, for fear of being blown away, she tied him to a thistle with a piece of fine thread. The cow soon observed Tom's oak-leaf hat, and liking the appearance of it, took poor Tom and the thistle at one mouthful. While the cow was chewing the thistle, Tom was afraid of her great teeth, which threatened to crush him in pieces, and he roared out as loud as he could:

"Mother, mother!"

"Where are you, Tommy, my dear Tommy?" said his mother.

"Here, mother," replied he, "in the red cow's mouth."

His mother began to cry and wring her hands; but the cow, surprised at the odd noise in her throat, opened her mouth and let Tom drop out. Fortunately his mother caught him in her apron as he was falling to the ground, or he would have been dreadfully hurt. She then put Tom in her bosom and ran home with him.

Tom's father made him a whip of a barley straw to drive the cattle with, and having one day gone into the fields, Tom slipped a foot and rolled into the furrow. A raven, which was flying over, picked him up, and flew with him over the sea, and there dropped him.

A large fish swallowed Tom the moment he fell into the sea, which was soon after caught, and bought for the table of King Arthur. When they opened the fish in order to cook it, everyone was astonished at finding such a little boy, and Tom was quite delighted at being free again. They carried him to the king, who made Tom his dwarf, and he soon grew a great favorite at court; for by his tricks and gambols he not only amused the king and queen, but also all the Knights of the Round Table.

It is said that when the king rode out on horseback, he often took Tom along with him, and if a shower came on, he used to creep into his majesty's waistcoat pocket where he slept till the rain was over.

King Arthur one day asked Tom about his parents, wishing to know if they were as small as he was, and whether they were well off. Tom told the king that his father and mother were as tall as anybody about the court, but in rather poor circumstances. On hearing this, the king carried Tom to his treasury, the place where he kept all his money, and told him to take as much money as he could carry home to his parents, which made the poor little fellow caper with joy. Tom went immediately to procure a purse, which was made of a water-bubble, and then returned to the treasury, where he received a silver three-penny-piece to put into it.

Our little hero had some difficulty in lifting the burden upon his back; but he at last succeeded in getting it placed to his mind, and set forward on his journey. However, without meeting with any accident, and after resting himself more than a hundred times by the way, in two days and two nights he reached his father's house in safety.

Tom had traveled forty-eight hours with a huge silver-piece on his back, and was almost tired to death, when his mother ran out to meet him, and carried him into the house. But he soon returned to court.

As Tom's clothes had suffered much in the batter-pudding, and the inside of the fish, his majesty ordered him a new suit of clothes, and to be mounted as a knight on a mouse.

> "Of Butterfly's wings his shirt was made,
>   His boots of chicken's hide;
> And by a nimble fairy blade,
> Well learned in the tailoring trade,
>   His clothing was supplied.
>   A needle dangled by his side;
>   A dapper mouse he used to ride;
>   Thus strutted Tom in stately pride!"

It was certainly very diverting to see Tom in this dress and mounted on the mouse, as he rode out a-hunting with the king and nobility, who were all ready to expire with laughter at Tom and his fine prancing charger.

The king was so charmed with his address that he ordered a little chair to be made, in order that Tom might sit upon his table, and also a palace of gold, a span high, with a door an inch wide, to live in. He also gave him a coach, drawn by six small mice.

The queen was so enraged at the honors conferred on Sir Thomas that she resolved to ruin him, and told the king that the little knight had been saucy to her.

The king sent for Tom in great haste; but being fully aware of the danger of royal anger, he crept into an empty snail-shell, where he lay for a long time until he was almost starved with hunger; but at last he ventured to peep out, and seeing a fine large butterfly on the ground, near the place of his concealment, he got close to it and jumping astride on it, was carried up into the air. The butterfly flew with him from tree to tree and from field to field, and at last returned to the court, where the king and nobility all strove to catch him; but at last poor Tom fell from his seat into a watering pot, in which he was almost drowned.

When the queen saw him, she was in a rage, and said he should be beheaded; and he was again put into a mouse trap until the time of his execution.

However, a cat, observing something alive in the trap, patted it about till the wires broke, and set Thomas at liberty.

The king received Tom again into favor, which he did not live to enjoy, for a large spider one day attacked him; and although he drew his sword and fought well, yet the spider's poisonous breath at last overcame him.

> "He fell dead on the ground where he stood,
> And the spider suck'd every drop of his blood."

King Arthur and his whole court were so sorry at the loss of their little favorite that they went into mourning and raised a fine white marble monument over his grave with the following epitaph:

> "Here lies Tom Thumb, King Arthur's knight,
> Who died by a spider's cruel bite.
> He was well known in Arthur's court,
> Where he afforded gallant sport;
> He rode a tilt and tournament,
> And on a mouse a-hunting went.
> Alive he filled the court with mirth;
> His death to sorrow soon gave birth.
> Wipe, wipe your eyes, and shake your head
> And cry—Alas! Tom Thumb is dead!"

CAP O' RUSHES

By JOSEPH JACOBS

WELL, there was once a very rich gentleman, and he had three daughters, and he thought he'd see how fond they were of him. So he says to the first, "How much do you love me, my dear?"

"Why," says she, "as I love my life."

"That's good," says he.

So he says to the second, "How much do *you* love me, my dear?"

"Why," says she, "better nor all the world."

"That's good," says he.

So he says to the third, "How much do *you* love me, my dear?"

"Why, I love you as fresh meat loves salt," says she.

Well, but he was angry. "You don't love me at all," says he, "and in my house you stay no more." So he drove her out there and then, and shut the door in her face.

Well, she went away on and on till she came to a fen, and there she gathered a lot of rushes and made them into a kind of a sort of a cloak with a hood, to cover her from head to foot, and to hide her fine clothes. And then she went on and on till she came to a great house.

"Do you want a maid?" says she.

"No, we don't," said they.

"I haven't nowhere to go," says she; "and I ask no wages, and do any sort of work," says she.

"Well," said they, "if you like to wash the pots and scrape the saucepans you may stay," said they.

So she stayed there and washed the pots and scraped the saucepans and did all the dirty work. And because she gave no name they called her "Cap o' Rushes."

Well, one day there was to be a great dance a little way off, and the servants were allowed to go and look on at the grand people. Cap o' Rushes said she was too tired to go, so she stayed at home.

But when they were gone, she offed with her cap o' rushes, and cleaned herself, and went to the dance. And no one there was so finely dressed as she.

Well, who should be there but her master's son, and what should he do but fall in love with her the minute he set eyes on her. He wouldn't dance with anyone else.

But before the dance was done, Cap o' Rushes slipped off, and away she went home. And when the other maids came back, she was pretending to be asleep with her cap o' rushes on.

Well, next morning they said to her, "You did miss a sight, Cap o' Rushes!"

"What was that?" says she.

"Why, the beautifullest lady you ever see, dressed right gay and ga'. The young master, he never took his eyes off her."

"Well, I should have liked to have seen her," says Cap o' Rushes.

"Well, there's to be another dance this evening, and perhaps she'll be there."

But, come the evening, Cap o' Rushes said she was too tired to go with them. Howsoever, when they were gone, she offed with her cap o' rushes and cleaned herself, and away she went to the dance.

The master's son had been reckoning on seeing her, and he danced with no one else, and never took his eyes off her. But, before the dance was over, she slipped off, and home she went, and when the maids came back she pretended to be asleep with her cap o' rushes on.

Next day they said to her again, "Well, Cap o' Rushes, you should ha' been there to see the lady. There she was again, gay and ga', and the young master he never took his eyes off her."

"Well, there," says she, "I should ha' liked to ha' seen her."

"Well," says they, "there's a dance again this evening, and you must go with us, for she's sure to be there."

Well, come this evening, Cap o' Rushes said she was too tired to go, and do what they would she stayed at home. But when they were gone, she offed with her cap o' rushes and cleaned herself, and away she went to the dance.

The master's son was rarely glad when he saw her. He danced

with none but her and never took his eyes off her. When she wouldn't tell him her name, nor where she came from, he gave her a ring and told her if he didn't see her again he should die.

Well, before the dance was over, off she slipped, and home she went, and when the maids came home she was pretending to be asleep with her cap o' rushes on.

Well, next day they says to her, "There, Cap o' Rushes, you didn't come last night, and now you won't see the lady, for there's no more dances."

"Well, I should have rarely liked to have seen her," says she.

The master's son he tried every way to find out where the lady was gone, but go where he might, and ask whom he might, he never heard anything about her. And he got worse and worse for the love of her till he had to keep his bed.

"Make some gruel for the young master," they said to the cook. "He's dying for the love of the lady." The cook set about making it when Cap o' Rushes came in.

"What are you a-doing of?" says she.

"I'm going to make some gruel for the young master," says the cook, "for he's dying for love of the lady."

"Let me make it," says Cap o' Rushes.

Well, the cook wouldn't at first, but at last she said yes, and Cap o' Rushes made the gruel. And when she had made it, she slipped the ring into it on the sly before the cook took it upstairs.

The young man he drank it and then he saw the ring at the bottom.

"Send for the cook," says he.

"Who made this gruel here?" says he.

"I did," says the cook, for she was frightened.

And he looked at her.

"No, you didn't," says he. "Say who did it, and you shan't be harmed."

"Well, then, 't was Cap o' Rushes," says she.

"Send Cap o' Rushes here," says he.

So Cap o' Rushes came.

"Did you make my gruel?" says he.

"Yes, I did," says she.

"Where did you get this ring?" says he.

"From him that gave it me," says she.

"Who are you, then?" says the young man.

"I'll show you," says she. And she offed with her cap o' rushes, and there she was in her beautiful clothes.

Well, the master's son he got well very soon, and they were to be married in a little time. It was to be a very grand wedding, and everyone was asked far and near. And Cap o' Rushes's father was asked. But she never told anybody who she was.

But before the wedding, she went to the cook, and says she:

"I want you to dress every dish without a mite o' salt.

"That'll be rare nasty," says the cook.

"That doesn't signify," says she.

"Very well," says the cook.

Well, the wedding day came, and they were married. And after they were married, all the company sat down to the dinner. When they began to eat the meat, it was so tasteless they couldn't eat it. But Cap o' Rushes's father tried first one dish and then another, and then he burst out crying.

"What is the matter?" said the master's son to him.

"Oh," says he, "I had a daughter. And I asked her how much she loved me. And she said 'As much as fresh meat loves salt.' And I turned her away from my door, for I thought she didn't love me. And now I see she loves me best of all. And she may be dead for ought I know."

"No, Father, here she is!" said Cap o' Rushes. And she goes up to him and puts her arms around him.

And so they were all happy ever after.

MOLLY WHUPPIE

By JOSEPH JACOBS

Illustration by JOHN D. BATTEN

ONCE upon a time there was a man and a wife had too many children, and they could not get meat for them, so they took the three youngest and left them in a wood. They traveled and traveled and could see never a house. It began to be dark, and they were hungry. At last they saw a light and made for it; it turned out to be a house. They knocked at the door, and a woman came to it, who said: "What do you want?" They said: "Please let us in and give us something to eat." The woman said: "I can't do that, as my man is a giant, and he would kill you if he comes home." They begged hard. "Let us stop for a little while," said they, "and we will go away before he comes."

So she took them in, and set them down before the fire, and gave them milk and bread; but just as they had begun to eat, a great knock came to the door, and a dreadful voice said:

> "Fee, fie, fo, fum,
> I smell the blood of some earthly one.

Who have you there, wife?"

"Eh," said the wife, "it's three poor lassies cold and hungry, and they will go away. Ye won't touch 'em, man." He said nothing, but ate up a big supper, and ordered them to stay all night.

Now he had three lassies of his own, and they were to sleep in the same bed with the three strangers. The youngest of the three strange lassies was called Molly Whuppie, and she was very clever. She noticed that before they went to bed the giant put straw ropes round her neck and her sisters', and round his own lassies' necks he put gold chains. So Molly took care and did not fall asleep, but waited till she was sure everyone was sleeping sound. Then she slipped out of the bed, and took the straw ropes off her own and her sisters' necks, and took the gold chains off the giant's lassies. She then put the straw ropes on the giant's lassies and the gold on herself and her sisters, and lay down.

And in the middle of the night up rose the giant, armed with a great club, and felt for the necks with the straw. It was dark. He took his own lassies out of bed on to the floor, and battered them until they were dead, and then lay down again, thinking he had managed finely.

Molly thought it time she and her sisters were off and away, so she wakened them and told them to be quiet, and they slipped out of the house.

They all got out safe, and they ran and ran, and never stopped until morning, when they saw a grand house before them. It turned out to be a king's house: so Molly went in, and told her story to the king.

He said: "Well, Molly, you are a clever girl, and you have managed well; but, if you would manage better, and go back, and steal the giant's sword that hangs on the back of his bed, I would give your eldest sister my eldest son to marry."

Molly said she would try. So she went back, and managed to slip into the giant's house, and crept in below the bed. The giant came home, and ate up a great supper, and went to bed. Molly waited until he was snoring, and she crept out, and reached over the giant and got down the sword; but just as she got it out over the bed it gave a rattle, and up jumped the giant, and Molly ran out at the door and the sword with her; and she ran, and he ran, till they came to the "Bridge of One Hair"; and she got over, but he couldn't, and he says, "Woe worth ye, Molly Whuppie! never ye come again." And she says: "Twice yet, carle," quoth she, "I'll come to Spain." So Molly took the sword to the king, and her sister was married to his son.

Well, the king he says: "Ye've managed well, Molly; but if ye would manage better, and steal the purse that lies below the giant's pillow, I would marry your second sister to my second son." And Molly said she would try. So she set out for the giant's house, and slipped in, and hid again below the bed, and waited till the giant had eaten his supper, and was snoring sound asleep. She slipped out and slipped her hand below the pillow, and got out the purse; but just as she was going out the giant wakened, and ran after her; and she ran, and he ran, till they came to the "Bridge of One Hair," and she got over, but he couldn't, and he said, "Woe worth ye, Molly

"Now I have caught you, Molly Whuppie."

Whuppie! never you come again." "Once yet, carle," quoth she, "I'll come to Spain." So Molly took the purse to the king, and her second sister was married to the king's second son.

After that the king says to Molly: "Molly, you are a clever girl, but if you would do better yet, and steal the giant's ring that he wears on his finger, I will give you my youngest son for yourself." Molly said she would try. So back she goes to the giant's house, and hides herself below the bed. The giant wasn't long ere he came home, and, after he had eaten a great big supper, he went to his bed, and shortly was snoring loud. Molly crept out and reached over the bed, and got hold of the giant's hand, and she pulled and she pulled until she got off the ring; but just as she got it off the giant got up, and gripped her by the hand and he says: "Now I have caught you, Molly Whuppie, and, if I had done as much ill to you as ye have done to me, what would ye do to me?"

Molly says: "I would put you into a sack, and I'd put the cat inside wi' you, and the dog aside you, and a needle and thread and a shears, and I'd hang you up upon the wall, and I'd go to the wood, and choose the thickest stick I could get, and I would come home, and take you down, and bang you till you were dead."

"Well, Molly," says the giant, "I'll just do that to you."

So he gets a sack, and puts Molly into it, and the cat and the dog beside her, and a needle and thread and shears, and hangs her up upon the wall, and goes to the wood to choose a stick.

Molly she sings out: "Oh, if ye saw what I see."

"Oh," says the giant's wife, "what do ye see, Molly?"

But Molly never said a word but, "Oh, if ye saw what I see!"

The giant's wife begged that Molly would take her up into the sack till she would see what Molly saw. So Molly took the shears and cut a hole in the sack, and took out the needle and thread with her, and jumped down and helped the giant's wife up into the sack, and sewed up the hole.

The giant's wife saw nothing, and began to ask to get down again; but Molly never minded, but hid herself at the back of the door. Home came the giant, and a great big tree in his hand, and he took down the sack, and began to batter it. His wife cried, "It's me, man"; but the dog barked and the cat mewed, and he did not know his wife's voice. But Molly came out from the back of the door, and the giant saw her and he after her; and he ran, and she ran, till they came to the "Bridge of One Hair," and she got over but he couldn't; and he said:

"Woe worth you, Molly Whuppie! never you come again."

"Never more, carle," quoth she, "will I come again to Spain."

So Molly took the ring to the king, and she was married to his youngest son, and she never saw the giant again.

THE THREE WISHES

By JOSEPH JACOBS

Illustration by JOHN D. BATTEN

ONCE upon a time, and be sure 'twas a long time ago, there lived a poor woodman in a great forest, and every day of his life he went out to fell timber. So one day he started out, and the goodwife filled his wallet and slung his bottle on his back, that he might have meat and drink in the forest. He had marked out a huge old oak, which, thought he, would furnish many and many a good plank. And when he was come to it, he took his ax in his hand and swung it round his head as though he were minded to fell the tree at one stroke. But he hadn't given one blow, when what should he hear but the pitifullest entreating, and there stood before him a fairy who prayed and beseeched him to spare the tree. He was dazed, as you may fancy, with wonderment and affright, and he couldn't open his mouth to utter a word. But he found his tongue at last, and, "Well," said he, "I'll e'en do as thou wishest."

"You've done better for yourself than you know," answered the fairy, "and to show I'm not ungrateful, I'll grant you your next three wishes, be they what they may." And therewith the fairy was no more to be seen, and the woodman slung his wallet over his shoulder and his bottle at his side, and off he started home.

But the way was long, and the poor man was regularly dazed with the wonderful thing that had befallen him, and when he got home there was nothing in his noddle but the wish to sit down and rest. Maybe, too, 'twas a trick of the fairy's. Who can tell? Anyhow down he sat by the blazing fire, and as he sat he waxed hungry, though it was a long way off supper-time yet.

"Hasn't thou naught for supper, dame?" said he to his wife.

"Nay, not for a couple of hours yet," said she.

"Ah!" groaned the woodman, "I wish I'd a good link of black pudding [sausage] here before me."

45

No sooner had he said the word, when clatter, clatter, rustle, rustle, what should come down the chimney but a link of the finest black pudding the heart of man could wish for.

If the woodman stared, the goodwife stared three times as much. "What's all this?" says she.

Then all the morning's work came back to the woodman, and he told his tale right out, from beginning to end, and as he told it the goodwife glowered and glowered, and when he had made an end of it she burst out,

"Thou bee'st but a fool, Jan, thou bee'st but a fool; and I wish the pudding were at thy nose, I do indeed."

And before you could say Jack Robinson, there the goodman sat and his nose was the longer for a noble link of black pudding.

He gave a pull but it stuck, and she gave a pull but it stuck, and they both pulled till they had nigh pulled the nose off, but it stuck and stuck.

"What's to be done now?" said he.

" 'T isn't so very unsightly," said she, looking hard at him.

Then the woodman saw that if he wished, he must need wish in a hurry; and wish he did, that the black pudding might come off his nose. Well! there it lay in a dish on the table, and if the goodman and goodwife didn't ride in a golden coach, or dress in silk and satin, why they had at least as fine a black pudding for their supper as the heart of man could desire.

THE KING O' THE CATS

By JOSEPH JACOBS

Illustration by JOHN D. BATTEN

ONE winter's evening the sexton's wife was sitting by the fire-side with her big black cat, Old Tom, on the other side, both half asleep and waiting for the master to come home. They waited and they waited, but still he didn't come, till at last he came rushing in, calling out, "Who's Tommy Tildrum?" in such a wild way that both his wife and his cat stared at him to know what was the matter.

"Why, what's the matter?" said his wife, "and why do you want to know who Tommy Tildrum is?"

"Oh, I've had such an adventure. I was digging away at old Mr. Fordyce's grave when I suppose I must have dropped asleep, and only woke up by hearing a cat's *Miaou.*"

"*Miaou!*" said Old Tom in answer.

"Yes, just like that! So I looked over the edge of the grave, and what do you think I saw?"

"Now, how can I tell?" said the sexton's wife.

"Why, nine black cats all like our friend Tom here, all with a white spot on their chestesses. And what do you think they were carrying? Why, a small coffin covered with a black velvet pall, and on the pall was a small coronet all of gold, and at every third step they took they cried all together, *Miaou——*"

"*Miaou!*" said Old Tom again.

"Yes, just like that!" said the Sexton. "And as they came nearer and nearer to me I could see them more distinctly, because their eyes shone out with a sort of green light. Well, they all came toward me, eight of them carrying the coffin, and the biggest cat of all walking in front for all the world like—but look at our Tom, how he's look-ing at me. You'd think he knew all I was saying."

"Go on, go on," said his wife; "never mind Old Tom."

"Well, as I was a-saying, they came toward me slowly and solemnly, and at every third step crying all together, *Miaou——*"

"*Miaou!*" said Old Tom again.

"Yes, just like that, till they came and stood right opposite Mr. Fordyce's grave, where I was, when they all stood still and looked straight at me. I did feel queer, that I did! But look at Old Tom; he's looking at me just like they did."

"Go on, go on," said his wife; "never mind Old Tom."

"Where was I? Oh, they all stood still looking at me, when the one that wasn't carrying the coffin came forward and, staring straight at me, said to me—yes, I tell 'ee, *said* to me, with a squeaky voice, 'Tell Tom Tildrum that Tim Toldrum's dead,' and that's why I asked you if you knew who Tom Tildrum was, for how can I tell Tom Tildrum Tim Toldrum's dead if I don't know who Tom Tildrum is?"

"Look at Old Tom, look at Old Tom!" screamed his wife.

And well he might look, for Tom was swelling and Tom was staring, and at last Tom shrieked out, "What—old Tim dead! then I'm the King o' the Cats!" and rushed up the chimney and was never more seen.

THE HOBYAHS

By JOSEPH JACOBS

Illustrations by JOHN D. BATTEN

ONCE there was an old man and woman and a little girl, and they all lived in a house made of hempstalks. Now the old man had a little dog named Turpie; and one night the Hobyahs came and said, "Hobyah! Hobyah! Hobyah! Tear down the hemp-

stalks, eat up the old man and woman, and carry off the little girl!" But little dog Turpie barked so that the Hobyahs ran off; and the old man said, "Little dog Turpie barks so that I cannot sleep nor slumber, and if I live till morning I will cut off his tail." So in the morning the old man cut off little dog Turpie's tail.

The next night the Hobyahs came again, and said, "Hobyah! Hobyah! Hobyah! Tear down the hempstalks, eat up the old man and woman, and carry off the little girl!" But little dog Turpie barked so that the Hobyahs ran off; and the old man said, "Little dog Turpie barks so that I cannot sleep nor slumber, and if I live till morning I will cut off one of his legs." So in the morning the old man cut off one of little dog Turpie's legs.

The next night the Hobyahs came again, and said, "Hobyah! Hobyah! Hobyah! Tear down the hempstalks, eat up the old man and woman, and carry off the little girl!" But little dog Turpie barked so that the Hobyahs ran off;

and the old man said, "Little dog Turpie barks so that I cannot sleep nor slumber, and if I live till morning I will cut off another of his legs." So in the morning the old man cut off another of little dog Turpie's legs.

The next night the Hobyahs came again, and said, "Hobyah! Hobyah! Hobyah! Tear down the hempstalks, eat up the old man and woman, and carry off the little girl!" But little dog Turpie barked so that the Hobyahs ran off; and the old man said, "Little dog Turpie barks so that I cannot sleep nor slumber, and if I live till morning I will cut off another of his legs." So in the morning the old man cut off another of little dog Turpie's legs.

The next night the Hobyahs came again, and said, "Hobyah! Hobyah! Hobyah! Tear down the hempstalks, eat up the old man and woman, and carry off the little girl!" But little dog Turpie barked so that the Hobyahs ran off; and the old man said, "Little dog Turpie barks so that I cannot sleep or slumber, and if I live till morning I will cut off another of his legs." So in the morning the old man cut off another of little dog Turpie's legs.

The next night the Hobyahs came again, and said, "Hobyah! Hobyah! Hobyah! Tear down the hempstalks, eat up the old man and woman, and carry off the little girl!" But little dog Turpie barked so that the Hobyahs ran off; and the old man said, "Little dog Turpie barks so that I cannot sleep or slumber, and if I live till morning I will cut off little dog Turpie's head." So in the morning the old man cut off little dog Turpie's head.

The next night the Hobyahs came again, and said, "Hobyah! Hobyah! Hobyah! Tear down the hempstalks, eat up the old man and woman, and carry off the little girl!" And when the Hobyahs found that little dog Turpie's head was off, they tore down the hempstalks, ate up the old man and woman, and carried the little girl off in a bag. And when the Hobyahs came to their home they hung up the bag with the little girl in it, and every Hobyah knocked on the top of the bag and said, "Look me! look me!" And then they went to sleep until the next night, for the Hobyahs slept in the daytime.

The little girl cried a great deal, and a man with a big dog came that way and heard her crying. When he asked her how she came there and she told him, he put the dog in the bag and took the little girl to his home.

The next night the Hobyahs took down the bag and knocked on the top of it, and said "Look me! look me!" and when they opened the bag——

the big dog jumped out and ate them all up; so there are no Hobyahs now.

HEREAFTERTHIS

By JOSEPH JACOBS

Illustration by JOHN D. BATTEN

ONCE upon a time there was a farmer called Jan, and he lived all alone by himself in a little farmhouse.

By-and-by he thought that he would like to have a wife to keep it all vitty for him.

So he went a-courting a fine maid, and he said to her: "Will you marry me?"

"That I will, to be sure," said she.

So they went to church, and were wed. After the wedding was over, she got up on his horse behind him, and he brought her home. And they lived as happy as the day was long.

One day, Jan said to his wife, "Wife, can you milk-y?"

"Oh, yes, Jan, I can milk-y. Mother used to milk-y, when I lived home."

So he went to market and bought her ten red cows. All went well till one day when she had driven them to the pond to drink, she thought they did not drink fast enough. So she drove them right into the pond to make them drink faster, and they were all drowned.

When Jan came home, she up and told him what she had done, and he said, "Oh, well, there, never mind, my dear, better luck next time."

So they went on for a bit, and then, one day, Jan said to his wife, "Wife, can you serve pigs?"

"Oh, yes, Jan, I can serve pigs. Mother used to serve pigs when I lived home."

So Jan went to market and bought her some pigs. All went well till one day, when she had put their food into the trough she thought they did not eat fast enough, and she pushed their heads into the trough to make them eat faster, and they were all choked.

When Jan came home, she up and told him what she had done,

and he said, "Oh, well, there, never mind, my dear, better luck next time."

So they went on for a bit, and then, one day, Jan said to his wife, "Wife, can you bake-y?"

"Oh, yes, Jan, I can bake-y. Mother used to bake-y when I lived home."

So he bought everything for his wife so that she could bake bread. All went well for a bit, till one day she thought she would bake white bread for a treat for Jan. So she carried her meal to the top of a high hill, and let the wind blow on it, for she thought to her-

"Oh, well, better luck next time."

self that the wind would blow out all the bran. But the wind blew away meal and bran and all—so there was an end of it.

When Jan came home, she up and told him what she had done, and he said, "Oh, well, there, never mind, my dear, better luck next time."

So they went on for a bit, and then, one day, Jan said to his wife, "Wife, can you brew-y?"

"Oh, yes, Jan, I can brew-y. Mother used to brew-y when I lived home."

So he bought everything proper for his wife to brew ale with. All went well for a bit, till one day when she had brewed her ale and put it in the barrel, a big black dog came in and looked up in her face. She drove him out of the house, but he stayed outside the door and still looked up in her face. And she got so angry that she pulled out the plug of the barrel, threw it at the dog, and said, "What dost look at me for? I be Jan's wife."

Then the dog ran down the road, and she after him to chase him right away. When she came back again, she found that the ale had all run out of the barrel, and so there was an end of it.

When Jan came home, she up and told him what she had done, and he said, "Oh, well, there, never mind, my dear, better luck next time."

So they went on for a bit, and then, one day, she thought to herself, " 'Tis time to clean up my house." When she was taking down her big bed she found a bag of groats on the tester. So when Jan came home, she up and said to him, "Jan, what is that bag of groats on the tester for?"

"That is for Hereafterthis, my dear."

Now, there was a robber outside the window, and he heard what Jan said. Next day, he waited till Jan had gone to market, and then he came and knocked at the door. "What do you please to want?" said Mally.

"I am Hereafterthis," said the robber. "I have come for the bag of groats."

Now the robber was dressed like a fine gentleman, so she thought to herself it was very kind of so fine a man to come for the bag of groats, so she ran upstairs and fetched the bag of groats, and gave it to the robber and he went away with it.

When Jan came home, she said to him, "Jan, Hereafterthis has been for the bag of groats."

"What do you mean, wife?" said Jan.

So she up and told him, and he said, "Then I'm a ruined man, for that money was to pay our rent with. The only thing we can do is to roam the world over till we find the bag of groats." Then Jan took the house door off its hinges. "That's all we shall have to lie on," he said. So Jan put the door on his back, and they both set out to look for Hereafterthis.

Many a long day they went, and in the night Jan used to put the door on the branches of a tree, and they would sleep on it. One night they came to a big hill, and there was a high tree at the foot. So Jan put the door up in it, and they got up in the tree and went to sleep. By and by Jan's wife heard a noise, and she looked to see what it was. It was an opening of a door in the side of the hill. Out came two fine gentlemen with a long table, and behind them fine ladies and gentlemen, each carrying a bag, and one of them was Hereafterthis with the bag of groats. They sat round the table, and began to drink and talk and count up all the money in the bags. So then Jan's wife woke him up, and asked what they should do.

"Now's our time," said Jan, and he pushed the door off the branches, and it fell right in the very middle of the table, and frightened the robbers so that they all ran away. Then Jan and his wife got down from the tree, took as many moneybags as they could carry on the door, and went straight home. And Jan bought his wife more cows, and more pigs, and they lived happy ever after.

THE BLACK BULL OF NORROWAY

By JOSEPH JACOBS

Illustrations by JOHN D. BATTEN

I N Norroway, long time ago, there lived a certain lady, and she had three daughters: The oldest of them said to her mother: "Mother, bake me a bannock, and roast me a collop[1], for I'm going away to seek my fortune." Her mother did so; and the daughter went away to an old witch washerwife and told her purpose. The old wife bade her stay that day, and look out of her back door, and see what she could see. She saw nought the first day. The second day she did the same, and saw nought. On the third day she looked again, and saw a coach-and-six coming along the road. She ran in and told the old wife what she saw. "Well," quoth the old woman, "yon's for you." So they took her into the coach and galloped off.

The second daughter next says to her mother: "Mother, bake me a bannock, and roast me a collop, for I'm going away to seek my fortune." Her mother did so; and away she went to the old wife, as her sister had done. On the third day she looked out of the back door, and saw a coach-and-four coming. "Well," quoth the old woman, "yon's for you." So they took her in, and off they set.

The third daughter says to her mother: "Mother, bake me a bannock, and roast me a collop, for I'm going away to seek my fortune." Her mother did so; and away she went to the old witch. She bade her look out of her back door, and see what she could see. She did so; and when she came back, said she saw nought. The second day she did the same, and saw nought. The third day she looked again, and on coming back said to the old wife she saw nought but a great Black Bull coming crooning along the road. "Well," quoth the old witch, "yon's for you." On hearing this she was next to distracted with grief and terror; but she was lifted up and set on his back, and away they went.

[1] A slice of meat.

Aye they traveled, and on they traveled, till the lady grew faint with hunger. "Eat out of my right ear," says the Black Bull, "and drink out of my left ear, and set by your leaving." So she did as he said, and was wonderfully refreshed. And long they rode, and hard they rode, till they came in sight of a very big and bonny castle.

She was set on his back, and away they went.

"Yonder we must be this night," quoth the Bull; " for my elder brother lives yonder"; and presently they were at the place. They lifted her off his back, and took her in, and sent him away to a park for the night. In the morning, when they brought the Bull home, they took the lady into a fine shining parlor, and gave her a beautiful apple, telling her not to break it till she was in the greatest strait ever mortal was in the world, and that would bring her out of it.

Again she was lifted on the Bull's back, and after she had ridden far, and farther than I can tell, they came in sight of a far bonnier castle, and far farther away than the last. Says the Bull to her: "Yonder we must be this night, for my second brother lives yonder"; and they were at the place directly. They lifted her down and took her in, and sent the Bull to the field for the night. In the morning they took the lady into a fine and rich room, and gave her the finest pear she had ever seen, bidding her not to break it till she was in the greatest strait ever mortal could be in, and that would get her out of it.

Again she was lifted and set on his back, and away they went. And long they rode, and hard they rode, till they came in sight of the far biggest castle, and far farthest off, they had yet seen. "We must be yonder tonight," says the Bull, "for my young brother lives yonder"; and they were there directly. They lifted her down, took her in, and sent the Bull to the field for the night. In the morning they took her into a room, the finest of all, and gave her a plum, telling her not to break it till she was in the greatest strait mortal could be in, and that would get her out of it. Presently they brought home the bull, set the lady on his back, and away they went.

And aye they rode, and on they rode, till they came to a dark and ugsome glen, where they stopped, and the lady lighted down. Says the Bull to her: "Here you must stay till I go and fight the Old One. You must seat yourself on that stone, and move neither hand nor foot till I come back, else I'll never find you again. And if everything round about you turns blue, I have beaten the Old One; but should all things turn red, he'll have conquered me."

She sat herself down on the stone, and by-and-by all around her turned blue. Overcome with joy, she lifted one of her feet, and crossed it over the other, so glad was she that her companion was victorious. The Bull returned and sought for her, but never could find her.

Long she sat, and aye she wept, till she wearied. At last she rose and went away, she didn't know where. On she wandered, till she came to a great hill of glass, that she tried all she could to climb, but wasn't able. Round the bottom of the hill she went, sobbing and seeking a passage over, till at last she came to a smith's house; and the smith promised, if she would serve him seven years, he would make her iron shoon, wherewith she could climb over the glassy hill.

At seven years' end she got her iron shoon, clomb the glassy hill, and chanced to come to the old washerwife's habitation. There she was told of a gallant young knight that had given in some clothes all over blood to wash, and whoever washed them was to be his wife.

She got her iron shoon and clomb the hill.

The old wife had washed till she was tired, and then she set her daughter at it, and both washed, and they washed, and they washed, in hopes of getting the young knight; but for all they could do they couldn't bring out a stain.

At length they set the stranger damsel to work; and whenever she began, the stains came out pure and clean, and the old wife made the knight believe it was her daughter had washed the clothes. So the knight and the eldest daughter were to be married, and the stranger damsel was distracted at the thought of it, for she was deeply in love with him. So she bethought her of her apple, and breaking it, found it filled with gold and precious jewelry, the richest she had ever seen. "All these," she said to the eldest daughter, "I will give you, on condition that you put off your marriage for one day, and allow me to go into his room alone at night."

The lady consented; but meanwhile the old wife had prepared a sleeping drink, and given it to the knight, who drank it, and never wakened till next morning. The live-long night the damsel sobbed and sang:

> "Seven long years I served for thee,
> The glassy hill I clomb for thee,
> Thy bloody clothes I wrang for thee;
> And wilt thou not waken and turn to me?"

Next day she knew not what to do for grief. Then she broke the pear, and found it filled with jewelry far richer than the contents of the apple. With these jewels she bargained for permission to be a second night in the young knight's chamber; but the old wife gave him another sleeping drink, and again he slept till morning. All night she kept singing and singing as before:

> "Seven long years I served for thee,
> The glassy hill I clomb for thee,
> Thy bloody clothes I wrang for thee;
> And wilt thou not waken and turn to me?"

Still he slept, and she nearly lost hope altogether. But that day, when he was out hunting, somebody asked him what noise and moaning was that they heard all last night in his bedchamber. He said: "I have heard no noise." But they assured him there was; and he resolved to keep waking that night to try what he could hear.

That being the third night, and the damsel being between hope and despair, she broke her plum, and it held far the richest jewelry of the three. She bargained as before; and the old wife, as before, took in the sleeping drink to the young knight's chamber; but he told her he couldn't drink it that night without sweetening. And when she went away for some honey to sweeten it with, he poured out the drink, and so made the old wife think he had drunk it. They all went to bed again, and the damsel began, as before, singing:

> "Seven long years I served for thee,
> The glassy hill I clomb for thee,
> Thy bloody clothes I wrang for thee;
> And wilt thou not waken and turn to me?"

He heard, and turned to her. And she told him all that had befallen her, and he told her all that had happened to him. And he caused the old washerwife and her daughter to be burnt. And they were married, and he and she are living happy to this day, for aught I know.

Tales From Ireland

THE FIELD OF BOLIAUNS

By JOSEPH JACOBS

Illustration by JOHN D. BATTEN

ONE fine day in harvest—it was indeed Lady-day in harvest, that everybody knows to be one of the greatest holidays in the year—Tom Fitzpatrick was taking a ramble through the ground, and went along the sunny side of a hedge; when all of a sudden he heard a clacking sort of noise a little before him in the hedge. "Dear me," said Tom, "but isn't it surprising to hear the stonechatters singing so late in the season?" So Tom stole on, going on the tops of his toes to try if he could get a sight of what was making the noise, to see if he was right in his guess. The noise stopped; but as Tom looked sharply through the bushes, what should he see in a nook of the hedge but a brown pitcher, that might hold about a gallon and a half of liquor; and by and by a little wee teeny tiny bit of an old man, with a little *motty* of a cocket hat stuck upon the top of his head, a deeshy daushy leather apron hanging before him, pulled out a little wooden stool, and stood up upon it, and dipped a little piggin into the pitcher, and took out the full of it, and put it beside the stool, and then sat down under the pitcher, and began to work at putting a heelpiece on a bit of a brogue just fit for himself.

"Well, by the powers," said Tom to himself, "I often heard tell of the Leprechauns, and to tell God's truth, I never rightly believed in them—but here's one of them in real earnest. If I go knowingly to work, I'm a made man. They say a body must never take their eyes off them, or they'll escape."

Tom now stole on a little farther, with his eye fixed on the little man just as a cat does with a mouse. So when he got up quite close to him, "God bless your work, neighbor," said Tom.

The little man raised up his head, and "Thank you kindly," said he.

"I wonder you'd be working on the holiday!" said **Tom.**

"That's my own business, not yours," was the reply.

"Well, maybe you'd be civil enough to tell *us* what you've got in the pitcher there?" said Tom.

A brown pitcher and a wee teeny bit of a man.

"That I will, with pleasure," said he; "it's good beer."

"Beer!" said Tom. "Thunder and fire! where did you get it?"

"Where did I get it, is it? Why, I made it. And what do you think I made it of?

"Devil a one of me knows," said Tom; "but of malt, I suppose, what else?"

"There you're out. I made it of heath."

"Of heath!" said Tom bursting out laughing; "sure you don't think me such a fool as to believe that?"

"Do as you please," said he, "but what I tell you is the truth. Did you never hear tell of the Danes?"

"Well, what about *them?*" said Tom.

"Why, all the about them there is, is that when they were here they taught us to make beer out of the heath, and the secret's in my family ever since."

"Will you give a body a taste of your beer?" said Tom.

"I'll tell you what it is, young man, it would be fitter for you to be looking after your father's property than to be bothering decent quiet people with your foolish questions. There now, while you're idling away your time here, there's the cows have broke into the oats, and are knocking the corn all about."

Tom was taken so by surprise with this that he was just on the very point of turning round when he recollected himself; so, afraid that the like might happen again, he made a grab at the Leprechaun, and caught him up in his hand; but in his hurry he overset the pitcher, and spilt all the beer, so that he could not get a taste of it to tell what sort it was. He then swore that he would kill him if he did not show him where his money was. Tom looked so wicked and so bloody-minded that the little man was quite frightened; so, says he, "Come along with me a couple of fields off, and I will show you a crock of gold."

So they went, and Tom held the Leprechaun fast in his hand, and never took his eyes from off him, though they had to cross hedges and ditches, and a crooked bit of bog, till at last they came to a great field all full of boliauns, and the Leprechaun pointed to a big boliaun, and says he:

"Dig under that boliaun, and you'll get the great crock all full of guineas."

Tom in his hurry had never thought of bringing a spade with him, so he made up his mind to run home and fetch one; and that he might know the place again he took off one of his red garters, and tied it round the boliaun.

Then he said to the Leprechaun: "Swear ye'll not take that garter away from that boliaun." And the Leprechaun swore right away not to touch it.

"I suppose," said the Leprechaun, very civilly, "you have no further occasion for me?"

"No," says Tom; "you may go away now, if you please, and God speed you, and may good luck attend you wherever you go."

"Well, good-bye to you, Tom Fitzpatrick," said the Leprechaun; "and much good may it do you when you get it."

So Tom ran for dear life, till he came home and got a spade, and then away with him, as hard as he could go, back to the field of boliauns; but when he got there, lo and behold! not a boliaun in the field but had a red garter, the very model of his own, tied about it; and as to digging up the whole field, that was all nonsense, for there were more than forty good Irish acres in it. So Tom came home again with the spade on his shoulder, a little cooler than he went, and many's the hearty curse he gave the Leprechaun every time he thought of the neat turn he had served him.

HUDDEN AND DUDDEN AND DONALD O'NEARY

By JOSEPH JACOBS

Illustrations by JOHN D. BATTEN

THERE was once upon a time two farmers, and their names were Hudden and Dudden. They had poultry in their yards, sheep on the uplands, and scores of cattle in the meadow land alongside the river. But for all that they weren't happy. For just between their two farms there lived a poor man by the name of Donald O'Neary. He had a hovel over his head and a strip of grass that was barely enough to keep his one cow, Daisy, from starving, and, though she did her best, it was but seldom that Donald got a drink of milk or a roll of butter from Daisy. You would think there was little here to make Hudden and Dudden jealous, but so it is, the more one has the more one wants, and Donald's neighbors lay awake of nights scheming how they might get hold of his little strip of grass-land. Daisy, poor thing, they never thought of; she was just a bag of bones. One day Hudden met Dudden, and they were soon grumbling as usual, and all to the tune of "If only we could get that vagabond Donald O'Neary out of the country."

"Let's kill Daisy," said Hudden at last; "if that doesn't make him clear out, nothing will."

No sooner said than agreed; and it wasn't dark before Hudden and Dudden crept up to the little shed where lay poor Daisy trying her best to chew the cud, though she hadn't had as much grass in the day as would cover your hand. And when Donald came to see if Daisy was all snug for the night, the poor beast had only time to lick his hand once before she died.

Well, Donald was a shrewd fellow, and downhearted though he was, began to think if he could get any good out of Daisy's death. He thought and he thought, and the next day you could have seen him trudging off early to the fair, Daisy's hide over his shoulder, every penny he had jingling in his pockets. Just before he got to the fair, he made several slits in the hide, put a penny in each slit, walked into the best inn of the town as bold as if it belonged to him, and, hanging the hide up to a nail in the wall, sat down.

"Some of your best whiskey," says he to the landlord. But the landlord didn't like his looks. "Is it fearing I won't pay you, you are?" says Donald. "Why, I have a hide here that gives me all the money I want." And with that he hit it a whack with his stick and out hopped a penny. The landlord opened his eyes.

"Let's kill Daisy," said Hudden at last.

"What'll you take for that hide?"

"It's not for sale, my good man."

"Will you take a gold piece?"

"It's not for sale, I tell you. Hasn't it kept me and mine for years?" and with that Donald hit the hide another whack and out jumped a second penny.

Well, the long and short of it was that Donald let the hide go, and, that evening, who but he should walk up to Hudden's door?

"Good evening, Hudden. Will you lend me your best scales?"

Hudden stared and scratched his head, but he lent the scales.

When Donald was safe at home, he pulled out his pocketful of bright gold and began to weigh each piece in the scales. But Hudden had put a lump of butter at the bottom, and so the last piece of gold stuck fast to the scales when he took them back to Hudden.

If Hudden had stared before, he stared ten times more now, and no sooner was Donald's back turned, than he was off as hard as he could pelt to Dudden's.

"Good evening, Dudden. That vagabond, bad luck to him——"

"You mean Donald O'Neary?"

"And who else should I mean? He's back here weighing out sackfuls of gold."

"How do you know that?"

"Here are my scales that he borrowed, and here's a gold piece still sticking to them."

Off they went together, and they came to Donald's door. Donald had finished making the last pile of ten gold pieces. And he couldn't finish because a piece had stuck to the scales.

In they walked without an "If you please" or "By your leave."

"Well, *I* never!" that was all *they* could say.

"Good evening, Hudden; good evening, Dudden. Ah! you thought you had played me a fine trick, but you never did me a better turn in all your lives. When I found poor Daisy dead, I thought to myself, 'Well, her hide may fetch something'; and it did. Hides are worth their weight in gold in the market just now."

Hudden nudged Dudden, and Dudden winked at Hudden.

"Good evening, Donald O'Neary."

"Good evening, kind friends."

The next day there wasn't a cow or a calf that belonged to Hudden or Dudden but her hide was going to the fair in Hudden's biggest cart drawn by Dudden's strongest pair of horses.

When they came to the fair, each one took a hide over his arm, and there they were walking through the fair, bawling out at the top of their voices: "Hides to sell! hides to sell!"

Out came the tanner: "How much for your hides, my good men?"

"Their weight in gold."

"It's early in the day to come out of the tavern." That was all the tanner said, and back he went to his yard.

"Hides to sell! Fine fresh hides to sell!"

Out came the cobbler: "How much for your hides, my men?"

"Their weight in gold."

"Is it making game of me you are! Take that for your pains," and the cobbler dealt Hudden a blow that made him stagger.

Up the people came running from one end of the fair to the other. "What's the matter? What's the matter?" cried they.

Donald had finished making the last pile of gold pieces.

"Here are a couple of vagabonds selling hides at their weight in gold," said the cobbler.

"Hold 'em fast; hold 'em fast!" bawled the innkeeper, who was the last to come up, he was so fat. "I'll wager it's one of the rogues who tricked me out of thirty gold pieces for a wretched hide."

It was more kicks than halfpence that Hudden and Dudden got before they were well on their way home again, and they didn't run the slower because all the dogs of the town were at their heels.

Well, as you may fancy, if they loved Donald little before, they loved him less now.

"What's the matter, friends?" said he, as he saw them tearing along, their hats knocked in, and their coats torn off, and their faces black and blue. "Is it fighting you've been? Or mayhap you met the police, ill luck to them?"

"We'll police you, you vagabond. It's mighty smart you thought yourself, deluding us with your lying tales."

"Who deluded you? Didn't you see the gold with your own two eyes?"

But it was no use talking. Pay for it he must, and should. There was a meal-sack handy, and into it Hudden and Dudden popped Donald O'Neary, tied him up tight, ran a pole through the knot, and off they started for the Brown Lake of the Bog, each with a pole-end on his shoulder, and Donald O'Neary between.

But the Brown Lake was far, the road was dusty, Hudden and Dudden were sore and weary, and parched with thirst. There was an inn by the roadside.

"Let's go in," said Hudden; "I'm dead beat. It's heavy he is for the little he had to eat."

If Hudden was willing, so was Dudden. As for Donald, you may be sure his leave wasn't asked, but he was lumped down at the inn door for all the world as if he had been a sack of potatoes.

"Sit still, you vagabond," said Dudden; "if we don't mind waiting, you needn't."

Donald held his peace, but after a while he heard the glasses clink, and Hudden singing away at the top of his voice.

"I won't have her, I tell you; I won't have her!" said Donald. But nobody heeded what he said.

"I won't have her, I tell you; I won't have her!" said Donald; and this time he said it louder; but nobody heeded what he said.

"I won't have her, I tell you; I won't have her!" said Donald; and this time he said it as loud as he could.

"And who won't you have, may I be so bold as to ask?" said a farmer, who had just come up with a drove of cattle, and was turning in for a glass.

"It's the king's daughter. They are bothering the life out of me to marry her."

"You're the lucky fellow. I'd give something to be in your shoes."

"Do you see that now! Wouldn't it be a fine thing for a farmer to be marrying a princess, all dressed in gold and jewels?"

"Jewels, do you say? Ah, now, couldn't you take me with you?"

"Well, you're an honest fellow, and as I don't care for the king's daughter, though she's as beautiful as the day, and is covered with jewels from top to toe, you shall have her. Undo the cord and let me out; they tied me tight, as they knew I'd run away from her."

Out crawled Donald; in crept the farmer.

"Now lie still, and don't mind the shaking; it's only rumbling over the palace steps you'll be. And maybe they'll abuse you for a vagabond, who won't have the king's daughter; but you needn't mind that. Ah! it's a deal I'm giving up for you, sure as it is that I don't care for the princess."

"Take my cattle in exchange," said the farmer; and you may guess it wasn't long before Donald was at their tails driving them homeward.

Out came Hudden and Dudden, and the one took one end of the pole, and the other the other. "I'm thinking he's heavier," said Hudden.

"Ah, never mind," said Dudden; "it's only a step now to the Brown Lake."

"I'll have her now! I'll have her now!" bawled the farmer, from inside the sack.

"By my faith and you shall, though," said Hudden, and he laid the stick across the sack.

"I'll have her! I'll have her!" bawled the farmer, louder than ever.

"Well, here you are," said Dudden, for they were now come to the Brown Lake, and, unslinging the sack, they pitched it plump into the lake.

"You'll not be playing your tricks on us any longer," said Hudden.

"True for you," said Dudden. "Ah, Donald, my boy, it was an ill day when you borrowed my scales."

Off they went, with a light step and an easy heart, but when they were near home, whom should they see but Donald O'Neary, and all around him the cows were grazing, and the calves were kicking up their heels and butting their heads together. "Is it you, Donald?" said Dudden. "Faith you've been quicker than we have."

"True for you, Dudden, and let me thank you kindly; the turn was good, if the will was ill. You'll have heard, like me, that the Brown Lake leads to the Land of Promise. I always put it down as lies, but it is just as true as my word. Look at the cattle."

Hudden stared, and Dudden gaped; but they couldn't get over the cattle; fine fat cattle they were, too.

"It's only the worst I could bring up with me," said Donald O'Neary; "the others were so fat, there was no driving them. Faith, too, it's little wonder they didn't care to leave, with grass as far as you could see, and as sweet and juicy as fresh butter."

"Ah, now, Donald, we haven't always been friends," said Dudden, "but, as I was just saying, you were ever a decent lad, and you'll show us the way, won't you?"

"I don't see that I'm called upon to do that; there is a power more cattle down there. Why shouldn't I have them all to myself?"

"Faith, they may well say, the richer you get, the harder the heart. You always were a neighborly lad, Donald. You wouldn't wish to keep the luck all to yourself?"

"True for you, Hudden, though 'tis a bad example you set me. But I'll not be thinking of old times. There is plenty for all there, so come along with me."

Off they trudged, with a light heart and an eager step. When they came to the Brown Lake the sky was full of little white clouds, and, if the sky was full, the lake was as full.

"Ah! now, look, there they are," cried Donald, as he pointed to the clouds in the lake.

"Where? where?" cried Hudden, and "Don't be greedy!" cried Dudden, as he jumped his hardest to be up first with the fat cattle. But if he jumped first, Hudden wasn't long behind.

They never came back. Maybe they got too fat, like the cattle. As for Donald O'Neary, he had cattle and sheep all his days to his heart's content.

ANDREW COFFEY

By JOSEPH JACOBS

Illustration by JOHN D. BATTEN

MY grandfather, Andrew Coffey, was known to the whole barony as a quiet, decent man. And if the whole barony knew him, he knew the whole barony, every inch, hill and dale, bog and pasture, field and covert. Fancy his surprise one evening, when he found himself in a part of the demesne he couldn't recognize a bit. He and his good horse were always stumbling up against some tree or stumbling down into some bog-hole that by rights didn't ought to be there. On the top of all this the rain came pelting down wherever there was a clearing, and the cold March wind tore through the trees. Glad he was when he saw a light in the distance, and drawing near found a cabin, though for the life of him he couldn't think how it came there. However, in he walked, after tying up his horse, and right welcome was the brushwood fire blazing on the hearth. And there stood a chair right and tight, that seemed to say, "Come, sit down in me." There wasn't a soul else in the room. Well, he did sit, and got a little warm and cheered after his drenching. But all the while he was wondering and wondering.

"Andrew Coffey! Andrew Coffey!"

Good heavens! who was calling him, and not a soul in sight? Look around as he might, indoors and out, he could find no creature with two legs or four, for his horse was gone.

"Andrew Coffey! Andrew Coffey! Tell me a story."

It was louder this time, and it was nearer. And then what a thing to ask for! It was bad enough not to be let sit by the fire and dry oneself, without being bothered for a story.

"Andrew Coffey! Andrew Coffey! Tell me a story, or it'll be the worse for you."

My poor grandfather was so dumbfounded that he could only stand and stare.

73

"Andrew Coffey! Andrew Coffey! I told you it'd be the worse for you."

And with that, out there bounced from a cupboard, that Andrew Coffey had never noticed before—*a man!* And the man was in a towering rage. But it wasn't that. And he carried as fine a blackthorn as you'd wish to crack a man's head with. But it wasn't that either. But when my grandfather clapped eyes on him, he knew him for Patrick Rooney, and all the world knew *he'd* gone overboard, fishing one night, long years before.

Andrew Coffey would neither stop nor stay, but he took to his heels and was out of the house as hard as he could. He ran and he ran, taking little thought of what was before till at last he ran up against a big tree. And then he sat down to rest.

He hadn't sat for a moment when he heard voices.

"It's heavy he is, the vagabond." "Steady now, we'll rest when we get under the big tree yonder." Now that happened to be the tree under which Andrew Coffey was sitting. At least he thought so, for seeing a branch handy he swung himself up by it, and was soon snugly hidden away. Better see than be seen, thought he.

The rain had stopped and the wind fallen. The night was blacker than ever, but Andrew Coffey could see four men, and they were carrying between them a long box. Under the tree they came, set the box down, opened it, and who should they bring out but—Patrick Rooney. Never a word did he say, and he looked as pale as old snow.

Well, one gathered brushwood, and another took out tinder and flint, and they soon had a big fire roaring, and my grandfather could see Patrick plainly enough. If he had kept still before, he kept stiller now. Soon they had four poles up and a pole across, right over the fire, for all the world like a spit, and on to the pole they slung Patrick Rooney.

"He'll do well enough," said one; "but who's to mind him whilst we're away; who'll turn the fire, who'll see that he doesn't burn?"

With that Patrick opened his lips: "Andrew Coffey!" said he.

"Andrew Coffey! Andrew Coffey! Andrew Coffey! Andrew Coffey!"

"I'm obliged to you, gentlemen," said Andrew Coffey, "but indeed I know nothing about the business."

"You'd better come down, Andrew Coffey," said Patrick. It was the second time he spoke, and Andrew Coffey decided he would come down. The four men went off, and he was left all alone with Patrick.

Then he sat and he kept the fire even, and he kept the spit turning, and all the while Patrick looked at him.

Poor Andrew Coffey couldn't make it all out, at all, at all, and he stared at Patrick and at the fire, and he thought of the little house in the wood, till he felt quite dazed.

"It's burning me, ye are!" said Patrick.

"Ah, but it's burning me, ye are!" says Patrick, very short and sharp.

"I'm sure I beg your pardon," said my grandfather, "but might I ask you a question?"

"If you want a crooked answer," said Patrick; "turn away, or it'll be the worse for you."

But my grandfather couldn't get it out of his head; hadn't everybody, far and near, said Patrick had fallen overboard. There was enough to think about, and my grandfather did think.

"Andrew Coffey! Andrew Coffey! It's burning me ye are."

Sorry enough my grandfather was, and he vowed he wouldn't do so again.

"You'd better not," said Patrick, and he gave him a cock of his eye, and a grin of his teeth, that just sent a shiver down Andrew Coffey's back. Well, it was odd, that here he should be in a thick wood he had never set eyes upon, turning Patrick Rooney upon a spit. You can't wonder at my grandfather thinking and thinking and not minding the fire.

"Andrew Coffey! Andrew Coffey! It's the death of you I'll be."

And with that what did my grandfather see, but Patrick unslinging himself from the spit, and his eyes glared and his teeth glistened.

It was neither stop nor stay my grandfather made, but out he ran into the night of the wood. It seemed to him there wasn't a stone but was for his stumbling, not a branch but beat his face, not a bramble but tore his skin. And wherever it was clear the rain pelted down and the cold March wind howled along.

Glad was he to see a light, and a minute after he was kneeling, dazed, drenched, and bedraggled by the hearth side. The brushwood flamed, and the brushwood crackled, and soon my grandfather began to feel a little warm and dry and easy in the mind.

"Andrew Coffey! Andrew Coffey!"

It's hard for a man to jump when he has been through all my grandfather had, but jump he did. And when he looked around, where should he find himself but in the very cabin he had first met Patrick in.

"Andrew Coffey, Andrew Coffey, tell me a story."

"Is it a story you want?" said my grandfather as bold as may be, for he was just tired of being frightened. "Well, if you can tell me the rights of this one, I'll be thankful."

And he told the tale of what had befallen him from first to last that night. The tale was long, and maybe Andrew Coffey was weary. It's asleep he must have fallen, for when he awoke he lay on the hillside under the open heavens, and his horse grazed at his side.

CONAL AND DONAL AND TAIG

By SEUMAS MAC MANUS

Illustration by VERBECK

ONCE there were three brothers named Conal, Donal and Taig, and they fell out regarding which of them owned a field of land. One of them had as good a claim to it as the other, and the claims of all of them were so equal that none of the judges, whomsoever they went before, could decide in favor of one more than the other.

At length they went to one judge who was very wise indeed and had a great name, and every one of them stated his case to him.

He sat on the bench, and heard Conal's case and Donal's case and Taig's case all through, with very great patience. When the three of them had finished, he said he would take a day and a night to think it all over, and on the day after, when they were all called into court again, the Judge said that he had weighed the evidence on all sides, with all the deliberation it was possible to give it, and he decided that one of them hadn't the shadow of a shade of a claim more than the others, so that he found himself facing the greatest puzzle he had ever faced in his life. "But," says he, "no puzzle puzzles me long. I'll very soon decide which of you will get the field. You seem to me to be three pretty lazy-looking fellows, and I'll give the field to whichever of the three of you is the laziest."

"Well, at that rate," says Conal, "it's me gets the field, for I'm the laziest man of the lot."

"How lazy are you?" says the Judge.

"Well," said Conal, "if I were lying in the middle of the road, and there was a regiment of troopers come galloping down it, I'd sooner let them ride over me than take the bother of getting up and going to the one side."

"Well, well," says the Judge, says he, "you are a lazy man surely, and I doubt if Donal or Taig can be as lazy as that."

77

"Oh, faith," says Donal, "I'm just every bit as lazy."

"Are you?" says the Judge. "How lazy are you?"

"Well," said Donal, "if I was sitting right close to a big fire, and you piled on it all the turf in a townland and all the wood in a baronry, sooner than have to move I'd sit there till the boiling marrow would run out of my bones."

"Well," says the Judge, "you're a pretty lazy man, Donal, and I doubt if Taig is as lazy as either of you."

"Indeed, then," says Taig, "I'm every bit as lazy."

"How can that be?" says the Judge.

"Well," says Taig, "if I was lying on the broad of my back in the middle of the floor and looking up at the rafters, and if soot drops were falling as thick as hailstones from the rafters into my open eyes, I would let them drop there for the length of the lee-long day sooner than take the bother of closing the eyes."

"Well," says the Judge, "that's very wonderful entirely, and," says he, "I'm in as great a quandary as before, for I see you are the three laziest men that ever were known since the world began, and which of you is the laziest it certainly beats me to say. But I'll tell you what I'll do," says the Judge, "I'll give the field to the oldest man of you."

"Then," says Conal, "it's me gets the field."

"How is that," says the Judge; "how old are you?"

"Well, I'm that old," says Conal, "that when I was twenty-one years of age I got a shipload of awls, and never lost nor broke one of them, and I wore out the last of them yesterday mending my shoes."

"Well, well," says the Judge, says he, "you're surely an old man, and I doubt very much that Donal and Taig can catch up to you."

"Can't I?" says Donal. "Take care of that."

"Why," said the Judge, "how old are you?"

"When I was twenty-one years of age," says Donal, "I got a shipload of needles, and yesterday I wore out the last of them mending my clothes."

"Well, well, well," says the Judge, says he, "you're two very, very old men, to be sure, and I'm afraid poor Taig is out of his chance anyhow."

"Take care of that," says Taig.

"Why," said the Judge, "how old are you, Taig?"

Says Taig, "When I was twenty-one years of age I got a shipload of razors, and yesterday I had the last of them worn to a stump shaving myself."

"Well," says the Judge, says he, "I've often heard tell of old men," he says, "but anything as old as what you three are never was known since Methusalem's cat died. The like of your ages," he says, "I never heard tell of, and which of you is the oldest, that surely beats me to decide, and I'm in a quandary again. But I'll tell you what I'll do," says the Judge, says he, "I'll give the field to whichever of you minds [remembers] the longest."

"Well, if that's it," says Conal, "it's me gets the field, for I mind the time when if a man tramped on a cat he usen't to give it a kick to console it."

"Well, well, well," says the Judge, "that must be a long mind entirely; and I'm afraid, Conal, you have the field."

"Not so quick," says Donal, says he, "for I mind the time when a woman wouldn't speak an ill word of her best friend."

"Well, well, well," says the Judge, "your memory, Donal, must certainly be a very wonderful one, if you can mind that time. Taig," says the Judge, says he, "I'm afraid your memory can't compare with Conal's and Donal's."

"Can't it?" says Taig, says he. "Take care of that, for I mind the time when you wouldn't find nine liars in a crowd of ten men."

"Oh, oh, oh!" says the Judge, says he. "That memory of yours, Taig, must be a wonderful one." Says he: "Such memories as you three men have were never known before, and which of you has the greatest memory it beats me to say. But I'll tell you what I'll do now," says he; "I'll give the field to whichever of you has the keenest sight."

"Then," says Conal, says he, "it's me gets the field; because," says he, "if there was a fly perched on the top of yon mountain, ten miles away, I could tell you every time he blinked."

"You have wonderful sight, Conal," says the Judge, says he, "and I'm afraid you've got the field."

"Take care," says Donal, says he, "but I've got as good. For I could tell you whether it was a mote in his eye that made him blink or not."

"Ah, ha, ha!" says the Judge, says he, "This is wonderful sight surely. Taig," says he, "I pity you, for you have no chance for the field now."

"Have I not?" says Taig. "I could tell you from here whether that fly was in good health or not by counting his heartbeats."

"Well, well, well," says the Judge, says he, "I'm in as great a quandary as ever. You are three of the most wonderful men that ever I met, and no mistake. But I'll tell you what I'll do," says he; "I'll give the field to the supplest man of you."

"Thank you," says Conal. "Then the field is mine."

"Why so?" says the Judge.

"Because," says Conal, says he, "if you filled that field with hares, and put a dog in the middle of them, and then tied one of my legs up my back, I would not let one of the hares get out."

"Then, Conal," says the Judge, says he, "I think the field is yours."

"By the leave of your Judgeship, not yet," says Donal.

"Why, Donal," says the Judge, says he, "surely you are not as supple as that?"

"Am I not?" says Donal. "Do you see that old castle over there without door, or window, or roof in it, and the wind blowing in and out through it like an iron gate?"

"I do," says the Judge. "What about that?"

"Well," says Donal, says he, "if on the stormiest day of the year you had that castle filled with feathers, I would not let a feather be lost, or go ten yards from the castle until I had caught and put it in again."

"Well, surely," says the Judge, says he, "you are a supple man, Donal, and no mistake. Taig," says he, "there's no chance for you now."

"Don't be too sure," says Taig, says he.

"Why," says the Judge, "you couldn't surely do anything to equal those things, Taig?"

Says Taig, says he: "I can shoe the swiftest race-horse in the

land when he is galloping at his topmost speed, by driving a nail every time he lifts his foot."

"Well, well, well," says the Judge, says he, "surely you are the three most wonderful men that ever I did meet. The likes of you never was known before, and I suppose the likes of you will never be on the earth again. There is only one other trial," says he, "and if this doesn't decide, I'll have to give it up. I'll give the field," says he, "to the cleverest man amongst you."

"Then," says Conal, says he, "you may as well give it to me at once."

"Why? Are you that clever, Conal?" says the Judge, says he.

"I am that clever," says Conal, "I am that clever, that I would make a skin-fit suit of clothes for a man without any more measurement than to tell me the color of his hair."

"Then, boys," says the Judge, says he, "I think the case is decided."

"Not so quick, my friend," says Donal, "not so quick."

"Why, Donal," says the Judge, says he, "you are surely not cleverer than that?"

"Am I not?" says Donal.

"Why," says the Judge, says he, "what can you do, Donal?"

"Why," says Donal, says he, "I would make a skin-fit suit for a man and give me no more measurement than let me hear him cough."

"Well, well, well," says the Judge, says he, "the cleverness of you two boys beats all I ever heard of. Taig," says he, "poor Taig, whatever chance either of these two may have for the field, I'm very, very sorry for you, but you have no chance."

"Don't be so very sure of that," says Taig, says he.

"Why," says the Judge, says he, "surely, Taig, you can't be as clever as either of them. How clever are you, Taig?"

"Well," says Taig, says he, "if I was a judge, and too stupid to decide a case that came up before me, I'd be that clever that I'd look wise and give some decision."

"Taig," says the Judge, says he, "I've gone into this case and deliberated upon it, and by all the laws of right and justice, I find and decide that you get the field."

THE OLD HAG'S LONG
LEATHER BAG

By SEUMAS MAC MANUS

Illustration by VERBECK

ONCE on a time, long, long ago, there was a widow woman who had three daughters. When their father died, their mother thought they never would want, for he had left her a long leather bag filled with gold and silver. But he was not long dead, when an old Hag came begging to the house one day and stole the long leather bag filled with gold and silver, and went away out of the country with it, no one knew where.

So from that day, the widow woman and her three daughters were poor, and she had a hard struggle to live and to bring up her three daughters.

But when they were grown up, the eldest said one day: "Mother, I'm a young woman now, and it's a shame for me to be here doing nothing to help you or myself. Bake me a bannock and cut me a callop[1], till I go away to push my fortune."

The mother baked her a whole bannock, and asked her if she would have half of it with her blessing or the whole of it without. She said to give her the whole bannock without.

So she took it and went away. She told them if she was not back in a year and a day from that, then they would know she was doing well, and making her fortune.

She traveled away and away before her, far farther than I could tell you, and twice as far as you could tell me, until she came into a strange country, and going up to a little house, she found an old Hag living in it. The Hag asked her where she was going. She said she was going to push her fortune.

Said the Hag: "How would you like to stay here with me? For I want a maid."

[1] Also "collop," a small slice of meat.

"What will I have to do?" said she.

"You will have to wash me and dress me, and sweep the hearth clean; but on the peril of your life, never look up the chimney," said the Hag.

"All right," she agreed to this.

The next day, when the Hag arose, she washed her and dressed her, and when the Hag went out, she swept the hearth clean, and she thought it would be no harm to have one wee look up the chimney. And there what did she see but her own mother's long leather bag of gold and silver? So she took it down at once, and getting it on her back, started away for home as fast as she could run.

But she had not gone far when she met a horse grazing in a field, and when he saw her, he said: "Rub me! Rub me! for I haven't been rubbed these seven years."

But she only struck him with a stick she had in her hand, and drove him out of her way.

She had not gone much farther when she met a sheep, who said: "Oh, shear me! Shear me! for I haven't been shorn these seven years."

But she struck the sheep, and sent it scurrying out of her way.

She had not gone much farther when she met a goat tethered, and he said: "Oh, change my tether! Change my tether! for it hasn't been changed these seven years."

But she flung a stone at him, and went on.

Next she came to a lime-kiln, and it said: "Oh, clean me! Clean me! for I haven't been cleaned these seven years."

But she only scowled at it, and hurried on.

After another bit she met a cow, and it said: "Oh, milk me! Milk me! for I haven't been milked these seven years."

She struck the cow out of her way, and went on.

Then she came to a mill. The mill said: "Oh, turn me! Turn me! for I haven't been turned these seven years."

But she did not heed what it said, only went in and lay down behind the mill door, with the bag under her head, for it was then night.

When the Hag came into her hut again and found the girl gone, she ran to the chimney and looked up to see if she had carried off the bag. She got into a great rage, and she started to run as fast as she could after her.

She had not gone far when she met the horse, and she said: "Oh, horse, horse of mine, did you see this maid of mine, with my tig, with my tag, with my long leather bag, and all the gold and silver I have earned since I was a maid?"

"Ay," said the horse, "it is not long since she passed here."

So on she ran, and it was not long till she met the sheep, and said she: "Sheep, sheep of mine, did you see this maid of mine, with my tig, with my tag, with my long leather bag, and all the gold and silver I have earned since I was a maid?"

"Ay," said the sheep, "it is not long since she passed here."

So she goes on, and it was not long before she met the goat, and said she: "Goat, goat of mine, did you see this maid of mine, with my tig, with my tag, with my long leather bag, and all the gold and silver I have earned since I was a maid?"

"Ay," said the goat, "it is not long since she passed here."

So she goes on, and it was not long before she met the lime-kiln, and said she: "Lime-kiln, lime-kiln of mine, did you see this maid of mine, with my tig, with my tag, with my long leather bag, and with all the gold and silver I have earned since I was a maid?"

"Ay," said the lime-kiln, "it is not long since she passed here."

So she goes on, and it was not long before she met the cow, and said she, "Cow, cow of mine, did you see this maid of mine, with my tig, with my tag, with my long leather bag, and all the gold and silver I have earned since I was a maid?"

"Ay," said the cow, "it is not long since she passed here."

So she goes on, and it was not long before she met the mill, and said she: "Mill, mill of mine, did you see this maid of mine, with my tig, with my tag, with my long leather bag, and all the gold and silver I have earned since I was a maid?"

And the mill said: "Yes, she is sleeping behind the door."

She went in and struck her with a white rod, and turned her into a stone. She then took the bag of gold and silver on her back, and went away back home.

A year and a day had gone by after the eldest daughter left home, and when they found she had not returned, the second daughter got up, and she said: "My sister must be doing well and making her fortune, and isn't it a shame for me to be sitting here doing nothing, either to help you, Mother, or myself. Bake me a bannock," said she, "and cut me a callop, till I go away to push my fortune."

The mother did this, and asked her would she have half the bannock with her blessing or the whole bannock without.

She said the whole bannock without, and she set off. Then she said: "If I am not back here in a year and a day, you may be sure that I am doing well and making my fortune," and then she went away.

She traveled away and away on before her, far farther than I could tell you, and twice as far as you could tell me, until she came into a strange country, and going up to a little house, she found an old Hag living in it. The old Hag asked her where she was going. She said she was going to push her fortune.

Said the Hag: "How would you like to stay here with me? For I want a maid."

"What will I have to do?" says she.

"You'll have to wash me and dress me, and sweep the hearth clean; and on the peril of your life never look up the chimney," said the Hag.

"All right," she agreed to this.

The next day, when the Hag arose, she washed her and dressed her, and when the Hag went out she swept the hearth, and she thought it would be no harm to have one wee look up the chimney.

And there what did she see but her own mother's long leather bag of gold and silver? So she took it down at once, and getting it on her back, started away for home as fast as she could run.

But she had not gone far when she met a horse grazing in a field, and when he saw her, he said: "Rub me! Rub me! for I haven't been rubbed these seven years."

But she only struck him with a stick she had in her hand, and drove him out of her way.

She had not gone much farther when she met the sheep, who said: "Oh, shear me! Shear me! for I haven't been shorn in seven years."

But she struck the sheep, and sent it scurrying out of her way.

She had not gone much farther when she met the goat tethered, and he said: "Oh, change my tether! Change my tether! for it hasn't been changed in seven years."

But she flung a stone at him, and went on.

Next she came to the lime-kiln, and that said: "Oh, clean me! Clean me! for I haven't been cleaned these seven years."

But she only scowled at it, and hurried on.

Then she came to the cow, and it said: "Oh, milk me! Milk me! for I haven't been milked these seven years."

She struck the cow out of her way, and went on.

Then she came to the mill. The mill said: "Oh, turn me! Turn me! for I haven't been turned these seven years."

But she did not heed what it said, only went in and lay down behind the mill door, with the bag under her head, for it was night.

When the Hag came into her hut again and found the girl gone, she ran to the chimney and looked up to see if she had carried off the bag. She got into a great rage, and she started to run as fast as she could after her.

She had not gone far when she met the horse, and she said: "Oh, horse, horse of mine, did you see this maid of mine, with my tig, with my tag, with my long leather bag, and all the gold and silver I have earned since I was a maid?"

"Ay," said the horse, "it is not long since she passed here."

So on she ran, and it was not long until she met the sheep, and said she: "Oh, sheep, sheep of mine, did you see this maid of mine, with my tig, with my tag, with my long leather bag, and all the gold and silver I have earned since I was a maid?"

"Ay," said the sheep, "it is not long since she passed here."

So she goes on, and it was not long before she met the goat, and said: "Goat, goat of mine, did you see this maid of mine, with my tig, with my tag, with my long leather bag, and all the gold and silver I have earned since I was a maid?"

"Ay," said the goat, "it is not long since she passed here."

So she goes on, and it was not long before she met the lime-kiln, and said she: "Lime-kiln, lime-kiln of mine, did you see this maid of mine, with my tig, with my tag, with my long leather bag, and all the gold and silver I have earned since I was a maid?"

"Ay," said the lime-kiln, "it is not long since she passed here."

So she goes on, and it was not long before she met the cow, and says she: "Cow, cow of mine, did you see this maid of mine, with my tig, with my tag, with my long leather bag, and all the gold and silver I have earned since I was a maid?"

"Ay," said the cow, "it is not long since she passed here."

So she goes on, and it was not long before she met the mill, and said she: "Mill, mill of mine, did you see this maid of mine, with my tig, with my tag, with my long leather bag, and all the gold and silver I have earned since I was a maid?"

And the mill said: "Yes, she is sleeping behind the door."

She went in and struck her with a white rod, and turned her into a stone. She then took the bag of gold and silver on her back and went home.

When the second daughter had been gone a year and a day, and she hadn't come back, the youngest daughter said: "My two sisters must be doing very well indeed, and making great fortunes when they are not coming back, and it's a shame for me to be sitting here doing nothing, either to help you, Mother, or myself. Make me a bannock and cut me a callop, till I go away and push my fortune."

The mother did this and asked her would she have half of the bannock with her blessing or the whole bannock without.

She said: "I will have half of the bannock with your blessing, Mother."

The mother gave her a blessing and half a bannock, and she set out. She traveled away and away on before her, far farther than I could tell you, and twice as far as you could tell me, until she came into a strange country, and going up to a little house, she found an old Hag living in it. The Hag asked her where she was going. She said she was going to push her fortune.

Said the Hag: "How would you like to stay here with me? For I want a maid."

"What will I have to do?" said she.

"You'll have to wash me and dress me, and sweep the hearth clean; and on the peril of your life never look up the chimney," said the Hag.

"All right," she agreed to this.

The next day, when the Hag arose, she washed her and dressed her, and when the Hag went out she swept the hearth, and she thought it would be no harm to have one wee look up the chimney, and there what did she see but her own mother's long leather bag of gold and silver! So she took it down at once, and getting it on her back, started away for home as fast as she could run.

When she got to the horse, the horse said: "Rub me! Rub me! for I haven't been rubbed these seven years."

"Oh, poor horse, poor horse," she said, "I'll surely do that." And she laid down her bag, and rubbed the horse.

Then she went on, and it wasn't long before she met the sheep, who said: "Oh, shear me! Shear me! for I haven't been shorn these seven years."

"Oh, poor sheep, poor sheep," she said, "I'll surely do that," and she laid down the bag, and sheared the sheep.

On she went till she met the goat, who said: "Oh, change my tether! Change my tether! for it hasn't been changed these seven years."

"Oh, poor goat, poor goat," she said, "I'll surely do that," and she laid down the bag, and changed the goat's tether.

Then she went on till she met the lime-kiln. The lime-kiln said:

"Oh, clean me! Clean me! for I haven't been cleaned these seven years."

"Oh, poor lime-kiln, poor lime-kiln," she said, "I'll surely do that," and she laid down the bag and cleaned the lime-kiln.

Then she went on and met the cow. The cow said: "Oh, milk me! Milk me! for I haven't been milked these seven years."

"Oh, poor cow, poor cow," she said, "I'll surely do that," and she laid down the bag and milked the cow.

At last she reached the mill. The mill said: "Oh, turn me! Turn me! for I haven't been turned these seven years."

"Oh, poor mill, poor mill," she said, "I'll surely do that," and she turned the mill, too. As night was on her, she went in and lay down behind the mill door to sleep.

When the Hag came into her hut again and found the girl gone, she ran to the chimney to see if she had carried off the bag. She got into a great rage, and started to run as fast as she could after her.

She had not gone far until she came up to the horse and said: "Oh, horse, horse of mine, did you see this maid of mine, with my tig, with my tag, with my long leather bag, and all the gold and silver I have earned since I was a maid?"

The horse said: "Do you think I have nothing to do only watch your maids for you? You may go somewhere else and look for information."

Then she came upon the sheep. "Oh, sheep, sheep of mine, have you seen this maid of mine, with my tig, with my tag, with my long leather bag, and all the gold and silver I have earned since I was a maid?"

The sheep said: "Do you think I have nothing to do only watch your maids for you? You may go somewhere else and look for information."

Then she went on till she met the goat. "Oh, goat, goat of mine, have you seen this maid of mine, with my tig, with my tag, with my long leather bag, and all the gold and silver I have earned since I was a maid?"

The goat said: "Do you think I have nothing to do only watch your maids for you? You can go somewhere else and look for information."

Then she went on till she came to the lime-kiln. "Oh, lime-kiln, lime-kiln, did you see this maid of mine, with my tig, with my tag, with my long leather bag, and all the gold and silver I have earned since I was a maid?"

Said the lime-kiln: "Do you think I have nothing to do only to watch your maids for you? You may go somewhere else and look for information."

Next she met the cow. "Oh, cow, cow of mine, have you seen this maid of mine, with my tig, with my tag, with my long leather bag, and all the gold and silver I have earned since I was a maid?"

The cow said: "Do you think I have nothing to do only watch your maids for you? You may go somewhere else and look for information."

Then she got to the mill. "Oh, mill, mill of mine, have you seen this maid of mine, with my tig, with my tag, with my long leather bag, and all the gold and silver I have earned since I was a maid?"

The mill said: "Come nearer and whisper to me."

She went nearer to whisper to the mill, and the mill dragged her under the wheels and ground her up.

The old Hag had dropped the white rod out of her hand, and the mill told the young girl to take this white rod and strike two stones behind the mill door. She did that, and her two sisters stood up. She hoisted the leather bag on her back, and the three of them set out and traveled away and away till they reached home.

The mother had been crying all the time while they were away, and was now ever so glad to see them, and rich and happy they all lived ever after.

MANIS THE MILLER

By SEUMAS MAC MANUS

Illustration by VERBECK

THERE was a man from the mountain, named Donal, once married the daughter of a stingy old couple who lived on the lowland. He used to stay and work on his own wee patch of land all the week round, till it came to Saturday evening, and on Saturday evening he went to his wife's father's to spend Sunday with him.

Coming and going he always passed the mill of Manis the miller; and Manis, who used to be watching him passing, always noticed, and thought it strange, that while he jumped the mill-race going to his wife's father's on a Saturday evening, he had always to wade through it coming back. And at last he stopped Donal one Monday morning, and asked him the meaning of it.

"Well, I'll tell you," says Donal, says he. "It's this: My old father-in-law is such a very small eater, that he says grace and blesses himself when I've only got a few pieces out of my meals; so I'm always weak coming back on Monday morning."

Manis, he thought over this to himself for a while, and then says he: "Would you mind letting me go with you next Saturday evening? If you do, I promise you that you'll leap the mill-race coming back."

"I'll be glad to have you," says Donal.

Very well and good. When Saturday evening came, Manis joined Donal and off they both trudged to Donal's father-in-law's.

The old man was not too well pleased at seeing Donal bringing a fresh hand, but Manis, he didn't pretend to see this, but made himself as welcome as the flowers in May. And when supper was laid down on Saturday night, Manis gave Donal the nudge, and both of them began to tie their shoes as if they had got loose, and they tied and tied away at their shoes, till the old man had eaten a couple of minutes and then said grace, and finished and got up from the table, thinking they wouldn't have the ill-manners to sit down after the meal was over.

But down to the table my brave Manis and Donal sat, and ate their hearty skinful. And when the old fellow saw this, he was gruff and grumpy enough, and it was little they could get out of him between that and bedtime.

But Manis kept a lively chat going, and told good stories that passed away the night; and when bedtime came and they offered Manis a bed in the room, Manis said no, that there was no place he could sleep only one, and that was along the fireside.

The old man and the old woman both objected to this, and said they couldn't think of allowing a stranger to sleep there; but all they could say or do wasn't any use, and Manis said he couldn't and wouldn't sleep in any other place, and lie down there he did in spite of them all, and they all went off to their beds.

But though Manis lay down, he was very careful not to let himself go to sleep; and when he was near about two hours lying, he hears the room door open easy, and the old woman puts her head out and listens, and Manis he snored as if he hadn't slept for ten days and ten nights before.

When the old woman heard this, she came on up the floor and looked at him, and saw him like as if he was dead asleep. Then she hastened to put a pot of water on the fire, and began to make a pot of stirabout for herself and the old man, for this was the way, as Manis had well suspected, that they used to cheat Donal.

But just in the middle of the cooking of the pot of stirabout, doesn't Manis roll over and pretend to waken up? Up he sits, and rubs his eyes, and looks about him, and looks at the woman and at the pot on the fire.

"Ah," says he, "is it here ye are, or is it mornin' with ye?"

"Well, no," says she, "it isn't morning, but we have a cow that's not well, and I had to put a mash on the fire here for her. I'm sorry I wakened ye."

"Oh, no, no!" says Manis, says he, "you haven't wakened me at all. It's this sore ankle I have here," says he, rubbing his ankle. "I've a very, very sore ankle," says he, "and it troubles me sometimes at night," he says, "and no matter how sound asleep I may be, it wakens me up, and I've got to sit up till I cure it." Says he: "There's nothin' cures it but soot—till I rub plenty of soot out of the chimney to it."

And Manis takes hold of the tongs, and he begins pulling the soot down out of the chimney from above the pot, and for every one piece that fell on the fire, there were five pieces that fell into the pot. And when Manis thought he had the posset well enough spiced with the soot, he raised up a little of the soot from the fire and rubbed his ankle with it.

"And now," says he, "that's all right, and I'll sleep sound and not waken again till mornin'." And he stretched himself out again, and began to snore.

The old woman was pretty well vexed that she had had her night's work spoiled, and she went up to the room to the old man and told him what had happened to the stirabout. He got into a bad rage entirely, and asked her was Manis asleep again, and she said he was. Then he ordered her to go down and make an oat scowder[1] and put it on the ashes for him.

She went down, and got the oatmeal, and made a good scowder, and set it on the ashes, and then sat by it for the short while it would be doing.

But she hadn't it many minutes on the ashes when Manis let a cry out of him, as if it was in his sleep, and up he jumps and rubs his eyes and looks about him; and when he saw her, he said: "Och! is it here ye are? And I'm glad ye are," says he; "because I've a great trouble on me mind, that's lying a load over me heart and wouldn't let me sleep, and I want to relieve me mind to ye," says Manis; "an' then I'll sleep hearty and sound all the night after. I'll tell you the story," says he.

So he catches hold of the tongs in his two hands, and as he told the story he would stir them about through the ashes.

[1] A hastily baked oat-cake.

Says he: "I want to tell you that my father afore he died was a very rich man and owned no end of land. He had three sons, myself and Teddy and Tom; and the three of us were three good hard workers. I always liked Teddy and Tom; but however it came out, Tom and Teddy hated me, and they never lost a chance of trying to damage me with my father and turn him against me. He sent Teddy and Tom to school and gave them a grand education, but he only gave me the spade in me fist and sent me out to the fields. And when Teddy and Tom came back from school, they were two gentlemen, and use to ride their horses and hunt with their hounds; and me they always made look after the horses and groom them and saddle them and bridle them, and be there in the yard to meet them when they would come in from their riding, and take charge of their horses, give them a rubbing down, and stable them for them.

"In my own mind, I use to think that this wasn't exactly fair or brotherly treatment; but I said nothing, for I liked both Teddy and Tom. And prouder and prouder of them every day got my father, and more and more every day he disliked me, until at long and at last, when he came to die, he liked Teddy and Tom that much, and he liked poor Manis that little, that he drew up his will and divided his land into four parts and left it in this way:

"Now, supposin'," says Manis, says he, digging the point of the tongs into the scowder, "supposin'," says he, "there was my father's farm. He cut it across this way," says he, drawing the tongs through the scowder in one way. "Then he cut it across this way," says he, drawing the tongs through the scowder in the other direction; "and that quarter," says he, tossing away a quarter of the scowder with the point of the tongs, "he gave to my mother. And that quarter there," says he, tossing off the other quarter into the dirt, "he gave to Teddy, and this quarter here," says he, tossing the third quarter, "he gave to Tom. And this last quarter," says Manis, says he, digging the point of the tongs right into the heart of the other quarter of the scowder, and lifting it up and looking at it, "this quarter," says he, "he gave to the priest," and he pitched it as far from him down the floor as he could. "And there," says he, throwing down the tongs, "he left poor Manis what he is today—a beggar and an outcast!

That, ma'am," says he, "is my story, and now that I've relieved my mind, I'll sleep sound and well till morning." And down he stretched himself by the fireside, and begins to snore again.

And the old woman she started up to the room, and she told the old man what had happened to the scowder; and the old fellow got into a mighty rage entirely, and was for getting up and going down to have the life of Manis, for he was starving with the hunger. But she tried to soothe him as well as she could. And then he told her to go down to the kitchen and make something else on the fire for him.

"Oh, it's no use," says she, "a-trying to make anything on the fire, for there'll be some other ache coming on that fellow's ankle or some other trouble on his mind, and he'll be getting up in the middle of it all to tell me about it. But I'll tell you what I'll do," says she, "I'll go out and I'll milk the cow, and give you a good jug of sweet milk to drink, and that will take the hunger off you till morning."

He told her to get up quick and do it, or she would find him dead of the hunger.

And off she went as quickly as she could, and took a jug off the kitchen dresser, and slipped out, leaving Manis snoring loudly in the kitchen. But when Manis thought that she had had time to have the jug near filled from the cow, he slips out to the byre, and as it was dark he talked like the old man: "And," says he, "I'll die with the hunger if you don't hurry with that."

So she filled the jug, and she reached it to him in the dark, and he drank it off, and gave her back the empty jug, and went in and lay down.

Then she milked off another jug for herself and drank it, and came slipping in, and put the jug easy on the dresser, so as not to waken Manis, and went up to the room.

When she came up, the old fellow was raging there. Says he: "You might have milked all the cows in the county since, an' me dead with hunger here waitin' on it. Give me my jug of milk," says he.

"And what do ye mean?" says she.

"What does yourself mean, you old blather-skite?" says the old man, says he.

Says she, "Didn't you come out to the byre and ask me for the jug of milk there, an' didn't I give it to you, and didn't you drink it all?"

"Be this and be that," says he, "but this is a nice how-do-ye-do. It's that scoundrel," says he, "in the kitchen, that's tricked ye again. An' be this an' be that," says he, "I'm goin' down now to have his life."

And when she heard how she had been tricked, she was not a bit sorry to let him go and have Manis's life.

But Manis had been listening with his ear to the keyhole to hear what was going on, and when he heard this, and while the man was preparing to go down and take his life, he hauled in a calf, and put it by the fireside where he had been lying, and threw the cover over it.

And when the man came down with the sledge hammer, he went to the place where he knew Manis had been lying, and he struck with all his might, and he drove the hammer through the calf's skull, and the calf only just gave one *moo!* and died. And then the old fellow went back to his bed content, and the miller went out and off home again.

When the old fellow and his woman got up in the morning early to go and bury the miller, they found the trick he had played on them, and they were in a pretty rage. But when the breakfast was made this morning, and Donal and all of them sat down, I can tell you the old fellow was in no hurry saying grace, and Donal he got his hearty fill for once in his life anyhow, and so did he at night.

And when Donal was going back home on Monday morning, he leapt the mill-race, and Manis came out, and gave him a cheer. He took Manis's both hands, and he shook them right hearty.

And every Monday morning after, for the three years that the old fellow lived, Manis always saw Donal leap the mill-race as easy as a sparrow might hop over a rod.

At the end of the three years, the old fellow died, and Donal went to live on the farm altogether, and there was no friend ever came to see him that was more heartily welcomed than Manis the Miller.

BILLY BEG AND THE BULL

By SEUMAS MAC MANUS

ONCE upon a time when pigs was swine, there was a King and a Queen, and they had one son, Billy, and the Queen gave Billy a bull that he was very fond of, and it was just as fond of him. After some time the Queen died, and she put it as her last request on the King that he would never part Billy and the bull, and the King promised that, come what might, come what may, he would not.

After the Queen died, the King married again, and the new Queen didn't take to Billy Beg, and no more did she like the bull, seeing himself and Billy so *thick*. But she couldn't get the King on no account to part Billy and the bull, so she consulted with a henwife what they could do as regards separating Billy and the bull. "What will you give me," says the henwife, "and I'll very soon part them?" "Whatever you ask," says the Queen. "Well and good, then," says the henwife, "you are to take to your bed, making pretend that you are bad with a complaint, and I'll do the rest of it." And, well and good, to her bed she took, and none of the doctors could do anything for her, or make out what was her complaint. So the Queen axed for the henwife to be sent for. And sent for she was, and when she came in and examined the Queen, she said there was one thing, and only one, could cure her. The King asked what was that, and the henwife said it was three mouthfuls of the blood of Billy Beg's bull. But the King wouldn't on no account hear of this, and the next day the Queen was worse, and the third day she was worse still, and told the King she was dying, and he'd have her death on his head. So, sooner nor this, the King had to consent to Billy Beg's bull being killed.

When Billy heard this he got very down in the heart entirely, and he went doitherin' about, and the bull saw him, and asked him what was wrong with him that he was so mournful, so Billy told the bull what was wrong with him, and the bull told him to never

98

mind, but keep up his heart, the Queen would never taste a drop
of his blood. The next day then the bull was to be killed, and the
Queen got up and went out to have the delight of seeing his death.
When the bull was led up to be killed, says he to Billy, "Jump up
on my back till we see what kind of a horseman you are." Up Billy
jumped on his back, and with that the bull leapt nine mile high,
nine mile deep and nine mile broad, and came down with Billy
sticking between his horns. Hundreds were looking on dazed at the
sight, and through them the bull rushed, and over the top of the
Queen, killing her dead, and away he galloped where you wouldn't
know day by night, or night by day, over high hills, low hills, sheep-
walks, and bullock-traces, the Cove of Cork, and old Tom Fox with
his bugle horn.

When at last they stopped, "Now then," says the bull to Billy,
"you and I must undergo great scenery, Billy. Put your hand," says
the bull, "in my left ear, and you'll get a napkin, that, when you
spread it out, will be covered with eating and drinking of all sorts,
fit for the King himself." Billy did this, and then he spread out the
napkin, and ate and drank to his heart's content, and he rolled up
the napkin and put it back in the bull's ear again. Then says the
bull, "Now put your hand into my right ear and you'll find a bit of
a stick; if you wind it over your head three times, it will be turned
into a sword and give you the strength of a thousand men besides
your own, and when you have no more need of it as a sword, it will
change back into a stick again." Billy did all this. Then says the
bull, "At twelve o'clock the morrow I'll have to meet and fight a
great bull."

Billy then got up again on the bull's back, and the bull started
off and away where you wouldn't know day by night, or night by
day, over high hills, low hills, sheep-walks and bullock-traces, the
Cove of Cork, and old Tom Fox with his bugle horn. There he met
the other bull, and both of them fought, and the like of their fight
was never seen before or since. They knocked the soft ground into
hard, and the hard into soft, the soft into spring wells, the spring
wells into rocks, and the rocks into high hills. They fought long,
and Billy Beg's bull killed the other, and drank his blood. Then

Billy took the napkin out of his ear again and spread it out and ate a hearty good dinner. Then says the bull to Billy, says he, "At twelve o'clock tomorrow, I'm to meet the bull's brother that I killed the day, and we'll have a hard fight."

Billy got on the bull's back again, and the bull started off and away where you wouldn't know day by night, or night by day, over high hills, low hills, sheep-walks and bullock-traces, the Cove of Cork, and old Tom Fox with his bugle horn. There he met the bull's brother that he killed the day before, and they set to, and they fought, and the like of the fight was never seen before or since. They knocked the soft ground into hard, the hard into soft, the soft into spring wells, the spring wells into rocks, and the rocks into high hills. They fought long, and at last Billy's bull killed the other bull and drank his blood. And then Billy took the napkin out of the bull's ear again and spread it out and ate another hearty dinner. Then says the bull to Billy, says he—"The morrow at twelve o'clock I'm to fight the brother to the two bulls I killed—he's a mighty great bull entirely, the strongest of them all; he's called the Black Bull of the Forest, and he'll be too able for me. When I'm dead," says the bull, "you, Billy, will take with you the napkin, and you'll never be hungry; and the stick, and you'll be able to overcome everything that comes in your way; and take out your knife and cut a strip of the hide off my back and another strip off my belly and make a belt of them, and as long as you wear them you cannot be killed."

Billy was very sorry to hear this, but he got up on the bull's back again, and they started off and away where you wouldn't know day by night or night by day, over high hills, low hills, sheep-walks and bullock-traces, the Cove of Cork and old Tom Fox with his bugle horn. And sure enough at twelve o'clock the next day they met the great Black Bull of the Forest, and both of the bulls set to it, and commenced to fight, and the like of the fight was never seen before or since; they knocked the soft ground into hard ground, and the hard ground into soft and the soft into spring wells, the spring wells into rocks, and the rocks into high hills. And they fought long, but at length the Black Bull of the Forest killed Billy Beg's bull, and

drank his blood. Billy Beg was so vexed at this that for two days he
sat over the bull neither eating or drinking, but crying salt tears all
the time.

Then he got up, and he spread out the napkin, and ate a hearty
dinner, for he was very hungry with his long fast; and after that he
cut a strip of the hide off the bull's back, and another off the belly,
and made a belt for himself, and taking it and the bit of stick, and
the napkin, he set out to push his fortune, and he traveled for three
days and three nights till at last he come to a great gentleman's place.
Billy asked the gentleman if he could give him employment, and the
gentleman said he wanted just such a boy as him for herding cattle.
Billy asked what cattle would he have to herd, and what wages
would he get. The gentleman said he had three goats, three cows,
three horses and three asses that he fed in an orchard, but that no
boy who went with them ever came back alive, for there were three
giants, brothers, that came to milk the cows and the goats every day,
and killed the boy that was herding; so if Billy liked to try, they
wouldn't fix the wages till they'd see if he would come back alive.
"Agreed, then," said Billy.

So the next morning he got up and drove out the three goats, the
three cows, the three horses, and the three asses to the orchard and
commenced to feed them. About the middle of the day Billy heard
three terrible roars that shook the apples off the bushes, shook the
horns on the cows, and made the hair stand up on Billy's head, and
in comes a frightful big giant with three heads, and begun to
threaten Billy. "You're too big," says the giant, "for one bite, and
too small for two. What will I do with you?" "I'll fight you," says
Billy, says he, stepping out to him and swinging the bit of stick three
times over his head, when it changed into a sword and gave him the
strength of a thousand men besides his own. The giant laughed at
the size of him, and says he, "Well, how will I kill you? Will it be
by a swing by the back,[1] a cut of the sword, or a square round of
boxing?" "With a swing by the back," says Billy, "if you can." So
they both laid holds, and Billy lifted the giant clean off the ground,
and fetching him down again sunk him in the earth up to his arm-

[1] A wrestle.

pits. "Oh, have mercy," says the giant. But Billy, taking his sword, killed the giant, and cut out his tongues. It was evening by this time, so Billy drove home the three goats, three cows, three horses, and three asses, and all the vessels in the house wasn't able to hold all the milk the cows give that night.

"Well," says the gentleman, "this beats me, for I never saw anyone coming back alive out of there before, nor the cows with a drop of milk. Did you see anything in the orchard?" says he. "Nothing worse nor myself," says Billy. "What about my wages, now," says Billy. "Well," says the gentleman, "you'll hardly come alive out of the orchard the morrow. So we'll wait till after that." Next morning his master told Billy that something must have happened to one of the giants, for he used to hear the cries of three every night, but last night he only heard two crying. "I don't know," says Billy, "anything about them."

That morning after he got his breakfast Billy drove the three goats, three cows, three horses, and three asses into the orchard again, and began to feed them. About twelve o'clock he heard three terrible roars that shook the apples off the bushes, the horns on the cows, and made the hair stand up on Billy's head, and in comes a frightful big giant, with six heads, and he told Billy he had killed his brother yesterday, but he would make him pay for it the day. "Ye're too big," says he, "for one bite, and too small for two, and what will I do with you?" "I'll fight you," says Billy, swinging his stick three times over his head, and turning it into a sword, and giving him the strength of a thousand men besides his own. The giant laughed at him, and says he, "How will I kill you—with a swing by the back, a cut of the sword, or a square round of boxing?" "With a swing by the back," says Billy, "if you can." So the both of them laid holds, and Billy lifted the giant clean off the ground, and fetching him down again, sunk him in it up to the armpits. "Oh, spare my life!" says the giant. But Billy taking up his sword, killed him and cut out his tongues. It was evening by this time, and Billy drove home his three goats, three cows, three horses, and three asses, and what milk the cows gave that night overflowed all the vessels in the house, and, running out, turned a rusty mill that hadn't been turned before for thirty years. If the master was surprised seeing Billy coming back the night before, he was ten times more surprised now.

"Did you see anything in the orchard the day!" says the gentleman. "Nothing worse nor myself," says Billy. "What about my wages now," says Billy. "Well, never mind about your wages," says the gentleman, "till the morrow, for I think you'll hardly come back alive again," says he. Well and good, Billy went to his bed, and the gentleman went to his bed, and when the gentleman rose in the morning says he to Billy, "I don't know what's wrong with two of the giants; I only heard one crying last night." "I don't know," says Billy, "they must be sick or something."

Well, when Billy got his breakfast that day again, he set out to the orchard, driving before him the three goats, three cows, three horses and three asses; and sure enough, about the middle of the day he hears three terrible roars again, and in comes another giant, this one with twelve heads on him, and if the other two were frightful, surely this one was ten times more so. "You villain, you," says he to Billy, "you killed my two brothers, and I'll have my revenge on you now. Prepare till I kill you," says he; "you're too big for one bite, and too small for two; what will I do with you?" "I'll fight you," says Billy, shaping out and winding the bit of stick three times over his head. The giant laughed heartily at the size of him, and says he, "What way do you prefer being killed? Is it with a swing by the back, a cut of the sword, or a square round of boxing?" "A swing by the back," says Billy. So both of them again laid holds, and my brave Billy lifts the giant clean off the ground, and fetching him down again, sunk him down to his armpits in it. "Oh, have mercy; spare my life," says the giant. But Billy took his sword, and, killing him, cut out his tongues. That evening he drove home his three goats, three cows, three horses, and three asses, and the milk of the cows had to be turned into a valley where it made a lough three miles long, three miles broad, and three miles deep, and that lough has been filled with salmon and white trout ever since. The gentleman wondered now more than ever to see Billy back the third day alive.

"Did you see nothing in the orchard the day, Billy?" says he. "No, nothing worse nor myself," says Billy. "Well, that beats me," says the gentleman. "What about my wages now?" says Billy. "Well, you're a good mindful boy, that I couldn't easy do without," says the gentleman, "and I'll give you any wages you ask for the future." The next morning, says the gentleman to Billy, "I heard none of the giants crying last night, however it comes. I don't know what has happened to them?" "I don't know," says Billy, "they must be sick or something." "Now, Billy," says the gentleman, "you must look after the cattle the day again, while I go to see the fight." "What fight?" says Billy. "Why," says the gentleman, "it's the king's daughter is going to be devoured by a fiery dragon, if the greatest fighter in the land, that they have been feeding specially for the last three months, isn't able to kill the dragon first. And if he's able to kill the dragon the king is to give him the daughter in marriage." "That will be fine," says Billy.

Billy drove out his three goats, three cows, three horses, and three asses to the orchard that day again, and the like of all that passed that day to see the fight with the man and the fiery dragon, Billy never witnessed before. They went in coaches and carriages, on horses and jackasses, riding and walking, crawling and creeping. "My tight little fellow," says a man that was passing to Billy, "why don't you come to see the great fight?" "What would take the likes of me there?" says Billy. But when Billy found them all gone he saddled and bridled the best black horse his master had, and put on the best suit of clothes he could get in his master's house, and rode off to the fight after the rest.

When Billy went there he saw the king's daughter with the whole court about her on a platform before the castle, and he thought he never saw anything half as beautiful, and the great warrior that was to fight the dragon was walking up and down on the lawn before her, with three men carrying his sword, and everyone in the whole country gathered there looking at him. But when the fiery dragon came up with twelve heads on him, and every mouth of him spitting fire, and let twelve roars out of him, the warrior ran away and hid himself up to the neck in a well of water, and all they could do they couldn't get him to come out and face the dragon. Then the king's daughter asked if there was no one there to save her from the dragon, and get her in marriage. But not one stirred. When Billy saw this, he tied the belt of the bull's hide round him, swung his stick over his head, and went in, and after a terrible fight entirely, killed the dragon. Everyone then gathered about to find who the stranger was. Billy jumped on his horse and darted away sooner than let them know; but just as he was getting away the king's daughter pulled the shoe off his foot. When the dragon was killed the warrior that had hid in the well of water came out, and cutting the heads off the dragon he brought them to the king, and said that it was he who killed the dragon, in disguise; and he claimed the king's daughter. But she tried the shoe on him and found it didn't fit him; so she said it wasn't him, and that she would marry no one only the man the shoe fitted.

When Billy got home he changed the clothes again, and had the horse in the stable, and the cattle all in before his master came. When the master came, he began telling Billy about the wonderful day they had entirely, and about the warrior hiding in the well of water, and about the grand stranger that came down out of the sky in a cloud on a black horse, and killed the fiery dragon, and then vanished in a cloud again. "And now," says he, "Billy, wasn't that wonderful?" "It was, indeed," says Billy, "very wonderful entirely."

After that it was given out over the country that all the people were to come to the king's castle on a certain day, till the king's daughter would try the shoe on them, and whoever it fitted she was to marry him. When the day arrived Billy was in the orchard with the three goats, three cows, three horses, and three asses, as usual, and the like of all the crowds that passed that day going to the king's castle to get the shoe tried on, he never saw before. They went in coaches and carriages, on horses and jackasses, riding and walking, and crawling and creeping. They all asked Billy was not he going to the king's castle, but Billy said, "Arrah, what would be bringin' the likes of me there?" At last when all the others had gone there passed an old man with a very scarecrow suit of rags on him, and Billy stopped him and asked him what boot would he take and swap clothes with him. "Just take care of yourself, now," says the old man, "and don't be playing off your jokes on my clothes, or maybe I'd make you feel the weight of this stick." But Billy soon let him see it was in earnest he was, and both of them swapped suits, Billy giving the old man boot.

Then off to the castle started Billy, with a suit of rags on his back and an old stick in his hand, and when he come there he found all in great commotion trying on the shoe, and some of them cutting down their foot, trying to get it to fit. But it was all of no use, the shoe could be got to fit none of them at all, and the king's daughter was going to give up in despair when the wee ragged-looking boy, which was Billy, elbowed his way through them, and says he, "Let me try it on; maybe it would fit me." But the people, when they saw him, all began to laugh at the sight of him, and "Go along out of that, you example you," says they shoving and pushing him back. But the king's daughter saw him, and called on them by all manner of means to let him come up and try on the shoe. So Billy went up, and all the people looked on, breaking their hearts laughing at the conceit of it. But what would you have of it, but to the dumfounding of them all, the shoe fitted Billy as nice as if it was made on his foot for a last.

So the king's daughter claimed Billy as her husband. He then confessed that it was he that killed the fiery dragon; and when the king had him dressed up in a silk and satin suit, with plenty of gold and silver ornaments, everyone gave in that his like they never saw afore. He was then married to the king's daughter, and the wedding lasted nine days, nine hours, nine minutes, nine half minutes and nine quarter minutes, and they lived happy and well from that day to this. I got brogues of *brochan*[1] and breeches of glass, a bit of pie for telling a lie, and then I came slithering home.

[1] Porridge.

Tales From Germany

THE WOLF AND THE SEVEN LITTLE GOATS

By WILLIAM AND JACOB GRIMM

Illustration by WALTER CRANE

THERE was once an old goat who had seven little ones, and was as fond of them as ever mother was of her children. One day she had to go into the wood to fetch food for them, so she called them all round her.

"Dear children," said she, "I am going out into the wood; and while I am gone, be on your guard against the wolf, for if he were once to get inside he would eat you up, skin, bones, and all. The wretch often disguises himself, but he may always be known by his hoarse voice and black paws."

"Dear mother," answered the kids, "you need not be afraid, we will take good care of ourselves." And the mother bleated good-bye, and went on her way with an easy mind.

It was not long before someone came knocking at the house door, and crying out,

"Open the door, my dear children, your mother is come back, and has brought each of you something."

But the little kids knew it was the wolf by the hoarse voice.

"We will not open the door," cried they; "you are not our mother; she has a delicate and sweet voice, and your voice is hoarse; you must be the wolf."

Then off went the wolf to a shop and bought a big lump of chalk, and ate it up to make his voice soft. And then he came back, knocked at the house door, and cried,

"Open the door, my dear children, your mother is here, and has brought each of you something."

But the wolf had put up his black paws against the window, and the kids seeing this, cried out,

"We will not open the door; our mother has no black paws like you; you must be the wolf."

The wolf then ran to a baker.

"Baker," said he, "I am hurt in the foot; pray spread some dough over the place."

And when the baker had plastered his feet, he ran to the miller.

"Miller," said he, "strew me some white meal over my paws." But the miller refused, thinking the wolf must be meaning harm to someone.

"If you don't do it," cried the wolf, "I'll eat you up!"

And the miller was afraid and did as he was told. And that just shows what men are.

And now came the rogue the third time to the door and knocked. "Open, children!" cried he. "Your dear mother has come home, and brought you each something from the wood."

"First show us your paws," said the kids, "so that we may know if you are really our mother or not."

And he put up his paws against the window, and when they saw that they were white, all seemed right, and they opened the door; and when he was inside they saw it was the wolf, and they were terrified and tried to hide themselves. One ran under the table, the second got into the bed, the third into the oven, the fourth ran into the kitchen, the fifth hid in the cupboard, the sixth under the sink, the seventh in the clock-case. But the wolf found them all, and gave them short shrift; one after the other he swallowed down, all but the youngest, who was hid in the clock-case. And so the wolf, having got what he wanted, strolled forth into the green meadows, and laying himself down under a tree, he fell asleep.

Not long after, the mother goat came back from the wood; and, oh! what a sight met her eyes! The door was standing wide open; table, chairs, and stools, all thrown about; dishes broken; quilt and pillows torn off the bed. She sought her children; they were no-where to be found. She called to each of them by name, but nobody answered, until she came to the name of the youngest.

"Here I am, Mother," a little voice cried.

"Here I am, Mother," a little voice cried, "here, in the clock-case."

And so she helped him out, and heard how the wolf had come, and eaten all the rest. And you may think how she cried for the loss of her dear children. At last in her grief she wandered out of doors, and the youngest kid with her; and when they came into the meadow, there they saw the wolf lying under a tree, and snoring so that the branches shook. The mother goat looked at him carefully on all sides and she noticed how something inside his body was moving and struggling.

"Dear me!" thought she. "Can it be that my poor children that he devoured for his evening meal are still alive?" And she sent the little kid back to the house for a pair of shears, and needle, and thread. Then she cut the wolf's body open, and no sooner had she made one snip than out came the head of one of the kids; and then another snip, and then one after the other the six little kids all jumped out alive and well, for in his greediness the rogue had swallowed them down whole. How delightful this was! So they comforted their dear mother and hopped about like tailors at a wedding.

"Now fetch some good hard stones," said the mother, "and we will fill his body with them, as he lies asleep."

And so they fetched some in all haste, and put them inside him, and the mother sewed him up so quickly again that he was none the wiser.

When the wolf at last awoke, and got up, the stones inside him made him feel very thirsty, and as he was going to the brook to drink, they struck and rattled one against another. And so he cried out:

> "What is this I feel inside me
> Knocking hard against my bones?
> How should such a thing betide me!
> They were kids, and now they're stones."

So he came to the brook, and stooped to drink, but the heavy stones weighed him down, so he fell over into the water and was drowned. And when the seven little kids saw it they came up running.

"The wolf is dead, the wolf is dead!" they cried, and taking hands, they danced with their mother all about the place.

THE ELVES AND THE SHOEMAKER

By *WILLIAM* AND *JACOB GRIMM*

THERE was once a shoemaker, who, through no fault of his own, became so poor that at last he had nothing left but just nough leather to make one pair of shoes. He cut out the shoes at ight, so as to set to work upon them next morning; and as he had good conscience, he laid himself quietly down in his bed, committed himself to heaven, and fell asleep. In the morning, after he ad said his prayers, and was going to get to work, he found the air of shoes made and finished, and standing on his table. He was ery much astonished, and could not tell what to think, and he took the shoes in his hand to examine them more nearly; and they were well made that every stitch was in its right place, just as if they ad come from the hand of a master-workman.

Soon after, a purchaser entered, and as the shoes fitted him very ell, he gave more than the usual price for them, so that the shoemaker had enough money to buy leather for two more pairs of shoes. He cut them out at night, and intended to set to work the next morning with fresh spirit; but that was not to be, for when he got p they were already finished, and a customer even was not lacking, who gave him so much money that he was able to buy leather nough for four new pairs. Early next morning he found the four airs also finished, and so it always happened; whatever he cut out the evening was worked up by the morning, so that he was soon the way of making a good living, and in the end became very ell to do.

One night, not long before Christmas, when the shoemaker had nished cutting out, and before he went to bed, he said to his wife, "How would it be if we were to sit up tonight and see who it is at does us this service?"

His wife agreed, and set a light to burn. Then they both hid in corner of the room, behind some coats that were hanging up, and en they began to watch. As soon as it was midnight they saw come in two neatly-formed naked little men, who seated themselves before the shoemaker's table, and took up the work that was already prepared, and began to stitch, to pierce, and to hammer so cleverly and quickly with their little fingers that the shoemaker's eyes could scarcely follow them, so full of wonder was he. And they never left off until everything was finished and was standing ready on the table, and then they jumped up and ran off.

The next morning the shoemaker's wife said to her husband, "Those little men have made us rich, and we ought to show ourselves grateful. With all their running about, and having nothing to cover them, they must be very cold. I'll tell you what: I will make little shirts, coats, waistcoats, and breeches for them, and knit each of them a pair of stockings, and you shall make each of them a pair of shoes."

The husband consented willingly, and at night, when everything was finished, they laid the gifts together on the table, instead of the cut-out work, and placed themselves so that they could observe how the little men would behave. When midnight came, they rushed in, ready to set to work, but when they found, instead of the pieces of prepared leather, the neat little garments put ready for them, they stood a moment in surprise, and then they testified the greatest delight. With the greatest swiftness they took up the pretty garments and slipped them on, singing,

> "What spruce and dandy boys are we!
> No longer cobblers we will be."

Then they hopped and danced about, jumping over the chairs and tables, and at last they danced out at the door.

From that time they were never seen again; but it always went well with the shoemaker as long as he lived, and whatever he took in hand prospered.

HANSEL AND GRETHEL

By WILLIAM AND *JACOB GRIMM*

NEAR a great forest there lived a poor woodcutter and his wife, and his two children; the boy's name was Hansel and the girl's Grethel. They had very little to bite or to sup, and once, when there was great dearth in the land, the man could not even gain the daily bread. As he lay in bed one night thinking of this, and turning and tossing, he sighed heavily, and said to his wife:

"What will become of us? We cannot even feed our children; there is nothing left for ourselves."

"I will tell you what, husband," answered the wife; "we will take the children early in the morning into the forest, where it is thickest; we will make them a fire, and we will give each of them a piece of bread, then we will go to our work and leave them alone; they will never find the way home again, and we shall be quit of them."

"No, wife," said the man, "I cannot do that; I cannot find in my heart to take my children into the forest and to leave them there alone; the wild animals would soon come and devour them."

"Oh, you fool," said she, "then we will all four starve; you had better get the coffins ready"—and she left him no peace until he consented.

"But I really pity the poor children," said the man.

The two children had not been able to sleep for hunger, and had heard what their stepmother had said to their father. Grethel wept bitterly, and said to Hansel:

"It is all over with us."

"Do be quiet, Grethel," said Hansel, "and do not fret; I will manage something." And when the parents had gone to sleep he got up, put on his little coat, opened the back door, and slipped out. The moon was shining brightly, and the white flints that lay in front of the house glistened like pieces of silver. Hansel stooped and filled the little pocket of his coat as full as it would hold. Then he went back again, and said to Grethel:

"Be easy, dear little sister, and go to sleep quietly; God will not forsake us," and laid himself down again in his bed.

When the day was breaking, and before the sun had risen, the wife came and awakened the two children, saying,

"Get up, you lazybones; we are going into the forest to cut wood."

Then she gave each of them a piece of bread, and said:

"That is for dinner, and you must not eat it before then, for you will get no more."

Grethel carried the bread under her apron, for Hansel had his pockets full of the flints. Then they set off all together on their way to the forest. When they had gone a little way Hansel stood still and looked back toward the house, and this he did again and again, till his father said to him:

"Hansel, what are you looking at? Take care not to forget your legs."

"Oh, father," said Hansel, "I am looking at my little white kitten who is sitting up on the roof to bid me good-bye."

"You young fool," said the woman, "that is not your kitten, but the sunshine on the chimney pot."

Of course Hansel had not been looking at his kitten, but had been taking every now and then a flint from his pocket and dropping it on the road.

When they reached the middle of the forest the father told the children to collect wood to make a fire to keep them warm; and Hansel and Grethel gathered brushwood enough for a little mountain; and it was set on fire, and when the flame was burning quite high the wife said:

"Now lie down by the fire and rest yourselves, you children, and we will go and cut wood; and when we are ready we will come and fetch you."

So Hansel and Grethel sat by the fire, and at noon they each ate their pieces of bread. They thought their father was in the wood all the time, as they seemed to hear the strokes of the ax: but really it was only a dry branch hanging to a withered tree that the wind moved to and fro. So when they had stayed there a long time their eyelids closed with weariness, and they fell fast asleep. When a ast they woke it was night, and Grethel began to cry, and said:

"How shall we ever get out of this wood?" But Hansel comforted
ıer, saying:

"Wait a little while longer, until the moon rises, and then we can
:asily find the way home."

And when the full moon got up Hansel took his little sister by
he hand, and followed the way where the flint stones shone like
ilver, and showed them the road. They walked on, the whole night
hrough, and at the break of day they came to their father's house.
They knocked at the door, and when the wife opened it and saw
hat it was Hansel and Grethel she said:

"You naughty children, why did you sleep so long in the wood?
We thought you were never coming home again!"

But the father was glad, for it had gone to his heart to leave them
·oth in the wood alone.

Not very long after that there was again great scarcity in those
·arts, and the children heard their mother say at night in bed to
heir father:

"Everything is finished up; we have only half a loaf, and after
hat the tale comes to an end. The children must be off; we will take
hem farther into the wood this time, so that they shall not be able
ɔ find the way back again; there is no other way to manage."

The man felt sad at heart, and he thought: "It would be better to
hare one's last morsel with one's children."

But the wife would listen to nothing that he said, but scolded
nd reproached him. He who says A must say B too, and when a
nan has given in once he has to do it a second time.

But the children were not asleep, and had heard all the talk. When
he parents had gone to sleep Hansel got up to go out and get more
int stones, as he did before, but the wife had locked the door, and
Iansel could not get out; but he comforted his little sister, and said:

"Don't cry, Grethel, and go to sleep quietly, and God will help us."

Early the next morning the wife came and pulled the children
ut of bed. She gave them each a little piece of bread—less than
·efore; and on the way to the wood Hansel crumbled the bread in
is pocket, and often stopped to throw a crumb on the ground.

"Hansel, what are you stopping behind and staring for?" said the father.

"I am looking at my little pigeon sitting on the roof, to say good-bye to me," answered Hansel.

"You fool," said the wife, "that is no pigeon, but the morning sun shining on the chimney pots."

Hansel went on as before, and strewed bread crumbs all along the road.

The woman led the children far into the wood, where they had never been before in all their lives. And again there was a large fire made, and the mother said:

"Sit still there, you children, and when you are tired you can go to sleep; we are going into the forest to cut wood, and in the evening, when we are ready to go home, we will come and fetch you."

So when noon came Grethel shared her bread with Hansel, who had strewed his along the road. Then they went to sleep, and the evening passed, and no one came for the poor children. When they awoke it was dark night, and Hansel comforted his little sister, and said: "Wait a little, Grethel, until the moon gets up, then we shall be able to see the way home by the crumbs of bread that I have scattered along it."

So when the moon rose they got up, but they could find no crumbs of bread, for the birds of the wood and of the field had come and picked them up. Hansel thought they might find the way all the same, but they could not. They went on all that night, and the next day from the morning until the evening, but they could not find the way out of the wood, and they were very hungry, for they had nothing to eat but the few berries they could pick up. And when they were so tired that they could no longer drag themselves along, they lay down under a tree and fell asleep.

It was now the third morning since they had left their father's house. They were always trying to get back to it, but instead of that they only found themselves farther in the wood, and if help had not soon come they would have been starved. About noon they saw a pretty snow-white bird sitting on a bough, and singing so sweetly that they stopped to listen. And when he had finished, the bird spread his wings and flew before them, and they followed after him until they came to a little house, and the bird perched on the roof. And when they came nearer they saw that the house was built of bread, and roofed with cakes; and the window was of transparent sugar.

"We will have some of this," said Hansel, "and make a fine meal. I will eat a piece of the roof, Grethel, and you can have some of the window—that will taste sweet."

So Hansel reached up and broke off a bit of the roof, just to see how it tasted, and Grethel stood by the window and gnawed at it. Then they heard a thin voice call out from inside:

> "Nibble, nibble, like a mouse,
> Who is nibbling at my house?"

And the children answered:

> "Never mind,
> It is the wind."

And they went on eating, never disturbing themselves. Hansel, who found that the roof tasted very nice, took down a great piece of it, and Grethel pulled out a large round window pane, and sat her down and began upon it. Then the door opened, and an aged woman came out, leaning upon a crutch. Hansel and Grethel felt very frightened, and let fall what they had in their hands. The old woman, however, nodded her head, and said:

"Ah, my dear children, how came you here? You must come indoors and stay with me; you will be no trouble."

So she took them each by the hand, and led them into her little house. And there they found a good meal laid out, of milk and pancakes, with sugar, apples, and nuts. After that she showed them two little white beds, and Hansel and Grethel laid themselves down on them, and thought they were in heaven.

The old woman, although her behavior was so kind, was a wicked witch, who lay in wait for children, and had built the little house on purpose to entice them. When they were once inside she used to kill

them, cook them, and eat them, and then it was a feast day with her
The witch's eyes were red, and she could not see very far, but she
had a keen scent, like the beasts, and knew very well when human
creatures were near. When she knew that Hansel and Grethel were
coming, she gave a spiteful laugh, and said triumphantly:

"I have them, and they shall not escape me!"

Early in the morning, before the children were awake, she got
up to look at them, and as they lay sleeping so peacefully with round
rosy cheeks, she said to herself:

"What a fine feast I shall have!"

Then she grasped Hansel with her withered hand, and led him
into a little stable, and shut him up behind a grating; and call and
scream as he might, it was no good. Then she went back to Grethel
and shook her, crying:

"Get up, lazybones; fetch water, and cook something nice for
your brother; he is outside in the stable, and must be fattened up
And when he is fat enough I will eat him."

Grethel began to weep bitterly, but it was of no use, she had to
do what the wicked witch bade her.

And so the best kind of victuals were cooked for poor Hansel
while Grethel got nothing but crab shells. Each morning the old
woman visited the little stable, and cried:

"Hansel, stretch out your finger, that I may tell if you will soon
be fat enough."

Hansel, however, used to hold out a little bone, and the old
woman, who had weak eyes, could not see what it was, and sup-
posing it to be Hansel's finger, wondered very much that it was not
getting fatter. When four weeks had passed and Hansel seemed to
remain so thin, she lost patience and could wait no longer.

"Now then, Grethel," cried she to the little girl; "be quick and
draw water; be Hansel fat or be he lean, tomorrow I must kill and
cook him."

Oh, what a grief for the poor little sister to have to fetch water,
and how the tears flowed down over her cheeks!

"Dear God, pray help us!" cried she. "If we had been devoured
by wild beasts in the wood at least we should have died together."

"Spare me your lamentations," said the old woman; "they are of no avail."

Early next morning Grethel had to get up, make the fire, and fill the kettle.

"First we will do the baking," said the old woman; "I have heated the oven already, and kneaded the dough."

She pushed poor Grethel toward the oven, out of which the flames were already shining.

"Creep in," said the witch, "and see if it is properly hot, so that the bread may be baked."

And Grethel once in, she meant to shut the door upon her and let her be baked, and then she would have eaten her. But Grethel perceived her intention, and said:

"I don't know how to do it: how shall I get in?"

"Stupid goose," said the old woman, "the opening is big enough, do you see? I could get in myself!" and she stooped down and put her head in the oven's mouth. Then Grethel gave her a push, so that she went in farther, and she shut the iron door upon her, and put up the bar. Oh, how frightfully she howled! But Grethel ran away, and left the wicked witch to burn miserably. Grethel went straight to Hansel, opened the stable door, and cried:

"Hansel, we are free! the old witch is dead!"

Then out flew Hansel like a bird from its cage as soon as the door is opened. How rejoiced they both were! how they fell each on the other's neck! and danced about, and kissed each other! And as they had nothing more to fear they went over all the old witch's house, and in very corner stood chests of pearls and precious stones.

"This is something better than flint stones," said Hansel, as he filled his pockets, and Grethel, thinking she also would like to carry something home with her, filled her apron full.

"Now, away we go," said Hansel—"if we only can get out of the witch's wood."

When they had journeyed a few hours they came to a great piece of water.

"We can never get across this," said Hansel; "I see no stepping-stones and no bridge."

"And there is no boat either," said Grethel; "but here comes a white duck; if I ask her she will help us over." So she cried:

> "Duck, duck, here we stand,
> Hansel and Grethel, on the land,
> Stepping-stones and bridge we lack,
> Carry us over on your nice white back."

And the duck came accordingly, and Hansel got upon her and told his sister to come, too.

"No," answered Grethel, "that would be too hard upon the duck; we can go separately, one after the other."

And that was how it was managed, and after that they went on happily, until they came to the wood and the way grew more and more familiar, till at last they saw in the distance their father's house. Then they ran till they came up to it, rushed in at the door, and fell on their father's neck. The man had not had a quiet hour since he left his children in the wood; but the wife was dead. And when Grethel opened her apron the pearls and precious stones were scattered all over the room, and Hansel took one handful after another out of his pocket. Then was all care at an end, and they lived in great joy together.

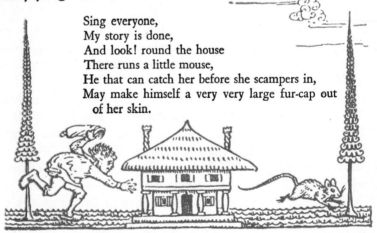

> Sing everyone,
> My story is done,
> And look! round the house
> There runs a little mouse,
> He that can catch her before she scampers in,
> May make himself a very very large fur-cap out
> of her skin.

LITTLE ONE EYE, LITTLE TWO EYES, LITTLE THREE EYES

By *WILLIAM* AND *JACOB GRIMM*

Illustration by ARTHUR RACKHAM

THERE was a woman who had three daughters, the eldest of whom was called Little One Eye, because she only had one eye in the middle of her forehead; the second, Little Two Eyes, because she had two eyes like other people; and the youngest, Little Three Eyes, because she had three eyes, one of them being also in the middle of the forehead. But because Little Two Eyes looked no different from other people her mother and sisters could not bear her. They said, "You with your two eyes are no better than anybody else; you do not belong to us." They knocked her about, and gave her shabby clothes, and food which was left over from their own meals; in short, they vexed her whenever they could.

It happened that Little Two Eyes had to go out into the fields to look after the goat; but she was still quite hungry, because her sisters had given her so little to eat. She sat down on a hillock and began to cry, and cried so much that a little stream ran down out of each eye. And as she looked up once in her sorrow, a woman stood near her, who asked, "Little Two Eyes, why do you cry?"

Little Two Eyes answered, "Have I not need to cry? Because I have two eyes, like other people, my sisters and my mother cannot bear me; they push me out of one corner into another, give me shabby clothes, and nothing to eat but what they leave. Today they have given me so little that I am still quite hungry."

The wise woman said, "Little Two Eyes, dry your eyes, and I will tell you something which will keep you from ever being hungry more. Only say to your goat, 'Little goat, bleat; little table, rise,' and a neatly-laid table will stand before you with the most delicious food on it, so that you can eat as much as you like. And when you are

satisfied and do not want the table any more, only say, 'Little goat
bleat; little table, away,' and it will disappear before your eyes.'
Then the wise woman went out of sight.

Little Two Eyes thought, "I must try directly if it be true what
she has said, for I am much too hungry to wait." So she said, "Little
goat, bleat; little table, rise"; and scarcely had she uttered the words
when there stood before her a little table, covered with a white cloth
on which were laid a plate, knife and fork, and silver spoon. The
most delicious food was there also, and smoking hot, as if just come
from the kitchen. Then Little Two Eyes said the shortest grace that
she knew, "Lord God, be our Guest at all times, Amen," began to
eat, and found it very good. And when she had had enough, she said
as the wise woman had taught her, "Little goat, bleat; little table,
away." In an instant the little table, and all that stood on it, had disappeared again. "That is a beautiful, easy way of housekeeping,"
thought Little Two Eyes, and was quite happy and merry.

In the evening, when she came home with her goat, she found a
little earthen dish with food, which her sisters had put aside for her,
but she did not touch anything—she had no need. On the next day
she went out again with her goat, and let the few crusts that were
given her remain uneaten. The first time and the second time the
sisters took no notice; but when the same thing happened every day
they remarked it, and said, "All is not right with Little Two Eyes,
she always leaves her food, and she used formerly to eat everything
that was given her; she must have found other ways of dining."

In order to discover the truth, they resolved that Little One Eye
should go with Little Two Eyes when she drove the goat into the
meadow, and see what she did there, and if anybody brought her
anything to eat and drink. So when Little Two Eyes set out again,
Little One Eye came to her and said, "I will go with you into the
field, and see that the goat is taken proper care of, and driven to
good pasture."

But Little Two Eyes saw what Little One Eye had in her mind,
and drove the goat into long grass, saying, "Come, Little One Eye,
we will sit down; I will sing you something." Little One Eye sat
down, being tired from the unusual walk and from the heat of the

un, and Little Two Eyes kept on singing, "Are you awake, Little One Eye? Are you asleep, Little One Eye?" Then Little One Eye shut her one eye and fell asleep. And when Little Two Eyes saw that Little One Eye was fast asleep, and could not betray anything, she said, "Little goat, bleat; little table, rise," and sat herself at her table, and ate and drank till she was satisfied; then she called out again, "Little goat, bleat; little table, away," and instantly everything disappeared.

Little Two Eyes now woke Little One Eye, and said, "Little One Eye, you pretend to watch, and fall asleep over it, and in the meantime the goat could have run all over the world; come, we will go home." Then they went home, and Little Two Eyes let her little dish again stand untouched; and Little One Eye, who could not tell the mother why her sister would not eat, said, as an excuse, "Oh, I fell asleep out there."

The next day the mother said to Little Three Eyes, "This time you shall go and see if Little Two Eyes eats out of doors, and if anyone brings her food and drink, for she must eat and drink secretly."

Then Little Three Eyes went to Little Two Eyes, and said, "I will go with you and see if the goat be taken proper care of, and driven to good pasture." But Little Two Eyes saw what Little Three Eyes had in her mind, and drove the goat into long grass, and said as before, "We will sit down here, Little Three Eyes; I will sing you something." Little Three Eyes seated herself, being tired from the walk and the heat of the sun, and Little Two Eyes began the same song again, and sang, "Are you awake, Little Three Eyes?" But instead of singing then as she should, "Are you asleep, Little *Three* Eyes?" she sang, through carelessness, "Are you asleep, Little *Two* Eyes?" and went on singing, "Are you awake, Little Three Eyes? Are you asleep, Little *Two* Eyes?" So the two eyes of Little Three Eyes fell asleep, but the third did not go to sleep, because it was not spoken to by the verse. Little Three Eyes, to be sure, shut it, and made believe to go to sleep, but only through slyness; for she winked with it, and could see everything quite well. And when Little Two Eyes thought that Little Three Eyes was fast asleep, she said her little sentence, "Little goat, bleat; little table, rise," ate and drank

"I know why the proud thing does not eat."

heartily, and then told the little table to go away again, "Little goat, bleat; little table, away." But Little Three Eyes had seen everything.

Then Little Two Eyes came to her, woke her, and said, "Ah, Little Three Eyes, have you been asleep? You keep watch well! Come, we will go home." And when they got home, Little Two Eyes again did not eat, and Little Three Eyes said to the mother, "I know why the proud thing does not eat: when she says to the goat out there, 'Little goat, bleat; little table, rise,' there stands a table before her, which is covered with the very best food, much better than we have here; and when she is satisfied, she says, 'Little goat, bleat; little table, away,' and everything is gone again; I have seen it all exactly. She put two of my eyes to sleep with her little verse, but the one in my forehead luckily remained awake."

Then the envious mother cried out, "Shall she be better off than we are?" fetched a butcher's knife, and stuck it into the goat's heart, so that it fell down dead.

When Little Two Eyes saw that, she went out full of grief, seated herself on a hillock, and wept bitter tears. All at once the wise woman stood near her again, and said, "Little Two Eyes, why do you cry?"

"Shall I not cry?" answered she. "The goat who every day, when

I said your little verse, laid the table so beautifully, has been killed by my mother; now I must suffer hunger and thirst again."

Then the wise woman said, "Little Two Eyes, I will give you some good advice; beg your sisters to give you the heart of the murdered goat, and bury it in the ground before the house door, and it will turn out lucky for you." Then she disappeared, and Little Two Eyes went home and said to her sisters, "Dear sisters, give me some part of my goat; I don't ask for anything good, only give me the heart."

Then they laughed, and said, "You can have that, if you do not want anything else." Little Two Eyes took the heart, and buried it quietly in the evening, before the house door, after the advice of the wise woman.

Next morning, when the sisters woke, and went to the house door together there stood a most wonderfully splendid tree, with leaves of silver and fruit of gold hanging between them. Nothing more beautiful or charming could be seen in the wide world. But they did not know how the tree had come there in the night. Little Two Eyes alone noticed that it had grown out of the heart of the goat, for it stood just where she had buried it in the ground.

Then the mother said to Little One Eye, "Climb up, my child, and gather us some fruit from the tree."

Little One Eye climbed up, but when she wanted to seize a golden apple, the branch sprang out of her hand: this happened every time, so that she could not gather a single apple, though she tried as hard as she could.

Then the mother said, "Little Three Eyes, do you climb up; you can see better about you with your three eyes than Little One Eye can."

Little One Eye scrambled down, and Little Three Eyes climbed up. But Little Three Eyes was no cleverer, and might look about her as much as she liked—the golden apples always sprang back from her grasp. At last the mother became impatient, and climbed up herself, but could touch the fruit just as little as Little One Eye or Little Three Eyes; she always grasped the empty air.

Then Little Two Eyes said, "I will go up myself; perhaps I shall prosper better."

"You!" cried the sisters. "With your two eyes, what can you do?"

But Little Two Eyes climbed up, and the golden apples did not spring away from her, but dropped of themselves into her hand, so that she could gather one after another, and brought down a whole apronful. Her mother took them from her, and instead of her sisters, Little One Eye and Little Three Eyes, behaving any better to poor Little Two Eyes for it, they were only envious because she alone could get the fruit, and behaved still more cruelly to her.

It happened, as they stood together by the tree, one day, that a young knight came riding by on a fine horse.

"Quick, Little Two Eyes," cried the two sisters, "creep under that we may not be ashamed of you"; and threw over poor Little Two Eyes, in a great hurry, an empty cask that stood just by the tree, and pushed also beside her the golden apples which she had broken off.

Now, as the knight came nearer, he proved to be a handsome prince, who stood still, admired the beautiful tree of gold and silver, and said to the two sisters:

"To whom does this beautiful tree belong? She who gives me a branch of it shall have whatever she wishes."

Then Little One Eye and Little Three Eyes answered that the tree was theirs, and they would break off a branch for him. Both gave themselves a great deal of trouble, but it was of no use, for the branches and fruit sprang back from them every time. Then the knight said:

"It is very wonderful that the tree belongs to you, and yet you have not the power of gathering anything from it."

They insisted, however, that the tree was their own property. But as they spoke, Little Two Eyes rolled a few golden apples from under the cask, so that they ran to the feet of the knight; for Little Two Eyes was angry that Little One Eye and Little Three Eyes did not tell the truth.

When the knight saw the apples, he was astonished, and asked where they came from. Little One Eye and Little Three Eyes answered that they had another sister, who might not, however, show herself, because she had only two eyes, like other common people. But the knight desired to see her, and called out, "Little Two Eyes,

come out." Then Little Two Eyes came out of the cask quite comforted, and the knight was astonished at her great beauty, and said:

"You, Little Two Eyes, can certainly gather me a branch from the
tree!"

"Yes," answered Little Two Eyes, "I can do that, for the tree
belongs to me." And she climbed up and easily broke off a branch,
with its silver leaves and golden fruit, and handed it to the knight.

Then the knight said, "Little Two Eyes, what shall I give you for
it?"

"Oh," answered Little Two Eyes, "I suffer hunger and thirst,
sorrow and want, from early morning till late evening; if you would
take me with you and free me, I should be happy."

Then the knight lifted Little Two Eyes upon his horse, and took
her home to his father's castle; there he gave her beautiful clothes,
food, and drink, as much as she wanted, and because he loved her so
much he married her, and the marriage was celebrated with great
joy.

Now, when Little Two Eyes was taken away by the handsome
knight, the two sisters envied her very much her happiness. "The
wonderful tree remains for us, though," thought they, "and even
though we cannot gather any fruit off it, everyone will stand before
it, come to us, and praise it." But next morning, the tree had disappeared, and all their hopes with it.

Little Two Eyes lived happily a long time. Once two poor women
came to her at the castle, and begged alms. Then Little Two Eyes
looked in their faces, and recognized her sisters, Little One Eye and
Little Three Eyes, who had fallen into such poverty that they had to
wander about, and seek their bread from door to door. Little Two
Eyes, however, bade them welcome, and was very good to them; for
they both repented from their hearts the evil they had done to their
sister in their youth.

SNOW-WHITE AND ROSE-RED

By WILLIAM AND JACOB GRIMM

Illustrations by WANDA GAG

THERE was once a poor widow who lived alone in her hut with her two children, who were called Snow-White and Rose-Red, because they were like the flowers which bloomed on two rose-bushes which grew before the cottage. But they were two as pious, good, industrious, and amiable children as any that were in the world, only Snow-White was more quiet and gentle than Rose-Red. For Rose-Red would run and jump about the meadows, seeking flowers and catching butterflies, while Snow-White sat at home helping her mother to keep house, or reading to her if there were nothing else to do. The two children loved one another dearly, and always walked hand in hand when they went out together; and ever when they talked of it they agreed that they would never separate from each other, and that whatever one had the other should share. Often they ran deep into the forest and gathered wild berries; but no beast ever harmed them. For the hare would eat cauliflowers out of their hands, the fawn would graze at their side, the goats would frisk about them in play, and the birds remained perched on the boughs singing as if nobody were near. No accident ever befell them; and if they stayed late in the forest, and night came upon them, they used to lie down on the moss and sleep till morning; and because their mother knew they would do so, she felt no concern about them. One time when they had thus passed the night in the forest, and the dawn of morning awoke them, they saw a beautiful child dressed in shining white sitting near their couch. She got up and looked at them kindly, but without saying anything went into the forest. The children saw they had slept close to the edge of a pit, into which they would have certainly fallen had they walked farther in the dark. Their mother told them the figure was doubtless the good angel who watches over children.

Snow-White and Rose-Red kept their mother's cottage so clean that it was a pleasure to enter it. Every morning in the summertime Rose-Red would first put the house in order, and then gather a nose-gay for her mother, in which she always placed a bud from each rose tree. Every winter's morning Snow-White would light the fire and put the kettle on to boil, and although the kettle was made of copper it yet shone like gold, because it was scoured so well. In the evenings, when the flakes of snow were falling, the mother would say: "Go, Snow-White, and bolt the door"; and then they used to sit down on the hearth, and the mother would put on her spectacles and read out of a great book while her children sat spinning. By their side, too, lay a little lamb, and on a perch behind them a little white dove reposed with her head under her wing.

One evening, when they were thus sitting comfortably together, there came a knock at the door as if somebody wished to come in. "Make haste, Rose-Red," cried her mother; "make haste and open the door; perhaps there is some traveler outside who needs shelter." So Red-Rose went and drew the bolt and opened the door, expecting to see some poor man outside, but instead, a great fat Bear poked his black head in. Rose-Red shrieked out and ran back, the little lamb bleated, the dove fluttered on her perch, and Snow-White hid herself behind her mother's bed. The Bear, however, began to speak, and said: "Be not afraid, I will do you no harm; but I am half frozen, and wish to come in and warm myself."

"Poor Bear!" cried the mother. "Come in and lie down before the fire; but take care you do not burn your skin"; and then she continued: "Come here, Rose-Red and Snow-White, the Bear will not harm you, he means honorably." So they both came back, and by degrees the lamb, too, and the dove overcame their fears and welcomed the rough visitor.

"You children," said the Bear, before he entered, "come and knock the snow off my coat." And they fetched their brooms and swept him clean. Then he stretched himself before the fire and grumbled out his satisfaction; and in a little while the children became familiar enough to play tricks with the unwieldly animal. They pulled his long, shaggy skin, set their feet upon his back and rolled him to and fro, and even ventured to beat him with a hazel stick, laughing when he grumbled. The Bear bore all their tricks good temperedly, and if they hit him too hard he cried out:

"Leave me my life, you children,
Snow-White and Rose-Red,
Or you'll never wed."

When bedtime came and the others were gone, the mother said to the Bear: "You may sleep here on the hearth if you like, and then you will be safely protected from the cold and bad weather."

As soon as day broke the two children let the Bear out again, and he trotted away over the snow, and ever afterwards he came every evening at a certain hour. He would lie down on the hearth and allow the children to play with him as much as they liked, till by degrees they became so accustomed to him that the door was left unbolted till their black friend arrived.

But as soon as spring returned, and everything out of doors was green again, the Bear one morning told Snow-White that he must leave her, and could not return during the whole summer. "Where are you going, then, dear Bear?" asked Snow-White. "I am obliged to go into the forest and guard my treasures from the evil Dwarfs; for in winter, when the ground is hard, they are obliged to keep in their holes, and cannot work through; but now, since the sun has thawed the earth and warmed it, the Dwarfs pierce through, and steal all they can find; and what has once passed into their hands, and gets concealed by them in their caves, is not easily brought to light." Snow-White, however, was very sad at the departure of the Bear, and opened the door so hesitatingly that when he pressed through it he left behind on the sneck a piece of his hairy coat; and through the hole which was made in his coat Snow-White fancied she saw the glittering of gold; but she was not quite certain of it. The Bear, however, ran hastily away, and was soon hidden behind the trees.

Some time afterwards the mother sent the children into the wood to gather sticks; and while doing so, they came to a tree which was lying across the path, on the trunk of which something kept bobbing up and down from the grass, and they could not imagine what it was. When they came nearer they saw a Dwarf, with an old wrinkled face and a snow-white beard a yard long. The end of this beard was fixed in a split of the tree, and the little man kept jumping about like a dog tied by a chain, for he did not know how to free himself. He glared at the maidens with his red fiery eyes, and exclaimed, "Why do you stand there? Are you going to pass without offering me any assistance?" "What have you done, little man?" asked Rose-Red. "You stupid, gaping goose!" exclaimed he. "I wanted to have split the tree, in order to get a little wood for my kitchen, for the little wood which we use is soon burned up with great fagots, not like what you rough, greedy people devour! I had

He snatched up his sack and marched off.

driven the wedge in properly, and everything was going on well, when the smooth wood flew upward, and the tree closed so suddenly together that I could not draw my beautiful beard out, and here it sticks and I cannot get away. There, don't laugh, you milk-faced things! Are you dumfounded?"

The children took all the pains they could to pull the Dwarf's beard out; but without success. "I will run and fetch some help," cried Rose-Red at length.

"Crack-brained sheepshead that you are!" snarled the Dwarf. "What are you going to call other people for? You are two too many now for me; can you think of nothing else?"

"Don't be impatient," replied Snow-White; "I have thought of something"; and pulling her scissors out of her pocket she cut off the end of the beard. As soon as the Dwarf found himself at liberty, he snatched up his sack, which lay between the roots of the tree, filled with gold, and throwing it over his shoulder marched off, grumbling and groaning and crying: "Stupid people! to cut off a piece of my beautiful beard. Plague take you!" and away he went without once looking at the children.

Some time afterwards Snow-White and Rose-Red went a-fishing, and as they neared the pond they saw something like a great locust hopping about on the bank, as if going to jump into the water. They ran up and recognized the Dwarf. "What are you after?" asked Rose-Red. "You will fall into the water." "I am not quite such a simpleton as that," replied the Dwarf; "but do you not see this fish will pull me in?" The little man had been sitting there angling, and unfortunately the wind had entangled his beard with the fishing line; and so, when a great fish bit at the bait, the strength of the weak little fellow was not able to draw it out, and the fish had the best of the struggle. The Dwarf held on by the reeds and rushes which grew near; but to no purpose, for the fish pulled him where it liked, and he must soon have been drawn into the pond. Luckily just then the two maidens arrived, and tried to release the beard of the Dwarf from the fishing line; but both were too closely entangled for it to be done. So the maiden pulled out her scissors again and cut off another piece of the beard. When the Dwarf saw this done he was in a great rage, and exclaimed: "You donkey! That is the way to disfigure my face. Was it not enough to cut it once, but you must now take away the best part of my fine beard? I dare not show myself again now to my own people. I wish you had run the soles off your boots before you had come here!" So saying, he took up a bag of pearls which lay among the rushes, and without speaking another word, slipped off and disappeared behind a stone.

Not many days after this adventure, it chanced that the mother sent the two maidens to the next town to buy thread, needles and pins, laces and ribbons. Their road passed over a common, on which here and there great pieces of rock were lying about. Just over their heads they saw a great bird flying round and round, and every now and then dropping lower and lower, till at last it flew down behind a rock. Immediately afterwards they heard a piercing shriek, and running up they saw with affright that the eagle had caught their old acquaintance, the Dwarf, and was trying to carry him off. The compassionate children thereupon laid hold of the little man, and held him fast till the bird gave up the struggle and flew off. As soon then as the Dwarf had recovered from his fright, he exclaimed in his squeaking voice: "Could you not hold me more gently? You have seized my fine brown coat in such a manner that it is all torn and full of holes, meddling and interfering rubbish that you are!" With these words he shouldered a bag filled with precious stones, and slipped away to his cave among the rocks.

The maidens were now accustomed to his ingratitude, and so they walked on to the town and transacted their business there. Coming home, they returned over the same common, and unawares walked up to a certain clean spot on which the Dwarf had shaken out his bag of precious stones, thinking nobody was near. The sun was shining, and the bright stones glittered in its beams and displayed such a variety of colors that the two maidens stopped to admire them.

"What are you standing there gaping for?" asked the Dwarf, while his face grew as red as copper with rage; he was continuing to abuse the poor maidens, when a loud roaring noise was heard, and presently a great black Bear came rolling out of the forest. The Dwarf jumped up terrified, but he could not gain his retreat before the Bear overtook him. Thereupon, he cried out: "Spare me, my dear Lord Bear! I will give you all my treasures. See these beautiful precious stones which lie here; only give me my life; for what have you to fear from a little weak fellow like me? You could not touch me with your big teeth. There are two wicked girls, take them; they would make nice morsels, as fat as young quails; eat them for heaven's sake."

The Bear, however, without troubling himself to speak, gave the bad-hearted Dwarf a single blow with his paw, and he never stirred after.

The maidens were then going to run away, but the Bear called after them: "Snow-White and Rose-Red, fear not! Wait a bit and I

"I am a king's son," he said.

will accompany you." They recognized his voice and stopped; and
when the Bear came, his rough coat suddenly fell off, and he stood
up a tall man, dressed entirely in gold. "I am a king's son," he said,
"and was condemned by the wicked Dwarf, who stole all my treasures, to wander about in this forest, in the form of a bear, till his
death released me. Now he has received his well-deserved punishment."

Then they went home, and Snow-White was married to the
prince, and Rose-Red to his brother, with whom they shared the
immense treasure which the Dwarf had collected. The old mother
also lived for many years happily with her two children, and the
rose trees which had stood before the cottage were planted now
before the palace, and produced every year beautiful red and white
roses.

THE FROG PRINCE

By WILLIAM AND JACOB GRIMM

Illustration by WALTER CRANE

IN the old times, when it was still of some use to wish for the thing one wanted, there lived a King whose daughters were all handsome, but the youngest was so beautiful that the sun himself, who has seen so much, wondered each time he shone over her because of her beauty. Near the royal castle there was a great dark wood, and in the wood under an old linden tree was a well; and when the day was hot, the King's daughter used to go forth into the wood and sit by the brink of the cool well, and if the time seemed long, she would take out a golden ball, and throw it up and catch it again, and this was her favorite pastime.

Now it happened one day that the golden ball, instead of falling back into the maiden's little hand which had sent it aloft, dropped to the ground near the edge of the well and rolled in. The King's daughter followed it with her eyes as it sank, but the well was deep, so deep that the bottom could not be seen. Then she began to weep, and she wept and wept as if she could never be comforted. And in the midst of her weeping she heard a voice saying to her.

"What ails thee, King's daughter? Thy tears would melt a heart of stone."

And when she looked to see where the voice came from, there was nothing but a frog stretching his thick ugly head out of the water.

"Oh, is it you, old waddler?" said she. "I weep because my golden ball has fallen into the well."

"Never mind, do not weep," answered the frog; "I can help you; but what will you give me if I fetch up your ball again?"

"Whatever you like, dear frog," said she; "any of my clothes, my pearls and jewels, or even the golden crown that I wear."

"Thy clothes, thy pearls and jewels, and thy golden crown are

not for me," answered the frog; "but if thou wouldst love me, and have me for thy companion and playfellow, and let me sit by thee at table, and eat from thy plate, and drink from thy cup, and sleep in thy little bed—if thou wouldst promise all this, then would I dive below the water and fetch thee thy golden ball again."

"Oh, yes," she answered; "I will promise it all, whatever you want, if you will only get me my ball again."

But she thought to herself, "What nonsense he talks! As if he could do anything but sit in the water and croak with the other frogs, or could possibly be anyone's companion."

But the frog, as soon as he heard her promise, drew his head under the water and sank down out of sight. But after a while he came to the surface again with the ball in his mouth, and he threw it on the grass.

The King's daughter was overjoyed to see her pretty plaything again, and she caught it up and ran off with it.

"Stop, stop!" cried the frog. "Take me up, too; I cannot run as fast as you!"

But it was of no use, for croak, croak after her as he might, she would not listen to him, but made haste home, and very soon forgot all about the poor frog, who had to betake himself to his well again.

The next day, when the King's daughter was sitting at table with the King and all the court, and eating from her golden plate, there came something pitter patter up the marble stairs, and then there came a knocking at the door, and a voice crying "Youngest King's daughter, let me in!"

And she got up and ran to see who it could be, but when she opened the door, there was the frog sitting outside. Then she shut the door hastily and went back to her seat, feeling very uneasy. The King noticed how quickly her heart was beating and said:

"My child, what are you afraid of? Is there a giant standing at the door ready to carry you away?"

"Oh, no," answered she; "no giant, but a horrid frog."

"And what does the frog want?" asked the King.

"O dear father," answered she, "when I was sitting by the well yesterday, and playing with my golden ball, it fell into the water, and while I was crying for the loss of it, the frog came and got it again for me on condition I would let him be my companion, but I never thought that he could leave the water and come after me; but now there he is outside the door, and he wants to come in to me."

And then they all heard him knocking the second time and crying:

> "Youngest King's daughter,
> Open to me!
> By the well water
> What promised you me?
> Youngest King's daughter
> Now open to me!"

"That which thou hast promised must thou perform," said the King; "so go now and let him in."

So she went and opened the door, and the frog hopped in, following at her heels, till she reached her chair. Then he stopped and cried:

"Lift me up to sit by you."

But she delayed doing so until the King ordered her. When once the frog was on the chair, he wanted to get on the table; and there he sat and said: "Now push your golden plate a little nearer, so that we may eat together."

And so she did; but everybody saw how unwilling she was, and the frog feasted heartily, but every morsel seemed to stick in her throat.

"I have had enough now," said the frog at last, "and as I am tired, you must carry me to your room, and make ready your silken bed, and we will lie down and go to sleep."

Then the King's daughter began to weep, and was afraid of the cold frog, that nothing would satisfy him but he must sleep in her pretty clean bed. Now the King grew angry with her, saying:

"That which thou hast promised in thy time of necessity, must thou now perform."

So she picked up the frog with her finger and thumb, carried him upstairs and put him in a corner, and when she had lain down to sleep, he came creeping up, saying: "I am tired and want sleep as much as you; take me up, or I will tell your father."

Then she felt beside herself with rage, and picking him up, she threw the frog with all her strength against the wall, crying:

"Now will you be quiet, you horrid frog!"

But as he fell, he ceased to be a frog, and became all at once a prince with beautiful kind eyes. And it came to pass that, with her father's consent, they became bride and bridegroom. And he told her how a wicked witch had bound him by her spells, and how no one but she alone could have released him, and that they two would go together to his father's kingdom. And there came to the door a carriage drawn by eight white horses, with white plumes on their heads, and with golden harness, and behind the carriage was standing faithful Henry, the servant of the young prince. Now, faithful Henry had suffered such care and pain when his master was turned into a frog, that he had been obliged to wear three iron bands over his heart, to keep it from breaking with trouble and anxiety. When the carriage started to take the prince to his kingdom, and faithful Henry had helped them both in, he got up behind, and was full of joy at his master's deliverance. And when they had gone a part of the way, the prince heard a sound at the back of the carriage, as if something had broken, and he turned round and cried:

"Henry, the wheel must be breaking!" but Henry answered:

"The wheel does not break,
'Tis the band round my heart
That, to lessen its ache,
When I grieved for your sake,
I bound round my heart."

Again, and yet once again there was the same sound, and the prince thought it must be the wheel breaking, but it was the breaking of the other bands from faithful Henry's heart, because it was now so relieved and happy.

CAT AND MOUSE IN PARTNERSHIP

By WILLIAM AND *JACOB GRIMM*

Illustration by WALTER CRANE

A CAT having made acquaintance with a mouse, professed such great love and friendship for her, that the mouse at last agreed that they should live and keep house together.

"We must make provision for the winter," said the cat, "or we shall suffer hunger, and you, little mouse, must not stir out, or you will be caught in a trap."

So they took counsel together and bought a little pot of fat. And then they could not tell where to put it for safety, but after long consideration the cat said there could not be a better place than the church, for nobody would steal there; and they would put it under the altar and not touch it until they were really in want. So this was done, and the little pot placed in safety.

But before long the cat was seized with a great wish to taste it.

"Listen to me, little mouse," said he; "I have been asked by my cousin to stand godfather to a little son she has brought into the world; he is white with brown spots; and they want to have the christening today, so let me go to it, and you stay at home and keep house."

"Oh, yes, certainly," answered the mouse; "pray go by all means; and when you are feasting on all the good things, think of me; I should so like a drop of the sweet red wine."

But there was not a word of truth in all this; the cat had no cousin, and had not been asked to stand godfather: he went to the church, straight up to the little pot, and licked the fat off the top; then he took a walk over the roofs of the town, saw his acquaintances, stretched himself in the sun, and licked his whiskers as often as he thought of the little pot of fat; and then when it was evening he went home. "Here you are at last," said the mouse; "I expect you have had a merry time."

"Oh, pretty well," answered the cat.

"And what name did you give the child?" asked the mouse.

"Top-off," answered the cat, dryly.

"Top-off!" cried the mouse, "that is a singular and wonderful name! Is it common in your family?"

"What does it matter?" said the cat. "It's not any worse than Crumb-picker, like your godchild."

A little time after this the cat was again seized with a longing.

"Again I must ask you," said he to the mouse, "to do me a favor, and keep house alone for a day. I have been asked a second time to stand godfather; and as the little one has a white ring round its neck, I cannot well refuse."

So the kind little mouse consented, and the cat crept along by the town wall until he reached the church, and going straight to the little pot of fat, devoured half of it.

"Nothing tastes so well as what one keeps to oneself," said he, feeling quite content with his day's work. When he reached home, the mouse asked what name had been given to the child.

"Half-gone," answered the cat.

"Half-gone!" cried the mouse. "I never heard such a name in my life! I'll bet it's not to be found in the calendar."

Soon after that the cat's mouth began to water again for the fat.

"Good things always come in threes," said he to the mouse; "again I have been asked to stand godfather, the little one is quite black with white feet, and not any white hair on its body. Such a thing does not happen every day, so you will let me go, won't you?"

"Top-off, Half-gone," murmured the mouse. "They are such curious names, I cannot but wonder at them!"

"That's because you are always sitting at home," said the cat, "in your little gray frock and hairy tail, never seeing the world, and fancying all sorts of things."

So the little mouse cleaned up the house and set it all in order. Meanwhile the greedy cat went and made an end of the little pot of fat.

"Now all is finished, one's mind will be easy," said he, and came home in the evening, quite sleek and comfortable. The mouse asked at once what name had been given to the third child.

"It won't please you any better than the others," answered the cat. "It is called All-gone."

"All-gone!" cried the mouse. "What an unheard-of-name! I never met with anything like it! All-gone! Whatever can it mean?" And shaking her head, she curled herself round and went to sleep. After that the cat was not again asked to stand godfather.

When the winter had come and there was nothing more to be had out of doors, the mouse began to think of their store.

"Come, cat," said she, "we will fetch our pot of fat. How good it will taste, to be sure!"

"Of course it will," said the cat; "just as good as if you stuck your tongue out of window!"

So they set out, and when they reached the place, they found the pot, but it was standing empty.

"Oh, now I know what it all meant," cried the mouse, "now I see what sort of a partner you have been! Instead of standing god-father, you have devoured it all up; first Top-off, then Half-gone, then"——

"Will you hold your tongue!" screamed the cat. "Another word, and I devour you, too!"

And the poor little mouse, having "All-gone" on her tongue, out it came, and the cat leaped upon her and made an end of her. And that is the way of the world.

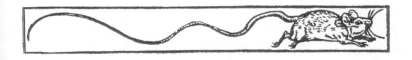

THE GOLDEN GOOSE

By *WILLIAM* AND *JACOB GRIMM*

THERE was a man who had three sons, the youngest of whom was called the Simpleton, and was despised, laughed at, and neglected, on every occasion. It happened one day that the eldest son wished to go into the forest to cut wood, and before he went his mother gave him a delicious pancake and a flask of wine, that he might not suffer from hunger or thirst. When he came into the forest a little old gray man met him, who wished him good day, and said,

"Give me a bit of cake out of your pocket, and let me have a drink of your wine; I am so hungry and thirsty."

But the prudent youth answered, "Give you my cake and my wine? I haven't got any; be off with you."

And leaving the little man standing there, he went off. Then he began to fell a tree, but he had not been at it long before he made a wrong stroke, and the hatchet hit him in the arm, so that he was obliged to go home and get it bound up. That was what came of the little gray man.

Afterwards the second son went into the wood, and the mother gave to him, as to the eldest, a pancake and a flask of wine. The little old gray man met him also, and begged for a little bit of cake and a drink of wine. But the second son spoke out plainly, saying, "What I give you I lose myself, so be off with you."

And leaving the little man standing there, he went off. The punishment followed; as he was chopping away at the tree, he hit himself in the leg so severely that he had to be carried home.

Then said the Simpleton, "Father, let me go for once into the forest to cut wood"; and the father answered, "Your brothers have hurt themselves by so doing; give it up, you understand nothing about it."

But the Simpleton went on begging so long, that the father said at last, "Well, be off with you; you will only learn by experience."

The mother gave him a cake (it was only made with water, and baked in the ashes), and with it a flask of sour beer. When he came into the forest the little old gray man met him, and greeted him, saying, "Give me a bit of your cake, and a drink from your flask; I am so hungry and thirsty."

And the Simpleton answered, "I have only a flour and water cake and sour beer; but if that is good enough for you, let us sit down together and eat." Then they sat down, and as the Simpleton took out his flour and water cake it became a rich pancake, and his sour beer became good wine; then they ate and drank, and afterwards the little man said: "You have such a kind heart, and share what you have so willingly, I will bestow good luck upon you. Yonder stands an old tree; cut it down. At its roots you will find something," and thereupon the little man took his departure.

The Simpleton went there, and hewed away at the tree, and when it fell he saw, sitting among the roots, a goose with feathers of pure gold. He lifted it out and took it with him to an inn where he intended to stay the night. The landlord had three daughters who, when they saw the goose, were curious to know what wonderful kind of bird it was, and ended by longing for one of its golden feathers. The eldest thought, "I will wait for a good opportunity, and then I will pull out one of its feathers for myself"; and so, when the Simpleton was gone out, she seized the goose by its wing—but there her finger and hand had to stay, held fast. Soon after came the second sister with the same idea of plucking out one of the golden feathers for herself; but scarcely had she touched her sister, than she also was obliged to stay, held fast. Lastly came the third with the same intentions; but the others screamed out,

"Stay away! for heaven's sake stay away!"

But she did not see why she should stay away, and thought, "If they do so, why should not I?" and went toward them. But when she reached her sisters there she stopped, hanging on with them. And so they had to stay, all night. The next morning the Simpleton took the goose under his arm and went away, unmindful of the three girls that hung on to it. The three had always to run after him, left and right, wherever his legs carried him. In the midst of the fields they met the parson, who, when he saw the procession, said:

"Shame on you, girls, running after a young fellow through the fields like this," and forthwith he seized hold of the youngest by the hand to drag her away, but hardly had he touched her when he, too, was obliged to run after them himself. Not long after the sexton came that way, and seeing the respected parson following at the heels of the three girls, he called out:

"Ho, your reverence, whither away so quickly? You forget that we have another christening today"; and he seized hold of him by his gown; but no sooner had he touched him than he was obliged to follow on, too. As the five tramped on, one after another, two peasants with their hoes came up from the field, and the parson cried out to them, and begged them to come and set him and the sexton free, but no sooner had they touched the sexton than they had to follow on, too; and now there were seven following the Simpleton and the goose.

By and by they came to a town where a king reigned, who had an only daughter who was so serious that no one could make her laugh; therefore the king had given out that whoever should make her laugh should have her in marriage. The Simpleton, when he heard this, went with his goose and his hangers-on into the presence of the king's daughter, and as soon as she saw the seven people following always one after the other, she burst out laughing, and seemed as if she could never stop. And so the Simpleton earned a right to her as his bride; but the king did not like him for a son-in-law and made all kinds of objections, and said he must first bring a man who could drink up a whole cellar of wine. The Simpleton thought that the little gray man would be able to help him, and went out into the forest, and there, on the very spot where he felled the tree, he saw a man sitting with a very sad countenance. The Simpleton asked him what was the matter, and he answered:

"I have a great thirst, which I cannot quench: cold water does not agree with me; I have indeed drunk up a whole cask of wine, but what good is a drop like that?" Then said the Simpleton, "I can help you; only come with me, and you shall have enough."

He took him straight to the king's cellar, and the man sat himself down before the big vats, and drank, and drank, and before a day was over he had drunk up the whole cellarful. The Simpleton again asked for his bride, but the king was annoyed that a wretched fellow, called the Simpleton by everybody, should carry off his daughter, and so he made new conditions. He was to produce a man who could eat up a mountain of bread. The Simpleton did not hesitate long, but ran quickly off to the forest, and there in the same place sat a man who had fastened a strap round his body, making a very piteous face, and saying: "I have eaten a whole bake-house full of rolls, but what is the use of that when one is so hungry as I am? My stomach feels quite empty, and I am obliged to strap myself together, that I may not die of hunger."

The Simpleton was quite glad of this, and said: "Get up quickly, and come along with me, and you shall have enough to eat."

He led him straight to the king's courtyard, where all the meal in the kingdom had been collected and baked into a mountain of bread. The man of the forest settled himself down before it and hastened to eat, and in one day the whole mountain disappeared.

Then the Simpleton asked for his bride the third time. The king, however, found one more excuse, and said he must have a ship that should be able to sail on land or on water.

"So soon," said he, "as you come sailing along with it, you shall have my daughter for your wife."

The Simpleton went straight to the forest, and there sat the little old gray man with whom he had shared his cake, and he said,

"I have eaten for you, and I have drunk for you, I will also give you the ship; and all because you were kind to me at the first."

Then he gave him the ship that could sail on land and on water. When the king saw it he could no longer withhold his daughter. The marriage took place, and at the death of the king the Simpleton possessed the kingdom, and lived long and happily with his wife.

RAPUNZEL

By WILLIAM AND JACOB GRIMM

Illustration by WALTER CRANE

THERE once lived a man and his wife, who had long wished for a child, but in vain. Now there was at the back of their house a little window which overlooked a beautiful garden full of the finest vegetables and flowers; but there was a high wall all round it, and no one ventured into it, for it belonged to a witch of great might, and of whom all the world was afraid. One day that the wife was standing at the window, and looking into the garden, she saw a bed filled with the finest rampion[1]; and it looked so fresh and green that she began to wish for some; and at length she longed for it greatly.

This went on for days, and as she knew she could not get the rampion, she pined away, and grew pale and miserable. Then the man was uneasy, and asked:

"What is the matter, dear wife?"

"Oh," answered she, "I shall die unless I can have some of that rampion to eat that grows in the garden at the back of our house."

The man, who loved her very much, thought to himself:

"Rather than lose my wife I will get some rampion, cost what it will."

So in the twilight he climbed over the wall into the witch's garden, plucked hastily a handful of rampion and brought it to his wife. She made a salad of it at once, and ate of it to her heart's content. But she liked it so much, and it tasted so good, that the next day she longed for it thrice as much as she had done before; if she was to have any rest the man must climb over the wall once more. So he went in the twilight again; and as he was climbing back, he saw, all at once, the witch standing before him, and was terribly frightened, as she cried, with angry eyes:

[1] A vegetable like a radish.

146

"How dare you climb over into my garden like a thief, and steal my rampion! It shall be the worse for you!"

"Oh," answered he, "be merciful rather than just. I have only done it through necessity; for my wife saw your rampion out of the window, and became possessed with so great a longing that she would have died if she could not have had some to eat." Then the witch said:

"If it is all as you say you may have as much rampion as you like, on one condition—the child that will come into the world must be given to me. It shall go well with the child, and I will care for it like a mother."

In his distress of mind the man promised everything; and, when the time came when the child was born, the witch appeared and, giving the child the name of Rapunzel (which is the same as rampion), she took it away with her.

Rapunzel was the most beautiful child in the world. When she was twelve years old the witch shut her up in a tower in the midst of a wood, and it had neither steps nor door, only a small window above. When the witch wished to be let in, she would stand below and would cry:

"Rapunzel, Rapunzel! let down your hair!"

Rapunzel had beautiful long hair that shone like gold. When she heard the voice of the witch she would undo the fastening of the upper window, unbind the plaits of her hair, and let it down twenty ells below, and the witch would climb up by it.

After they had lived thus a few years it happened that as the King's son was riding through the wood, he came to the tower; and as he drew near he heard a voice singing so sweetly that he stood still and listened. It was Rapunzel in her loneliness trying to pass away the time with sweet songs. The King's son wished to go in to her, and sought to find a door in the tower, but there was none. So he rode home, but the song had entered into his heart, and every day he went into the wood and listened to it. Once, as he was standing there under a tree, he saw the witch come up, and listened while she called out:

"O Rapunzel, Rapunzel! let down your hair."

Then he saw how Rapunzel let down her long tresses, and how the witch climbed up by it and went in to her, and he said to himself:

"Since that is the ladder, I will climb it, and seek my fortune." And the next day, as soon as it began to grow dusk, he went to the tower and cried:

"O Rapunzel, Rapunzel! let down your hair."

And she let down her hair, and the King's son climbed up by it.

Rapunzel was greatly terrified when she saw that a man had come in to her, for she had never seen one before; but the King's son began speaking so kindly to her, and told how her singing had entered into his heart, so that he could have no peace until he had seen her herself. Then Rapunzel forgot her terror, and when he asked her to take him for her husband, and she saw that he was young and beautiful, she thought to herself:

"I certainly like him much better than old mother Gothel," and she put her hand into his hand, saying:

"I would willingly go with thee, but I do not know how I shall get out. When thou comest, bring each time a silken rope, and I will make a ladder, and when it is quite ready I will get down by it out of the tower, and thou shalt take me away on thy horse." They agreed that he should come to her every evening, as the old woman came in the daytime. So the witch knew nothing of all this until once Rapunzel said to her unwittingly:

"Mother Gothel, how is it that you climb up here so slowly, and the King's son is with me in a moment?"

"O wicked child," cried the witch, "what is this I hear! I thought I had hidden thee from all the world, and thou hast betrayed me!"

In her anger she seized Rapunzel by her beautiful hair, struck her several times with her left hand, and then grasping a pair of shears in her right—snip, snap—the beautiful locks lay on the ground. And she was so hard-hearted that she took Rapunzel and put her in a waste and desert place, where she lived in great woe and misery.

The same day on which she took Rapunzel away she went back to the tower in the evening and made fast the severed locks of hair to the window hasp, and the King's son came and cried:

"Rapunzel, Rapunzel! let down your hair."

Then she let the hair down, and the King's son climbed up, but instead of his dearest Rapunzel he found the witch looking at him with wicked, glittering eyes.

"Aha!" cried she, mocking him, "you came for your darling, but the sweet bird sits no longer in the nest, and sings no more; the cat has got her, and will scratch out your eyes as well! Rapunzel is lost to you; you will see her no more."

The King's son was beside himself with grief, and in his agony he sprang from the tower: he escaped with life, but the thorns on which he fell put out his eyes. Then he wandered blind through the wood, eating nothing but roots and berries, and doing nothing but lament and weep for the loss of his dearest wife.

So he wandered several years in misery until at last he came to the desert place where Rapunzel lived with her twin-children that she had borne, a boy and a girl. At first he heard a voice that he thought he knew, and when he reached the place from which it seemed to come Rapunzel knew him, and fell on his neck and wept. And when her tears touched his eyes they became clear again, and he could see with them as well as ever.

Then he took her to his kingdom, where he was received with great joy, and there they lived long and happily.

THE NOSE

By *WILLIAM* AND *JACOB GRIMM*

DID YOU ever hear the story of the three poor soldiers, who, after having fought hard in the wars, set out on their road home, begging their way as they went?

They had journeyed on a long way, sick at heart with their bad luck at thus being turned loose on the world in their old days, when one evening they reached a deep gloomy wood through which they must pass; night came fast upon them, and they found that they must, however unwillingly, sleep in the wood. So, to make all as safe as they could, it was agreed that two should lie down and sleep, while a third sat up and watched lest wild beasts should break in and tear them to pieces; when he was tired he was to wake one of the others and sleep in his turn, and so on with the third, that they might share the work fairly among them.

The two who were to rest first soon lay down and fell fast asleep, and the other made himself a good fire under the trees and sat down by the side to keep watch. He had not sat long before all of a sudden up came a little man in a red jacket. "Who's there?" said he. "A friend," said the soldier. "What sort of a friend?" "An old broken soldier," said the other, "with his two comrades who have nothing left to live on; come, sit down and warm yourself." "Well, my worthy fellow," said the little man, "I will do what I can for you; take this and show it to your comrades in the morning." So he took out an old cloak and gave it to the soldier, telling him that whenever he put it over his shoulders anything that he wished for would be fulfilled; then the little man made him a bow and walked away.

The second soldier's turn to watch soon came, and the first laid himself down to sleep; but the second man had not sat by himself long before up came the little man in the red jacket again. The soldier treated him in a friendly way as his comrade had done, and the little man gave him for his part a purse, which he told him was always full of gold, let him draw as much as he would from it.

Then the third soldier's turn to watch came, and he also had the little man for his guest, who gave him a wonderful horn that drew crowds around it whenever it was played; and made everyone forget his business to come and dance to its beautiful music.

In the morning each told his story and showed his treasure; and as they all liked each other very much and were old friends, they agreed to travel together to see the world, and for a while only to make use of the wonderful purse. And thus they spent their time very joyously, till at last they began to be tired of this roving life, and thought they should like to have a home of their own. So the first soldier put his old cloak on, and wished for a fine castle. In a moment it stood before their eyes; fine gardens and green lawns spread round it, and flocks of sheep and goats and herds of oxen were grazing about, and out of the gate came a fine coach with three dapple gray horses to meet them and bring them home.

All was very well for a time; but it would not do to stay at home always, so they got together all their rich clothes and trappings and servants, and ordered their coach with three horses, and set out on a journey to see a neighboring king. Now this king had an only daughter, and as he took the three soldiers for kings' sons, he gave them a kind welcome. One day, as the second soldier was walking with the princess, she saw him with the wonderful purse in his hand; and having asked him what it was, he was foolish enough to tell her; though, indeed, it did not much signify, for she was a witch and knew all the wonderful things that the three soldiers brought. Now this princess was very cunning and artful; so she set to work and made a purse so like the soldier's that no one would know one from the other, and then asked him to come and see her, and made him drink some wine that she had got ready for him, till he fell fast asleep. Then she felt in his pocket, and took away the wonderful purse and left the one she had made in its place.

The next morning the soldiers set out for home, and soon after they reached their castle, happening to want some money, they went to their purse for it, and found something indeed in it, but to their great sorrow when they had emptied it none came in the place of what they took. Then the cheat was soon found out: for the second soldier knew where he had been, and how he had told the story to the princess, and he guessed that she had betrayed him. "Alas!" cried he, "poor wretches that we are, what shall we do?" "Oh," said the first soldier, "let no gray hairs grow for this mishap; I will soon get the purse back." So he threw his cloak across his shoulders and wished himself in the princess's chamber. There he found her sitting alone, telling her gold that fell around her in a shower from the purse. But the soldier stood looking at her too long, for the moment she saw him she started up and cried out with all her force, "Thieves! Thieves!" so that the whole court came running in and tried to seize him. The poor soldier now began to be dreadfully frightened in his turn, and thought it was high time to make the best of his way off; so, without thinking of the ready way of traveling that his cloak gave him, he ran to the window, opened it, and jumped out; and, unluckily, in his haste his cloak caught and was left hanging, to the great joy of the princess, who knew its worth.

The poor soldier made the best of his way home to his comrades, on foot and in a very downcast mood; but the third soldier told him to keep up his heart, and took his horn and blew a merry tune. At the first blast a countless troop of foot and horse came rushing to their aid, and they set out to make war against their enemy. Then the king's palace was besieged, and he was told that he must give up the purse and cloak, or that not one stone should be left upon another. And the king went into his daughter's chamber and talked with her; but she said, "Let me try first if I cannot beat them some other way." So she thought of a cunning scheme to overreach them; and, dressing herself as a poor girl with a basket on her arm, set out by night with her maid, and went into the enemy's camp as if she wanted to sell trinkets.

In the morning she began to ramble about, singing ballads so beautifully that all the tents were left empty, and the soldiers ran round in crowds and thought of nothing but hearing her sing. Amongst the rest came the soldier to whom the horn belonged, and as soon as she saw him she winked to her maid, who slipped slyly through the crowd and went into his tent where the horn hung, and stole it away. This done, they both got safely back to the palace; the besieging army went away, the three wonderful gifts were all left in the hands of the princess, and the three soldiers were as penniless and forlorn as when the little man in the red jacket found them in the wood.

Poor fellows! they began to think what was now to be done. "Comrades," at last said the second soldier, who had had the purse, "we had better part, we cannot live together, let each seek his bread as well as he can." So he turned to the right; and the other two to the left, for they said they would rather travel together. Then on he strayed till he came to a wood (now this was the same wood where they had met with so much luck before); and he walked on a long time till evening began to fall, when he sat down tired beneath a tree, and soon fell asleep.

Morning dawned, and he was greatly delighted at opening his eyes, to see that the tree was laden with the most beautiful apples. He was hungry enough, so he soon plucked and ate first one, then a second, then a third apple. A strange feeling came over his nose: when he put the apple to his mouth something was in the way; he felt it; it was his nose, that grew and grew till it hung down to his breast. It did not stop there; still it grew and grew. "Heavens!" thought he, "when will it have done growing?" And well might he ask, for by this time it reached the ground as he sat on the grass, and thus it kept creeping on till he could not bear its weight, or raise himself up; and it seemed as if it would never end, for already it stretched its enormous length all through the wood.

Meantime his comrades were journeying on, till on a sudden one of them stumbled against something. "What can it be?" said the other. They looked, and could think of nothing that it was like but a nose. "We will follow it and find its owner, however," said they; so they traced it till at last they found their poor comrade lying stretched under the apple tree. What was to be done? They tried to carry him, but in vain. They caught an ass that was passing by and raised him upon its back; but it was soon tired of carrying such a load. So they sat down in despair, when up came the little man in the red jacket. "Well, how now, friend?" said he, laughing. "Well, I must find a cure for you, I see." So he told them to gather a pear from a tree that grew close by, and the nose would come right again. No time was lost, and the nose was soon brought to its proper size, to the poor soldier's joy.

"I will do something more for you yet," said the little man; "take some of these pears and apples with you; whoever eats one of the apples will have his nose grow like yours just now; but if you give him a pear, all will come right again. Go to the princess and get her to eat some of your apples; her nose will grow twenty times as long as yours did; then look sharp, and you will get what you want of her."

Then they thanked their old friend very heartily for all his kindness, and it was agreed that the poor soldier who had already tried the power of the apple should undertake the task. So he dressed himself up as a gardener's boy, and went to the king's palace, and said he had apples to sell, such as were never seen there before. Everyone that saw them was delighted and wanted to taste, but he said they were only for the princess; and she soon sent her maid to buy his stock. They were so ripe and rosy that she soon began eating, and had already eaten three, when she, too, began to wonder what was the matter with her nose, for it grew and grew, down to the ground, out at the window, and over the garden, nobody knows where.

Then the king made known to all his kingdom, that whoever would heal her of this dreadful disease should be richly rewarded. Many tried, but the princess got no relief. And now the old soldier dressed himself very sprucely as a doctor, who said he could cure her; so he chopped up some of the apple, and to punish her a little more gave her a dose, saying he would call tomorrow and see her again. The morrow came, and of course, instead of being better, the nose had been growing fast all night, and the poor princess was in a dreadful fright. So the doctor chopped up a very little of the pear and gave it to her, and said he was sure that would do good, and he would call again the next day. Next day came, and the nose was, to be sure, a little smaller, but yet it was bigger than it was when the doctor first began to meddle with it.

Then he thought to himself, "I must frighten this cunning princess a little more before I shall get what I want of her"; so he gave her another dose of the apple, and said he would call on the morrow. The morrow came, and the nose was ten times as bad as before. "My good lady," said the doctor, "something works against my medicine, and is too strong for it; but I know by the force of my art what it is; you have stolen goods about you, I am sure, and if you do not give them back, I can do nothing for you." But the princess denied very stoutly that she had anything of the kind. "Very well," said the doctor, "you may do as you please, but I am sure I am right, and you will die if you do not own it." Then he went to the king, and told how the matter stood. "Daughter," said he, "send back the cloak, the purse, and the horn, that you stole from the right owners."

Then she ordered her maid to fetch all three, and gave them to the doctor, and begged him to give them back to the soldiers; and the moment he had them safe, he gave her a whole pear to eat, and the nose came right. And as for the doctor, he put on the cloak, wished the king and all his court a good day, and was in a short time with his two friends, who lived from that time happily at home in their palace, except when they took airings in their coach with the three dapple gray horses.

THE GOOSE-GIRL

By WILLIAM AND JACOB GRIMM

Illustration by WALTER CRANE

THERE lived once an old Queen, whose husband had been dead many years. She had a beautiful daughter who was promised in marriage to a King's son living a great way off. When the time appointed for the wedding drew near, and the old Queen had to send her daughter into the foreign land, she got together many costly things, furniture and cups and jewels and adornments, both of gold and silver, everything proper for the dowry of a royal Princess, for she loved her daughter dearly. She gave her also a waiting gentlewoman to attend her and to give her into the bridegroom's hands; and they were each to have a horse for the journey, and the Princess's horse was named Falada, and he could speak. When the time for parting came, the old Queen took her daughter to her chamber, and with a little knife she cut her own finger so that it bled; and she held beneath it a white napkin, and on it fell three drops of blood; and she gave it to her daughter, bidding her take care of it, for it would be needful to her on the way. Then they took leave of each other; and the Princess put the napkin in her bosom, got on her horse, and set out to go to the bridegroom. After she had ridden an hour, she began to feel very thirsty, and she said to the waiting woman: "Get down, and fill my cup that you are carrying with water from the brook; I have great desire to drink."

"Get down yourself," said the waiting woman, "and if you are thirsty stoop down and drink; I will not be your slave."

And as her thirst was so great, the Princess had to get down and to stoop and drink of the water of the brook, and could not have her gold cup to serve her. "Oh, dear!" said the poor Princess. And the three drops of blood heard her, and said:

"If your mother knew of this, it would break her heart."

But the Princess answered nothing, and quietly mounted her horse again. So they rode on some miles farther; the day was warm.

the sun shone hot, and the Princess grew thirsty once more. And when they came to a watercourse she called again to the waiting woman and said:

"Get down, and give me to drink out of my golden cup." For she had forgotten all that had gone before. But the waiting woman spoke still more scornfully and said:

"If you want a drink, you may get it yourself; I am not going to be your slave."

So, as her thirst was so great, the Princess had to get off her horse and to stoop toward the running water to drink, and as she stooped, she wept and said, "Oh, dear!" And the three drops of blood heard her and answered:

"If your mother knew of this, it would break her heart!"

And as she drank and stooped over, the napkin on which were the three drops of blood fell out of her bosom and floated down the stream, and in her distress she never noticed it; not so the waiting woman, who rejoiced because she should have power over the bride, who, now that she had lost the three drops of blood, had become weak, and unable to defend herself. And when she was going to mount her horse again the waiting woman cried:

"Falada belongs to me, and this jade to you." And the Princess had to give way and let it be as she said. Then the waiting woman ordered the Princess with many hard words to take off her rich clothing and to put on her plain garments, and then she made her swear to say nothing of the matter when they came to the royal court; threatening to take her life if she refused. And all the while Falada noticed and remembered.

The waiting woman then mounting Falada, and the Princess the sorry jade, they journeyed on till they reached the royal castle. There was great joy at their coming, and the King's son hastened to meet them, and lifted the waiting woman from her horse, thinking she was his bride; and then he led her up the stairs, while the real Princess had to remain below. But the old King, who was looking out of the window, saw her standing in the yard, and noticed how delicate and gentle and beautiful she was, and he went down and asked the seeming bride who it was that she had brought with her and that was now standing in the courtyard.

"Oh!" answered the bride, "I only brought her with me for company; give the maid something to do, that she may not be forever standing idle."

But the old King had no work to give her; until he bethought him of a boy he had who took care of the geese, and that she might help him. And so the real Princess was sent to keep geese with the goose-boy, who was called Conrad.

Soon after the false bride said to the Prince:

"Dearest husband, I pray thee do me a pleasure."

"With all my heart," answered he.

"Then," said she, "send for the knacker, that he may carry off the horse I came here upon, and make away with him; he was very troublesome to me on the journey." For she was afraid that the horse might tell how she had behaved to the Princess. And when the order had been given that Falada should die, it came to the Princess's ears, and she came to the knacker's man secretly, and promised him a piece of gold if he would do her a service. There was in the town a great dark gateway through which she had to pass morning and evening with her geese, and she asked the man to take Falada's head and to nail it on the gate, that she might always see it as she passed by. And the man promised, and he took Falada's head and nailed it fast in the dark gateway.

Early next morning as she and Conrad drove their geese through the gate, she said as she went by:

"O Falada, dost thou hang there?"

And the head answered:

"Princess, dost thou so meanly fare?
But if thy mother knew thy pain,
Her heart would surely break in twain."

But she went on through the town, driving her geese to the field And when they came into the meadows, she sat down and undid her hair, which was all of gold, and when Conrad saw how it glistened, he wanted to pull out a few hairs for himself. And she said:

> "O wind, blow Conrad's hat away,
> Make him run after as it flies,
> While I with my gold hair will play,
> And twist it up in seemly wise."

Then there came a wind strong enough to blow Conrad's hat far away over the fields, and he had to run after it; and by the time he came back she had put up her hair with combs and pins, and he could not get at any to pull it out; and he was sulky and would not speak to her; so they looked after the geese until the evening came, and then they went home.

The next morning, as they passed under the dark gateway, the Princess said:

> "O Falada, dost thou hang there?"

And Falada answered:

> "Princess, dost thou so meanly fare?
> But if thy mother knew thy pain,
> Her heart would surely break in twain."

And when they reached the fields she sat down and began to comb out her hair; then Conrad came up and wanted to seize upon some of it, and she cried:

> "O wind, blow Conrad's hat away,
> Make him run after as it flies,
> While I with my gold hair will play,
> And do it up in seemly wise."

Then the wind came and blew Conrad's hat very far away, so that he had to run after it, and when he came back her hair was put up again, so that he could pull none of it out; and they tended the geese until the evening. And after they had got home, Conrad went to the old King and said:

"I will tend the geese no longer with that girl!"

"Why not?" asked the old King.

"Because she vexes me the whole day long," answered Conrad. Then the old King ordered him to tell how it was.

"Every morning," said Conrad, "as we pass under the dark gateway with the geese, there is an old horse's head hanging on the wall, and she says to it:

"O Falada, dost thou hang there?"

And the head answers:

"Princess, dost thou so meanly fare?
But if thy mother knew thy pain,
Her heart would surely break in twain."

And besides this, Conrad related all that happened in the fields, and how he was obliged to run after his hat.

The old King told him to go to drive the geese next morning as usual, and he himself went behind the gate and listened how the maiden spoke to Falada; and then he followed them into the fields, and hid himself behind a bush; and he watched the goose-boy and the goose-girl tend the geese; and after a while he saw the girl make her hair all loose, and how it gleamed and shone. Soon she said:

"O wind, blow Conrad's hat away,
And make him follow as it flies,
While I with my gold hair will play,
And bind it up in seemly wise."

Then there came a gust of wind and away went Conrad's hat, and he after it, while the maiden combed and bound up her hair; and the old King saw all that went on. At last he went unnoticed away, and when the goose-girl came back in the evening he sent for her, and asked the reason of her doing all this.

"That I dare not tell you," she answered, "nor can I tell any man of my woe, for when I was in danger of my life I swore an oath not to reveal it." And he pressed her sore, and left her no peace, but he could get nothing out of her. At last he said:

"If you will not tell it to me, tell it to the iron oven," and he went

Walter Crane

A strong wind blew Conrad's hat away.

[See page 159]

away. Then she crept into the iron oven, and began to weep and to lament, and at last she opened her heart and said:

"Here I sit forsaken of all the world, and I am a King's daughter, and a wicked waiting woman forced me to give up my royal garments and my place at the bridegroom's side, and I am made a goose-girl, and have to do mean service. And if my mother knew, it would break her heart."

Now the old King was standing outside by the oven-door listening, and he heard all she said, and he called to her and told her to come out of the oven. And he caused royal clothing to be put upon her, and it was a marvel to see how beautiful she was. The old King then called his son and proved to him that he had the wrong bride, for she was really only a waiting woman, and that the true bride was here at hand, she who had been the goose-girl. The Prince was glad at heart when he saw her beauty and gentleness; and a great feast was made ready, and all the court people and good friends were bidden to it. The bridegroom sat in the midst with the Princess on one side and the waiting woman on the other; and the false bride did not know the true one, because she was dazzled with her glittering braveries. When all the company had eaten and drunk and were merry, the old King gave the waiting woman a question to answer, as to what such a one deserved, who had deceived her masters in such and such a manner, telling the whole story, and ending by asking: "Now, what doom does such a one deserve?"

"No better than this," answered the false bride, "that she be put naked into a cask, studded inside with sharp nails, and be dragged along in it by two horses from street to street, till she be dead."

"Thou hast spoken thy own doom," said the old King; "as thou hast said, so shall it be done." And when the sentence was fulfilled, the Prince married the true bride, and ever after they ruled over their kingdom in peace and blessedness.

THE BREMEN TOWN MUSICIANS

By *WILLIAM* AND *JACOB GRIMM*

Illustration by WALTER CRANE

THERE was once an ass whose master had made him carry sacks to the mill for many a long year, but whose strength began at last to fail, so that each day as it came found him less capable of work. Then his master began to think of turning him out, but the ass, guessing that something was in the wind that boded him no good, ran away, taking the road to Bremen; for here, he thought, he might get an engagement as town musician. When he had gone a little way he found a hound lying by the side of the road, panting, as if he had run a long way.

"Now, Holdfast, what are you so out of breath about?" said the ass.

"Oh, dear!" said the dog, "now I am old, I get weaker every day, and can do no good in the hunt, so, as my master was going to have me killed, I have made my escape; but now, how am I to gain a living?"

"I will tell you what," said the ass. "I am going to Bremen to become town musician. You may as well go with me, and take up music, too. I can play the lute, and you can beat the drum."

And the dog consented, and they walked on together. It was not long before they came to a cat sitting in the road, looking as dismal as three wet days.

"Now then, what is the matter with you, old shaver?" said the ass.

"I should like to know who would be cheerful when his neck is in danger?" answered the cat. "Now that I am old my teeth are getting blunt, and I would rather sit by the oven and purr than run about after mice, and my mistress wanted to drown me; so I took myself off; but good advice is scarce, and I do not know what is to become of me."

"Go with us to Bremen," said the ass, "and become town musician. You understand serenading."

The cat thought well of the idea, and went with them accordingly. After that the three travelers passed by a yard, and a cock was perched on the gate crowing with all his might.

"Your cries are enough to pierce bone and marrow," said the ass; "what is the matter?"

"I have foretold good weather for Lady-day, so that all the shirts may be washed and dried; and now on Sunday morning company is coming, and the mistress has told the cook that I must be made into the soup, and this evening my neck is to be wrung, so that I am crowing with all my might while I can."

"You had much better go with us, Chanticleer," said the ass. "We are going to Bremen. At any rate, that will be better than dying. You have a powerful voice, and when we are all performing together it will have a very good effect."

So the cock consented, and they went on all four together.

But Bremen was too far off to be reached in one day, and toward evening they came to a wood, where they determined to pass the night. The ass and the dog lay down under a large tree; the cat got up among the branches, and the cock flew up to the top, as that was the safest place for him. Before he went to sleep he looked all round him to the four points of the compass, and perceived in the distance a little light shining, and he called out to his companions that there must be a house not far off, as he could see a light, so the ass said:

"We had better get up and go there, for these are uncomfortable quarters." The dog began to fancy a few bones, not quite bare, would do him good. And they all set off in the direction of the light, and it grew larger and brighter, until at last it led them to a robber's house, all lighted up. The ass, being the biggest, went up to the window, and looked in.

"Well, what do you see?" asked the dog.

"What do I see?" answered the ass; "here is a table set out with splendid eatables and drinkables, and robbers sitting at it and making themselves very comfortable."

"That would just suit us," said the cock.

"Yes, indeed, I wish we were there," said the ass. Then they consulted together how it should be managed so as to get the robbers out of the house, and at last they hit on a plan. The ass was to place his forefeet on the window sill, the dog was to get on the ass's back, the cat on the top of the dog, and lastly the cock was to fly up and perch on the cat's head. When that was done, at a given signal they all began to perform their music. The ass brayed, the dog barked, the cat mewed, and the cock crowed; then they burst through into the room, breaking all the panes of glass. The robbers fled at the dreadful sound; they thought it was some goblin, and fled to the wood in the utmost terror. Then the four companions sat down to table, made free with the remains of the meal, and feasted as if they had been hungry for a month. And when they had finished they put out the lights, and each sought out a sleeping place to suit his nature and habits. The ass laid himself down outside on the dunghill, the dog behind the door, the cat on the hearth by the warm ashes, and the cock settled himself in the cockloft, and as they were all tired with their long journey they soon fell fast asleep.

When midnight drew near, and the robbers from afar saw that no light was burning, and that everything appeared quiet, their captain said to them that he thought that they had run away without reason, telling one of them to go and reconnoiter. So one of them went, and found everything quite quiet; he went into the kitchen to strike a light, and taking the glowing fiery eyes of the cat for burning coals, he held a match to them in order to kindle it. But the cat, not seeing the joke, flew into his face, spitting and scratching. Then he cried out in terror, and ran to get out at the back door, but the dog, who was lying there, ran at him and bit his leg; and as he was rushing through the yard by the dunghill the ass struck out and gave him a great kick with his hindfoot; and the cock, who had been wakened with the noise, and felt quite brisk, cried out. "Cock-a-doodle-doo!"

Then the robber got back as well as he could to his captain, and said, "Oh, dear! in that house there is a gruesome witch, and I felt her breath and her long nails in my face; and by the door there stands a man who stabbed me in the leg with a knife; and in the yard there lies a black specter, who beat me with his wooden club; and above, upon the roof, there sits the justice, who cried, 'Bring that rogue here!' And so I ran away from the place as fast as I could."

From that time forward the robbers never ventured to that house, and the four Bremen town musicians found themselves so well off where they were, that there they stayed. And the person who last related this tale is still living, as you see.

THE FISHERMAN AND HIS WIFE

By WILLIAM AND JACOB GRIMM

Illustration by WALTER CRANE

THERE was once a fisherman and his wife who lived together in a hovel by the seashore, and the fisherman went out every day with his hook and line to catch fish, and he angled and angled.

One day he was sitting with his rod and looking into the clear water, and he sat and sat.

At last down went the line to the bottom of the water, and when he drew it up he found a great flounder on the hook. And the flounder said to him:

"Fisherman, listen to me; let me go, I am not a real fish but an enchanted prince. What good shall I be to you if you land me? I shall not taste well; so put me back into the water again, and let me swim away."

"Well," said the fisherman, "no need of so many words about the matter; as you can speak I had much rather let you swim away."

Then he put him back into the clear water, and the flounder sank to the bottom, leaving a long streak of blood behind him. Then the fisherman got up and went home to his wife in their hovel.

"Well, husband," said the wife, "have you caught nothing today?"

"No," said the man—"that is, I did catch a flounder, but as he said he was an enchanted prince, I let him go again."

"Then, did you wish for nothing?" said the wife.

"No," said the man; "what should I wish for?"

"Oh, dear!" said the wife; "and it is so dreadful always to live in this evil-smelling hovel. You might as well have wished for a little cottage. Go again and call him; tell him we want a little cottage. I daresay he will give it us; go, and be quick."

And when he went back, the sea was green and yellow, and not nearly so clear. So he stood and said:

"O man, O man!—if man you be,
Or flounder, flounder, in the sea—
Such a tiresome wife I've got,
For she wants what I do not."

Then the flounder came swimming up, and said:
"Now then, what does she want?"
"Oh," said the man, "you know when I caught you my wife says
ought to have wished for something. She does not want to live
any longer in the hovel, and would rather have a cottage.

"Go home with you," said the flounder, "she has it already."
So the man went home, and found, instead of the hovel, a little
cottage, and his wife was sitting on a bench before the door. And
he took him by the hand, and said to him:
"Come in and see if this is not a great improvement."
So they went in, and there was a little house place and a beautiful
little bedroom, a kitchen and larder, with all sorts of furniture, and
iron and brass ware of the very best. And at the back was a little
yard with fowls and ducks, and a little garden full of green vegetables and fruit.

"Look," said the wife, "is not that nice?"

"Yes," said the man, "if this can only last we shall be very well contented."

"We will see about that," said the wife. And after a meal they went to bed.

So all went well for a week or fortnight, when the wife said:

"Look here, husband, the cottage is really too confined, and the yard and garden are so small; I think the flounder had better get us a larger house; I should like very much to live in a large stone castle; so go to your fish and he will send us a castle."

"Oh, my dear wife," said the man, "the cottage is good enough; what do we want a castle for?"

"We want one," said the wife; "go along with you; the flounder can give us one."

"Now, wife," said the man, "the flounder gave us the cottage; I do not like to go to him again, he may be angry."

"Go along," said the wife, "he might just as well give us it as not; do as I say!"

The man felt very reluctant and unwilling; and he said to himself: "It is not the right thing to do"; nevertheless he went.

So when he came to the seaside, the water was purple and dark blue and gray and thick, and not green and yellow as before. And he stood and said:

> "O man, O man!—if man you be,
> Or flounder, flounder, in the sea—
> Such a tiresome wife I've got,
> For she wants what I do not."

"Now then, what does she want?" said the flounder.

"Oh," said the man, half frightened, "she wants to live in a large stone castle."

"Go home with you, she is already standing before the door," said the flounder.

Then the man went home, as he supposed, but when he got there, there stood in the place of the cottage a great castle of stone, and his wife was standing on the steps, about to go in; so she took him by the hand, and said: "Let us enter."

With that he went in with her, and in the castle was a great hall with a marble pavement, and there were a great many servants, who led them through large doors, and the passages were decked with tapestry, and the rooms with golden chairs and tables, and crystal chandeliers hanging from the ceiling; and all the rooms had carpets. And the tables were covered with eatables and the best wine for any-one who wanted them. And at the back of the house was a great stable-yard for horses and cattle, and carriages of the finest; besides, there was a splendid large garden, with the most beautiful flowers and fine fruit trees, and a pleasance full half a mile long, with deer and oxen and sheep, and everything that heart could wish for.

"There!" said the wife, "is not this beautiful?"

"Oh, yes," said the man, "if it will only last we can live in this fine castle and be very well contented."

"We will see about that," said the wife; "in the meanwhile we will sleep upon it." With that they went to bed.

The next morning the wife was awake first, just at the break of day, and she looked out and saw from her bed the beautiful country lying all round. The man took no notice of it, so she poked him in the side with her elbow, and said:

"Husband, get up and just look out of the window. Look, just think if we could be king over all this country: Just go to your fish and tell him we should like to be king."

"Now, wife," said the man, "what should we be kings for? I don't want to be king."

"Well," said the wife, "if you don't want to be king, I will be king."

"Now, wife," said the man, "what do you want to be king for? I could not ask him such a thing."

"Why not?" said the wife, "you must go directly all the same; I must be king."

So the man went, very much put out that his wife should want to be king.

"It is not the right thing to do—not at all the right thing," thought the man. He did not at all want to go, and yet he went all the same.

And when he came to the sea the water was quite dark gray,

and rushed far inland, and had an ill smell. And he stood and said:

> "O man, O man!—if man you be,
> Or flounder, flounder, in the sea—
> Such a tiresome wife I've got,
> For she wants what I do not."

"Now then, what does she want?" said the fish.

"Oh, dear!" said the man, "she wants to be king."

"Go home with you, she is so already," said the fish.

So the man went back, and as he came to the palace he saw it was very much larger, and had great towers and splendid gateways; the herald stood before the door, and a number of soldiers with kettledrums and trumpets.

And when he came inside everything was of marble and gold, and there were many curtains with great golden tassels. Then he went through the doors of the saloon to where the great throne room was, and there was his wife sitting upon a throne of gold and diamonds, and she had a great golden crown on, and the scepter in her hand was of pure gold and jewels, and on each side stood six pages in a row, each one a head shorter than the other. So the man went up to her and said:

"Well, wife, so now you are king!"

"Yes," said the wife, "now I am king."

So then he stood and looked at her, and when he had gazed at her for some time he said:

"Well, wife, this is fine for you to be king! Now there is nothing more to wish for."

"Oh, husband," said the wife, seeming quite restless, "I am tired of this already! Go to your fish and tell him that now I am king I must be emperor."

"Now, wife," said the man, "what do you want to be emperor for?"

"Husband," said she, "go and tell the fish I want to be emperor."

"Oh, dear!" said the man, "he could not do it—I cannot ask him such a thing. There is but one emperor at a time; the fish can't possibly make anyone emperor—indeed he can't."

"Now, look here," said the wife, "I am king, and you are only my husband, so will you go at once? Go along! for if he was able to make me king he is able to make me emperor; and I will and must be emperor, so go along!"

So he was obliged to go; and as he went he felt very uncomfortable about it, and he thought to himself:

"It is not at all the right thing to do; to want to be emperor is really going too far; the flounder will soon be beginning to get tired of this."

With that he came to the sea, and the water was quite black and thick, and the foam flew, and the wind blew, and the man was terrified. But he stood and said:

> "O man, O man!—if man you be,
> Or flounder, flounder, in the sea—
> Such a tiresome wife I've got,
> For she wants what I do not."

"What is it now?" said the fish.

"Oh, dear!" said the man, "my wife wants to be emperor."

"Go home with you," said the fish, "she is emperor already."

So the man went home, and found the castle adorned with polished marble and alabaster figures, and golden gates. The troops were being marshaled before the door, and they were blowing trumpets and beating drums and cymbals; and when he entered he saw barons and earls and dukes waiting about like servants; and the doors were of bright gold. And he saw his wife sitting upon a throne made of one entire piece of gold, and it was about two miles high; and she had a great golden crown on, which was about three yards high, set with brilliants and carbuncles; and in one hand she held the scepter, and the other the globe; and on both sides of her stood pages in two rows, all arranged according to their size, from the most enormous giant of two miles high to the tiniest dwarf of the size of my little finger; and before her stood earls and dukes in crowds. So the man went up to her and said:

"Well, wife, so now you are emperor."

"Yes," said she, "now I am emperor."

Then he went and sat down and had a good look at her, and then he said: "Well, now, wife, there is nothing left to be, now you are emperor."

"What are you talking about, husband?" said she. "I am emperor, and next I will be pope! So go and tell the fish so."

"Oh, dear!" said the man. "What is it that you don't want? You can never become pope; there is but one pope in Christendom, and the fish can't possibly do it."

"Husband," said she, "no more words about it; I must and will be pope; so go along to the fish."

"Now, wife," said the man, "how can I ask him such a thing? It is too bad—it is asking a little too much; and, besides, he could not do it."

"What rubbish!" said the wife; "if he could make me emperor he can make me pope. Go along and ask him; I am emperor, and you are only my husband, so go you must."

So he went, feeling very frightened, and he shivered and shook, and his knees trembled; and there arose a great wind, and the clouds flew by, and it grew very dark, and the sea rose mountains high, and the ships were tossed about, and the sky was partly blue in the middle, but at the sides very dark and red, as in a great tempest. And he felt very desponding, and stood trembling and said:

> "O man, O man!—if man you be,
> Or flounder, flounder, in the sea—
> Such a tiresome wife I've got,
> For she wants what I do not."

"Well, what now?" said the fish.

"Oh, dear!" said the man, "she wants to be pope."

"Go home with you, she is pope already," said the fish.

So he went home, and he found himself before a great church, with palaces all round. He had to make his way through a crowd of people; and when he got inside he found the place lighted up with thousands and thousands of lights; and his wife was clothed in a golden garment, and sat upon a very high throne, and had three golden crowns on, all in the greatest priestly pomp; and on both sides of her there stood two rows of lights of all sizes—from the size of the longest tower to the smallest rushlight, and all the emperors and kings were kneeling before her and kissing her foot.

"Well, wife," said the man, and sat and stared at her, "so you are pope."

"Yes," said she, "now I am pope!"

And he went on gazing at her till he felt dazzled, as if he were sitting in the sun. And after a little time he said:

"Well, now, wife, what is there left to be, now you are pope?"

And she sat up very stiff and straight, and said nothing.

And he said again, "Well, wife, I hope you are contented at last with being pope; you can be nothing more."

"We will see about that," said the wife. With that they both went to bed; but she was as far as ever from being contented, and she could not get to sleep for thinking of what she should like to be next.

The husband, however, slept as fast as a top after his busy day; but the wife tossed and turned from side to side the whole night through, thinking all the while what she could be next, but nothing would occur to her; and when she saw the red dawn she slipped off the bed, and sat before the window to see the sun rise, and as it came up she said: "Ah, I have it! what if I should make the sun and moon to rise—husband!" she cried, and stuck her elbow in his ribs "wake up, and go to your fish, and tell him I want power over the sun and moon."

The man was so fast asleep that when he started up he fell out of bed. Then he shook himself together, and opened his eyes and said:

"Oh—wife, what did you say?"

"Husband," said she, "if I cannot get the power of making the sun and moon rise when I want them, I shall never have another quiet hour. Go to the fish and tell him so."

"Oh, wife!" said the man, and fell on his knees to her, "the fish can really not do that for you. I grant you he could make you emperor and pope; do be contented with that, I beg of you."

And she became wild with impatience, and screamed out:

"I can wait no longer, go at once!"

And so off he went as well as he could for fright. And a dreadful storm arose, so that he could hardly keep his feet; and the houses and trees were blown down, and the mountains trembled, and rocks fell in the sea; the sky was quite black, and it thundered and lightened; and the waves, crowned with foam, ran mountains high. So he cried out, without being able to hear his own words:

> "O man, O man!—if man you be,
> Or flounder, flounder, in the sea—
> Such a tiresome wife I've got,
> For she wants what I do not."

"Well, what now?" said the flounder.

"Oh, dear!" said the man, "she wants to order about the sun and moon."

"Go home with you!" said the flounder, "you will find her in the old hovel."

And there they are sitting to this very day.

Tales From Norway

THE GOLDEN BIRD

By P. C. ASBJORNSEN

Illustration by T. KITTELSEN

THERE was once upon a time a king who had a garden; in that garden there was an apple tree, and on that apple tree there grew a golden apple every year; but when the time came to pluck the apple it was gone, and no one knew who took it or what became of it; but gone it was.

The king had three sons, and one day he told them that he who could bring him the apple, or get hold of the thief, should have the kingdom after him, no matter whether he was the eldest, the second, or the younger son. The eldest set out first and sat down under the tree to keep watch for the thief. Soon after dark a golden bird came flying, and the light from it was so strong and dazzling that it could be seen a long way off. When the prince saw the bird and the dazzling light he became so frightened that he dared not stay any longer, but rushed indoors as fast as he could.

Next morning the apple was gone; the prince had then, however, recovered his courage and began to get ready for his journey and wanted to set off to find the bird. The king fitted him out in grand style and spared neither money nor fine raiment. When the prince had gone a bit on the way he became hungry, opened his scrip and sat down to his breakfast by the roadside. A fox then came out of the wood and sat down and looked at him.

"Do give me a little to eat," said the fox.

"I'll give you some powder and shot," said the prince; "my food I shall want myself; nobody can tell how far and how long I may have to travel," said he.

"Just so," said the fox, and he went back into the wood again.

When the prince had finished his meal and rested awhile he set out on his way again. After a long time he came to a big city, and in that city there was an inn where there was always joy and never any sorrow; he thought that would be a nice place to stop at, and so he remained. And there was such dancing and drinking and joy and merrymaking that he forgot the bird and his father and his journey and the whole kingdom. Away he was and away he stopped.

The next year the second prince was to watch for the thief in the garden; he also sat down under the tree when the apple began to ripen. But one night, all of a sudden, the golden bird came flying, shining like the sun; the prince became so afraid that he took to his heels and ran indoors as fast as he could.

In the morning the apple was gone, but the prince had then recovered his courage and wanted to set out and find the bird. He began to get ready and the king fitted him out in grand style and spared neither money nor fine raiment. But the same thing happened to him as to his brother; when he had got a bit on the way he became hungry, opened his scrip and sat down to his breakfast by the roadside. A fox came out from the wood, sat down and looked at him.

"Do give me a little to eat," said the fox.

"I'll give you some powder and shot," said the prince; "my food I shall want myself; nobody can tell how far and how long I may have to travel," said he.

"Just so," said the fox, and so he went back into the wood again.

When the prince had finished his meal and rested awhile, he set out on his way again. After a long time he came to the same city, and the same inn where there was always joy and never any sorrow: and there he also thought it would be nice to stop, and the first he met was his brother, and so he remained. The brother had been leading a gay and reckless life and had scarcely any clothes left on his back; but now he began afresh, and there was such dancing and drinking and joy and merriment that the second prince also forgot the bird and his father and his journey and the whole kingdom. Away he was and away he stopped.

When the time came for the apple to ripen again the youngest prince was to go into the garden and watch for the thief. He took a companion with him who was to help him up into the tree, and he also took with him a keg of beer and a pack of cards to pass away the time with so that he should not fall asleep. All of a sudden they saw a bright light, as if from the sun; every feather of the bird could be seen long before it came to the tree. The prince climbed up into the tree and at the same time the golden bird swooped down and took the apple; the prince tried to seize the bird, but he only caught a feather out of its tail.

So he went to the king's bedroom, and as he came in with the feather, it became as light as day.

He also wanted to try if he could find his brothers and catch the bird, for he had been so near to it that he had got a feather from its tail and would know it again anywhere, he said.

Well, the king went and pondered long whether he should let him go, for he thought the youngest would not fare any better than the two eldest, who ought to have more knowledge of the world, and he was afraid he should lose him also. But the prince begged so earnestly that at last he got permission to go.

He then began to get ready and the king fitted him out in grand style, both with clothes and money, and so he set off.

When he had traveled for some time he became hungry and took his scrip and sat down to have his breakfast, but just as he was in the midst of it a fox came out of the wood and sat down close by his side and looked at him.

"Do give me a little to eat," said the fox.

"I shall want the food myself," said the prince, "for I cannot tell how far I shall travel; but I have enough to give you a little."

When the fox had got the piece of meat he asked the prince where he was going. Yes, that he would tell him.

"If you will listen to me, I will help you, and you will have good luck," said the fox.

The prince promised he would, and so they set off together. They traveled awhile till they came to the same city, and the same inn where there was always joy but no sorrow.

"I must keep outside here; the dogs are rather a nuisance," said the fox; and so he told the prince where his brothers were to be found and what they were doing. "And if you go in there you will not get any further either," said he.

The prince promised he would not go in there, and gave him his hand on it, and so each went his way. But when the prince came to the inn and heard the noise and merriment going on he felt he must go in; there was no help for it. And when he met his brothers there was such rejoicing that he forgot both the fox and the journey and the bird and his father. But when he had been there awhile the fox came—he had ventured into the city after all— and opened the door a little and made a sign to the prince, saying that now they must be off. So the prince bethought himself, and they went their way.

When they had traveled awhile they saw a big mountain far away. The fox said, "Three hundred miles at the back of that mountain there is a gilded linden tree with golden leaves, and in that tree sits the golden bird from which you took the feather."

Thither they traveled together. When the prince was going to catch the bird, the fox gave him some bright feathers which he was to wave in his hands, and so attract the bird, which would then fly down and sit on his hand.

But the fox said he must not touch the linden tree, for inside it was a big troll, who owned it, and if the prince only touched the smallest twig the troll would come out and kill him on the spot.

No, he would not touch it, said the prince; but when he had got the bird on his hand he thought he must have a twig of the tree; there was no help for it, it was so bright and beautiful. So he took a tiny little sprig, but the same moment the troll came out.

"Who is that stealing my tree and my bird?" roared the troll, and he was so angry that he spurted sparks of fire.

"Thieves believe that all men steal," said the prince, "but only those get hanged who do not steal properly," said he.

The troll said that made no difference, and was going to kill him, but the prince begged him to spare his life.

"Well," said the troll, "if you can bring me back the horse which my nearest neighbor has taken, you will get off with your life."

"Where shall I find it, then?" said the prince.

"Oh, he lives three hundred miles at the back of that big blue mountain against the horizon yonder," said the troll.

The prince promised he would do his best. But when he came back to the fox he found him in rather a bad temper.

"Now you have got yourself into trouble," said the fox; "if you had listened to me we could have been on our way home by this," said he.

So they had to make a fresh start, for the prince had pledged his word, and his life depended on his finding the horse.

At last they got there, but as the prince was going to take the horse the fox said: "When you come into the stable you will find all sorts of bridles hanging on the wall, both of gold and silver; you must not touch them, for then the troll will come and kill you right away; you must take the ugliest and shabbiest you see."

Yes, the prince promised he would; but when he came into the stable he thought it was quite unreasonable not to take a fine bridle, for there were plenty of them, and so he took the brightest he could find. It was as bright as gold, but just then the troll came and was so angry that sparks flew from him.

"Who is that stealing my horse and my bridle?" he shrieked.

"Thieves believe that all men steal," said the prince; "but only those get hanged who do not steal properly," said he.

"Well, that makes no difference. I'll kill you on the spot," shouted the troll. But the prince begged him to spare his life.

"Well," said the troll, "if you can bring me back the fair damsel which my nearest neighbor has taken from me I will spare you."

"Whereabouts does he live, then?" asked the prince.

"Oh, he lives three hundred miles at the back of that big blue mountain against the horizon yonder," said the troll.

The prince promised he would fetch the damsel, and was allowed to go, and so he escaped with his life.

But when he came out you may imagine how angry the fox was.

"Now you've got yourself into trouble again," said he; "if you had listened to me we could have been on our way home long ago. I almost think I will not go with you any farther."

But the prince begged and prayed and promised he would never do anything else but what the fox told him, if he would only remain with him. At last the fox gave in, and they became firm friends again; so they set off once more and came at last to where the fair damsel was.

"Well," said the fox, "I have your promise, but I dare not let you in to the troll, after all; this time I must go myself." So he went in, and after awhile he came out with the damsel, and so they went back the same way they had come.

When they got to the troll, who had the horse, they took both the horse and the brightest bridle; and when they got to the troll who had the linden tree and the bird, they took both the tree and the bird and started off with them.

When they had got a bit on the way they came to a field of rye, and the fox then said:

"I hear a thundering noise; you had better go on ahead; I will remain here awhile," he said. He then plaited himself a gown of rye straw, in which he looked like a preacher. All at once the three trolls came rushing along, hoping to overtake the prince.

"Have you seen anyone passing here with a fair damsel, a horse with a golden bridle, a golden bird, and a gilded linden tree?" they shouted to the fox as he stood there preaching.

"Well, I've heard from my grandmother's grandmother that something of the kind passed this way, but that was in the good old times, when my grandmother's grandmother baked halfpenny cakes and gave back the halfpenny."

Then all the trolls burst out laughing: "Ha, ha, ha!" they laughed and held on to one another.

"If we have slept so long we may as well turn our noses homeward, and go to sleep again," they said, and so they went back the way they came.

The fox then set off after the prince, but when they came to the city where the inn and his brothers were, he said:

"I dare not go through the town on account of the dogs; I must go my own way just above here, but you must take good care your brothers do not get hold of you."

But when the prince came into the city he thought it would be too bad if he did not look in upon his brothers and have a word with them, and so he tarried there for awhile.

When the brothers saw him they came out and took both the damsel, and the horse, and the bird, and the linden tree, and everything from him, and they put him in a barrel, and threw him into

They put him in a barrel and threw him into the sea.

the sea; and so they set off home to the king's palace, with the damsel, and the horse, and the bird, and the linden tree, and everything. But the damsel would not speak, and she became pale and wretched to look upon; the horse got so thin and miserable that it could hardly hang together; the bird became silent and shone no more, and the linden tree withered.

In the meantime, the fox was sneaking about outside the city where the inn and the merriment were, and was waiting for the prince and the damsel, and wondered why they did not return.

He went hither and thither, waiting and watching for them, and at last he came down to the shore, and when he saw the barrel, which was lying out at sea drifting, he shouted: "Why are you drifting about there, you empty barrel?"

"Oh, it is I," said the prince in the barrel.

The fox then swam out to sea as fast as he could, got hold of the barrel, and towed it to land; then he began to gnaw the hoops, and when he had got some off the barrel, he said to the prince: "Stamp and kick."

The prince stamped and kicked till all the staves flew about, and out he jumped from the barrel.

So they went together to the king's palace, and when they got there the damsel regained her beauty and began to talk; the horse became so fat and sleek that every hair glistened; the light shone from the bird and it began to sing; the linden tree began to blossom and its leaves to sparkle, and the damsel said, "He is the one who has saved us."

They planted the linden tree in the garden, and the youngest prince was to marry the princess, for such the damsel really was; but the two eldest brothers were put each in a spiked barrel and rolled down a high mountain.

Then they began to prepare for the wedding, but the fox first asked the prince to put him on the block and cut his head off, and although the prince both prayed and cried, there was no help for it; he would have to do it. But as he cut the head off, the fox turned into a handsome prince, and he was the brother of the princess, whom they had rescued from the troll.

So the wedding came off and everything was so grand and splendid, that the news of the festivities reached all the way here.

THE PRINCESS WHOM NOBODY COULD SILENCE

By P. C. ASBJORNSEN

THERE was once upon a time a king, and he had a daughter who would always have the last word; she was so perverse and contrary in her speech that no one could silence her. So the king therefore promised that he who could outwit her should have the princess in marriage and half the kingdom besides. There were plenty of those who wanted to try, I can assure you; for it isn't every day that a princess and half a kingdom are to be had.

The gate to the palace hardly ever stood still. The suitors came in swarms and flocks from east and west, both riding and walking. But there was no one who could silence the princess. At last the king announced that those who tried and did not succeed should be branded on both ears with a large iron; he would not have all this running about the palace for nothing.

So there were three brothers who had also heard about the princess, and as they were rather badly off at home, they thought they would try their luck and see if they could win the princess and half the kingdom. They were good friends and so they agreed to set out together. When they had got a bit on the way, Ashiepattle found a dead magpie.

"I have found something! I have found something!" cried he.

"What have you found?" asked the brothers.

"I have found a dead magpie," said he.

"Faugh! Throw it away; what can you do with that?" said the other two, who always believed they were the wisest.

"Oh, I've nothing else to do. I can easily carry it," said Ashiepattle.

When they had gone on a bit farther Ashiepattle found an old willow twig, which he picked up.

"I have found something! I have found something!" he cried.

"What have you found now?" said the brothers.

"I have found a willow twig," said he.

"Pooh! What are you going to do with that? Throw it away," said the two.

"I have nothing else to do, I can easily carry it with me," said Ashiepattle.

When they had gone still farther he found a broken saucer, which he also picked up.

"Here, lads, I have found something! I have found something!" said he.

"Well, what have you found now?" asked the brothers.

"A broken saucer," said he.

"Pshaw! Is it worth while dragging that along with you, too? Throw it away!" said the brothers.

"Oh, I've nothing else to do, I can easily carry it with me," said Ashiepattle.

When they had gone a little bit farther he found a crooked goat-horn and soon after he found the fellow to it.

"I have found something! I have found something, lads!" said he.

"What have you found now?" said the others.

"Two goat-horns," answered Ashiepattle.

"Ugh! Throw them away! What are you going to do with them?" said they.

"Oh, I have nothing else to do. I can easily carry them with me," said Ashiepattle.

In a little while he found a wedge.

"I say, lads, I have found something! I have found something!" he cried.

"You are everlastingly finding something! What have you found now?" asked the two eldest.

"I have found a wedge," he answered. "Oh, throw it away! What are you going to do with it?" said they.

"Oh, I have nothing else to do. I can easily carry it with me," said Ashiepattle.

As he went across the king's fields, which had been freshly manured, he stooped down and took up an old boot-sole.

"Hullo, lads! I have found something, I have found something!" said he.

"Heaven grant you may find a little sense before you get to the palace!" said the two. "What is it you have found now?"

"An old boot-sole," said he.

"Is that anything worth picking up? Throw it away? What are you going to do with it?" said the brothers.

"Oh, I have nothing else to do. I can easily carry it with me, and —who knows?—it may help me to win the princess and half the kingdom," said Ashiepattle.

"Yes, you look a likely one, don't you?" said the other two. So they went in to the princess, the eldest first.

"Good day!" said he.

"Good day to you!" answered she, with a shrug.

"It's terribly hot here," said he.

"It's hotter in the fire," said the princess. The branding iron was lying waiting in the fire.

When he saw this he was struck speechless, and so it was all over with him.

The second brother fared no better. "Good day!" said he.

"Good day to you," said she with a wriggle.

"It's terribly hot here!" said he.

"It's hotter in the fire," said she. With that he lost both speech and wits, and so the iron had to be brought out.

Then came Ashiepattle's turn.

"Good day!" said he.

"Good day to you!" said she, with a shrug and a wriggle.

"It is very nice and warm here!" said Ashiepattle.

"It's warmer in the fire," she answered. She was in no better humor now she saw the third suitor.

"Then there's a chance for me to roast my magpie on it," said he, bringing it out.

"I'm afraid it will sputter," said the princess.

"No fear of that! I'll tie this willow twig round it," said the lad.

"You can't tie it tight enough," said she.

"Then I'll drive in a wedge," said the lad, and brought out the wedge.

"The fat will be running off it," said the princess.

"Then I'll hold this under it," said the lad, and showed her the broken saucer.

"You are so crooked in your speech," said the princess.

"No, I am not crooked," answered the lad; "but this is crooked." And he brought out one of the goat-horns.

"Well, I've never seen the like!" cried the princess.

"Here you see the like," said he, and brought out the other horn.

"It seems you have come here to wear out my soul!" she said.

"No, I have not come here to wear out your soul, for I have one here which is already worn out," answered the lad, and brought out the old boot-sole.

The princess was so dumfounded at this that she was completely silenced.

"Now you are mine!" said Ashiepattle, and so he got her and half the kingdom into the bargain.

THE DOLL IN THE GRASS

By P. C. ASBJORNSEN

ONCE upon a time there was a king who had twelve sons. When they were grown up he told them they must go out into the world and find themselves wives, who must all be able to spin and weave and make a shirt in one day, else he would not have them for daughters-in-law. He gave each of his sons a horse and a new suit of armor, and so they set out in the world to look for wives.

When they had traveled a bit on the way they said they would not take Ashiepattle with them, for he was good for nothing. Ashiepattle must stop behind; there was no help for it. He did not know what he should do or which way he should turn; he became so sad that he got off the horse and sat down on the grass and began to cry.

When he had sat awhile one of the tussocks among the grass began to move, and out of it came a small white figure; as it came nearer Ashiepattle saw that it was a beautiful little girl, but she was so tiny, so very, very tiny.

She went up to him and asked him if he would come below and pay a visit to the doll in the grass.

Yes, that he would; and so he did. When he came down below the doll in the grass was sitting in a chair dressed very finely and looking still more beautiful. She asked Ashiepattle where he was going and what was his errand.

He told her they were twelve brothers, and that the king had given them each a horse and a suit of armor, and told them to go out in the world and find themselves wives, but they must all be able to spin and weave and make a shirt in a day.

"If you can do that and will become my wife, I will not travel any farther," said Ashiepattle to the doll in the grass.

Yes, that she would, and she set to work at once to get the shirt spun, woven and made; but it was so tiny, so very, very tiny, no bigger than—so!

Ashiepattle then returned home, taking the shirt with him; but when he brought it out he felt very shy because it was so small. But the king said he could have her for all that, and you can imagine how happy and joyful Ashiepattle then became.

The road did not seem long to him as he set out to fetch his little sweetheart. When he came to the doll in the grass he wanted her to sit with him on his horse; but no, that she wouldn't; she said she would sit and drive in a silver spoon, and she had two small white horses which would draw her. So they set out, he on his horse and she in the silver spoon; and the horses which drew her were two small white mice.

Ashiepattle always kept to one side of the road, for he was so afraid he should ride over her; she was so very, very tiny.

When they had traveled a bit on the way they came to a large lake; there Ashiepattle's horse took fright and shied over to the other side of the road, and upset the spoon, so that the doll in the grass fell into the water. Ashiepattle became very sad, for he did not know how he should get her out again; but after awhile a merman brought her up. But now she had become just as big as any other grown-up being, and was much more beautiful than she was before. So he placed her in front of him on the horse and rode home.

When Ashiepattle got there all his brothers had also returned, each with a sweetheart; but they were so ugly and ill-favored and bad-tempered that they had come to blows with their sweethearts on their way home. On their heads they had hats which were painted with tar and soot, and this had run from their hats down their faces, so that they were still uglier and more ill-favored to behold.

When the brothers saw Ashiepattle's sweetheart they all became envious of him, but the king was so pleased with Ashiepattle and his sweetheart that he drove all the others away, and so Ashiepattle was married to the doll in the grass; and afterwards they lived happy and comfortable for a long, long while; and if they are not dead, they must be still alive.

GUDBRAND ON THE HILLSIDE

By P. C. ASBJORNSEN

THERE was once upon a time a man whose name was Gudbrand. He had a farm which lay far away up on the side of a hill, and therefore they called him Gudbrand on the Hillside.

He and his wife lived so happily together, and agreed so well, that whatever the man did the wife thought it so well done that no one could do it better. No matter what he did, she thought it was always the right thing.

They lived on their own farm, and had a hundred dollars at the bottom of their chest and two cows in their cowshed. One day the woman said to Gudbrand:

"I think we ought to go to town with one of the cows and sell it, so that we may have some ready money by us. We are pretty well off, and ought to have a few shillings in our pocket like other people; the hundred dollars in the chest we mustn't touch, but I can't see what we want with more than one cow, and it will be much better for us, as I shall have only one to look after instead of the two I have now to mind and feed."

Yes, Gudbrand thought, that was well and sensibly spoken. He took the cow at once and went to town to sell it; but when he got there no one would buy the cow.

"Ah, well!" thought Gudbrand, "I may as well take the cow home again. I know I have both stall and food for it, and the way home is no longer than it was here." So he strolled homeward again with the cow.

When he had got a bit on the way he met a man who had a horse to sell, and Gudbrand thought it was better to have a horse than a cow, and so he changed the cow for the horse.

When he had gone a bit farther he met a man who was driving a fat pig before him, and then he thought it would be better to have a fat pig than a horse, and so he changed with the man.

He now went a bit farther, and then he met a man with a goat, and so he thought it was surely better to have a goat than a pig, and changed with the man who had the goat.

Then he went a long way, till he met a man who had a sheep; he changed with him, for he thought it was always better to have a sheep than a goat.

When he had got a bit farther he met a man with a goose, and so he changed the sheep for the goose. And when he had gone a long, long way he met a man with a cock; he changed the goose with him, for he thought this wise: "It is surely better to have a cock than a goose."

He walked on till late in the day, when he began to feel hungry. So he sold the cock for six pence and bought some food for himself. "For it is always better to keep body and soul together than to have a cock," thought Gudbrand.

He then set off again homeward till he came to his neighbor's farm and there he went in.

"How did you get on in town?" asked the people.

"Oh, only so-so," said the man. "I can't boast of my luck, nor can I grumble at it either." And then he told them how it had gone with him from first to last.

"Well, you'll have a fine reception when you get home to your wife," said the man. "Heaven help you! I should not like to be in your place."

"I think I might have fared much worse," said Gudbrand; "but whether I have fared well or ill, I have such a kind wife that she never says anything, no matter what I do."

"Ay, so you say; but you won't get me to believe it," said the neighbor.

"Shall we have a wager on it?" said Gudbrand. "I have a hundred dollars in my chest at home; will you lay the same?"

So they made the wager and Gudbrand remained there till the evening, when it began to get dark, and then they went together to the farm. The neighbor was to remain outside the door and listen while Gudbrand went in to his wife.

"Good evening!" said Gudbrand when he came in.

"Good evening!" said the wife. "Heaven be praised you are back again."

"Yes, here I am!" said the man. And then the wife asked him how he had got on in town.

"Oh, so-so," answered Gudbrand; "not much to brag of. When I came to town no one would buy the cow, so I changed it for a horse."

"Oh, I'm so glad of that," said the woman; "we are pretty well off and we ought to drive to church like other people, and when we can afford to keep a horse I don't see why we should not have one. Run out, children, and put the horse in the stable."

"Well, I haven't got the horse after all," said Gudbrand; "for when I had got a bit on the way I changed it for a pig."

"Dear me!" cried the woman. "That's the very thing I should have done myself. I'm so glad of that, for now we can have some bacon in the house and something to offer people when they come to see us. What do we want with a horse? People would only say we had become so grand that we could no longer walk to church. Run out, children, and let the pig in."

"But I haven't got the pig either," said Gudbrand; "for when I had got a bit farther on the road I changed it into a milch goat."

"Dear! dear! how well you manage everything!" cried the wife. "When I really come to think of it, what do I want with the pig? People would only say, 'Over yonder they eat up everything they have.' No, now I have a goat I can have both milk and cheese, and keep the goat into the bargain. Let in the goat, children."

"But I haven't got the goat either," said Gudbrand; "when I got a bit on the way I changed the goat and got a fine sheep for it."

"Well!" shouted the woman, "you do everything just as I should wish it—just as if I had been there myself. What do we want with a goat? I should have to climb up hill and down dale to get it home at night. No, when I have a sheep I can have wool and clothes in the house, and food as well. Run out, children, and let in the sheep."

"But I haven't got the sheep any longer," said Gudbrand; "for when I had got a bit on the way I changed it for a goose."

"Well, thank you for that!" said the woman; "and many thanks,

too! What do I want with a sheep? I have neither wheel nor
spindle, and I do not care either to toil and drudge making clothes;
we can buy clothes now as before. Now I can have goose fat, which
I have so long been wishing for, and some feathers to stuff that
little pillow of mine. Run, children, and let in the goose."

"Well, I haven't got the goose either," said Gudbrand; "when
I had got a bit farther on the way I changed it for a cock."

"Well, I don't know how you can think of it all!" cried the
woman. "It's just as if I had done it all myself. A cock! Why, it's
just the same as if you'd bought an eight-day clock, for every morning the cock will crow at four, so we can be up in good time. What
do we want with a goose? I can't make goose fat and I can easily fill
my pillow with some soft grass. Run, children, and let in the cock."

"But I haven't got a cock either," said Gudbrand; "for when I
had got a bit farther I became so terribly hungry I had to sell the
cock for sixpence and get some food to keep body and soul together."

"Heaven be praised you did that!" cried the woman. "Whatever
you do, you always do the very thing I could have wished. Besides,
what did we want with the cock? We are our own masters and
can lie as long as we like in the mornings. Heaven be praised! As
long as I have got you back again, who manage everything so well,
I shall neither want cock, nor goose, nor pig, nor cows."

Gudbrand then opened the door. "Have I won the hundred dollars now?" he asked. And the neighbor was obliged to confess that
he had.

THE SQUIRE'S BRIDE

By P. C. ASBJORNSEN

ONCE upon a time there was a rich squire who owned a large farm, and had plenty of silver at the bottom of his chest and money in the bank besides; but he felt there was something wanting, for he was a widower.

One day the daughter of a neighboring farmer was working for him in the hayfield. The squire saw her and liked her very much, and as she was the child of poor parents he thought if he only hinted that he wanted her she would be ready to marry him at once.

So he told her he had been thinking of getting married again.

"Ay! one may think of many things," said the girl, laughing slyly. In her opinion the old fellow ought to be thinking of something that behooved him better than getting married.

"Well, you see, I thought that you should be my wife!"

"No, thank you all the same," said she, "that's not at all likely."

The squire was not accustomed to be gainsaid, and the more she refused him the more determined he was to get her.

But as he made no progress in her favor he sent for her father and told him that if he could arrange the matter with his daughter he would forgive him the money he had lent him, and he would also give him the piece of land which lay close to his meadow into the bargain.

"Yes, you may be sure I'll bring my daughter to her senses," said the father. "She is only a child, and she doesn't know what's best for her." But all his coaxing and talking did not help matters. She would not have the squire, she said, if he sat buried in gold up to his ears.

The squire waited day after day, but at last he became so angry and impatient that he told the father, if he expected him to stand by his promise, he would have to put his foot down and settle the matter now, for he would not wait any longer.

The man knew no other way out of it but to let the squire get everything ready for the wedding; and when the parson and the wedding guests had arrived the squire should send for the girl as if she were wanted for some work on the farm. When she arrived she would have to be married right away, so that she would have no time to think it over.

The squire thought this was well and good, and so he began brewing and baking and getting ready for the wedding in grand style. When the guests had arrived the squire called one of his farm lads and told him to run down to his neighbor and ask him to send him what he had promised.

"But if you are not back in a twinkling," he said, shaking his fist at him, "I'll——"

He did not say more, for the lad ran off as if he had been shot at.

"My master has sent me to ask for that you promised him," said the lad, when he got to the neighbor, "but there is no time to be lost, for he is terribly busy today."

"Yes, yes! Run down into the meadow and take her with you. There she goes!" answered the neighbor.

The lad ran off and when he came to the meadow he found the daughter there raking the hay.

"I am to fetch what your father has promised my master," said the lad.

"Ah, ha!" thought she. "Is that what they are up to?"

"Ah, indeed!" she said. "I suppose it's that little bay mare of ours. You had better go and take her. She stands there tethered on the other side of the peas field," said the girl.

The boy jumped on the back of the bay mare and rode home at full gallop.

"Have you got her with you?" asked the squire.

"She is down at the door," said the lad.

"Take her up to the room my mother had," said the squire.

"But, master, how can that be managed?" said the lad.

"You must just do as I tell you," said the squire. "If you cannot manage her alone you must get the men to help you," for he thought the girl might turn obstreperous.

When the lad saw his master's face he knew it would be no use to gainsay him. So he went and got all the farm-tenants who were there to help him. Some pulled at the head and the forelegs of the mare and others pushed from behind, and at last they got her up the stairs and into the room. There lay all the wedding finery ready.

"Now, that's done, master!" said the lad; "but it was a terrible job. It was the worst I have ever had here on the farm."

"Never mind, you shall not have done it for nothing," said his master. "Now send the women up to dress her."

"But I say, master—!" said the lad.

"None of your talk!" said the squire. "Tell them they must dress her and mind and not forget either wreath or crown."

The lad ran into the kitchen.

"Look here, lasses," he said; "you must go upstairs and dress up the bay mare as bride. I expect the master wants to give the guests a laugh."

The women dressed the bay mare in everything that was there, and then the lad went and told his master that now she was ready dressed, with wreath and crown and all.

"Very well, bring her down!" said the squire. "I will receive her myself at the door," said he.

There was a terrible clatter on the stairs; for that bride, you know, had no silken shoes on.

When the door was opened and the squire's bride entered the parlor, you can imagine there was a good deal of tittering and grinning.

And as for the squire you may be sure he had had enough of that bride, and they say he never went courting again.

THE CAT ON THE DOVREFELL

By SIR GEORGE W. DASENT

Illustration by J. M. CORNER

ONCE ON A TIME there was a man up in Finnmark who had caught a great white bear, which he was going to take to the King of Denmark. Now, it so fell out, that he came to the Dovrefell just about Christmas Eve, and there he turned into a cottage where a man lived, whose name was Halvor, and asked the man if he could get house-room there, for his bear and himself.

"Heaven never help me, if what I say isn't true!" said the man; "but we can't give anyone house-room now, for every Christmas Eve such a pack of trolls come down upon us, that we are forced to flit, and haven't so much as a house over our own heads, to say nothing of lending one to anyone else."

"Oh!" said the man, "if that's all, you can very well lend me your house; my bear can lie under the stove yonder, and I can sleep in the side room."

Well, he begged so hard, that at last he got leave to stay there; so the people of the house flitted out, and before they went, everything was got ready for the Trolls; the tables were laid, and there were rice porridge, and fish boiled in lye, and sausages, and all else that was good, just as for any other grand feast.

So, when everything was ready, down came the Trolls. Some were great and some were small; some had long tails and some had no tails at all; some, too, had long, long noses; and they ate and drank, and tasted everything. Just then, one of the little Trolls caught sight of the white bear, who lay under the stove; so he took a piece of sausage and stuck it on a fork, and went and poked it up against the bear's nose, screaming out:

"Pussy, will you have some sausage?"

Then the white bear rose up and growled, and hunted the whole pack of them out of doors, both great and small.

Next year Halvor was out in the wood, on the afternoon of Christmas Eve, cutting wood before the holidays, for he thought the Trolls would come again; and just as he was hard at work, he heard a voice in the wood calling out:

"Halvor, Halvor!"

"Well," said Halvor, "here I am."

The white bear rose up and hunted the whole pack out of doors.

"Have you got your big cat with you still?"

"Yes, that I have," said Halvor; "she's lying at home under the stove, and what's more, she has now got seven kittens, far bigger and fiercer than she is herself."

"Oh, then, we'll never come to see you again," bawled out the Troll away in the wood, and he kept his word; for since that time the Trolls have never eaten their Christmas brose with Halvor on the Dovrefell.

THE HUSBAND WHO WAS TO MIND THE HOUSE

By SIR GEORGE W. DASENT

ONCE upon a time there was a man so surly and cross, he never thought his wife did anything right in the house. So, one evening in hay-making time, he came home, scolding and swearing, and showing his teeth and making a dust.

"Dear love, don't be so angry; there's a good man," said his goody; "tomorrow let's change our work. I'll go out with the mowers and mow, and you shall mind the house at home."

Yes, the husband thought that would do very well. He was quite willing, he said.

So early next morning his goody took a scythe over her neck, and went out into the hayfield with the mowers and began to mow; but the man was to mind the house, and do the work at home.

First of all he wanted to churn the butter; but when he had churned a while, he got thirsty, and went down to the cellar to tap a barrel of ale. So, just when he had knocked in the bung, and was putting the tap into the cask, he heard overhead the pig come into the kitchen. Then off he ran up the cellar steps, with the tap in his hand, as fast as he could, to look after the pig, lest it should upset the churn; but when he got up, and saw that the pig had already knocked the churn over, and stood there, routing and grunting amid the cream which was running all over the floor, he got so wild with rage that he quite forgot his ale barrel and ran at the pig as hard as he could. He caught it, too, just as it ran out of doors, and gave it such a kick that piggy lay for dead on the spot. Then all at once he remembered he had the tap in his hand; but when he got down to the cellar, every drop of ale had run out of the cask.

Then he went into the dairy and found enough cream left to fill the churn again, and so he began to churn, for butter they must have for dinner. When he had churned a bit, he remembered that their milking cow was still shut up in the byre, and hadn't had a bit to eat or a drop to drink all the morning, though the sun was high. Then all at once he thought 'twas too far to take her down to the meadow, so he'd just get her up on the housetop—for the house, you must know, was thatched with sods, and a fine crop of grass was growing there. Now their house lay close up against a steep down, and he thought if he laid a plank across to the thatch at the back he'd easily get the cow up.

But still he couldn't leave the churn, for there was his little babe crawling about the floor, and "if I leave it," he thought, "the child is sure to upset it!" So he took the churn on his back and went out with it; but then he thought he'd better first water the cow before he turned her out on the thatch; so he took up a bucket to draw water out of the well; but, as he stooped down at the well's brink, all the cream ran out of the churn over his shoulders, down the well.

Now it was near dinner time, and he hadn't even got the butter yet; so he thought he'd best boil the porridge, and filled the pot with water, and hung it over the fire. When he had done that, he thought the cow might perhaps fall off the thatch and break her legs or her neck. So he got up on the house to tie her up. One end of the rope he made fast to the cow's neck, and the other he slipped down the chimney and tied round his own thigh; and he had to make haste, for the water now began to boil in the pot, and he had still to grind the oatmeal.

So he began to grind away; but while he was hard at it, down fell the cow off the housetop after all, and as she fell, she dragged the man up the chimney by the rope. There he stuck fast; and as for the cow, she hung halfway down the wall. . . .

And now the goody had waited seven lengths and seven breadths for her husband to come and call them home to dinner; but never a call they had. At last she thought she'd waited long enough, and went home. But when she got there and saw the cow hanging in such an ugly place, she ran up and cut the rope in two with her scythe. But as she did this, down came her husband out of the chimney; and so when his old dame came inside the kitchen, there she found him standing on his head in the porridge pot.

WHY THE BEAR IS STUMPY-TAILED

By SIR GEORGE W. DASENT

ONE day the Bear met the Fox, who came slinking along with a string of fish he had stolen.

"Whence did you get those from?" asked the Bear.

"Oh! my Lord Bruin, I've been out fishing and caught them," said the Fox.

So the Bear had a mind to learn to fish, too, and bade the Fox tell him how he was to set about it.

"Oh! it's an easy craft for you," answered the Fox, "and soon learned. You've only got to go upon the ice, and cut a hole and stick your tail down into it; and so you must go on holding it there as long as you can. You're not to mind if your tail smarts a little; that's when the fish bite. The longer you hold it there the more fish you'll get; and then all at once out with it, with a cross pull sideways, and with a strong pull, too."

Yes; the Bear did as the Fox had said, and held his tail a long, long time down in the hole, till it was fast frozen in. Then he pulled it out with a cross pull, and it snapped short off. That's why Bruin goes about with a stumpy tail this very day.

THE LAD WHO WENT TO THE NORTH WIND

By SIR GEORGE W. DASENT

ONCE upon a time there was an old widow who had one son, and as she was poorly and weak, her son had to go up into the safe to fetch meal for cooking; but when he got outside the safe, and was just going down the steps, there came the North Wind, puffing and blowing, caught up the meal, and so away with it through the air. Then the lad went back into the safe for more; but when he came out again on the steps, if the North Wind didn't come again and carry off the meal with a puff; and more than that, he did so the third time. At this the lad got very angry; and as he thought it hard that the North Wind should behave so, he thought he'd just look him up and ask him to give up his meal.

So off he went, but the way was long, and he walked and walked; but at last he came to the North Wind's house.

"Good day!" said the lad, and "Thank you for coming to see us yesterday."

"GOOD DAY!" answered the North Wind, for his voice was loud and gruff. "AND THANKS FOR COMING TO SEE ME. WHAT DO YOU WANT?"

"Oh!" answered the lad, "I only wished to ask you to be so good as to let me have back that meal you took from me on the safe steps, for we haven't much to live on; and if you're to go on snapping up the morsel we have there'll be nothing for it but to starve."

"I haven't got your meal," said the North Wind; "but if you are in such need, I'll give you a cloth which will get you everything you want, if you only say, 'Cloth, spread yourself, and serve up all kinds of good dishes!'"

With this the lad was well content. But, as the way was so long, he couldn't get home in one day, so he stopped at an inn on the way; and when they were going to sit down to supper, he laid the cloth on a table which stood in the corner and said: "Cloth, spread yourself, and serve up all kinds of good dishes."

He had scarce said so before the cloth did as it was bid; and all who stood by thought it a fine thing, but most of all the landlady. So, when all were fast asleep, at dead of night, she took the lad's cloth, and put another in its stead, just like the one he had got from the North Wind, but which couldn't so much as serve up a bit of dry bread.

So, when the lad awoke, he took his cloth and went off with it, and that day he got home to his mother.

"Now," said he, "I've been to the North Wind's house, and a good fellow he is, for he gave me this cloth, and when I only say to it, 'Cloth, spread yourself, and serve up all kinds of good dishes,' I get any sort of food I please."

"All very true, I dare say," said his mother, "but seeing is believing, and I shan't believe it till I see it."

So the lad made haste, drew out a table, laid the cloth on it, and said:

"Cloth, spread yourself, and serve up all kinds of good dishes."

But never a bit of dry bread did the cloth serve up.

"Well," said the lad, "there's no help for it but to go to the North Wind again"; and away he went.

So he came late in the afternoon to where the North Wind lived.

"Good evening!" said the lad.

"Good evening!" said the North Wind.

"I want my rights for that meal of ours which you took," said the lad; "for, as for that cloth I got, it isn't worth a penny."

"I've got no meal," said the North Wind; "but yonder you have a ram which coins nothing but golden ducats as soon as you say to it, 'Ram, ram! Make money!'"

So the lad thought this a fine thing; but as it was too far to get home that day, he turned in for the night at the same inn where he had slept before.

Before he called for anything, he tried the truth of what the North Wind had said of the ram, and found it was all right; but, when the landlord saw that, he thought it was a famous ram, and, when the lad had fallen asleep, he took another which couldn't coin gold ducats, and changed the two.

Next morning off went the lad; and when he got home to his mother, he said: "After all, the North Wind is a jolly fellow; for now he has given me a ram which can coin golden ducats if I only say, 'Ram, ram! Make money!'"

"All very true, I dare say," said his mother; "but I shan't believe any such stuff until I see the ducats made."

"Ram, ram! Make money!" said the lad; but if the ram made anything, it wasn't money.

So the lad went back again to the North Wind, and blew him up, and said the ram was worth nothing, and he must have his rights for the meal.

"Well!" said the North Wind, "I've nothing else to give you but that old stick in the corner yonder; but it's a stick of that kind that if you say, 'Stick, stick! lay on!' it lays on till you say, 'Stick, stick! now stop!'"

So, as the way was long the lad turned in this night, too, to the landlord; but as he could pretty well guess how things stood as to the cloth and the ram, he lay down at once on the bench and began to snore as if he were asleep.

Now the landlord, who easily saw that the stick must be worth something, hunted up one which was like it, and when he heard the lad snore, was going to change the two; but just as the landlord was about to take it, the lad bawled out: "Stick, stick! lay on!"

So the stick began to beat the landlord, till he jumped over chairs, and tables, and benches, and yelled and roared:

"Oh, my! oh, my! bid the stick be still, else it will beat me to death, and you shall have back both your cloth and your ram."

When the lad thought the landlord had got enough, he said: "Stick, stick! now stop!"

Then he took the cloth and put it into his pocket, and went home with his stick in his hand, leading the ram by a cord round its horns; and so he got his rights for the meal he had lost.

BOOTS WHO MADE THE PRINCESS SAY "THAT'S A STORY"

By *SIR GEORGE W. DASENT*

Illustration by E. WERENSKIOLD

ONCE upon a time there was a King who had a daughter, and she was such a dreadful story-teller that the like of her was not to be found far or near. So the King gave out, that if anyone could tell such a string of lies as would get her to say, "That's a story," he should have her to wife, and half the kingdom besides. Well, many came, as you may fancy, to try their luck, for everyone would have been very glad to have the Princess, to say nothing of the kingdom; but they all cut a sorry figure, for the Princess was so given to story-telling, that all their lies went in at one ear and out of the other. Among the rest came three brothers to try their luck, and the two elder went first, but they fared no better than those who had gone before them. Last of all, the third, Boots, set off and found the Princess in the farmyard.

"Good morning," he said, "and thank you for nothing."

"Good morning," said she, "and the same to you."

Then she went on, "You haven't such a fine farmyard as ours, I'll be bound; for when two shepherds stand, one at each end of it, and blow their ram's horns, the one can't hear the other."

"Haven't we though!" answered Boots; "ours is far bigger; for when a calf starts to cross a field, it is a full-grown cow when it reaches the other end."

"I dare say!" said the Princess. "Well, but you haven't such a big ox, after all, as ours yonder; for when two men sit, one on each horn, they can't touch each other with a twenty-foot rule."

"Stuff!" said Boots. "Is that all? Why, we have an ox who is so big, that when two men sit, one on each horn, and each blows his great mountain-trumpet, they can't hear one another."

"I dare say!" said the Princess. "But you haven't so much milk as we, I'll be bound; for we milk our cows into great pails, and carry them indoors, and empty them into great tubs, and so we make great, great cheeses."

"Oh! you do, do you?" said Boots. "Well, we milk ours into great tubs, and then we put them in carts and drive them indoors, and then we turn them out into great brewing vats, and so we make cheeses as big as a great house. We had, too, a dun mare to tread the cheese well together when it was making; but once she tumbled down into the cheese, and we lost her; and after we had eaten at this cheese seven years, we came upon a great dun mare, alive and kicking. Well, once after that I was going to drive this mare to the mill, and her backbone snapped in two; but I wasn't put out, not I; for I took a spruce sapling, and put it into her for a backbone, and she had no other backbone all the while we had her. But the sapling grew up into such a tall tree, that I climbed right up to the sky by it, and when I got there I saw a lady sitting and spinning the foam of the sea into pigs'-bristle ropes; but just then the spruce-fir broke short off, and I couldn't get down again; so the lady let me down by one of the ropes, and down I slipped straight into a fox's hole, and who should sit there but my mother and your father cobbling shoes; and just as I stepped in, my mother gave your father such a box on the ear that it made his whiskers curl."

"That's a story!" said the Princess, "my father never did any such thing in all his born days!"

So Boots got the Princess to wife, and half the kingdom besides.

Tales From France

LITTLE RED RIDING-HOOD

By *CHARLES PERRAULT*

ONCE upon a time there lived in a certain village a little country girl, the prettiest creature ever seen. Her mother was very fond of her, and her grandmother doted on her still more. This good woman had made for her a little red riding-hood, which became the girl so well that everybody called her Little Red Riding-Hood.

One day her mother, having made some custards, said to her:

"Go, my dear, and see how thy grandmamma does, for I hear she has been very ill; carry her a custard and this little pot of butter."

Little Red Riding-Hood set out immediately to go to her grandmother, who lived in another village.

As she was going through the wood she met with Gaffer Wolf, who had a very great mind to eat her up, but he durst not, because of some fagot makers hard by in the forest. He asked her whither she was going. The poor child, who did not know that it was dangerous to stop and listen to a wolf, said to him:

"I am going to see my grandmamma and carry her a custard and a little pot of butter from my mamma."

"Does she live far off?" said the Wolf.

"Oh! yes," answered Little Red Riding-Hood; "it is beyond that mill you see there, at the first house in the village."

"Well," said the Wolf, "I'll go and see her, too. I'll go this way and you go that, and we shall see who will be there soonest."

The Wolf began to run as fast as he could, taking the nearest way, and the little girl went by the longest, diverting herself in gathering nuts, running after butterflies, and making nosegays of such little flowers as she met with. The Wolf was not long before he got to the old woman's house. He knocked at the door—tap, tap.

"Who's there?"

"Your grandchild, Little Red Riding-Hood," replied the Wolf, imitating her voice; "who has brought you a custard and a little pot of butter sent you by mamma."

The good grandmother, who was in bed, because she was ill, cried out:

"Pull the bobbin, and the latch will go up."

The Wolf pulled the bobbin, and the door opened, and he fell upon the good woman and ate her up in a moment, for it was above

"Grandmamma, what great teeth you've got!"

three days that he had not touched a bit. He then shut the door and went into the grandmother's bed, expecting Little Red Riding-Hood, who came some time afterwards and knocked at the door—tap, tap.

"Who's there?"

Little Red Riding-Hood, hearing the big voice of the Wolf, was at first afraid; but believing her grandmother had got a cold, and was hoarse, answered:

" 'Tis your grandchild, Little Red Riding-Hood, who has brought you a custard and a little pot of butter mamma sends you."

The Wolf cried out to her, softening his voice as much as he could:

"Pull the bobbin and the latch will go up."

Little Red Riding-Hood pulled the bobbin and the door opened.

The Wolf, seeing her come in, said to her, hiding himself under the bedclothes:

"Put the custard and the little pot of butter upon the stool, and come and lie down with me."

Little Red Riding-Hood undressed herself and stood by the bed, where, being greatly amazed to see how her grandmother looked in her night clothes, she said to her:

"Grandmamma, what great arms you've got!"

"That is the better to hug thee, my dear."

"Grandmamma, what great legs you've got!"

"The better to run, my child."

"Grandmamma, what great ears you've got!"

"The better to hear, my child!"

"Grandmamma, what great eyes you've got!"

"The better to see, my child."

"Grandmamma, what great teeth you've got!"

"To eat thee up!"

And saying these words, the wicked Wolf fell upon Little Red Riding-Hood and ate her all up.

PUSS IN BOOTS

By CHARLES PERRAULT

Illustration by GUSTAVE DORÉ

A MILLER, dying, divided all his property between his three children. This was a very simple matter, as he had nothing to leave but his mill, his ass, and his cat; so he made no will, and called in no lawyer, who would, probably, have taken a large slice out of these poor possessions. The eldest son took the mill, the second the ass, while the third was obliged to content himself with the cat, at which he grumbled very much. "My brothers," said he, "by putting their property together, may gain an honest living, but there is nothing left for me except to die of hunger; unless, indeed, I were to kill my cat and eat him, and make a coat out of his skin, which would be very scanty clothing."

The cat, who heard the young man talking to himself, sat up on his four paws, and looking at him with a grave and wise air, said: "Master, I think you had better not kill me; I shall be much more useful to you alive."

"How so?" asked his master.

"You have but to give me a sack, and a pair of boots, such as gentlemen wear when they go shooting, and you will find you are not so ill off as you suppose."

Now, though the young miller did not much depend upon the cat's words, still he thought it rather surprising that a cat should speak at all. And he had before now seen him show so much adroitness and cleverness in catching rats and mice, that it seemed advisable to trust him a little farther; especially as—poor young fellow—he had nobody else to trust.

When the cat got his boots, he drew them on with a grand air, and slinging his sack over his shoulder, and drawing the cords of it round his neck, he marched bravely to a rabbit warren hard by, with which he was well acquainted. Then, putting some bran and lettuces into his bag, and stretching himself out beside it as if he were dead, he waited till some fine, fat young rabbit, ignorant of the wickedness and deceit of the world, should peep into the sack to eat the food that was inside. This happened very shortly, for there are plenty of foolish young rabbits in every warren; and when one of them, who really was a splendid fat fellow, put his head inside, Master Puss drew the cords immediately, and took him and killed him without mercy. Then, very proud of his prey, he marched direct to the palace, and begged to speak with the King.

He was desired to ascend to the apartment of his majesty, where, making a low bow, he said: "Sire, here is a magnificent rabbit, killed in the warren which belongs to my lord the Marquis of Carabas, and which he has desired me to offer humbly to your majesty."

"Tell your master," replied the King, politely, "that I accept his present, and am very much obliged to him."

Another time, Puss went out and hid himself and his sack in a wheat field, and there caught two splendid fat partridges in the same manner as he had done the rabbit. When he presented them to the King, with a similar message as before, his majesty was so pleased that he ordered the cat to be taken down into the kitchen and given something to eat and drink; where, while enjoying himself, the faithful animal did not cease to talk in the most cunning way of the large preserves and abundant game which belonged to his lord the Marquis of Carabas.

One day, hearing that the King was intending to take a drive along the riverside with his daughter, the most beautiful princess in the world, Puss said to his master: "Sir, if you would only follow my advice, your fortune is made."

"Be it so," said the miller's son, who was growing disconsolate, and cared very little what he did: "Say your say, cat."

"It is but little," replied Puss, looking wise, as cats can. "You have only to go and bathe in the river at a place which I shall show you, and leave all the rest to me. Only remember that you are no longer yourself, but my lord the Marquis of Carabas."

"Just so," said the miller's son, "it's all the same to me"; but he did as the cat told him.

While he was bathing, the King and all the court passed by, and were startled to hear loud cries of "Help! help! my lord the Marquis of Carabas is drowning." The King put his head out of the car-

"Help, Help! the Marquis of Carabas is drowning."

riage, and saw nobody but the cat, who had at different times brought him so many presents of game; however, he ordered his guards to fly quickly to the succor of my lord the Marquis of Carabas. While they were pulling the unfortunate marquis out of the water, the cat came up, bowing, to the side of the King's carriage, and told a long and pitiful story about some thieves who, while his master was bathing, had come and carried away all his clothes, so that it would be impossible for him to appear before his majesty and the illustrious princess.

"Oh, we will soon remedy that," answered the King, kindly; and immediately ordered one of the first officers of the household to ride back to the palace with all speed, and bring back the most elegant supply of clothes for the young gentleman, who kept out of sight until they arrived. Then, being handsome and well-made, his new clothes became him so well, that he looked as if he had been a marquis all his days, and advanced with an air of respectful ease to offer his thanks to his majesty.

The King received him courteously, and the princess admired him very much. Indeed, so charming did he appear to her, that she hinted to her father to invite him into the carriage with them, which, you may be sure, the young man did not refuse. The cat, delighted at the success of his scheme, went away as fast as he could, and ran so swiftly that he kept a long way ahead of the royal carriage. He went on and on, till he came to some peasants who were mowing in a meadow. "Good people," said he, in a very firm voice, "the King is coming past here shortly, and if you do not say that the field you are mowing belongs to my lord the Marquis of Carabas, you shall all be chopped as small as mincemeat."

So when the King drove by, and asked whose meadow it was where there was such a splendid crop of hay, the mowers all answered, trembling, that it belonged to my lord the Marquis of Carabas.

"You have very fine land, Marquis," said his majesty to the miller's son, who bowed, and answered that "it was not a bad meadow, take it altogether."

Then the cat came to a wheat field, where the reapers were reaping with all their might. He bounced in upon them: "The King is coming past today, and if you do not tell him that this wheat belongs to my lord the Marquis of Carabas, I will have you everyone chopped as small as mincemeat." The reapers, very much alarmed, did as they were bid, and the King congratulated the marquis upon possessing such beautiful fields, laden with an abundant harvest.

They drove on—the cat always running before and saying the same thing to everybody he met, that they were to declare that the whole country belonged to his master; so that even the King was astonished at the vast estate of my lord the Marquis of Carabas.

But now the cat arrived at a great castle where dwelt an Ogre, to whom belonged all the land through which the royal equipage had been driving. This Ogre was a cruel tyrant, and his tenants and servants were terribly afraid of him, which accounted for their being so ready to say whatever they were told to say by the cat, who had taken pains to inform himself all about the Ogre. So, putting on the boldest face he could assume, Puss marched up to the castle with his boots on, and asked to see the owner of it, saying that he was on his travels, but did not wish to pass so near the castle of such a noble gentleman without paying his respects to him. When the Ogre heard this message, he went to the door, received the cat as civilly as an Ogre can, and begged him to walk in and repose himself.

"Thank you, sir," said the cat; "but first I hope you will satisfy a traveler's curiosity. I have heard in far countries of your many re-markable qualities, and especially how you have the power to change yourself into any sort of beast you choose—a lion, for instance, or an elephant."

"That is quite true," replied the Ogre; "and lest you should doubt it I will immediately become a lion."

He did so; and the cat was so frightened that he sprang up to the roof of the castle and hid himself in the gutter—a proceeding rather inconvenient on account of his boots, which were not exactly fitted to walk with upon tiles. At length, perceiving that the Ogre had resumed his original form, he came down again stealthily, and confessed that he had been very much frightened.

"But, sir," said he, "it may be easy enough for such a big gentle-man as you to change himself into a large animal; I do not suppose you could become a small one—a rat, or mouse, for instance. I have heard that you can; still, for my part, I consider it quite impossible."

"Impossible!" cried the other, indignantly. "You shall see!" and immediately the cat saw the Ogre no longer, but a little mouse running along on the floor.

This was exactly what he wanted; and he did the very best a cat could do, and the most natural under the circumstances—he sprang upon the mouse and gobbled it up in a trice. So there was an end of the Ogre.

By this time the King had arrived opposite the castle, and was seized with a strong desire to enter it. The cat, hearing the noise of the carriage wheels, ran forward in a great hurry, and, standing at the gate, said, in a loud voice: "Welcome, sire, to the castle of my lord the Marquis of Carabas."

"What!" cried his majesty, very much surprised, "does the castle also belong to you? Truly, Marquis, you have kept your secret well up to the last minute. I have never seen anything finer than this courtyard and these battlements. I have nothing like them in the whole of my dominions."

The marquis, without speaking, offered his hand to the princess to assist her to descend, and, standing aside that the King might enter first—for he had already acquired all the manners of a court—followed his majesty to the great hall, where a magnificent dinner was laid, and where, without more delay, they sat down to feast.

Before the banquet was over, the King, charmed with the good qualities of the Marquis of Carabas—and likewise with his wine, of which he had drunk several cups—said, bowing across the table at which the princess and the miller's son were talking very confidentially together: "It rests with you, Marquis, whether you will not become my son-in-law."

"I shall be only too happy," said the complaisant marquis, and the princess's cast-down eyes declared the same.

So they were married the very next day, and took possession of the Ogre's castle, and of everything that had belonged to him.

As for the cat, he became at once a grand personage, and had nevermore any need to run after mice, except for his own diversion.

CINDERELLA

By *CHARLES PERRAULT*

Illustrations by GEORGE CRUIKSHANK

THERE was once an honest gentleman who took for his second wife a lady, the proudest and most disagreeable in the whole country. She had two daughters exactly like herself in all things. He also had one little girl, who resembled her dead mother, the best woman in all the world. Scarcely had the second marriage taken place, than the stepmother became jealous of the good qualities of the little girl who was so great a contrast to her own two daughters. She gave her all the menial occupations of the house; compelled her to wash the floors and staircases, to dust the bedrooms, and clean the grates; and while her sisters occupied carpeted chambers hung with mirrors, where they could see themselves from head to foot, this poor little damsel was sent to sleep in an attic, on an old straw mattress, with only one chair and not a looking-glass in the room.

She suffered all in silence, not daring to complain to her father, who was entirely ruled by his new wife. When her daily work was done, she used to sit down in the chimney corner among the ashes; from which the two sisters gave her the nickname of *Cinderella*. But Cinderella, however shabbily clad, was handsomer than they were with all their fine clothes.

It happened that the king's son gave a series of balls, to which were invited all the rank and fashion of the city, and among the rest the two elder sisters. They were very proud and happy, and occupied their whole time in deciding what they should wear; a source of new trouble to Cinderella, whose duty it was to get up their fine linen and laces, and who never could please them however much she tried. They talked of nothing but their clothes.

"I," said the elder, "shall wear my velvet gown and my trimmings of English lace."

"And I," added the younger, "will have but my ordinary silk petticoat, but I shall adorn it with an upper skirt of flowered brocade, and shall put on my diamond tiara, which is a great deal finer than anything of yours."

Here the elder sister grew angry, and the dispute began to run so high that Cinderella, who was known to have excellent taste, was called upon to decide between them. She gave them the best advice she could, and gently and submissively offered to dress them herself, and especially to arrange their hair, an accomplishment in which she

She gave her all the menial occupations.

excelled many a noted coiffeur. The important evening came, and she exercised all her skill to adorn the two young ladies. While she was combing out the elder's hair, this ill-natured girl said sharply, "Cinderella, do you not wish you were going to the ball?"

"Ah, madam" (they obliged her always to say madam), "you are only mocking me; it is not my fortune to have any such pleasure."

"You are right; people would only laugh to see a little cinderwench at a ball."

Any other than Cinderella would have dressed the hair all awry, but she was good, and dressed it perfectly even and smooth, and as prettily as she could.

The sisters had scarcely eaten for two days, and had broken a dozen stay-laces a day, in trying to make themselves slender; but tonight they broke a dozen more, and lost their tempers over and over again before they had completed their toilette. When at last the happy moment arrived, Cinderella followed them to the coach; after it had whirled them away, she sat down by the kitchen fire and cried.

Immediately her godmother, who was a fairy, appeared beside her. "What are you crying for, my little maid?"

"Oh, I wish—I wish—" Her sobs stopped her.

"You wish to go to the ball; isn't it so?"

Cinderella nodded.

"Well then, be a good girl, and you shall go. First run into the garden and fetch me the largest pumpkin you can find."

Cinderella did not comprehend what this had to do with her going to the ball, but being obedient and obliging, she went. Her godmother took the pumpkin, and having scooped out all its inside, struck it with her wand; it became a splendid gilt coach, lined with rose-colored satin.

"Now fetch me the mousetrap out of the pantry, my dear."

Cinderella brought it; it contained six of the fattest, sleekest mice.

The fairy lifted up the wire door, and as each mouse ran out she struck it and changed it into a beautiful black horse.

"But what shall I do for your coachman, Cinderella?"

Cinderella suggested that she had seen a large black rat in the rat trap, and he might do for want of better.

"You are right; go and look again for him."

He was found; and the fairy made him into a most respectable coachman, with the finest whiskers imaginable. She afterwards took six lizards from behind the pumpkin frame, and changed them into six footmen, all in splendid livery, who immediately jumped up behind the carriage, as if they had been footmen all their days. "Well, Cinderella, now you can go to the ball."

"What, in these clothes?" said Cinderella piteously, looking down on her ragged frock.

Her godmother laughed, and touched her also with the wand; at which her wretched threadbare jacket became stiff with gold, and sparkling with jewels; her woolen petticoat lengthened into a gown of sweeping satin, from underneath which peeped out her little feet, no longer bare, but covered with silk stockings, and the prettiest glass slippers in the world. "Now, Cinderella, depart; but remember, if you stay one instant after midnight, your carriage will be-

She touched Cinderella with the wand.

come a pumpkin, your coachman a rat, your horses mice, and your footmen lizards; while you, yourself, will be the little cinder-wench you were an hour ago."

Cinderella promised without fear, her heart was so full of joy.

Arrived at the palace, the king's son, whom some one, probably the fairy, had told to await the coming of an uninvited princess, whom nobody knew, was standing at the entrance, ready to receive her. He offered her his hand, and led her with the utmost courtesy through the assembled guests, who stood aside to let her pass, whispering to one another, "Oh, how beautiful she is!" It might have turned the head of anyone but poor Cinderella, who was so used to be despised, that she took it all as if it were something happening in a dream.

Her triumph was complete; even the old king said to the queen, that never since her majesty's young days had he seen so charming and elegant a person. All the court ladies scanned her eagerly, clothes and all, determining to have theirs made next day of exactly the same pattern. The king's son himself led her out to dance, and she danced so gracefully that he admired her more and more. Indeed, at supper, which was fortunately early, his admiration quite took away his appetite. For Cinderella herself, with an involuntary shyness, she sought out her sisters; placed herself beside them and offered them all sorts of civil attentions, which coming as they supposed from a stranger, and so magnificent a lady, almost overwhelmed them with delight.

While she was talking with them, she heard the clock strike a quarter to twelve, and making a courteous adieu to the royal family, she re-entered her carriage, escorted tenderly by the king's son, and arrived in safety at her own door. There she found her godmother, who smiled approval; and of whom she begged permission to go to a second ball, the following night, to which the queen had earnestly invited her. While she was talking, the two sisters were heard knocking at the gate, and the fairy godmother vanished, leaving Cinderella sitting in the chimney corner, rubbing her eyes and pretending to be very sleepy.

"Ah," cried the eldest sister maliciously, "it has been the most delightful ball, and there was present the most beautiful princess I ever saw, who was so exceedingly polite to us both."

"Was she?" said Cinderella indifferently; "and who might she be?"

"Nobody knows, though everybody would give their eyes to know, especially the king's son."

"Indeed!" replied Cinderella, a little more interested; "I should like to see her. Miss Javotte"—that was the elder sister's name—"will you not let me go tomorrow, and lend me your yellow gown that you wear on Sundays?"

"What, lend my yellow gown to a cinder-wench! I am not so mad as that"; at which refusal Cinderella did not complain, for if her sister really had lent her the gown, she would have been considerably embarrassed.

The next night came, and the two young ladies, richly dressed in different toilettes, went to the ball.

Cinderella, more splendidly attired and beautiful than ever, followed them shortly after. "Now remember twelve o'clock," was her godmother's parting speech; and she thought she certainly should. But the prince's attentions to her were greater even than the first evening, and in the delight of listening to his pleasant conversation, time slipped by unperceived. While she was sitting beside him in a lovely alcove, and looking at the moon from under a bower of orange blossoms, she heard a clock strike the first stroke of twelve. She started up, and fled away as lightly as a deer.

Amazed, the prince followed, but could not catch her. Indeed he missed his lovely princess altogether, and only saw running out of the palace doors, a little dirty lass whom he had never beheld before, and of whom he certainly would never have taken the least notice. Cinderella arrived at home breathless and weary, ragged and cold, without carriage, or footmen, or coachman; the only remnant of her past magnificence being one of her little glass slippers—the other she had dropped in the ballroom as she ran away.

When the two sisters returned, they were full of this strange adventure, how the beautiful lady had appeared at the ball more beautiful than ever, and enchanted everyone who looked at her; and how as the clock was striking twelve she had suddenly risen up and fled through the ballroom, disappearing no one knew how or where, and dropping one of her glass slippers behind her in her flight. How the king's son had remained inconsolable, until he chanced to pick up the little glass slipper, which he carried away in his pocket, and was seen to take it out continually, and look at it affectionately, with the air of a man very much in love; in fact, from his behavior during the remainder of the evening, all the court and royal family were convinced that he had become desperately enamored of the wearer of the little glass slipper.

Cinderella listened in silence, turning her face to the kitchen fire, and perhaps it was that which made her look so rosy, but nobody ever noticed or admired her at home, so it did not signify, and next morning she went to her weary work again just as before.

A few days after, the whole city was attracted by the sight of a herald going round with a little glass slipper in his hand, publishing

She drew from her pocket the fellow slipper.

with a flourish of trumpets, that the king's son ordered this to be fitted on the foot of every lady in the kingdom, and that he wished to marry the lady whom it fitted best, or to whom it and the fellow slipper belonged. Princesses, duchesses, countesses, and simple gentlewomen all tried it on, but being a fairy slipper, it fitted nobody; and besides, nobody could produce its fellow slipper, which lay all the time safely in the pocket of Cinderella's old linsey gown.

At last the herald came to the house of the two sisters, and though they well knew neither of themselves was the beautiful lady, they made every attempt to get their clumsy feet into the glass slipper, but in vain.

"Let me try it on," said Cinderella from the chimney corner.

"What, you?" cried the others, bursting into shouts of laughter; but Cinderella only smiled, and held out her hand.

Her sisters could not prevent her, since the command was that every young maiden in the city should try on the slipper, in order that no chance might be left untried, for the prince was nearly breaking his heart; and his father and mother were afraid that, though a prince, he would actually die for love of the beautiful unknown lady.

So the herald bade Cinderella sit down on a three-legged stool in the kitchen, and himself put the slipper on her pretty little foot, which it fitted exactly; she then drew from her pocket the fellow slipper, which she also put on, and stood up—for with the touch of the magic shoes all her dress was changed likewise—no longer the poor despised cinder-wench, but the beautiful lady whom the king's son loved.

Her sisters recognized her at once. Filled with astonishment, mingled with no little alarm, they threw themselves at her feet, begging her pardon for all their former unkindness. She raised and embraced them; told them she forgave them with all her heart, and only hoped they would love her always. Then she departed with the herald to the king's palace, and told her whole story to his majesty and the royal family, who were not in the least surprised, for everybody believed in fairies, and everybody longed to have a fairy god-mother.

For the young prince, he found her more lovely and lovable than ever, and insisted upon marrying her immediately. Cinderella never went home again, but she sent for her two sisters to the palace, and with the consent of all parties married them shortly after to two rich gentlemen of the court.

THE SLEEPING BEAUTY IN
THE WOOD

By *CHARLES PERRAULT*

Illustration by GUSTAVE DORÉ

ONCE there was a royal couple who grieved excessively because they had no children. When at last, after long waiting, the queen presented her husband with a little daughter, his majesty showed his joy by giving a christening feast so grand that the like of it was never known. He invited all the fairies in the land—there were seven altogether—to stand godmothers to the little princess; hoping that each might bestow on her some good gift, as was the custom of good fairies in those days.

After the ceremony all the guests returned to the palace, where there was placed before each fairy godmother a magnificent covered dish with an embroidered table napkin, and a knife and fork of pure gold, studded with diamonds and rubies. But alas! as they placed themselves at table, there entered an old fairy who had never been invited, because more than fifty years since she had left the king's dominion on a tour of pleasure, and had not been heard of until this day. His majesty, much troubled, desired a cover to be placed for her, but it was of common delft, for he had ordered from his jeweler only seven gold dishes, for the seven fairies aforesaid. The old fairy thought herself neglected, and muttered angry threats, which were overheard by one of the younger fairies, who chanced to sit beside her. This good godmother, afraid of harm to the pretty baby, hastened to hide herself behind the hangings in the hall. She did this because she wished all the others to speak first—so that if any ill gift were bestowed on the child, she could counteract it.

The six now offered their good wishes—which, unlike most wishes, were sure to come true. The fortunate little princess was to grow up the fairest woman in the world; to have a temper sweet as an angel; to be perfectly graceful and gracious; to sing like a nightingale; to dance like a leaf on a tree; and to possess every accomplishment under the sun. Then the old fairy's turn came. Shaking her head spitefully, she uttered the wish that when the baby grew up into a young lady, and learned to spin, she might prick her finger with the spindle and die of the wound.

At this terrible prophecy, all the guests shuddered; and some of the more tender-hearted began to weep. The lately happy parents were almost out of their wits with grief. Upon which the wise young fairy appeared from behind the tapestry, saying cheerfully, "Your Majesties may comfort themselves; the princess shall not die. I have no power to alter the ill-fortune just wished her by my ancient sister—her finger must be pierced; and she shall then sink, not into the sleep of death, but into a sleep that will last a hundred years. After that time is ended, the son of a King shall come and awake her." Then all the fairies vanished.

The King, in the hope of avoiding his daughter's doom, issued an edict forbidding all persons to spin, and even to have spinning wheels in their houses, on pain of instant death. But it was in vain. One day when she was just fifteen years of age, the King and Queen left their daughter alone in one of their castles, where, wandering about at her will, she came to an ancient donjon tower, climbed to the top of it, and there found a very old woman—so old and deaf that she had never heard of the King's edict—busy with her wheel.

"What are you doing, good old woman?" said the Princess.

"I'm spinning, my pretty child."

"Ah, how charming! Let me try if I can spin also."

She had no sooner taken up the spindle than, being lively and obstinate, she handled it so awkwardly and carelessly that the point pierced her finger. Though it was so small a wound, she fainted away at once and dropped silently down on the floor. The poor old woman called for help; shortly came the ladies-in-waiting, who tried every means to restore their young mistress; but all their care was useless. She lay, beautiful as an angel, the color still lingering in her lips and cheeks, her fair bosom softly stirred with her breath; only her eyes were fast closed. When the King, her father, and the Queen, her mother, beheld her thus, they knew regret was idle—all had happened as the cruel fairy meant. But they also knew that their daughter would not sleep forever, though after one hundred years it was not likely they would either of them behold her awakening. Until that happy hour should arrive, they determined to leave her in repose. They sent away all the physicians and attendants, and themselves sorrowfully laid her upon a bed of embroidery, in the most elegant apartment in the palace. There she slept, and looked like a sleeping angel still.

When this misfortune happened, the kindly young fairy who had saved the Princess by changing her sleep of death into this sleep of a hundred years, was twelve thousand leagues away, in the kingdom of Mataquin. But, being informed of everything, she arrived speedily in a chariot of fire drawn by dragons.

The King was somewhat startled by the sight, but nevertheless went to the door of his palace, and, with a mournful countenance, presented her his hand to descend.

The fairy condoled with his Majesty, and approved of all he had done. Then, being a fairy of great common sense and foresight, she suggested that the Princess, awakening after a hundred years in this old castle, might be a good deal embarrassed, especially with a young Prince by her side, to find herself alone. Accordingly, without asking anyone's leave, she touched with her magic wand the entire population of the palace—except the King and Queen: governesses, ladies of honor, waiting maids, gentlemen ushers, cooks, kitchen girls, pages, footmen—down to the horses that were in the stables, and the grooms that attended them, she touched each and all. Nay, with kind consideration for the feelings of the Princess, she even touched the little fat lapdog, Puffy, who had laid himself down beside his mistress on her splendid bed. He, like all the rest, fell fast asleep in a moment. The very spits that were before the kitchen fire ceased turning, and the fire itself went out, and everything became as silent as if it were the middle of the night, or as if the palace were a palace of the dead.

The King and Queen—having kissed their daughter and wept over her a little, but not much, she looked so sweet and content—departed from the castle, giving orders that it was to be approached no more. The command was unnecessary, for in one quarter of an hour there sprang up around it a wood so thick and thorny that neither beasts nor men could attempt to penetrate there. Above this dense mass of forest could only be seen the top of the high tower where the lovely Princess slept.

A great many changes happen in a hundred years. The King, who never had a second child, died, and his throne passed into another royal family. So entirely was the story of the poor Princess forgotten, that when the reigning king's son, being one day out hunting and stopped in the chase by this formidable wood, inquired what wood it was and what were those towers which he saw appearing out of the midst of it, no one could answer him. At length an old peasant was found who remembered having heard his grandfather say to his father that in this tower was a Princess, beautiful as the day, who was doomed to sleep there for one hundred years, until awakened by a king's son, her destined bridegroom.

At this the young Prince, who had the spirit of a hero, determined to find out the truth for himself. Spurred on by both generosity and curiosity, he leaped from his horse and began to force his way through the thick wood. To his amazement the stiff branches all gave way, and the ugly thorns of their own accord, and the brambles buried themselves in the earth to let him pass. This done, they closed behind him, allowing none of his suite to follow; but, ardent and young, he went boldly on alone.

The first thing he saw was enough to smite him with fear. Bodies of men and horses lay extended on the ground; but the men had faces, not death-white, but red as peonies, and beside them were glasses half filled with wine, showing that they had gone to sleep drinking. Next he entered a large court paved with marble, where stood rows of guards presenting arms, but as if cut out of stone; then he passed through many chambers where gentlemen and ladies, all in the dress of the past century, slept at their ease, some standing, some sitting. The pages were lurking in corners, the ladies of honor were stooping over their embroidery frames or listening, apparently with polite attention, to the gentlemen of the court; but all were as

A young girl of wonderful beauty lay asleep.

silent as statues and as immovable. Their clothes, strange to say, were fresh and new as ever; and not a particle of dust or spider-web had gathered over the furniture, though it had not known a broom for a hundred years. Finally the astonished Prince came to an inner chamber, where was the fairest sight his eyes had ever beheld.

A young girl of wonderful beauty lay asleep on an embroidered bed, and she looked as if she had only just closed her eyes. Trembling, the Prince approached and knelt beside her. Some say he kissed her; but as nobody saw it, and she never told, we cannot be quite sure of the fact. However, as the end of the enchantment had come, the Princess waked at once, and, looking at him with eyes of the tenderest regard, said drowsily: "Is it you, my Prince? I have waited for you very long."

Charmed with these words, and still more with the tone in which they were uttered, the Prince assured her that he loved her more than his life. Nevertheless, he was the most embarrassed of the two; for, thanks to the kind fairy, the princess had plenty of time to dream of him during her century of slumber, while he had never even heard of her till an hour before. For a long time did they sit talking, and yet had not said half enough. Their only interruption was the little dog Puffy, who had awakened with his mistress, and now began to be exceedingly jealous.

Meantime all the attendants, whose enchantment was also broken, not being in love were ready to die of hunger after their fast of a hundred years. A lady of honor ventured to say that dinner was served, whereupon the Prince handed his beloved Princess at once to the great hall. She did not wait to dress for dinner, being already perfectly and magnificently attired, though in a fashion somewhat out of date. However, her lover had the politeness not to notice this, nor to remind her that she was dressed exactly like her royal grandmother, whose portrait still hung on the palace walls.

During dinner a concert by the attendant musicians took place, and, considering they had not touched their instruments for a century, they played extremely well. They ended with a wedding march; for that very evening the marriage of the Prince and Princess was celebrated, and although the bride was nearly one hundred years older than the bridegroom, it is remarkable that the fact would never have been discovered by anyone unacquainted therewith.

After a few days they went together out of the castle and enchanted wood, both of which immediately vanished, and were nevermore beheld by mortal eyes. The Princess was restored to her ancestral kingdom, and after a few years the Prince and she became King and Queen, and ruled long and happily.

BLUE BEARD

By *CHARLES PERRAULT*

Illustration by GUSTAVE DORÉ

T HERE was once a man who had fine houses, both in town and country, a deal of silver and gold plate, embroidered furniture, and coaches gilded all over with gold. But this man was so unlucky as to have a blue beard, which made him so ugly that all the women and girls ran away from him.

One of his neighbors, a lady of quality, had two daughters who were perfect beauties. He asked her for one of them in marriage, but neither of them could bear the thought of marrying a man who had a blue beard. Besides, he had already been married several times, and nobody ever knew what became of his wives.

In the hope of making them like him, Blue Beard took them, with their mother and three or four ladies of their acquaintance, and other young people of the neighborhood, to one of his country houses, where they stayed a whole week. There were parties of pleasure, hunting, fishing, dancing, mirth, and feasting all the time. Nobody went to bed, but all passed the time in merrymaking and joking with one another. Everything succeeded so well that the youngest daughter began to think the master of the house was a very civil gentleman, and his beard was not so very blue after all.

As soon as they returned home, the marriage took place. About a month afterwards, Blue Beard told his wife that he was obliged to take a journey for six weeks, about affairs of great consequence, desiring her to amuse herself in his absence, to send for her friends and acquaintances, to carry them into the country if she pleased, and to have a good time wherever she was.

"Here," said he, "are the keys of the two great wardrobes wherein I have my best furniture; these are of my silver and gold plate, which is not every day in use; these open my strong boxes, which hold my money, both gold and silver; these my caskets of jewels and this is the master key to all my apartments. This little one here is the key of the closet at the end of the great gallery on the ground floor. Open them all; go into all and every one of them, except that little closet, which I forbid you; if you open it, there's nothing that you may not expect from my just anger and resentment."

She promised to observe exactly whatever he ordered; so, having embraced her, he got into his coach and proceeded on his journey.

Her neighbors and good friends did not wait to be sent for, so great was their impatience to see all the rich furniture of her house. They ran through all the rooms, closets, and wardrobes, which were all so fine and rich that they seemed to surpass one another.

After that they went up into the two great rooms, where were the best and richest furniture. They could not sufficiently admire the number and beauty of the tapestries, beds, couches, cabinets, stands, tables, and looking-glasses in which you might see yourself from head to foot; some of them were framed with glass, others with silver, plain and gilded, the finest and most magnificent ever seen.

They ceased not to compliment and envy their friend, but she was so much pressed by her curiosity to open the closet on the ground floor that, without considering that it was very uncivil to leave her company, she went down a little back staircase with such haste that she had twice or thrice like to have broken her neck.

Arriving at the closet door, she hesitated, thinking of her husband's orders and considering what unhappiness might attend her if she was disobedient; but the temptation was so strong she could not overcome it. She took the little key and opened it, trembling, but could not at first see anything plainly because the windows were shut. After some moments she began to perceive that the floor was covered with blood, which reflected the bodies of several dead women, ranged against the walls. (These were the wives whom Blue Beard had married and murdered, one after another.) She thought she would die for fear, and the key, which she pulled out of the lock, fell out of her hand.

After having somewhat recovered from the shock, she took up the key, locked the door, and went upstairs to her bedroom to rest. Having observed that the key of the closet was stained with blood, she tried two or three times to wipe it off, but the stain would not come out; in vain did she wash it, and even rub it with soap and sand, the blood still remained, for the key was magical; when the blood was removed from one side it came again on the other.

Blue Beard returned from his journey the same evening, and said he had received letters upon the road informing him that the affair he went about was ended to his advantage. His wife did all she could to convince him she was extremely glad of his speedy return.

Next morning he asked for the keys, which she gave him, with such a trembling hand that he easily guessed what had happened.

"What!" said he, "is not the key of my closet among the rest?"

"I must certainly," said she, "have left it above upon the table."

"Fail not," said Blue Beard, "to bring it to me presently."

After several goings backward and forward she was forced to bring him the key. Blue Beard attentively considered it and said to his wife: "How comes this blood upon the key?"

"I do not know," cried the poor woman, paler than death.

"You do not know!" replied Blue Beard. "I very well know. You were resolved to go into the closet, were you not? Very well, madam; you shall go in and take your place among the ladies you saw there."

Upon this she threw herself at her husband's feet, and begged his pardon with all the signs of a true repentance, vowing that she would never again be disobedient. She would have melted a rock, so beautiful and sorrowful was she; but Blue Beard had a heart harder than rock! "You must die, madam," said he, "and that very soon."

"Since I must die," answered she, her eyes bathed in tears, "give me some little time to say my prayers."

"I give you," replied Blue Beard, "half a quarter of an hour."

When she was alone she called out to her sister:

"Sister Anne, go up, I beg you, on top of the tower and see if my brothers are not coming; they promised me that they would come today, and if you see them, give them a sign to make haste."

Sister Anne went to the tower, and the poor wife cried out from time to time: "Anne, sister Anne, do you see anyone coming?"

And sister Anne replied: "I see nothing but the sun, which makes a dust, and the grass, which looks green."

In the meanwhile Blue Beard, holding a great saber in his hand, cried out as loud as he could bawl to his wife:

"Come down instantly, or I shall come up after you."

"One moment longer, if you please," said his wife; and then she cried out softly: "Anne, sister Anne, dost thou see anybody coming?"

And sister Anne answered: "I see nothing but the sun, which makes a dust, and the grass, which is green."

"Come down quickly," shouted Blue Beard, "or I will come up."

"I am coming," answered his wife; and then she cried: "Anne, sister Anne, dost thou not see anyone coming?"

"I see," replied sister Anne, "a great dust, which comes on this side."

"Are they my brothers?"

"Alas! no, my dear sister, I see a flock of sheep."

"Will you not come down?" roared Blue Beard.

"One moment longer," said his wife, and then she cried out: "Anne, sister Anne, dost thou see nobody coming?"

"I see," said she, "two horsemen, but they are yet a great way off."

"God be praised!" replied the poor wife: "they are my brothers."

Then Blue Beard bawled out so loud that he made the whole house tremble. The distressed wife came down and threw herself at his feet, all in tears, with her hair about her shoulders.

"That will not help you," said Blue Beard; "you must die"; then, taking hold of her hair with one hand, and lifting up the sword with the other, he was going to cut off her head. The poor lady, looking at him with dying eyes, begged him to give her one little moment more.

"No," said he; "say your prayers," and was about to strike . . .

At this very instant there was such a loud knocking at the gate that Blue Beard looked up in alarm. The gate was opened and two horsemen entered, who drew their swords and ran directly at Blue Beard. He knew them to be his wife's brothers, one a dragoon, the other a musketeer; so that he quickly ran to save himself; but the two brothers pursued so close that they overtook him before he could get to the steps of the porch, and ran their swords through his body and left him dead.

Blue Beard had no heirs, and so his wife became mistress of all.

Gustav Doré

The two brothers near Blue Beard's castle.

his estate. She made use of one part of it to marry her sister Anne to a young gentleman who had loved her a long while; another part to buy captains' commissions for her brothers, and the rest to marry herself to a very worthy gentleman, who made her forget the unhappy time she had passed with Blue Beard.

BEAUTY AND THE BEAST

By *MME. LEPRINCE DE BEAUMONT*

Illustrations by WALTER CRANE

T HERE was once a very rich merchant, who had six children, three boys and three girls. As he was himself a man of great sense, he spared no expense for their education. The three daughters were all handsome, but particularly the youngest; indeed, she was so very beautiful, that in her childhood everyone called her the Little Beauty; and being equally lovely when she was grown up, nobody called her by any other name, which made her sisters very jealous of her. This youngest daughter was not only more handsome than her sisters, but also was better tempered. The two eldest were vain of their wealth and position. They gave themselves a thousand airs, and refused to visit other merchants' daughters; nor would they condescend to be seen except with persons of quality.

They went every day to balls, plays, and public walks, and always made game of their youngest sister for spending her time in reading or other useful employments. As it was well known that these young ladies would have large fortunes, many great merchants wished to get them for wives; but the two eldest always answered, that, for their parts, they had no thoughts of marrying anyone below a duke or an earl at least. Beauty had quite as many offers as her sisters, but she always answered, with the greatest civility, that though she was much obliged to her lovers, she would rather live some years longer with her father, as she thought herself too young to marry.

It happened that, by some unlucky accident, the merchant suddenly lost all his fortune, and had nothing left but a small cottage in the country. Upon this he said to his daughters, while the tears ran down his cheeks, "My children, we must now go and dwell in the cottage, and try to get a living by labor, for we have no other means of support." The two eldest replied that they did not know how to work, and would not leave town; for they had lovers enough who would be glad to marry them, though they had no longer any fortune. But in this they were mistaken; for when the lovers heard what had happened, they said: "The girls were so proud and ill-tempered, that all we wanted was their fortune; we are not sorry at all to see their pride brought down; let them show off their airs to their cows and sheep." But everybody pitied poor Beauty, because she was so sweet-tempered and kind to all, and several gentlemen offered to marry her, though she had not a penny; but Beauty still refused, and said she could not think of leaving her poor father in this trouble. At first Beauty could not help sometimes crying in secret for the hardships she was now obliged to suffer; but in a very short time she said to herself, "All the crying in the world will do me no good, so I will try to be happy without a fortune."

When they had removed to their cottage, the merchant and his three sons employed themselves in plowing and sowing the fields, and working in the garden. Beauty also did her part, for she rose by four o'clock every morning, lighted the fires, cleaned the house, and got ready the breakfast for the whole family. At first she found all this very hard; but she soon grew quite used to it, and thought it no hardship; indeed, the work greatly benefited her health. When she had done, she used to amuse herself with reading, playing her music, or singing while she spun. But her two sisters were at a loss what to do to pass the time away; they had their breakfast in bed, and did not rise till ten o'clock. Then they commonly walked out, but always found themselves very soon tired; when they would often sit down under a shady tree, and grieve for the loss of their carriage and fine clothes, and say to each other, "What a mean-spirited, poor stupid creature our young sister is, to be so content with this low way of life!" But their father thought differently; and loved and admired his youngest child more than ever.

After they had lived in this manner about a year the merchant received a letter, which informed him that one of his richest ships, which he thought was lost, had just come into port. This news made the two eldest sisters almost mad with joy; for they thought they should now leave the cottage, and have all their finery again. When

they found that their father must take a journey to the ship, the two
eldest begged he would not fail to bring them back some new gowns,
caps, rings, and all sorts of trinkets. But Beauty asked for nothing;
for she thought in herself that all the ship was worth would hardly
buy everything her sisters wished for. "Beauty," said the merchant,
"you ask for nothing: what can I bring you, my child?"

"Since you are so kind as to think of me, dear father," she answered, "I should be glad if you would bring me a rose, for we have
none in our garden." Now Beauty did not indeed wish for a rose,
nor anything else, but she only said this that she might not affront
her sisters; otherwise they would have said she wanted her father
to praise her for desiring nothing. The merchant took his leave of
them, and set out on his journey; but when he got to the ship, some
persons went to law with him about the cargo, and after a deal of
trouble he came back to his cottage as poor as he had left it. When
he was within thirty miles of his home, and thinking of the joy of
again meeting his children, he lost his way in the midst of a dense
forest. It rained and snowed very hard, and, besides, the wind was so
high as to throw him twice from his horse. Night came on, and he
feared he should die of cold and hunger, or be torn to pieces by the
wolves that he heard howling round him. All at once, he cast his
eyes toward a long avenue, and saw at the end a light, but it seemed
a great way off. He made the best of his way toward it, and found
that it came from a splendid palace, the windows of which were all
blazing with light. It had great bronze gates, standing wide open,
and fine courtyards, through which the merchant passed; but not a
living soul was to be seen. There were stables, too, which his poor,
starved horse, less scrupulous than himself, entered at once, and took
a good meal of oats and hay. His master then tied him up, and
walked toward the entrance hall, but still without seeing a single
creature. He went on to a large dining parlor, where he found a
good fire, and a table covered with some very nice dishes, but only
one plate with a knife and fork. As the snow and rain had wetted
him to the skin, he went up to the fire to dry himself. "I hope," said
he, "the master of the house or his servants will excuse me, for it
surely will not be long now before I see them." He waited some

time, but still nobody came: at last the clock struck eleven, and the merchant, being quite faint for the want of food, helped himself to a chicken, and to a few glasses of wine, yet all the time trembling with fear. He sat till the clock struck twelve, and then, taking courage, began to think he might as well look about him: so he opened a door at the end of the hall, and went through it into a very grand room, in which there was a fine bed; and he was feeling very weary, he shut the door, took off his clothes, and got into it.

It was ten o'clock in the morning before he awoke, when he was amazed to see a handsome new suit of clothes laid ready for him, instead of his own, which were all torn and spoiled. "To be sure," said he to himself, "this place belongs to some good fairy, who has taken pity on my ill luck." He looked out of the window, and instead of the snow-covered wood, where he had lost himself the previous night, he saw the most charming arbors covered with all kinds of flowers. Returning to the hall where he had supper, he found a breakfast table, ready prepared. "Indeed, my good fairy," said the merchant aloud, "I am vastly obliged to you for your kind care of me." He then made a hearty breakfast, took his hat, and was going to the stable to pay his horse a visit; but as he passed under one of the arbors, which was loaded with roses, he thought of what Beauty had asked him to bring back to her, and so he took a bunch of roses to carry home. At the same moment he heard a loud noise, and saw coming toward him a beast, so frightful to look at that he was ready to faint with fear. "Ungrateful man!" said the beast in a terrible voice, "I have saved your life by admitting you into my palace, and in return you steal my roses, which I value more than anything I possess. But you shall atone for your fault—die in a quarter of an hour."

The merchant fell on his knees, and clasping his hands, said, "Sir, I humbly beg your pardon: I did not think it would offend you to gather a rose for one of my daughters, who had entreated me to bring her one home. Do not kill me, my lord!"

"I am not a lord, but a beast," replied the monster. "I hate false compliments: so do not fancy that you can coax me by any such ways. You tell me that you have daughters; now I will suffer you to escape, if one of them will come and die in your stead. If not, promise you will yourself return in three months, to be dealt with as I may choose."

The tender-hearted merchant had no thoughts of letting any one of his daughters die for his sake; but he knew that if he seemed to accept the beast's terms, he should at least have the pleasure of seeing them once again. So he gave his promise, and was told that he might then set off as soon as he liked. "But," said the beast, "I do not wish you to go back empty-handed. Go to the room you slept in, and you will find a chest there; fill it with whatsoever you like best, and I will have it taken to your own house for you."

When the beast said this, he went away. The good merchant, left to himself, began to consider that, as he must die—for he had no thought of breaking a promise, made even to a beast—he might as well have the comfort of leaving his children provided for. He returned to the room he had slept in, and found there heaps of gold pieces lying about. He filled the chest with them to the very brim, locked it, and mounting his horse, left the palace as sorrowful as he had been glad when he first beheld it. The horse took a path across the forest of his own accord, and in a few hours they reached the merchant's house. His children came running round him, but, instead of kissing them with joy, he could not help weeping as he looked at them. He held in his hand the bunch of roses, which he gave to Beauty, saying, "Take these roses, Beauty; but little do you think how dear they have cost your poor father"; and then he gave them an account of all that he had seen or heard in the palace of the beast.

The two eldest sisters now began to shed tears, and to lay the blame upon Beauty, who, they said, would be the cause of her father's death. "See," said they, "what happens from the pride of the little wretch; why did not she ask for such things as we did? But, to be sure, Miss must not be like other people; and though she will be the cause of her father's death, yet she does not shed a tear."

"It would be useless," replied Beauty, "for my father shall not die. As the beast will accept one of his daughters, I will give myself up, and be only too happy to prove my love for the best of fathers."

"No, sister," said the three brothers with one voice, "that cannot be; we will go in search of this monster, and either he or we will perish."

"Do not hope to kill him," said the merchant, "his power is far too great. But Beauty's young life shall not be sacrificed; I am old,

Walter Crane

Take these roses, Beauty; they cost your father dear!"

and cannot expect to live much longer; so I shall but give up a few years of my life, and shall only grieve for the sake of my children."

"Never, father," cried Beauty; "if you go back to the palace, you cannot hinder my going after you! Though young, I am not over-fond of life; and I would much rather be eaten up by the monster, than die of grief for your loss."

The merchant tried in vain to reason with Beauty who still obstinately kept to her purpose; which, in truth, made her two sisters glad, for they were jealous of her, because everybody loved her.

The merchant was so grieved at the thought of losing his child, that he never once thought of the chest filled with gold, but at night, to his great surprise, he found it standing by his bedside. He said nothing about his riches to his eldest daughters, for he knew very well it would at once make them want to return to town; but he told Beauty his secret, and she then said, that while he was away, two gentlemen had been on a visit at her cottage, who had fallen in love with her two sisters. She entreated her father to marry them without delay, for she was so sweet-natured she only wished them to be happy.

Three months went by, only too fast, and then the merchant and Beauty got ready to set out for the palace of the beast. Upon this, the two sisters rubbed their eyes with an onion, to make believe they were crying; both the merchant and his sons cried in earnest. Only Beauty shed no tears. They reached the palace in a very few hours, and the horse, without bidding, went into the stable as before. The merchant and Beauty walked toward the large hall, where they found a table covered with every dainty and two plates laid already. The merchant had very little appetite; but Beauty, that she might the better hide her grief, placed herself at the table, and helped her father; she then began to eat herself, and thought all the time that, to be sure, the beast had a mind to fatten her before he ate her up, since he had provided such good cheer for her. When they had done their supper, they heard a great noise, and the good old man began to bid his poor child farewell, for he knew that it was the beast coming to them. When Beauty first saw that frightful form, she was very much terrified, but tried to hide her fear. The creature walked up to her, and eyed her all over—then asked her in a dreadful voice if she had come quite of her own accord.

"Yes," said Beauty.

"Then you are a good girl, and I am very much obliged to you."

This was such an astonishingly civil answer that Beauty's courage rose: but it sank again when the beast, addressing the merchant, desired him to leave the palace next morning, and never return to it again. "And so good night, merchant. And good night, Beauty."

"Good night, beast," she answered, as the monster shuffled out.

"Ah! my dear child," said the merchant, kissing his daughter, "I am half dead already, at the thought of leaving you with this dreadful beast; you shall go back and let me stay in your place."

"No," said Beauty boldly, "I will never agree to that; you must go home tomorrow morning."

They then wished each other good night, and went to bed, both of them thinking they should not be able to close their eyes; but as soon as ever they had lain down, they fell into a deep sleep, and did not awake till morning. Beauty dreamed that a lady came up to her, who said, "I am very much pleased, Beauty, with the goodness you have shown, in being willing to give your life to save that of your father. Do not be afraid of anything; you shall not go without a reward."

As soon as Beauty awoke she told her father this dream; but though it gave him some comfort, he was a long time before he could be persuaded to leave the palace. At last Beauty succeeded in getting him safely away.

When her father was out of sight, poor Beauty began to weep sorely; still, having naturally a courageous spirit, she soon resolved not to make her sad case still worse by sorrow, which she knew was vain, but to wait and be patient. She walked about to take a view of all the palace, and the elegance of every part of it much charmed her.

But what was her surprise, when she came to a door on which was written, BEAUTY's ROOM! She opened it in haste, and her eyes were dazzled by the splendor and taste of the apartment. What made her wonder more than all the rest, was a large library filled with books, a harpsichord, and many pieces of music. "The beast surely does not mean to eat me up immediately," said she, "since he takes care I shall not be at a loss how to amuse myself." She opened the library and saw these verses written in letters of gold in the back of one of the books:

> "Beauteous lady, dry your tears,
>   Here's no cause for sighs or fears.
>   Command as freely as you may,
>   For you command and I obey."

"Alas!" said she, sighing: "I wish I could only command a sight of my poor father, and to know what he is doing at this moment." Just then, by chance, she cast her eyes upon a looking-glass that stood near her, and in it she saw a picture of her old home, and her father riding mournfully up to the door. Her sisters came out to meet him, and although they tried to look sorry, it was easy to see that in their hearts they were very glad. In a short time all this picture disappeared, but it caused Beauty to think that the beast, besides being very powerful, was also very kind. About the middle of the day she found a table laid ready for her, and a sweet concert of music played all the time she was dining, without her seeing anybody. But at supper, when she was going to seat herself at table, she heard the noise of the beast, and could not help trembling with fear..

"Beauty," said he, "will you give me leave to see you sup?"

"That is as you please," answered she, very much afraid.

"Not in the least," said the beast. "You alone command in this place. If you should not like my company, you need only say so, and I will leave you that moment. But tell me, Beauty, do you not think me very ugly?"

"Why, yes," said she, "for I cannot tell a falsehood; but then I think you are very good."

"Am I?" sadly replied the beast. "Yet, besides being ugly, I am also very stupid; I know well enough that I am but a beast."

"Stupid people," said Beauty, "are never aware of it themselves."

At which kindly speech the beast looked pleased, and replied, not without an awkward sort of politeness, "Pray do not let me detain you from supper, and be sure that you are well served. All you see is your own, and I should be deeply grieved if you wanted for any-thing."

"You are very kind—so kind that I almost forgot you are so ugly," said Beauty, earnestly.

"Ah! yes," answered the beast, with a great sigh; "I hope I am good-tempered, but still I am only a monster."

"There is many a monster who wears the form of a man; it is better of the two to have the heart of a man and the form of a monster."

"I would thank you, Beauty, for this speech, but I am too senseless to say anything that would please you," returned the beast in a melancholy voice; and altogether he seemed so gentle and so un-happy that Beauty, who had the tenderest heart in the world, felt her fear of him gradually vanish.

She ate her supper with a good appetite, and conversed in her own sensible and charming way, till at last, when the beast rose to depart, he terrified her more than ever by saying abruptly, in his gruff voice, "Beauty, will you marry me?"

Now Beauty, frightened as she was, would speak only the exact truth; besides her father had told her that the beast liked only to have the truth spoken to him. So she answered, in a very firm tone, "No, beast."

He did not get into a passion, but sighed deeply and departed.

When Beauty found herself alone, she began to feel pity for the poor beast. "Oh," she said, "what a sad thing it is that he should be so very frightful, since he is so good-tempered!"

Beauty lived three months in this palace very well pleased. The beast came to see her every night, and talked with her while she supped; and though what he said was not very clever, yet, as she saw in him every day some new goodness, instead of dreading the time of his coming, she soon began continually looking at her watch, to see if it were nine o'clock; for that was the hour when he never failed to visit her. One thing only vexed her, which was that every night before he went away, he always made it a rule to ask her if she would be his wife, and seemed very much grieved at her stead-fastly replying "No." At last, one night, she said to him, "You wound me greatly, beast, by forcing me to refuse you so often; I wish I could take such a liking to you as to agree to marry you; but I must tell you plainly that I do not think it will ever happen. I shall always be your friend; so try to let that content you."

"I must," sighed the beast, "for I know well enough how frightful I am; but I love you better than myself. Yet I think I am very lucky in your being pleased to stay with me; now promise, Beauty, that you will never leave me."

Beauty would almost have agreed to this, so sorry was she for him, but she had that day seen in her magic glass, which she looked at constantly, that her father was dying of grief for her sake.

"Alas!" she said. "I long so much to see my father, that if you do not give me leave to visit him, I shall break my heart."

"I would rather break mine, Beauty," answered the beast; "I will send you to your father's cottage: you shall stay there, and your poor beast shall die of sorrow."

"No," said Beauty, crying, "I love you too well to be the cause of your death; I promise to return in a week. You have shown me that my sisters are married, and my brothers are gone for soldiers, so that my father is left all alone. Let me stay a week with him."

"You shall find yourself with him tomorrow morning," replied the beast; "but mind, do not forget your promise. When you wish to return, you have nothing to do but to put your ring on a table when you go to bed. Good-bye, Beauty!" The beast sighed as he said these words, and Beauty went to bed very sorry to see him so much grieved. When she awoke in the morning, she found herself in her father's cottage. She rang a bell that was at her bedside, and a servant entered; but as soon as she saw Beauty, the woman gave a loud shriek; upon which the merchant ran upstairs, and when he beheld his daughter he ran to her, and kissed her a hundred times. At last Beauty began to remember that she had brought no clothes with her to put on; but the servant told her she had just found in the next room a large chest full of dresses, trimmed all over with gold, and adorned with pearls and diamonds.

Beauty, in her own mind, thanked the beast for his kindness, and put on the plainest gown she could find among them all. She then

Walter Crane

Forgetting all his ugliness, she threw herself upon his body.

[See page 246]

desired the servant to lay the rest aside, for she intended to give
them to her sisters; but, as soon as she had spoken these words, the
chest was gone out of sight in a moment. Her father then suggested,
perhaps the beast chose for her to keep them all for herself: and as
soon as he had said this, they saw the chest standing again in the
same place. While Beauty was dressing herself, a servant brought
word to her that her sisters were come with their husbands to pay
her a visit. They both lived unhappily with the gentlemen they had
married. The husband of the eldest was very handsome, but was so
proud of this that he thought of nothing else from morning till
night, and did not care a pin for the beauty of his wife. The second
had married a man of great learning; but he made no use of it,
except to torment and affront all his friends, and his wife more than
any of them. The two sisters were ready to burst with spite when
they saw Beauty dressed like a princess, and looking so very charming. All the kindness that she showed them was of no use; for they
were vexed more than ever when she told them how happy she lived
at the palace of the beast. The spiteful creatures went by themselves
into the garden, where they cried to think of her good fortune.

"Why should the little wretch be better off than we?" said they.
"We are much handsomer than she is."

"Sister," said the eldest, "a thought has just come into my head;
let us try to keep her here longer than the week for which the beast
gave her leave; and then he will be so angry that perhaps when she
goes back to him he will eat her up in a moment."

"That is well thought of," answered the other, "but to do this, we
must pretend to be very kind."

They then went to join her in the cottage, where they showed
her so much false love that Beauty could not help crying for joy.

When the week was ended, the two sisters began to pretend such
grief at the thought of her leaving them that she agreed to stay a
week more; but all that time Beauty could not help fretting for the
sorrow that she knew her absence would give her poor beast; for
she tenderly loved him, and much wished for his company again.
Among all the grand and clever people she saw, she found nobody
who was half so sensible, so affectionate, so thoughtful, or so kind.

The tenth night of her being at the cottage, she dreamed she was in the garden of the palace, that the beast lay dying on a grass plot, and with his last breath put her in mind of her promise, and laid his death to her forsaking him. Beauty awoke in a great fright, and she burst into tears. "Am not I wicked," said she, "to behave so ill to a beast who has shown me so much kindness? Why will I not marry him? I am sure I should be more happy with him than my sisters are with their husbands. He shall not be wretched any longer on my account; for I should do nothing but blame myself all the rest of my life."

She then rose, put her ring on the table, got into bed again, and soon fell asleep. In the morning she with joy found herself in the palace of the beast. She dressed herself very carefully, that she might please him the better, and thought she had never known a day pass away so slowly. At last the clock struck nine, but the beast did not come. Beauty, dreading lest she might truly have caused his death, ran from room to room, calling out: "Beast, dear beast"; but there was no answer. At last she remembered her dream, rushed to the grass plot, and there saw him lying apparently dead beside the fountain. Forgetting all his ugliness, she threw herself upon his body, and finding his heart still beating, she fetched some water and sprinkled it over him, weeping and sobbing the while.

The beast opened his eyes. "You forgot your promise, Beauty, and so I determined to die; for I could not live without you. I have starved myself to death, but I shall die content since I have seen your face once more."

"No, dear beast," cried Beauty, passionately, "you shall not die; you shall live to be my husband. I thought it was only friendship I felt for you, but now I know it was love."

The moment Beauty had spoken these words, the palace was suddenly lighted up, and all kinds of rejoicings were heard around them, none of which she noticed, but hung over her dear beast with the utmost tenderness. At last, unable to restrain herself, she dropped her head over her hands, covered her eyes, and cried for joy; and, when she looked up again, the beast was gone. In his stead she saw at her feet a handsome, graceful young prince, who thanked her with the tenderest expressions for having freed him from en-chantment.

"But where is my poor beast? I only want him and nobody else," sobbed Beauty.

"I am he," replied the prince. "A wicked fairy condemned me to this form, and forbade me to show that I had any wit or sense, till a beautiful lady should consent to marry me. You alone, dearest Beauty, judged me neither by my looks nor by my talents, but by my heart alone. Take it then, and all that I have besides, for all is yours."

Beauty, full of surprise, but very happy, suffered the prince to lead her to his palace, where she found her father and sisters, who had been brought there by the fairy lady whom she had seen in a dream the first night she came.

"Beauty," said the fairy, "you have chosen well, and you have your reward, for a true heart is better than either good looks or clever brains. As for you, ladies," and she turned to the two elder sisters, "I know all your ill deeds, but I have no worse punishment for you than to see your sister happy. You shall stand as statues at the door of her palace, and when you repent of and have amended your faults, you shall become women again. But, to tell you the truth, I very much fear you will remain statues forever."

Tales From Czechoslovakia

##

BUDULINEK

By PARKER FILLMORE

THERE was once a little boy named Budulinek. He lived with his old Granny in a cottage near a forest.

Granny went out to work every day. In the morning when she went away she always said:

"There, Budulinek, there's your dinner on the table, and mind, you mustn't open the door no matter who knocks!"

One morning Granny said:

"Now, Budulinek, today I'm leaving you some soup for your dinner. Eat it when dinner time comes. And remember what I always say: don't open the door no matter who knocks."

She went away and pretty soon Lishka, the sly old mother fox, came and knocked on the door.

"Budulinek!" she called. "You know me! Open the door! Please!"

Budulinek called back: "No, I mustn't open the door."

But Lishka, the sly old mother fox, kept on knocking.

"Listen, Budulinek," she said: "if you open the door, do you know what I'll do? I'll give you a ride on my tail!"

Now Budulinek thought to himself:

"Oh, that would be fun to ride on the tail of Lishka, the fox!"

So Budulinek forgot all about what Granny said to him every day and opened the door.

Lishka, the sly old thing, came into the room and what do you think she did? Do you think she gave Budulinek a ride on her tail? Well, she didn't. She just went over to the table and gobbled up the bowl of soup that Granny had put there for Budulinek's dinner and then she ran away.

When dinner time came Budulinek hadn't anything to eat.

In the evening when Granny came home, she said:

"Budulinek, did you open the door and let anyone in?"

Budulinek was crying because he was so hungry, and he said:

"Yes, I let in Lishka, the old mother fox, and she ate up all my dinner, too!

Granny said:

"Now, Budulinek, you see what happens when you open the door and let someone in. Another time, remember what Granny says and don't open the door."

The next morning Granny cooked some porridge for Budulinek's dinner and said:

"Now, Budulinek, here's some porridge for your dinner. Remember: while I'm gone you must not open the door no matter who knocks."

Granny was no sooner out of sight than Lishka came again and knocked on the door.

"Oh, Budulinek!" she called. "Open the door and let me in!"

But Budulinek said:

"No, I won't open the door!"

"Oh, now, Budulinek, please open the door!" Lishka begged. "You know me! Do you know what I'll do if you open the door? I'll give you a ride on my tail! Truly I will!"

Budulinek thought to himself:

"This time maybe she will give me a ride on her tail."

So he opened the door.

Lishka came into the room, gobbled up Budulinek's porridge, and ran away without giving him any ride at all.

When dinner time came Budulinek hadn't anything to eat.

In the evening when Granny came home she said:

"Budulinek, did you open the door and let anyone in?"

Budulinek was crying again because he was so hungry, and he said:

"Yes, I let in Lishka, the old mother fox, and she ate up all my porridge, too!"

"Budulinek, you're a bad boy!" Granny said. "If you open the door again, I'll have to spank you! Do you hear?"

The next morning before she went to work, Granny cooked some peas for Budulinek's dinner.

As soon as Granny was gone he began eating the peas, they were so good.

Presently Lishka, the fox, came and knocked on the door.

"Budulinek!" she called. "Open the door! I want to come in!"

But Budulinek wouldn't open the door. He took his bowl of peas and went to the window and started to eat them there where Lishka could see them.

"Oh, Budulinek!" Lishka begged. "You know me! Please open the door! This time I promise you I'll give you a ride on my tail! Truly I will!"

She just begged and begged until at last Budulinek opened the door. Then Lishka jumped into the room and do you know what she did? She put her nose right into the bowl of peas and gobbled them all up!

Then she said to Budulinek:

"Now get on my tail and I'll give you a ride!"

So Budulinek climbed on Lishka's tail and Lishka went running around the room faster and faster until Budulinek was dizzy and just had to hold on with all his might.

Then, before Budulinek knew what was happening, Lishka slipped out of the house and ran swiftly off into the forest, home to her hole, with Budulinek still on her tail! She hid Budulinek down in her hole with her own three children and she wouldn't let him out. He had to stay there with the three little foxes and they all teased him and bit him. And then wasn't he sorry he had disobeyed his Granny! And, oh, how he cried!

When Granny came home she found the door open and no little Budulinek anywhere. She looked high and low, but no, there was no little Budulinek. She asked everyone she met had they seen her little Budulinek, but nobody had. So poor Granny just cried and cried, she was so lonely and sad.

One day an organ grinder with a wooden leg began playing in front of Granny's cottage. The music made her think of Budulinek.

"Organ grinder," Granny said, "here's a penny for you. But,

please, don't play any more. Your music makes me cry."

"Why does it make you cry?" the organ grinder asked.

"Because it reminds me of Budulinek," Granny said, and she told the organ grinder all about Budulinek and how somebody had stolen him away.

The organ grinder said:

"Poor Granny! I tell you what I'll do: as I go around and play my organ I'll keep my eyes open for Budulinek. If I find him I'll bring him back to you."

"Will you?" Granny cried. "If you bring me back my little Budulinek I'll give you a measure of rye and a measure of millet and a measure of poppy seed and a measure of everything in the house!"

So the organ grinder went off, and everywhere he played his organ he looked for Budulinek. But he couldn't find him.

At last one day while he was walking through the forest he thought he heard a little boy crying. He looked around everywhere until he found a fox's hole.

"Oho!" he said to himself. "I believe that wicked old Lishka must have stolen Budulinek! She's probably keeping him here with her own three children! I'll soon find out."

So he put down his organ and began to play. And as he played he sang softly:

> "One old fox
> And two, three, four,
> And Budulinek
> He makes one more!"

Old Lishka heard the music playing and she said to her oldest child:

"Here, son, give the old man a penny and tell him to go away because my head aches."

So the oldest little fox climbed out of the hole and gave the organ grinder a penny and said:

"My mother says, please will you go away because her head aches."

As the organ grinder reached over to take the penny, he caught the oldest little fox and stuffed him into a sack. Then he went on playing and singing:

> "One old fox
> And two and three
> And Budulinek
> Makes four for me!"

Presently Lishka sent out her second child with a penny, and the organ grinder caught the second little fox in the same way and stuffed it also into the sack. Then he went on grinding his organ and softly singing:

> "One old fox
> And another for me,
> And Budulinek
> He makes the three."

"I wonder why that old man still plays his organ," Lishka said and sent out her third child with a penny.

So the organ grinder caught the third little fox and stuffed it also into the sack. Then he kept on playing and singing softly:

> "One old fox—
> I'll soon get you!—
> And Budulinek
> He makes just two.

At last Lishka herself came out. So he caught her, too, and stuffed her in with her children. Then he sang:

> "Four naughty foxes
> Caught alive!
> And Budulinek
> He makes the five!"

The organ grinder went to the hole and called down: "Budulinek! Budulinek! Come out!"

As there were no foxes left to hold him back, Budulinek was able to crawl out.

When he saw the organ grinder he cried and said:

"Oh, please, Mr. Organ Grinder, I want to go home to my Granny!"

"I'll take you home to your Granny," the organ grinder said, "but first I must punish these naughty foxes."

The organ grinder cut a strong switch and gave the four foxes in the sack a terrible beating, until they begged him to stop and promised that they would never again do anything to Budulinek.

Then the organ grinder let them go and he took Budulinek home to Granny.

Granny was delighted to see her little Budulinek and she gave the organ grinder a measure of rye and a measure of millet and a measure of poppy seed and a measure of everything else in the house.

And Budulinek never again opened the door!

ZLATOVLASKA
THE GOLDEN-HAIRED

By PARKER FILLMORE

THERE was once an old king who was so wise that he was able to understand the speech of all the animals in the world. This is how it happened. An old woman came to him one day bringing him a snake in a basket.

"If you have this snake cooked," she told him, "and eat it as you would a fish, then you will be able to understand the birds of the air, the beasts of the earth, and the fishes of the sea."

The king was delighted. He made the old wise woman a handsome present and at once ordered his cook, a youth named Yirik, to prepare the "fish" for dinner.

"But understand, Yirik," he said severely, "you're to cook this 'fish,' not eat it! You're not to taste one morsel of it. If you do, you forfeit your head!"

Yirik thought this a strange order.

"What kind of a cook am I," he said to himself, "that I'm not to sample my own cooking?"

When he opened the basket and saw the "fish," he was further mystified.

"Um," he murmured, "it looks like a snake to me."

He put it on the fire and, when it was broiled to a turn, he ate a morsel. It had a fine flavor. He was about to take a second bite when suddenly he heard a little voice that buzzed in his ear these words: "Give us some, too! Give us some, too!"

He looked around to see who was speaking, but there was no one in the kitchen. Only some flies were buzzing about.

Just then outside a hissing voice called out:

"Where shall we go? Where shall we go?"

A higher voice answered:

"To the miller's barley field! To the miller's barley field!"

Yirik looked out the window and saw a gander with a flock of geese.

"Oho!" he said to himself, shaking his head. "Now I understand! Now I know what kind of 'fish' this is! Now I know why the poor cook was not to take a bite!"

He slipped another morsel into his mouth, garnished the "fish" carefully on a platter, and carried it to the king.

After dinner the king ordered his horse and told Yirik to come with him for a ride. The king rode on ahead and Yirik followed.

As they cantered across a green meadow, Yirik's horse began to prance and neigh.

"Ho! Ho!" he said. "I feel so light that I could jump over a mountain!"

"So could I," the king's horse said, "but I have to remember the old bag of bones that is perched on my back. If I were to jump he'd tumble off and break his neck."

"And a good thing, too!" said Yirik's horse. "Why not? Then instead of such an old bag of bones you'd get a young man to ride you, like Yirik."

Yirik almost burst out laughing as he listened to the horses' talk, but he suppressed his merriment lest the king should know that he had eaten some of the magic snake.

Now of course the king, too, understood what the horses were saying. He glanced apprehensively at Yirik and it seemed to him that Yirik was grinning.

"What are you laughing at, Yirik?"

"Me?" Yirik said. "I'm not laughing. I was just thinking of something funny."

"Um," said the king.

His suspicions against Yirik were aroused. Moreover he was afraid to trust himself to his horse any longer. So he turned back to the palace at once.

There he ordered Yirik to pour him out a goblet of wine.

"And I warn you," he said, "that you forfeit your head if you pour a drop too much or too little."

Yirik carefully tilted a great tankard and began filling a goblet. As he poured, a bird suddenly flew into the window pursued by another bird. The first bird had in its beak three golden hairs.

"Give them to me! Give them to me! They're mine!" screamed the second bird.

"I won't! I won't! They're mine!" the first bird answered. "I picked them up!"

"Yes, but I saw them first!" the other cried. "I saw them fall as the maiden sat and combed her golden tresses. Give me two of them and I'll let you keep the third."

"No! No! No! I won't let you have one of them!"

The second bird darted angrily at the first, and after a struggle succeeded in capturing one of the golden hairs. One hair dropped to the marble floor, making as it struck a musical tinkle, and the first bird escaped still holding in its bill a single hair.

In his excitement over the struggle, Yirik overflowed the goblet.

"Ha! Ha!" said the king. "See what you've done! You forfeit your head! However, I'll suspend sentence on condition that you find this golden-haired maiden and bring her to me for a wife."

Poor Yirik didn't know who the maiden was nor where she lived. But what could he say? If he wanted to keep his head, he must undertake the quest. So he saddled his horse and started off at random.

His road led him through a forest. Here he came upon a bush under which some shepherds had kindled a fire. Sparks were falling on an ant hill nearby, and the ants in great excitement were running hither and thither with their eggs.

"Yirik!" they cried. "Help! Help, or we shall all be burned to death, we and our young ones in the eggs!"

Yirik instantly dismounted, cut down the burning bush, and put out the fire.

"Thank you, Yirik, thank you!" the ants said. "Your kindness to us this day will not go unrewarded. If ever you are in trouble, think of us and we will help you."

As Yirik rode on through the forest, he came upon two fledgling ravens lying by the path.

"Help us, Yirik, help us!" they cawed. "Our father and mother have thrown us out of the nest in yonder tall fir tree to fend for ourselves. We are young and helpless and not yet able to fly. Give us some meat to eat or we shall perish with hunger."

The sight of the helpless fledglings touched Yirik to pity. He dismounted instantly, drew his sword, and killed his horse. Then he fed the starving birds the meat they needed.

"Thank you, Yirik, thank you!" the little ravens croaked. "You have saved our lives this day. Your kindness will not go unrewarded. If ever you are in trouble, think of us and we will help you."

Yirik left the young ravens and pushed on afoot. The path through the forest was long and wearisome. It led out finally on the seashore. On the beach two fishermen were quarreling over a big fish with golden scales that lay gasping on the sand.

"It's mine, I tell you!" one of the men was shouting. "It was caught in my net, so of course it's mine!"

To this the other one shouted back:

"But your net would never have caught a fish if you hadn't been out in my boat and if I hadn't helped you!"

"Give me this one," the first man said, "and I'll let you have the next one."

"No! You take the next one!" the other said, "This one's mine!"

So they kept on arguing to no purpose until Yirik went up to them and said: "Let me decide this for you. Suppose you sell me the fish and then divide the money."

He offered them all the money the king had given him for his journey. The fishermen, delighted at the offer, at once agreed. Yirik handed them over the money and then, taking the gasping fish in his hand, he threw it back into the sea.

When the fish had caught its breath, it rose on a wave and called out to Yirik: "Thank you, Yirik, thank you. You have saved my life this day. Your kindness will not go unrewarded. If ever you are in trouble, think of me and I will help you."

With that the golden fish flicked its tail and disappeared in the water.

"Where are you going, Yirik?" the fisherman asked.

"I'm going in quest of a golden-haired maiden whom my master, the king, wishes to make his wife."

"He must mean the Princess Zlatovlaska," the fishermen said to each other.

"The Princess Zlatovlaska?" Yirik repeated. "Who is she?"

"She's the golden-haired daughter of the King of the Crystal Palace. Do you see the faint outlines of an island over yonder? That's where she lives. The king has twelve daughters, but Zlatovlaska alone has golden hair. Each morning at dawn a wonderful glow spreads over land and sea. That's Zlatovlaska combing her golden hair."

The fisherman conferred apart for a moment and then said:

"Yirik, you settled our dispute for us and now in return we'll row you over to the island."

So they rowed Yirik over to the Island of the Crystal Palace and left him there, with the warning that the king would probably try to palm off on him one of the dark-haired princesses.

Yirik at once presented himself at the palace, got an audience with the king, and declared his mission.

"H'm," the king said. "So your master desires the hand of my daughter, the Princess Zlatovlaska, eh? H'm, h'm. Well, I see no objection to your master as a son-in-law, but of course before I entrust the princess into your hands you must prove yourself worthy. I tell you what I'll do: I'll give you three tasks to perform. Be ready for the first one tomorrow."

Early the next day the king said to Yirik:

"My daughter, Zlatovlaska, had a precious necklace of pearls. She was walking in the meadow over yonder when the string broke and the pearls rolled away in the tall grasses. Now your first task is to gather up every last one of those pearls and hand them to me before sundown."

Yirik went to the meadow and when he saw how broad it was and how thickly covered with tall grasses his heart sank, for he realized that he could never search over the whole of it in one day. However, he got down on his hands and knees and began to hunt.

Midday came and he had not yet found a single pearl.

"Oh, dear," he thought to himself in despair, "if only my ants were here, they could help me!"

He had no sooner spoken than a million little voices answered:
"We are here, and we're here to help you!"

And sure enough there they were, the very ants that he supposed were far away!

"What do you want us to do?" they asked.

"Find me all the pearls that are scattered in this meadow. I can't find one of them."

Instantly the ants scurried hither and thither and soon they began bringing him the pearls one by one. Yirik strung them together until the necklace seemed complete.

"Are there any more?" he asked.

He was about to tie the string together when a lame ant, whose foot had been burned in the fire, hobbled up, crying.

"Wait, Yirik, don't tie the string yet! Here's the last pearl!"

Yirik thanked the ants for their help and at sundown carried the string of pearls to the king. The king counted the pearls and, to his surprise, found that not one was missing.

"You've done this well," he said. "Tomorrow I'll give you your second task."

The next day when Yirik presented himself, the king said:

"While my daughter, Zlatovlaska, was bathing in the sea, a golden ring slipped from her finger and disappeared. Your task is to find me this ring before sundown."

Yirik went down to the seashore and as he walked along the beach his heart grew heavy as he realized the difficulty of the task before him. The sea was clear, but so deep that he couldn't even see the bottom. How then could he find the ring?

"Oh, dear," he said aloud, "if only the golden fish were here! It could help me."

"I am here," a voice said, "and I'm here to help you."

And there was the golden fish on the crest of a wave, gleaming like a flash of fire!

"What do you want me to do?" it said.

"Find me a golden ring that lies somewhere on the bottom of the sea."

"Ah, a golden ring? A moment ago I met a pike," the fish said, "that had just such a golden ring. Wait for me here and I'll go find the pike."

In a few moments the golden fish returned with the pike and sure enough it was Zlatovlaska's ring that the pike was carrying.

That evening at sundown the king acknowledged that Yirik had accomplished his second task.

The next day the king said:

"I could never allow my daughter, Zlatovlaska, the Golden-Haired, to go to the kingdom of your master unless she carried with her two flasks, one filled with the Water of Life, the other with the Water of Death. So, for a third task I set you this: to bring the princess a flask of the Water of Life and a flask of the Water of Death."

Yirik had no idea which way to turn. He had heard of the Waters of Life and Death, but all he knew about them was that their springs were far away beyond the Red Sea. He left the Crystal Palace and walked off aimlessly until his feet had carried him of themselves into a dark forest.

"If only those young ravens were here," he said aloud, "they could help me!"

Instantly he heard a loud, "Caw! Caw!" and two ravens flew down to him, saying:

"We are here! We are here to help you! What do you want us to do?"

"I have to bring the king a flask of the Water of Life and a flask of the Water of Death and I don't know where the springs are. Do you know?"

"Yes, we know," the ravens said. "Wait here and we'll soon fetch you water from both springs."

They flew off and in a short time returned, each bearing a gourd of the precious water.

Yirik thanked the ravens and carefully filled his two flasks.

As he was leaving the forest, he came upon a great spider web. An ugly spider sat in the middle of it sucking a fly. Yirik took a drop of the Water of Death and flicked it on the spider. The spider doubled up dead and fell to the ground like a ripe cherry.

Then Yirik sprinkled a drop of Living Water on the fly. The fly instantly revived, pulled itself out of the web, and flew about happy and free once again.

"Thank you, Yirik," it buzzed, "thank you for bringing me back to life. You won't be sorry. Just wait and you'll soon see that I'll reward you!"

When Yirik returned to the palace and presented the two flasks, the king said:

"But one thing yet remains. You may take Zlatovlaska, the Golden-Haired, but you must yourself pick her out from among the twelve sisters."

The king led Yirik into a great hall. The twelve princesses were seated about a table, beautiful maidens all and each looking much like the others. Yirik could not tell which was Zlatovlaska, the Golden-Haired, for each princess wore a long heavy white veil so draped over her head and shoulders that it completely covered her hair.

"Here are my twelve daughters," the king said. "One of them is Zlatovlaska, the Golden-Haired. Pick her out and you may lead her at once to your master. If you fail to pick her out, then you must depart without her."

In dismay Yirik looked from sister to sister. There was nothing to show him which was Zlatovlaska, the Golden-Haired. How was he to find out?

Suddenly he heard a buzzing in his ear and a little voice whispered: "Courage, Yirik, courage! I'll help you!"

He turned his head quickly and there was the fly he had rescued from the spider.

"Walk slowly by each princess," the fly said, "and I'll tell you when you come to Zlatovlaska, the Golden-Haired."

Yirik did as the fly ordered. He stopped a moment before the first princess until the fly buzzed: "Not that one! Not that one!"

He went on to the next princess and again the fly buzzed: "Not that one! Not that one!"

So he went on from princess to princess until at last the fly buzzed out: "Yes, that one! That one!"

So Yirik remained standing where he was and said to the king: "This, I think, is Zlatovlaska, the Golden-Haired."

"You have guessed right," the king said.

At that Zlatovlaska removed the white veil from her head, and her lovely hair tumbled down to her feet like a golden cascade. It shimmered and glowed like the sun in the early morning when he peeps over the mountain top. Yirik stared until the brightness dimmed his sight.

The king immediately prepared Zlatovlaska, the Golden-Haired, for her journey. He gave her the two precious flasks of water; he arranged a fitting escort; and then with his blessing he sent her forth under Yirik's care.

Yirik conducted her safely to his master.

When the old king saw the lovely princess that Yirik had found for him, his eyes blinked with satisfaction, he capered about like a spring lamb, and he ordered that immediate preparations be made for the wedding. He was most grateful to Yirik and thanked him again and again.

"My dear boy," he said, "I had expected to have you hanged for your disobedience and let the ravens pick your bones. But now, to show you how grateful I am for the beautiful bride you have found me, I'm not going to have you hanged at all. Instead, I shall have you beheaded and then given a decent burial."

The execution took place at once in order to be out of the way before the wedding.

"It's a great pity he had to die," the king said as the executioner cut off Yirik's head. "He has certainly been a faithful servant."

Zlatovlaska, the Golden-Haired, asked if she might have his severed head and body. The king who was too madly in love to refuse her anything said: "Yes."

So Zlatovlaska took the body and the head and put them together. Then she sprinkled them with the Water of Death. Instantly the wound closed and soon it healed so completely that there wasn't even a scar left.

Yirik lay there lifeless but looking merely as if he were asleep. Zlatovlaska sprinkled him with the Water of Life and immediately his head and limbs stirred. Then he opened his eyes and sat up. Life poured through his veins and he sprang to his feet younger, fresher, handsomer than before.

The old king was filled with envy.

"I, too," he cried, "wish to be made young and handsome!"

He commanded the executioner to cut off his head and he told Zlatovlaska to sprinkle him afterwards with the Water of Life.

The executioner did as he was told. Then Zlatovlaska sprinkled the old king's head and body with the Water of Life. Nothing happened. Zlatovlaska kept on sprinkling the Water of Life until there was no more left.

"Do you know," the princess said to Yirik, "I believe I should have used the Water of Death first."

So now she sprinkled the body and head with the Water of Death and, sure enough, they grew together at once. But of course there was no life in them. And of course there was no possible way of putting life into them because the Water of Life was all gone. So the old king remained dead.

"This will never do," the people said. "We must have a king. And with the wedding feast and everything prepared we simply must have a wedding, too. If Zlatovlaska, the Golden-Haired, cannot marry the old king, she'll have to marry someone else. Now who shall it be?

Some one suggested Yirik because he was young and handsome, and because, like the old king, he could understand the birds and the beasts.

"Yirik!" the people cried. "Let Yirik be our king!"

And Zlatovlaska, the Golden-Haired, who had long since fallen in love with handsome Yirik, consented to have the wedding at once in order that the feast already prepared might not be wasted.

So Yirik and Zlatovlaska, the Golden-Haired, were married and they ruled so well and they lived so happily that to this day when people say of someone: "He's as happy as a king," they are thinking of King Yirik, and when they say of someone: "She's as beautiful as a queen," they are thinking of Zlatovlaska, the Golden-Haired.

LONGSHANKS, GIRTH, AND KEEN

By PARKER FILLMORE

Illustration by WARREN CHAPPELL

THERE was once an aged king who had an only son. One day he called the prince to him and said: "My dear son, you know that ripe fruit falls in order to make room for other fruit. This my old head is like ripe fruit and soon the sun will no longer shine upon it. Now before I die I should like to see you happily married. Get you a wife, my son."

"I would, my father, that I could please you in this," the prince answered, "but I know of no one who would make you a worthy daughter-in-law."

The old king reached into his pocket, drew out a golden key, and handed it to the prince. He said:

"Go up into the tower to the very top. There look about you and when you have decided what you like best of all you see, come back and tell me."

The prince took the key and at once mounted the tower. He had never before gone to the very top and he had never heard what was there. He went up and up until at last he saw a small iron door in the ceiling. He opened this with the golden key, pushed it back, and entered a large circular hall. The ceiling was blue and silver, like the heavens on a bright night when the stars shine, and the floor was covered with a green silken carpet. There were twelve tall windows set in gold frames, and on the crystal glass of each window a beautiful young girl was pictured in glowing colors. Every one of them was a princess with a royal crown upon her head. As the prince looked at them it seemed to him that each was more lovely than the last, and for the life of him he knew not which was the loveliest. Then they began to move as if alive, and they smiled at the prince and nodded, and looked as if they were about to speak.

Suddenly the prince noticed that one of the twelve windows was covered with a white curtain. He pulled the curtain aside and there without any question was the most beautiful princess of them all, clothed in pure white, with a silver girdle and a crown of pearls. Her face was deathly pale, and sad as the grave.

For a long time the prince stood before this picture in utter amazement and as he looked at it a pain seemed to enter his heart.

"This one I want for my bride," he said aloud, "this one and no other."

At these words the maiden bowed, flushed like a rose, and then instantly all the pictures disappeared.

When the prince told his father what he had seen and which maiden he had chosen, the old king was greatly troubled.

"My son," he said, "you did ill to uncover what was covered and in declaring this, your choice, you have exposed yourself to a great danger. This maiden is in the power of a black magician who holds her captive in an iron castle. Of all who have gone to rescue her not one has ever returned. However, what's done is done, and you have given your word. Go, then, try what fortune has in store for you, and may Heaven bring you back safe and sound."

So the prince bade his father farewell, mounted his horse, and rode forth to find his bride. His first adventure was to lose his way in a deep forest. He wandered about some time not knowing where to turn when suddenly he was hailed from behind with these words:

"Hey, there, master, wait a minute!"

He looked around and saw a tall man running toward him.

"Take me into your service, master," the tall man said. "If you do you won't regret it."

"What is your name," the prince asked, "and what can you do?"

"People call me Longshanks because I can stretch myself out. I'll show you. Do you see a bird's nest in the top of that tall fir? I'll get it down for you, and not by climbing the tree either."

So saying he began to stretch out and his body shot up and up until he was as tall as the fir tree. He reached over and got the nest and then, in a shorter time than it had taken him to stretch out, he reduced himself to his natural size.

"You do your trick very well," the prince said, "but just now a bird's nest isn't of much use to me. What I need is someone to show me the way out of this forest."

"H'm," Longshanks said, "that's an easy enough matter."

Again he began to stretch himself up and up and up until he was three times as tall as the highest pine. He looked around and said: "Over there, in that direction, is the nearest way out."

Then he made himself small again, took the horse by the bridle, walked ahead, and in a short time they emerged from the forest.

A broad plain stretched out before them and beyond it they could see tall gray rocks that looked like the walls of a great city and mountains overgrown with forests.

Longshanks pointed off across the plain and said: "There, master, goes a comrade of mine who would be very useful to you. You ought to take him into your service, too."

"Very well," said the prince, "call him here that I may find out what sort of a fellow he is."

"He is too far away to call," Longshanks said. "He wouldn't hear my voice and if he did he would be a long time in reaching us, for he has much to carry. I had better step over and get him myself."

As he said this, Longshanks stretched out and out until his head was lost in the clouds. He took two or three strides, reached his comrade, set him on his shoulder, and brought him to the prince.

The new man was heavily built and round as a barrel.

"Who are you?" the prince asked. "And what can you do?"

"I am called Girth," the man said. "I can widen myself."

"Let me see you do it," the prince said.

"Very well, master," said Girth, beginning to puff out, "I will. But take care! Ride off into the forest as fast as you can!"

The prince did not understand the warning, but he saw that Longshanks was in full flight, so he spurred his horse and galloped after him. It was well he did, for in another moment Girth would have crushed both him and his horse, so fast did he spread out, so huge did he become. In a short time he filled the whole plain until it looked as though a mountain had fallen upon it.

When the plain was entirely covered, he stopped expanding,

heaved a deep breath that shook the forest trees, and returned to his natural size.

"You made me run for my life!" the prince said. "I tell you I don't meet a fellow like you every day! By all means join me."

They went across the plain and as they neared the rocks they met a man whose eyes were bandaged with a handkerchief.

"Master," said Longshanks, "there is my other comrade. Take him into your service, too, and I can tell you you won't regret the bread he eats."

"Who are you?" the prince asked. "And why do you keep your eyes bandaged? You can't see where you're going."

"On the contrary, master, it is just because I see too well that I have to bandage my eyes. With bandaged eyes I see as well as other people whose eyes are uncovered. When I take the handkerchief off, my sight is so keen it goes straight through everything. When I look at anything intently it catches fire, and if it can't burn, it crumbles to pieces. On account of my sight I'm called Keen."

He untied the handkerchief, turned to one of the rocks opposite, and gazed at it with glowing eyes. Soon the rock began to crumble and fall to pieces. In a few moments it was reduced to a heap of sand. In the sand something gleamed like fire. Keen picked it up and handed it to the prince. It was a lump of pure gold.

"Ha, ha!" said the prince. "You are a fine fellow and worth more than wages! I should be a fool not to take you into my service. Since you have such keen eyes, look and tell me how much farther it is to the Iron Castle and what is happening there now."

"If you rode there alone," Keen answered, "you might get there within a year, but with us to help you, you will arrive this very day. Our coming is not unexpected, either, for at this very moment they are preparing supper for us."

"What is the captive princess doing?"

"She is sitting on a high tower behind an iron grating. The magician stands on guard."

"If you are real men," the prince cried, "you will help to free her."

The three comrades promised they would.

They led the prince straight through the gray rocks by a defile which Keen made with his eyes, and on and on through high mountains and deep forests. Whatever obstacle was in the way one or another of the three comrades was able to remove it.

By late afternoon they had crossed the last mountain, had left behind them the last stretch of dark forest, and they saw looming up ahead of them the Iron Castle.

Just as the sun sank, the prince and his followers crossed the drawbridge and entered the courtyard gate. Instantly the drawbridge lifted and the gate clanged shut.

They went through the courtyard and the prince put his horse in the stable, where he found a place all in readiness. Then the four of them marched boldly into the castle.

Everywhere—in the courtyard, in the stables, and now in the various rooms of the castle—they saw great numbers of richly clad men all of whom, masters and servants, had been turned to stone.

They went on from one room to another until they reached the banquet hall. This was brilliantly lighted and the table, with food and drink in abundance, was set for four persons. They waited, expecting someone to appear, but no one came. At last, overpowered by hunger, they sat down and ate and drank most heartily.

After supper they began to look about for a place to sleep. It was then without warning that the doors burst open and the magician appeared. He was a bent old man with a bald head and a gray beard that reached to his knees. He was dressed in a long black robe and he had, instead of a belt, three iron bands about his waist.

He led in a beautiful lady dressed in white, with a silver girdle and a crown of pearls. Her face was deathly pale and as sad as the grave. The prince recognized her instantly and sprang forward to meet her. Before he could speak, the magician raised his hand and said:

"I know why you have come. It is to carry off this princess. Very well, take her. If you can guard her for three nights so that she won't escape you, she is yours. But if she escapes you, then you and your men will suffer the fate of all those who have come before you, and be turned into stone."

Then, when he had motioned the princess to a seat, he turned and left the hall. The prince could not take his eyes from the princess, she was so beautiful. He tried to talk to her, asking her many questions, but she made him no answer. She might have been marble the way she never smiled and never looked at any of them.

He seated himself beside her, determined to stay all night on guard in order to prevent her escape. For greater security Longshanks stretched himself out on the floor like a strap and wound himself around the room the whole length of the wall. Girth sat in the doorway and puffed himself out until he filled that space so completely that not even a mouse could slip through. Keen took his place by a pillar in the middle of the hall.

But, alas, in a few moments they all grew heavy with drowsiness and in the end slept soundly all night long.

In the morning, in the early dawn the prince awoke, and with a pain in his heart that was like a blow from a dagger, he saw that the princess was gone. Instantly he aroused his men and asked them what was to be done.

"It's all right, master, don't worry," said Keen as he took a long look through the window. "I see her now. A hundred miles from here is a forest, in the midst of the forest an ancient oak, on the top of the oak an acorn. The princess is that acorn. Let Longshanks take me on his shoulders and we'll go get her."

Longshanks picked Keen up, stretched himself out, and set forth. He took ten miles at a stride and in the time it would take you or me to run around a cottage, here he was back again with the acorn in his hand. He gave it to the prince.

"Drop it, master, on the floor."

The prince dropped the acorn, and instantly the princess appeared.

As the sun came over the mountain tops the doors slammed open and the magician entered. A crafty smile was on his face. But when he saw the princess the smile changed to a scowl, he growled in rage, and bang! one of the iron bands about his waist burst asunder. Then he took the princess by the hand and dragged her off.

That whole day the prince had nothing to do but wander about the castle and look at all the strange and curious things it contained. It seemed as if at some one instant all life had been arrested. In one hall he saw a prince who had been turned into stone while he was brandishing his sword. The sword was still uplifted. In another room there was a stone knight who was taken in the act of flight. He had stumbled on the threshold but he had not yet fallen. A serving man sat under the chimney eating his supper. With one hand he was reaching a piece of roast meat to his mouth. Days, months, perhaps years had gone by, but the meat had not yet touched his lips. There were many others, all of them still in whatever position they happened to be when the magician had cried: "Be ye turned into stone!"

In the courtyard and the stables the prince found many fine horses overtaken by the same fate.

Outside the castle everything was equally dead and silent. There were trees but they had no leaves, there was a river but it didn't flow, and no fish could live in its waters. There wasn't a singing bird anywhere, and there wasn't even one tiny flower.

In the morning, at noon, and at supper-time the prince and his companions found a rich feast prepared for them. Unseen hands served them food and poured them wine.

Then after supper, as on the preceding night, the doors burst open and the magician led in the princess, whom he handed over to the prince to guard for the second night.

Of course, the prince and his men determined to fight off drowsiness this time with all their strength. But in spite of this determination again they fell asleep. At dawn the prince awoke and saw that the princess was gone.

He jumped up and shook Keen by the shoulder.

"Wake up, Keen, wake up! Where is the princess?"

Keen rubbed his eyes, took one look out of the window, and said:

"There, I see her. Two hundred miles from here is a mountain, in the mountain is a rock, in the rock a precious stone. That stone is the princess. If Longshanks will carry me over there we'll get her."

Longshanks put Keen on his shoulder, stretched himself out until he was able to go twenty miles at a stride, and off he went. Keen fixed his glowing eyes on the mountain and the mountain crumbled. Then the rock that was inside the mountain broke into a thousand

Longshanks, Girth and Keen.

pieces and there was the precious stone glittering among the pieces.

They picked it up and carried it back to the prince. As soon as he dropped it on the floor the princess reappeared.

When the magician came in and found her there, his eyes sparkled with anger, and bang! the second of his iron bands cracked and burst asunder. Rumbling and growling he led the princess away.

That day passed as the day before. After supper the magician brought back the princess and, looking fiercely at the prince, he sneered and said: "Now we'll see who wins, you or I."

This night the prince and his men tried harder than ever to stay awake. They didn't even allow themselves to sit down, but kept walking. All in vain. One after another they fell asleep on their feet and again the princess escaped.

In the morning the prince, as usual, was the first to awake. When he saw the princess was gone, he aroused Keen. "Wake up, Keen!" he cried. "Look out and tell me where the princess is."

This time Keen had to look long before he saw her.

"Master, she is far away. Three hundred miles from here there is a black sea. At the bottom of that sea is a shell. In that shell is a golden ring. That ring is the princess. But don't be worried, master, we'll get her. This time let Longshanks take Girth as well as me, for we may need him."

So Longshanks put Keen on one shoulder and Girth on the other. Then he stretched himself out until he was able to cover thirty miles at a stride. When they reached the black sea Keen showed Longshanks where to reach down in the water for the shell. Longshanks reached down as far as he could but not far enough to touch bottom.

"Wait, comrades, wait," said Girth. "Now it's my turn to help."

With that he puffed himself out and out as far as he could. Then he lay down on the beach and began drinking up the sea. He drank it in such great gulps that soon Longshanks was able to reach bottom and to get the shell. Longshanks took out the ring and then, putting his comrades on his shoulders, started back for the castle. He was not able to go fast, for Girth, with half the sea in his stomach, was very heavy. At last in desperation Longshanks turned Girth upside down and shook him and instantly the great plain upon which he emptied him turned into a huge lake. It was all poor Girth could do to scramble out of the water and back to Longshanks' shoulder.

Meanwhile at the castle the prince was awaiting his men in great anxiety. Morning was breaking and still they did not come. As the first rays of the sun shot over the mountain tops, the doors slammed open and the magician stood on the threshold. He glanced around and when he saw that the princess was not there he gave a mocking laugh and entered. But at that very instant there was the crash of a breaking window, a golden ring struck the floor, and lo! the princess! Keen had seen in time the danger that was threatening the prince, and Longshanks had hurled the ring through the window.

The magician bellowed with rage until the castle shook, and then, bang! the third iron band burst asunder and from what had once been the magician a black crow arose and flew out of the broken window and was never seen again.

Instantly the beautiful princess blushed like a rose and was able to speak and to thank the prince for delivering her.

Everything in the castle came to life. The prince with the up-lifted sword finished his stroke and put the sword into its scabbard. The knight who was stumbling fell, and jumped up holding his nose to see whether he still had it. The serving man under the chimney put the meat into his mouth and kept on eating. And so every one finished what he had been doing at the moment of enchantment. The horses, too, came to life and stamped and neighed.

Around the castle the trees burst into leaf. Flowers covered the meadows. High in the heavens the lark sang, and in the flowing river there were shoals of tiny fish. Everything was alive again, everything happy.

The knights who had been restored to life gathered in the hall to thank the prince for their deliverance. But the prince said to them:

"You have nothing to thank me for. If it had not been for these, my three trusty servants, Longshanks, Girth, and Keen I should have met the same fate as you."

The prince set out at once on his journey home with his bride and his three serving men. When he reached home, the old king, who had given him up for lost, wept for joy at his unexpected return.

All the knights whom the prince had rescued were invited to the wedding, which took place at once and lasted for three weeks.

When it was over, Longshanks, Girth, and Keen presented them-selves to the young king and told him that they were again going out into the world to look for work. The young king urged them to stay.

"I will give you everything you need as long as you live," he promised them, "and you won't have to exert yourselves at all."

But such an idle life was not to their liking. So they took their leave and started out again and to this day they are still knocking around somewhere.

Tales From Russia

THE BUN

By *VALERY CARRICK*

With illustrations by THE AUTHOR

ONCE upon a time there was an old man, and one day he wanted something nice to eat, so he said to his wife: "My dear, please make me a bun."

But she answered: "What am I to make it of? We have no flour."

"What nonsense," he said, "of course we have! You've only got to scrape the sides of the bin and sweep its floor and you'll get plenty!"

So his wife took a feather brush, and she scraped the sides and swept the floor of the bin, and so got a little flour together. Then she kneaded the dough with cream, rolled out the bun, spread it over with butter and then put it in the oven.

And the bun turned out simply splendid! She took it out of the oven and put it on the window sill to get cold.

"What am I to make it of?"

And there the bun lay and lay, and he began to feel lonely, so he just took and rolled off!

From the window sill he rolled down on to the bench, from the bench on to the floor, and over the floor to the door.

274

Then he rolled right over the threshold into the lobby, out of the lobby onto the front door steps and down the steps right out of doors, and rolled straight along the road into the field.

Suddenly he met a hare, and the hare said to him: "Mr. Bun, Mr. Bun, I shall eat you up!"

"No, you sha'n't, Mr. Hare, for I'll sing you a song." And he started singing: "I'm Mr. Bun, I'm Mr. Bun, I was scraped from the sides and swept from the floor of the bin, I was kneaded with cream and fried in butter,

"She put it in the oven."

and was put to cool on the window sill, but I got away from gaffer and I got away from grannie, and I sha'n't find it hard to get away from you!" And when he had finished his song he went on rolling farther, and was out of sight before Mr. Hare had time to look.

"I was put on the window sill."

And he went on rolling, when suddenly he met a wolf, and the wolf said to him: "Mr. Bun, Mr. Bun, I shall eat you up!"

"No, you sha'n't, Mr. Wolf, for I'll sing you a song." And he started singing: "I'm Mr. Bun, I'm Mr. Bun, I was scraped from the sides and swept from the floor of the bin, I was kneaded with cream and fried in butter, and was put to cool on the window sill, but I got away from gaffer and I got away from grannie and I got away from Mr. Hare, and I think I'll find it easy enough to get away from you!"

And he went on rolling farther, when suddenly he met a bear. And the bear said to him: "Mr. Bun, Mr. Bun, I shall eat you up!"

"Indeed you shall not, you old crooked-paws, you couldn't if you tried." And he started singing: "For I'm Mr. Bun, I'm Mr. Bun, I was scraped from the sides, and swept from the floor of the bin, I was kneaded with cream and fried in butter, and was put to cool on the window sill, but I got away from gaffer and I got away from grannie, I got away from Mr. Hare, and got away from Mr. Wolf —Good-bye, Bruin!"

"I got away from gaffer and grannie."

And he went on rolling farther, when suddenly he met a fox, and the fox said to him: "How do you do, Mr. Bun, how pretty you are, and how well-baked you are!"

And Mr. Bun was pleased at being praised, and he started singing: "I'm Mr. Bun, I'm Mr. Bun, I was scraped from the sides and swept from the floor of the bin, I was kneaded with cream and fried in butter, and was put to cool on the window sill, but I got away from gaffer and I got away from grannie, I got away from Mr. Hare, and got away from Mr. Wolf, I got away from Bruin and I'll get away from you!"

"And I'll run away from you."

"That's a fine song," said the fox, "please sing it me again, but come and sit on my nose; I've got so deaf lately."

So Mr. Bun jumped up on Mr. Fox's nose and sang his song again. And the fox said: "Thank you, Mr. Bun, but please sing it just once again. And come and sit on my tongue, then I shall hear still better." And Mr. Fox put out his tongue and Mr. Bun jumped on to it, and Mr. Fox just closed his mouth and ate Mr. Bun up.

MR. SAMSON CAT

By *VALERY CARRICK*

With illustrations by THE AUTHOR

ONCE upon a time a cat came running out of a certain village, and a fox came running out of a certain forest, and they met.

"How do you do?" said the fox. "How do you do?" said the cat. "What's your name?" said the fox. "Mr. Samson Cat, and what's yours?" "They call me Widow Fox." "Let's live together," said the cat. "Very well," said the fox. And so they settled down in the Widow Fox's cottage.

"How do you do?" said the fox.
"How do you do?" said the cat.

One day Mr. Cat went out for a walk to gather berries in the forest, when a hare came running along. He never noticed the cat and jumped right on to the top of him.

Mr. Cat said: "F-r-r-r!" and the hare took fright and set off running so fast, that you could just see his heels twinkle, and he was gone!

Then the hare met a wolf, and said to him: "As I was running past Widow Fox's cottage, an unheard-of beast jumped right on to the top of me, he was so big and so dreadful! He was just going to swallow me up alive, only my legs saved me!"

"I must go and have a look," said the wolf.

"Don't, he will eat you up!" said the hare.

Nevertheless the wolf went off to Widow Fox's cottage.

And just then Widow Fox and Mr. Samson Cat had dragged a dead sheep into their courtyard, and were hard at it behind the fence, gobbling him up.

"F-r-r-r!" said the cat, and the hare took fright.

When Widow Fox had had enough, she came out at the gate, and there Mr. Wolf came up to her. He could hear how Mr. Cat was going on behind the fence, and said to Widow Fox: "Who is that there in your courtyard, Widow Fox?"

"That's the mighty Mr. Samson Cat. He killed a sheep in a fight and now he's eating it. You'd better go away quickly, or else the same thing will happen to you."

Meantime Mr. Cat was working hard at the sheep and crying: "Mee-*ow*, mee-*ow!*" And Mr. Wolf thought he was saying: "Not en*ough,* not en*ough,*" and he thought: "Good gracious, he hasn't had enough after eating a sheep!" and he grew frightened and ran away.

And as he was running he saw a pig rubbing his side against a tree. And he said to him: "Have you heard the news? We sha'n't be able to make a living in *this* forest any more; Widow Fox has got a dreadful animal living with her, the mighty Mr. Samson Cat. He eats four sheep a day, and then says he hasn't had enough."

And Mr. Pig flapped his ears and winked his eye and said: "I should like to have a look at this beast!"

"What are you thinking of?" said Mr. Wolf. "You'd better not go near the place!"

And while they were standing and talking, a bear come up, and Mr. Pig said to him: "Uncle Bruin, have you heard the news? Widow Fox has a beast living with her called the mighty Mr. Samson Cat. He eats ten oxen a day, and then says he hasn't had enough!"

"What a terrible thing," said Bruin, "I *should* like to see that beast!"

So they discussed this way and that, and sent Mr. Pig to Widow Fox to ask if they might just with one eye have a peep at Mr. Samson Cat. And Mr. Pig came to Widow Fox and said: "How do you do? how do you do, Widow Fox? We have heard tell of your Mr. Samson Cat and we should so like to have a look at him. Do please tell us how this could be arranged without the danger of his eating us up!"

And Widow Fox thought for a bit and then said: "This is how you must arrange it: bake a *lot* of pies and get a *lot* of honey, and invite us to come and see you. *Perhaps* he won't harm you then."

And Mr. Pig was delighted and ran back to his friends and told Mr. Wolf and Mr. Bruin: "Widow Fox says: 'Bake a *lot* of pies and get a *lot* of honey, and we will come and see you, and *perhaps* the mighty Mr. Samson Cat won't eat you all up."

And so Bruin began to get the honey, Mr. Wolf began to bake the pies, and Mr. Pig began to tidy up, and get ready to receive the expected guests.

And they baked a *lot* of pies, and got a *lot* of honey, and Bruin said: "I shall get up into a tree; from there I shall see better when the guests begin to arrive." And so he climbed up.

And Mr. Wolf said: "For a whole day I've been working at those pies. I shall go and rest for a bit under this log." And he crawled under the log and lay down there.

And Mr. Pig said: "I have got hot all over, making everything

There was nothing to be done but start eating without their hosts.

tidy. I shall go and get into the shade for a bit." And he went and hid in the brushwood.

Meanwhile Widow Fox and the mighty Mr. Samson Cat came along, and their hosts were not there! Bruin was up an oak, Mr. Wolf under a log, and Mr. Pig in the brushwood. So there was nothing to be done but start eating without their hosts, and Widow Fox went for the honey while Mr. Cat got to work on the stuffed pies.

Suddenly Mr. Cat heard something rustling in the grass, and this was Mr. Pig's tail rustling from fright. Mr. Cat thought: "I expect that's a mouse," and dashed off and caught Mr. Pig by the tail.

Mr. Pig squealed and ran off as hard as he could, and ran his snout straight into the stump of a tree.

Mr. Cat was really just as much frightened himself, and jumped on to the tree. At this, Bruin's paws grew weak from fright, and he fell plump down from the tree right on to the top of the log under which Mr. Wolf was lying.

And Mr. Wolf thought: "My end has come," and he jumped out from under the log and started off running as hard as he could go. And it was not till evening that Mr. Wolf, Mr. Pig and Bruin met again and told each other their experiences.

Mr. Pig said: "Well, I never! The way he caught hold of my tail and dashed my head against the stump!"

And Bruin said: "The stump was nothing! He tore out the whole oak tree by the roots and began to shake it. How could I possibly hold on? I was lucky not to fall into his jaws."

And Mr. Wolf said: "And the way he put one on me with that oak tree! Well, that *is* a beast, if you like!"

And they all began to shake their heads and said: "Well, that *is* a beast, if you like! There's no mistake about Mr. Samson Cat!"

THE LITTLE HUMPBACKED HORSE

By POST WHEELER

Illustrations by MICHAEL G. PERTS

ACROSS the wide sea-ocean, on the farther side of high mountains, beyond thick forests, in a village that faced the sky, there once lived an old peasant who had three sons. The eldest, Danilo, was the most knowing lad in the place; the second, Gavrilo, was neither clever nor dull; and the youngest, who was named Ivan, was called a dullard, because while his brothers, after they had sowed their wheat and threshed it, drove to town and went merry-making, he cared to do nothing but lie in the corner on the stove and sleep. So the whole neighborhood called him "Little Fool Ivan."

Now one morning when the peasant went to his stack, he found to his dismay that someone in the night had stolen some of the hay; so that evening he sent his eldest son to watch for the thief.

Danilo, accordingly, took his ax and his hay-fork and went to the field. On this night there was a biting frost and heavy snow, and he said to himself, "Why should I freeze myself stiff to save a little worthless fodder?" So, finding a warm corner, he lay down, wrapped himself in his thick fur coat and went to sleep.

In the morning he saw that some of the hay had been stolen. He rolled himself well in the snow, went home and knocked at the door till his father let him in.

"Didst thou see the thief?" asked the peasant.

"I heard him prowling not far off," answered Danilo, "but I shouted and he dared not come nearer. However, I have had a terrible night, thou mayst be sure! It was bitter cold and I am frozen to the marrow!"

His father praised him, calling him a good son, and the next night sent his second son to watch.

So Gavrilo took his hatchet and his long knife and went to the field. Now on this night it was raining, and he said to himself,

"They say my brother is cleverer than I, but I am at least knowing enough to take care of myself, and why should I stand all night wet to the skin for the sake of a little dried grass?" So, having found a sheltered spot, he lay down, covered himself with his warm cloak and went to sleep.

In the morning he saw that more of the hay had been stolen. He went to a brook, poured water over his clothing so that it was drenched, went home and knocked at the door till it was opened.

"Didst thou see the thief?" asked his father.

"I did," Gavrilo answered, "and laid hold of his coat and gave him such a beating that he will remember it. But the rascal tore away and ran so fast that I could not catch him. But I have had a night for my pains, I can tell you! The rain poured every minute and I am soaked to the bones!"

His father praised him likewise, calling him a brave fellow till he was as proud as a cock with five hens; and the next evening said to Little Fool Ivan: "Now, my son, it is thy turn to watch, but thou art such a simpleton thou canst not even keep the sparrows from the peas. It will be small use for thee to go."

However, Little Fool Ivan climbed down from the stove, put a crust of bread under his coat and went whistling off to the field. He did not lie down as his brothers had done, but went about the whole field, looking on every side, and when the moon rose he sat down under a bush, counted the stars in the sky and ate his crust with a good appetite.

Suddenly, just at midnight, he heard the neigh of a horse, and looking out from the bush he saw a wonderful mare, as white as snow, with a golden mane curled in little rings.

"So," said Little Fool Ivan to himself, "thou art, then, the thief of our hay! Only come a little nearer and I will be on thy back as tight as a locust!" The mare came nearer and nearer and at last, choosing the right moment, Ivan leaped out, seized her tail and jumped on to her back, wrong side before.

The white mare's eyes darted forth lightning. She curled her neck like a snake, reared on her hind legs and shot off like an arrow. She raced over fields, she flew like a bird over ditches, she galloped like the wind along mountains and dashed through thick forests. But run as she would, and rear and snort as she might, she could not throw off Little Fool Ivan. He clung to her tail and stuck to her back like a burr.

At last, just as day was beginning to dawn, the mare stopped and, panting, spoke to him with a human voice. "Well, Ivan," she said, "since thou canst sit me, it seems thou must possess me. Take me home and give me a place to rest for three days. Only, each morning, just at sunrise, let me out to roll in the dew. And when the three days are up, I will bear thee three such colts as were never heard of before. Two of them will be Tzar's horses, of brown and gray, and these thou mayst sell if thou choosest. But the third will be a little humpbacked stallion only three feet high, with ears a foot long, and him thou shalt neither sell for gold nor give a gift to anyone whatsoever. So long as thou art in the white world he shall be thy faithful servant. In winter he will show thee how to be warm, and when thou dost hunger he will show thee where to find bread. In return for these three colts, thou shalt release me and give me my freedom."

Little Fool Ivan agreed. He rode the white mare home, hid her in an empty shepherd's corral, whose entrance he covered with a horse-cloth, and went home and knocked at the door till his brothers let him in.

When they saw him, they began to question him. "Well, no doubt thou didst see the thief! Perhaps thou didst even catch him! Tell us."

"To be sure I did," he replied. "I jumped on the thief's back and laid hold of the villain's tail, and we ran a thousand versts or more. My neck was nearly broken in the end and ye may believe I am tired!" So saying he climbed on to the stove without taking off even his bark sandals, and went to sleep, while his brothers and his father roared with laughter at the story, not a word of which, of course, they believed.

Little Fool Ivan kept the white mare hidden from all other eyes. For three mornings he rose at daybreak and let her out to roll on the dewy meadow and on the fourth morning, when he went to the corral, he found beside her, as she had promised, three colts. Two were most beautiful to see; they were of brown and gray, their eyes were like blue sapphires, their manes and tails were golden and curled in little rings, and their hoofs were of diamond, studded with pearls. But the third was a tiny horse like a toy, with two humps on his back and ears a foot long.

Ivan was overjoyed. He thanked the white mare and she, released, curled her neck like a snake, reared on her hind legs and shot off like an arrow. Then he began to admire the three colts, especially the little humpbacked one which frisked like a dog about Ivan's knees, clapping his long ears together from playfulness and dancing up and down on his little hoofs. He kept them hidden, as he had the white mare, in the shepherd's corral, letting them out each morning at sunrise to roll in the dew and spending many hours petting them, talking to them, currying their coats till they shone like silver, and braiding their golden manes.

Time went on (but whether it was three weeks or three years that flew away matters little, since one need not run after them) till it befell, one day, that his eldest brother, Danilo, who had been to town for a holiday, returned late at night and, missing his way in the darkness, stumbled into the shepherd's corral. Hearing a sound, he made a light and to his astonishment saw the three young horses.

"So—ho!" he thought. "Now I understand why Little Fool Ivan spends so much time in this old corral!" He ran to the house and woke his brother Gavrilo. "Come quickly," he said, "and see what three horses our young idiot of a brother has found for himself!" And Gavrilo followed him as fast as he could, straight across a nettlefield barefoot, since he did not wait to put on his boots.

When they came to the corral the two fine horses were neighing and snorting. Their eyes were burning like beautiful blue candles and their curling gold manes and tails and their hoofs of diamond and pearls filled the two brothers with envy. Each looked at them so long that he was nearly made blind of one eye. Then Danilo said:

"They say it takes a fool to find a treasure. But where in the white world could Little Fool Ivan have got these marvelous steeds?

As for thee and me, brother, we might search our heads off and we would find not even two *roubles!*"[1]

"That is true," answered Gavrilo. "We should have the horses, and not Little Fool Ivan. Now I have an idea. Next week is the Fair at the capital. Many foreigners will come in ships to buy linen, and it is said that even Tzar Saltan will be there. Let us come here by night and take the horses thither and sell them. They will fetch a great price and we will divide it equally between us two. Thou knowest what a good time we could have with the money, and while we are slapping our full purses and enjoying ourselves our dolt of an Ivan will not be able to guess where his horses have gone visiting. What sayest thou? Let us shake hands upon it."

So the two brothers agreed, kissed each other, crossed themselves, and went home planning how to spend the money they should get for the horses.

When the next week came round, accordingly, they said a prayer before the holy images, asked their father's blessing and departed to the Fair. When they had gone some distance, however, they returned to the village secretly after nightfall, took the two fine horses out of the corral and again set out for the capital.

Next morning, when Ivan came to the corral, he found to his grief that the beautiful pair had vanished. There was left only the little humpbacked horse that was turning round and round before him, capering, clapping his long ears together and dancing up and down from joy. Ivan began to weep salt tears. "O my horses, brown and gray!" he cried; "my good steeds with golden manes! Did I not caress you enough? What wretch—may he tumble through a bridge!—hath stolen you away?"

At this the humpbacked horse neighed and spoke in a human voice: "Don't worry, little master," he said. "It was thy brothers who took them away, and I can take thee to them. Sit on my back and hold fast by my ears, and have a care not to fall off!" So Little Fool Ivan sat on his back, holding up his feet lest they drag on the ground, and laid hold of his ears, and the pony shook himself till his little mane quivered, reared on his hind legs, snorted three times

---

[1] One *rouble* = about fifty-two cents.

and shot away like an arrow, so fast that the dust curled under his feet. And almost before Ivan had time to take breath, he was versts away on the highroad to the capital.

When his brothers saw Little Fool Ivan coming after them like the wind on his toy horse, they knew not what to do. "For shame, ye rascals!" shouted he as he overtook them. "Ye may be more clever than I, but I have never stolen your steeds!"

"Our dear little brother!" said Danilo. "There is little use denying. We took thy two horses, but we did so with no thought of wrong to thee. As thou knowest, this has been a poor season with our crops and a bad harvest, and for despair I and Gavrilo have been like to hang ourselves. When we came by chance upon these two steeds, we considered that thou hadst little knowledge of bargaining and trading, and doubtless knew not their worth, whereas we could get for them at least a thousand roubles at the Fair. With this money we could help our little father, as thou wouldst wish, and we purposed to buy besides for thee a red cap and new boots with red heels. So if we have erred, do thou forgive us."

"Well," answered Little Fool Ivan, "thy words sound fair enough. If this was your thought, go and sell my two horses, but I will go with you." So, though they wished him well strangled, the two brothers had no choice but to take him with them, and thus they came to the capital.

Now when they reached the market place where the traders were assembled, so wonderful were the two steeds that the people swarmed about them, buzzing like bees in a hive, till for the press no one could pass either in or out, and there was great commotion. Perceiving this, the head man sent a crier who blew on a gold trumpet and shouted in a loud voice: "O merchants and buyers! crowd not, but disperse one and all!" But they would not move from the horses. Then the head man rode out himself, in slippers and fur cap, with a body of soldiers who cleared the way with their whips, so that he came to the middle of the market and saw the horses with his own eyes.

"God's world is wonderful!" he cried, rubbing his head. "What marvels doth it hold!" And bidding the crier proclaim that no buyer should buy them, he rode to the Palace, came to the presence of the Tzar, and told him of them.

The Tzar could not sit still for curiosity. He ordered his state carriage and rode at once to the market, and when he saw the horses, tugging at their halters and gnawing their bits, with eyes shining like sapphires, their curling golden manes, and hoofs of diamonds and pearls, he could not take his eyes from them. He examined them on both sides, called to them with caressing words, patted their backs and stroked their manes, and asked who owned them.

"O Tzar's Majesty," said Little Fool Ivan, "I am their master."

"What wilt thou take for them?" asked the Tzar.

"Thrice five caps full of silver," answered Ivan, "and five roubles beside."

"Good," said the Tzar, and ordered the money given him. Then ten grooms, with gray hair and golden uniforms, led the pair to the royal stables. On the way, however, the horses knocked the grooms down, bit to pieces their bridles, and ran neighing back to Ivan.

Then the Tzar called him to his presence, and said: "It seems that my wonderful steeds will obey only thee. There is no help but that I make thee my Chief Equerry and Master of my Stables." And he ordered the crier at once to proclaim the appointment. So Little Fool Ivan called his brothers Danilo and Gavrilo, gave to them the fifteen caps full of silver, and the five roubles beside, kissed them, bade them not neglect their father but to care for him in his old age, and led the two horses to the royal stables, while a great throng of people followed, watching the little humpbacked horse who went dancing after them up the street.

The telling of a tale is quick, but time itself passes slowly. Five weeks went by, while Ivan wore red robes, ate sweet food and slept his fill. Each morning at sunrise he took the horses to roll in the dew on the open field, and fed them with honey and white wheat till their coats shone like satin. But the more the Tzar praised him, the more envious many in the Court were of him. As the saying is, one need not be rich only so he have curly hair and is clever; and because Little Fool Ivan had succeeded so easily, people hated him, and the one who hated him most was the officer who had been the Tzar's

Master of Horse before his coming. Each day this man pondered how he might bring about Ivan's ruin, and at night he crept to the stables and hid in the wheat bins, hoping to catch his rival in some fault.

When this failed, he went to all those Court officials who were envious of the new favorite, and bade them hang their heads and go about with sorrowful faces, promising, when the Tzar asked the cause, to tell him what would ruin Little Fool Ivan. They did so, and the Tzar, noticing their sad looks asked:

"O Boyars, why are ye cast down and crestfallen?"

Then he who had given this counsel stood forth, and said: "O Tzar's Majesty! not for ourselves do we grieve, but we fear thy new Master of the Stables is a wizard and an evildoer and familiar with Black Magic. For he doth boast openly that he could fetch thee, if he chose, in addition to thy two wonderful steeds, the fabled Pig with the Golden Bristles and the Silver Tusks, with her twenty sucklings, who live in the hidden valley of the Land of the South."

Hearing this, the Tzar was wroth. "Bring before me this wild boaster," he said, "and he shall make good his words without delay!" Thereupon they ran to the stables, where Little Fool Ivan lay asleep, and kicked him wide awake and brought him to the Tzar, who looked at him angrily, and said: "Hear my command. If in three days thou hast not brought hither, from the hidden valley of the Land of the South, the Pig with the Golden Bristles and Silver Tusks, together with her twenty sucklings, I will deliver thee to an evil death!"

Little Fool Ivan went out to the stable weeping bitterly. Hearing him coming, the little humpbacked horse began to dance and to flap its ears together for joy, but as soon as he saw his master's tears he almost began to sob himself. "Why are thou not merry, little master?" he asked. "Why does thy head hang lower than thy shoulders?"

Ivan embraced and kissed the little horse, and told him the task the Tzar had laid upon him. "Do not weep," said the pony; "I can help thee. Nor is this service so hard a one. Go thou to the Tzar and ask of him a bucket of golden corn, a bucket of silver wheat, and a silken lasso."

So Ivan went before the Tzar and asked, as he had been bidden, for the wheat, the corn, and the silken lasso, and brought them to the stables. "Now," said the little humpbacked horse, "lie down and sleep, for the morning holds more wisdom than the evening."

Little Fool Ivan lay down to sleep, and next morning the pony waked him at dawn. "Mount me now," he said, "with thy grain and thy silken rope, and we will be off, for the way is far."

Ivan put the silver wheat and the golden corn into stout bags, slung them across the pony's neck, and with his silken lasso wound about his waist, mounted, and the little humpbacked horse darted away like an eagle. He scoured wide plains, leaped across swift rivers, and sped along mountain ridges, and after running without pause for a day and night, he stopped in a deep valley on the edge of a dreary wood, and said: "Little master, this is the Land of the South, and in this valley lives the Pig with the Golden Bristles. She comes each day to root in this forest. Take thou the golden corn and the silver wheat and pour them on the ground in two piles, at some distance apart, and conceal thyself. When the Pig comes she will run to the corn, but the sucklings will begin to eat the wheat, and while the mother is not by, thou mayest secure them. Bring them to me and tie them to my saddle with the silken lasso, and I will bear thee back. As for the Pig, she will follow her sucklings."

Little Fool Ivan did all as the little horse bade him. He entered the forest, put the corn and wheat in two piles, hid himself in a thicket near the latter, and rested till evening, when there came a sound of grunting and the Pig with the Golden Bristles and Silver Tusks led her young into the forest. She saw the corn, and at once began to eat it, while the twenty sucklings ran to the wheat. He caught them, one by one, tied them with the silken lasso, and, hastening to the little horse, made them fast to his saddle bow. Scarce had he mounted when the Pig perceived them, and seeing her sucklings borne away, came running after them, erecting her golden bristles and gnashing her silver tusks.

The little humpbacked horse sped away like a flash back along the road they had come, with the Pig pursuing them, and, after running without stop for a night and a day, they arrived after dark at the Tzar's capital. Little Fool Ivan rode to the Palace courtyard, set down there the twenty suckling-pigs, still tied by the silken lasso, went to the stable and fell asleep.

In the morning the Tzar was greatly astonished to see that Little Fool Ivan had performed the task, and was delighted to possess the new treasure. He sent for his Master of Horse, praised him and gave him a rich present, so the envious ones were made still more envious.

So, after some days, these came to the Tzar and said: "Thy Master of Horse, O Tzar's Majesty, doth boast now that the bringing of the wonderful Pig with her twenty sucklings was but a small service, and that he could, if he but chose, bring to thee the Mare with Seven Manes and her seven fierce stallions that graze on a green meadow between the crystal hills of the Caucasus."

Then, in more anger than before, the Tzar bade them bring Little Fool Ivan to his presence and said sternly: "Heed my royal word. If in seven days thou hast not brought hither from between the crystal hills of the Caucasus the Seven-Maned Mare with her seven stallions, I will send thee where the crows shall pick thy bones!"

Little Fool Ivan went weeping to the little humpbacked horse and told him of the Tzar's new command. "Grieve not, little master," said the other; "let not thy bright head droop. I can aid thee. Nor is this service too hard a one. Go thou to the Tzar and demand that he prepare at once a stone stable with one door opening into it and another opening out. Ask also for a horse's skin and an iron hammer of twelve *poods*[1] weight."

Ivan obeyed. He demanded the stable, the horse's skin and the iron hammer, and when all was ready the little horse said: "Lie down and sleep now, little master. The morning is wiser than the evening." Little Fool Ivan lay down and slept, and next morning at daybreak the pony waked him. Ivan tied the horse's skin to the saddle bow, slung the hammer about his neck and mounted, and the little humpbacked horse darted away like a swallow, till the dust

[1] One *pood* = about forty pounds.

curled about his legs like a whirlwind. When he had run three days and four nights without rest, he stopped between two crystal hills and said:

"Yonder lies the green meadow whereon each evening grazes the Mare with Seven Manes and her seven fierce stallions. Take now thy

"Grieve not, little master," said the little horse.

horse's skin and sew me within it, and presently the mare will come and will set upon me with her teeth. While she rends the skin from me, do thou run and strike her between her two ears with thy twelve pood hammer, so that she will be stunned. Mount me then in haste, and thou mayst lead her after thee, and as for the seven stallions, they will follow."

So Little Fool Ivan sewed the little horse in the horse's skin, and when the mare with the seven stallions came, the stallions stood afar off, but the mare set upon him and rent the skin from him. Then Ivan ran and struck her with the iron hammer and stunned her, and instantly, holding by her seven manes, leaped to the back of the little humpbacked horse.

Scarce had he mounted, when the seven fierce stallions saw him, and came galloping after them, screaming with rage. But the little humpbacked horse was off like a dart back along the road they had come, and when they had traveled without stopping three nights and four days, they arrived at the Tzar's capital. Little Fool Ivan rode to the stone stable that had been built, went in at one door, and leaving therein the Mare with the Seven Manes, rode out of the other and barred it behind him, and the seven stallions, following the mare, were caught. Then Ivan went to his own place and went to sleep.

When they reported to the Tzar that this time also Little Fool Ivan had performed his task, the Tzar was more rejoiced than before and bestowed high rank and all manner of honors upon him, till, for hatred and malice the envious ones were beside themselves.

They conferred together, and coming before the Tzar, they said: "O Tzar's Majesty! to bring thee the mare and the stallions, thy Master of Horse boasteth now, was but a small service, saying that, if he willed, he could fetch thee from across three times nine lands, where the little red sun rises, the beautiful Girl-Tzar, whom thou hast so long desired for thy bride, who lives on the sea-ocean in a golden boat, which she rows with silver oars."

Then was the Tzar mightily angered. "Summon this boaster again before me," he commanded, and when Little Fool Ivan was come in, he bade him bring him the lovely Girl-Tzar within twelve days or pay the forfeit with his head. So, for the third time, Ivan went weeping to the little humpbacked horse and told him the Tzar's will.

"Dry thy tears, little master," said the other, "for I can assist thee. This is not, after all, the hardest service. Go thou to the Tzar and ask for two handkerchiefs cunningly embroidered in gold, a silken tent woven with gold thread and with golden tent-poles, gold and silver dishes, and all manner of wines and sweetmeats."

Ivan lost no time in obeying and when they were ready brought them to the stables. "Lie down and sleep now," said the little horse. "Tomorrow is wiser than today." Accordingly Little Fool Ivan lay down and slept till the little horse woke him at daybreak. He put all that had been prepared into a bag and mounted, and the little humpbacked horse sped away like the wind.

For six days they rode, a hundred thousand versts, till they reached a forest at the very end of the world, where the little red sun rises out of the blue sea-ocean. Here they stopped and Ivan alighted.

"Pitch now thy tent on the white sand," said the little horse. "In it spread thy embroidered handkerchiefs and on them put the wine and the gold and silver plates piled with sweetmeats. As for thee, do thou hide behind the tent and watch. From her golden boat the Girl-Tzar will see the tent and will approach it. Let her enter it and eat and drink her fill. Then go in, seize and hold her, and call for me." So saying, he ran to hide himself in the forest.

Ivan pitched the tent, prepared the food and wine, and lying down behind the tent, made a tiny hole in the silk through which to see, and waited. And before long the golden boat came sailing over the blue sea-ocean. The beautiful Girl-Tzar alighted to look at the splendid tent and, seeing the wine and sweetmeats, entered and began to eat and drink. So graceful and lovely was she that no tale could describe her and Little Fool Ivan could not gaze enough. He forgot what the little horse had told him and he was still peering through the hole in the silk when the beautiful maiden sprang up, left the tent, leaped into her golden boat, and the silver oars carried her far away on the sea-ocean.

When the little humpbacked horse came running up, Ivan too late repented of his folly. "I am guilty before thee!" he said. "And now I shall never see her again!" and he began to shed tears.

"Never mind," said the little horse. "She will come again tomorrow, but if thou failest next time we must needs go back without her and thy head will be lost."

Next day Little Fool Ivan spread the wines and sweetmeats and lay down to watch as before; and again the lovely Girl-Tzar came rowing in her golden boat and entered the tent and began to regale herself. And while she ate and drank Ivan ran in and seized and held her and called to the little horse. The girl cried out and fought to be free, but when she saw how handsome Little Fool Ivan was, she quite forgot to struggle. He mounted and put her before him on the saddle, and the humpbacked horse dashed away like lightning along the road they had come.

They rode six days and on the seventh they came again to the capital, and Little Fool Ivan—with a sad heart, since he had fallen in love with her himself—brought the lovely girl to the Palace.

The Tzar was overjoyed. He came out to meet them, took the maiden by her white hand, seated her beside him beneath a silken curtain on a cushion of purple velvet, and spoke to her tender words. "O Girl-Tzar, to whom none can be compared!" he said. "My Tzaritza that is to be! For how long have I not slept, either by night or in the white day, for thinking of thine eyes!"

But the beautiful Girl-Tzar turned from him and would not answer and again and again he tried his wooing, till at length she said: "O Tzar, thou art wrinkled and gray, and hast left sixty years behind thee, while I am but sixteen. Should I wed thee, the Tzars of all Tzardoms would laugh, saying that a grandfather had taken to wife his grandchild."

Hearing this, the Tzar was angry. "It is true," he said, "that flowers do not bloom in winter and that I am no longer young. But I am nevertheless a great Tzar."

Then she replied: "I will wed no one who hath gray hairs and who lacks teeth in his head. If thou wilt but grow young again, then will I wed thee right willingly."

"How can a man grow young again?" he asked.

"There is a way, O Tzar," she said, "and it is thus: Order three great caldrons to be placed in thy courtyard. Fill the first with cold water, the second with boiling water, and the third with boiling mare's milk. He who bathes one minute in the boiling milk, two in the boiling water, and three in the cold water, becomes instantly young and so handsome that it cannot be told. Do this and I will become thy Tzaritza, but not otherwise."

The Tzar at once bade them prepare in the courtyard the three caldrons, one of cold water, one of boiling water, and one of boiling mare's milk, minded to make the test. The envious courtiers, however, came to him and said: "O Tzar's Majesty! this is a strange thing and we have never heard that a man can plunge into boiling liquid and not be scalded. We pray thee, therefore, bid thy Master of Horse bathe before thee; then mayest thou be assured that all is well." And this counsel seemed to the Tzar good and he straightway summoned Little Fool Ivan and bade him prepare to make the trial.

When Ivan heard the Tzar's command he said to himself, "So I am to be killed like a sucking-pig or a chicken!" and he went sorrowfully to the stables and told the little humpbacked horse. "Thou hast found for me the Pig with the Golden Bristles," he said, "the Seven-Maned Mare, and the beautiful Girl-Tzar; but now these are all as nothing and my life is as worthless as a boot sole!" And he began to weep bitterly.

"Weep not, little master," said the little horse. "This is indeed a real service that I shall serve thee. Now listen well to what I say. When thou goest to the courtyard, before thou strippest off thy clothes to bathe, ask of the Tzar to permit them to bring to thee thy little humpbacked horse, that thou mayest bid him farewell for the last time. He will agree, and when I am brought there I shall gallop three times around the three kettles, dip my nose in each and sprinkle thee. Lose not a moment then, but jump instantly in the caldron of boiling milk, then into the boiling water, and last into the cold water."

Scarcely had he instructed him when the Boyars came to bring Ivan to the courtyard. All the Court Ministers were there to see and the place was crowded with people, while the Tzar looked on from a balcony. The two caldrons were boiling hot and servants fed the great fires beneath them with heaps of fuel. Little Fool Ivan bowed low before the Tzar and prepared for the bath.

But having taken off his coat, he bowed again and said: "O Tzar's

Majesty! I have but one favor to ask. Bid them bring hither my little humpbacked horse that I may embrace him once more for the last time!" The Tzar was in good humor, thinking he was so soon to regain his youth, and he consented, and presently the little horse came running into the courtyard, dancing up and down and clapping his long ears together. But as soon as he came to the three caldrons he galloped three times round them, dipped his nose into each and sprinkled his master; and without waiting a moment Little Fool Ivan threw off his clothes and jumped into the caldrons, one after the other. And while he had been good-looking before, he came from the last caldron so handsome that his beauty could neither be described with a pen nor written in a tale.

Now when the Tzar saw this, he could wait no longer. He hastened down from the balcony and without waiting to undress, crossed himself and jumped into the boiling milk. But the charm

The people shouted, "Health to Tzar Ivan!"

did not work in his case, and he was instantly scalded to death.

Seeing the Tzar was dead, the Girl-Tzar came to the balcony and spoke to the people, saying: "Thy Tzar chose me to be his Tzaritza. If thou wilt, I will rule this Tzardom, but it shall be only as the wife of him who brought me from mine own!"

The people, well pleased, shouted: "Health to Tzar Ivan!" And so Little Fool Ivan led the lovely Girl-Tzar to the church and they were married that same day.

Then Tzar Ivan ordered the trumpeters to blow their hammered trumpets and the butlers to open the bins, and he made in the Palace a feast like a hill, and the Boyars and Princes sat at oak tables and drank from golden goblets and made merry till they could not stand on their feet.

But Little Fool Ivan, with his Tzaritza, ruled the Tzardom wisely and well, and grew never too wise to take counsel of his little humpbacked horse.

WASSILISSA THE BEAUTIFUL

By POST WHEELER

IN a certain Tzardom, across three times nine kingdoms, beyond high mountain chains, there once lived a merchant. He had been married for twelve years, but in that time there had been born to him only one child, a daughter, who from her cradle was called Wassilissa the Beautiful. When the little girl was eight years old the mother fell ill, and before many days it was plain to be seen that she must die. So she called her little daughter to her, and taking a tiny wooden doll from under the blanket of the bed, put it into her hands and said:

"My little Wassilissa, my dear daughter, listen to what I say, remember well my last words and fail not to carry out my wishes. I am dying, and with my blessing I leave to thee this little doll. It is very precious, for there is no other like it in the whole world. Carry it always about with thee in thy pocket and never show it to anyone. When evil threatens thee or sorrow befalls thee, go into a corner, take it from thy pocket and give it something to eat and drink. It will eat and drink a little, and then thou mayest tell it thy trouble and ask its advice, and it will tell thee how to act in thy time of need." So saying, she kissed her little daughter on the forehead, blessed her, and shortly after died.

Little Wassilissa grieved greatly for her mother, and her sorrow was so deep that when the dark night came, she lay in her bed and wept and did not sleep. At length she bethought herself of the tiny doll, so she rose and took it from the pocket of her gown and finding a piece of wheat bread and a cup of *kwas*,[1] she set them before it, and said: "There, my little doll, take it. Eat a little, and drink a little, and listen to my grief. My dear mother is dead and I am lonely for her."

Then the doll's eyes began to shine like fireflies, and suddenly it became alive. It ate a morsel of the bread and took a sip of the kwas,

[1] Beer.

and when it had eaten and drunk, it said: "Don't weep, little Wassilissa. Grief is worst at night. Lie down, shut thine eyes, comfort thyself and go to sleep. The morning is wiser than the evening." So Wassilissa the Beautiful lay down, comforted herself and went to sleep, and the next day her grieving was not so deep and her tears were less bitter.

Now after the death of his wife, the merchant sorrowed for many days as was right, but at the end of that time he began to desire to marry again and to look about him for a suitable wife. This was not difficult to find, for he had a fine house, with a stable of swift horses, besides being a good man who gave much to the poor. Of all the women he saw, however, the one who, to his mind, suited him best of all, was a widow of about his own age with two daughters of her own, and she, he thought, besides being a good housekeeper, would be a kind foster mother to his little Wassilissa.

So the merchant married the widow and brought her home as his wife, but the little girl soon found that her foster mother was very far from being what her father had thought. She was a cold, cruel woman, who had desired the merchant for the sake of his wealth, and had no love for his daughter. Wassilissa was the greatest beauty in the whole village, while her own daughters were as spare and homely as two crows, and because of this all three envied and hated her. They gave her all sorts of errands to run and difficult tasks to perform, in order that the toil might make her thin and worn and that her face might grow brown from sun and wind, and they treated her so cruelly as to leave few joys in life for her. But all this the little Wassilissa endured without complaint, and while the stepmother's two daughters grew always thinner and uglier, in spite of the fact that they had no hard tasks to do, never went out in cold or rain, and sat always with their arms folded like ladies of a Court, she herself had cheeks like blood and milk and grew every day more and more beautiful.

Now the reason for this was the tiny doll, without whose help little Wassilissa could never have managed to do all the work that was laid upon her. Each night, when everyone else was sound asleep, she would get up from her bed, take the doll into a closet, and locking the door, give it something to eat and drink, and say: "There, my little doll, take it. Eat a little, drink a little, and listen to my grief. I live in my father's house, but my spiteful stepmother wishes to drive me out of the white world. Tell me! How shall I act, and what shall I do?"

Then the little doll's eyes would begin to shine like glowworms, and it would become alive. It would eat a little food, and sip a little drink, and then it would comfort her and tell her how to act. While Wassilissa slept, it would get ready all her work for the next day, so that she had only to rest in the shade and gather flowers, for the doll would have the kitchen garden weeded, and the beds of cabbage watered, and plenty of fresh water brought from the well, and the stoves heated exactly right. And, besides this, the little doll told her how to make, from a certain herb, an ointment which prevented her from ever being sunburnt. So all the joy in life that came to Wassilissa came to her through the tiny doll that she always carried in her pocket.

Years passed, till Wassilissa grew up and became of an age when it is good to marry. All the young men in the village, high and low, rich and poor, asked for her hand, while not one of them stopped even to look at the stepmother's two daughters, so ill-favored were they. This angered their mother still more against Wassilissa; she answered every gallant who came with the same words: "Never shall the younger be wed before the older ones!" And each time, when she had let a suitor out of the door, she would soothe her anger and hatred by beating her stepdaughter. So while Wassilissa grew each day more lovely and graceful, she was often miserable, and but for the little doll in her pocket, would have longed to leave the white world.

Now there came a time when it became necessary for the merchant to leave his home and to travel to a distant Tzardom. He bade farewell to his wife and her two daughters, kissed Wassilissa and gave her his blessing and departed, bidding them say a prayer each day for his safe return. Scarce was he out of sight of the village, however, when his wife sold his house, packed all his goods and moved with them to another dwelling far from the town, in a gloomy neighborhood on the edge of a wild forest. Here every day, while her two daughters were working indoors, the merchant's wife would send Wassilissa on one errand or other into the forest, either to find a branch of a certain rare bush or to bring her flowers or berries.

Now deep in this forest, as the stepmother well knew, there was a green lawn and on the lawn stood a miserable little hut on hens' legs, where lived a certain Baba-Yaga, an old witch grandmother. She lived alone and none dared go near the hut, for she ate people as one eats chickens. The merchant's wife sent Wassilissa into the forest each day, hoping she might meet the old witch and be devoured; but always the girl came home safe and sound, because the little doll showed her where the bush, the flowers and the berries grew, and did not let her go near the hut that stood on hens' legs. And each time the stepmother hated her more and more because she came to no harm.

One autumn evening the merchant's wife called the three girls to her and gave them each a task. One of her daughters she bade make a piece of lace, the other to knit a pair of hose, and to Wassilissa she gave a basket of flax to be spun. She bade each finish a certain amount. Then she put out all the fires in the house, leaving only a single candle lighted in the room where the three girls worked, and she herself went to sleep.

They worked an hour, they worked two hours, they worked three hours, when one of the elder daughters took up the tongs to straighten the wick of the candle. She pretended to do this awkwardly (as her mother had bidden her) and put the candle out, as if by accident.

"What are we to do now?" asked her sister. "The fires are all out, there is no other light in all the house, and our tasks are not done."

"We must go and fetch fire," said the first. "The only house near is a hut in the forest, where a Baba-Yaga lives. One of us must go and borrow fire from her."

"I have enough light from my steel pins," said the one who was making the lace, "and I will not go."

"And I have plenty of light from my silver needles," said the other, who was knitting the hose, "and *I* will not go."

"Thou, Wassilissa," they both said, "shalt go and fetch the fire, for thou hast neither steel pins nor silver needles and cannot see to spin thy flax!" They both rose up, pushed Wassilissa out of the house and locked the door, crying: "Thou shalt not come in till thou hast fetched the fire."

Wassilissa sat down on the doorstep, took the tiny doll from one pocket and from another the supper she had ready for it, put the food before it and said: "There, my little doll, take it. Eat a little and listen to my sorrow. I must go to the hut of the old Baba-Yaga in the dark forest to borrow some fire and I fear she will eat me. Tell me! What shall I do?"

Then the doll's eyes began to shine like two stars and it became alive. It ate a little and said: "Do not fear, little Wassilissa. Go where thou hast been sent. While I am with thee no harm shall come to thee from the old witch." So Wassilissa put the doll back into her pocket, crossed herself and started out into the dark, wild forest.

Whether she walked a short way or a long way the telling is easy, but the journey was hard. The wood was very dark, and she could not help trembling from fear. Suddenly she heard the sound of a horse's hoofs and a man on horseback galloped past her. He was dressed all in white, the horse under him was milk-white and the harness was white, and just as he passed her it became twilight.

She went a little further and again she heard the sound of a horse's hoofs and there came another man on horseback galloping past her. He was dressed all in red, and the horse under him was blood-red and its harness was red, and just as he passed her the sun rose.

That whole day Wassilissa walked, for she had lost her way. She could find no path at all in the dark wood and she had no food to set before the little doll to make it alive.

But at evening she came all at once to the green lawn where the wretched little hut stood on its hens' legs. The wall around the hut was made of human bones and on its top were skulls. There was a gate in the wall, whose hinges were the bones of human feet and whose locks were jawbones set with sharp teeth. The sight filled Wassilissa with horror and she stopped as still as a post buried in the ground.

As she stood there a third man on horseback came galloping up. His face was black, he was dressed all in black, and the horse he rode was coal-black. He galloped up to the gate of the hut and disappeared there as if he had sunk through the ground, and at that moment the night came and the forest grew dark.

But it was not dark on the green lawn, for instantly the eyes of all the skulls on the wall were lighted up and shone till the place was as bright as day. When she saw this Wassilissa trembled so with fear that she could not run away.

Then suddenly the wood became full of a terrible noise; the trees began to groan, the branches to creak and the dry leaves to rustle, and the Baba-Yaga came flying from the forest. She was riding in a great iron mortar and driving it with the pestle, and as she came she swept away her trail behind her with a kitchen broom.

She rode up to the gate and stopping, said:

> "Little House, little House,
>   Stand the way thy mother placed thee,
>   Turn thy back to the forest and thy face to me!"

And the little hut turned facing her and stood still. Then smelling all around her, she cried: "Foo! Foo! I smell a smell that is Russian. Who is there?"

Wassilissa, in great fright, came nearer to the old woman and bowing very low, said: "It is only Wassilissa, Grandmother. My stepmother's daughters sent me to thee to borrow some fire."

"Well," said the old witch, "I know them. But if I give thee the fire thou shalt stay with me some time and do some work to pay for it. If not, thou shalt be eaten for my supper." Then she turned to the gate and shouted: "Ho! Ye, my solid locks, unlock! Thou, my stout gate, open!" Instantly the locks unlocked, the gate opened of itself, and the Baba-Yaga rode in whistling. Wassilissa entered behind her and immediately the gate shut again and the locks snapped tight.

When they had entered the hut the old witch threw herself down on the stove, stretched out her bony legs and said: "Come, fetch and put on the table at once everything that is in the oven. I am hungry." So Wassilissa ran and lighted a splinter of wood from one of the skulls on the wall and took the food from the oven and set it before her. There was enough cooked meat for three strong men. She brought also from the cellar, kwas, honey, beer and wine, and the Baba-Yaga ate and drank the whole, leaving the girl only a little cabbage soup, a crust of bread and a morsel of suckling-pig.

When her hunger was satisfied, the old witch, growing drowsy, lay down on the stove and said: "Listen to me well, and do what I bid thee. Tomorrow when I drive away, do thou clean the yard, sweep the floors and cook my supper. Then take a quarter of a measure of wheat from my storehouse and pick out of it all the black grains and the wild peas. Mind thou dost all that I have bade; if not, thou shalt be eaten for my supper."

Presently the Baba-Yaga turned toward the wall and began to snore and Wassilissa knew that she was fast asleep. Then she went into the corner, took the tiny doll from her pocket, put before it a bit of bread and a little cabbage soup that she had saved, burst into tears and said:

"There, my little doll, take it. Eat a little, drink a little, and listen to my grief. Here I am in the house of the old witch and the gate in the wall is locked and I am afraid. She has given me a difficult task and if I do not do all she has bade, she will eat me tomorrow. Tell me; what shall I do?"

Then the eyes of the little doll began to shine like two candles. It ate a little of the bread and drank a little of the soup and said: "Do not be afraid, Wassilissa the Beautiful. Be comforted. Say thy prayers, and go to sleep. The morning is wiser than the evening." So Wassilissa trusted the little doll and was comforted. She said her prayers, lay down on the floor and went fast asleep.

When she woke next morning, very early, it was still dark. She rose and looked out of the window, and she saw that the eyes of the skulls on the wall were growing dim. As she looked, the man dressed all in white, riding the milk-white horse, galloped swiftly around the corner of the hut, leaped the wall and disappeared, and as he went, it became quite light and the eyes of the skulls flickered and went out. The old witch was in the yard; now she began to whistle and the great iron mortar and pestle and the kitchen broom flew out of the hut to her. As she got into the mortar the man dressed all in red, mounted on the blood-red horse, galloped like the wind around the corner of the hut, leaped the wall and was gone, and at that moment the sun rose. Then the Baba-Yaga shouted: "Ho! Ye, my solid locks, unlock! Thou, my stout gate, open!" And the locks unlocked and the gate opened and she rode away in the mortar, driving with the pestle and sweeping away her path behind her with the broom.

When Wassilissa found herself left alone, she examined the hut, wondering to find it filled with such an abundance of everything. Then she stood still, remembering all the work that she had been bidden to do and wondering what to begin first. But as she looked she rubbed her eyes, for the yard was already neatly cleaned and the floors were nicely swept, and the little doll was sitting in the storehouse picking the last black grains and wild peas out of the quarter-measure of wheat.

Wassilissa ran and took the little doll in her arms. "My dearest little doll!" she cried. "Thou hast saved me from my trouble! Now I have only to cook the Baba-Yaga's supper, since all the rest of the tasks are done!"

"Cook it, with God's help," said the doll, "and then rest, and may the cooking of it make thee healthy!" And so saying it crept into her pocket and became again only a little wooden doll.

So Wassilissa rested all day and was refreshed; and when it grew toward evening she laid the table for the old witch's supper, and sat looking out of the window, waiting for her coming. After awhile she heard the sound of a horse's hoofs and the man in black, on the coal-black horse, galloped up to the wall gate and disappeared like a great dark shadow. And instantly it became quite dark and the eyes of all the skulls began to glitter and shine.

Then all at once the trees of the forest began to creak and groan and the leaves and the bushes to moan and sigh, and the Baba-Yaga came riding out of the dark wood in the huge iron mortar, driving with the pestle and sweeping out the trail behind her with the kitchen broom. Wassilissa let her in; and the witch, smelling all around her, asked: "Well, hast thou done perfectly all the tasks I gave thee to do, or am I to eat thee for my supper?"

"Be so good as to look for thyself, Grandmother," answered Wassilissa.

The Baba-Yaga went all about the place, tapping with her iron pestle, and carefully examining everything. But so well had the little doll done its work that, try as hard as she might, she could not find anything to complain of. There was not a weed left in the yard, nor a speck of dust on the floors, nor a single black grain or wild pea in the wheat.

The old witch was greatly angered, but was obliged to pretend to be pleased. "Well," she said, "thou has done all well." Then, clapping her hands, she shouted: "Ho! my faithful servants! Friends of my heart! Haste and grind my wheat!" Immediately three pairs of hands appeared, seized the measure of wheat and carried it away.

The Baba-Yaga sat down to supper, and Wassilissa put before her all the food from the oven, with kwas, honey, beer, and wine. The old witch ate it, bones and all, almost to the last morsel, enough for four strong men, and then, growing drowsy, stretched her bony legs on the stove and said: "Tomorrow do as thou hast done today, and besides these tasks take from my storehouse a half-measure of poppy seeds and clean them one by one. Someone has mixed earth with them to do me a mischief and to anger me, and I will have them made perfectly clean." So saying she turned to the wall and soon began to snore.

When she was fast asleep, Wassilissa went into the corner, took the little doll from her pocket, set before it a part of the food that was left and asked its advice. And the doll, when it had become alive, and eaten a little food and sipped a little drink, said: "Don't worry, beautiful Wassilissa! Be comforted. Do as thou didst last night: say thy prayers and go to sleep." So Wassilissa was comforted. She said her prayers and went to sleep and did not wake till next morning when she heard the old witch in the yard whistling. She ran to the window just in time to see her take her place in the big iron mortar, and as she did so the man dressed all in red, riding on the blood-red horse, leaped over the wall and was gone, just as the sun rose over the wild forest.

As it had happened on the first morning, so it happened now. When Wassilissa looked she found that the little doll had finished all the tasks except the cooking of the supper. The yard was swept and in order, the floors were as clean as new wood, and there was not a grain of earth left in the half-measure of poppy seeds. She rested and refreshed herself till the afternoon, when she cooked the supper, and when evening came she laid the table and sat down to wait for the old witch's coming.

Soon the man in black, on the coal-black horse, galloped up to the gate, and the dark fell and the eyes of the skulls began to shine like day; then the ground began to quake, and the trees of the forest began to creak and the dry leaves to rustle, and the Baba-Yaga came riding in her iron mortar, driving with her pestle and sweeping away her path with her broom.

When she came in, she smelled around her and went all about the hut, tapping with the pestle; but pry and examine as she might, again she could see no reason to find fault and was angrier than ever. She clapped her hands and shouted: "Ho! my trusty servants! Friends of my soul! Haste and press the oil out of my poppy seeds!" And instantly the three pair of hands appeared, seized the measure of poppy seeds and carried it away.

Presently the old witch sat down to supper and Wassilissa brought all she had cooked, enough for five grown men, and set it before her, and brought beer and honey, and then she herself stood silently waiting. The Baba-Yaga ate and drank it all, every morsel, leaving not so much as a crumb of bread; then she said snappishly:

"Well, why dost thou say nothing, but stand there as if thou wast dumb?"

"I spoke not," Wassilissa answered, "because I dared not. But if thou wilt allow me, Grandmother, I wish to ask thee some questions."

"Well," said the old witch, "only remember that every question does not lead to good. If thou knowest overmuch, thou wilt grow old too soon. What wilt thou ask?"

"I would ask thee," said Wassilissa, "of the men on horseback. When I came to thy hut, a rider passed me. He was dressed all in white and he rode a milk-white horse. Who was he?"

"That was my white, bright day," answered the Baba-Yaga angrily. "He is a servant of mine, but he cannot hurt thee. Ask me more."

"Afterwards," said Wassilissa, "a second rider overtook me. He was dressed in red and the horse he rode was blood-red. Who was he?"

"That was my servant, the round, red sun," answered the Baba-Yaga, "and he, too, cannot injure thee," and she ground her teeth. "Ask me more."

"A third rider," said Wassilissa, "came galloping up to the gate. He was black, his clothes were black and the horse was coal-black. Who was he?"

"That was my servant, the black, dark night," answered the old witch furiously; "but he also cannot harm thee. Ask me more."

But Wassilissa, remembering what the Baba-Yaga had said, that not every question led to good, was silent.

"Ask me more!" cried the old witch. "Why dost thou not ask me more? Ask me of the three pair of hands that serve me!"

But Wassilissa saw how she snarled at her and she answered: "The three questions are enough for me. As thou hast said, Grandmother, I would not, through knowing overmuch, become too soon old."

"It is well for thee," said the Baba-Yaga, "that thou didst not ask of them, but only of what thou didst see outside of this hut. Hadst thou asked of them, my servants, the three pair of hands would have seized thee also, as they did the wheat and poppy seeds, to be my food. Now I would ask a question in my turn: How is it that thou hast been able, in a little time, to do perfectly all the tasks I gave thee? Tell me!"

Wassilissa was so frightened to see how the old witch ground her teeth that she almost told her of the little doll; but she bethought herself just in time, and answered: "The blessing of my dead mother helps me."

Then the Baba-Yaga sprang up in a fury. "Get thee out of my house this moment!" she shrieked. "I want no one who bears a blessing to cross my threshold! Get thee gone!"

Wassilissa ran to the yard, and behind her she heard the old witch shouting to the locks and the gate. The locks opened, the gate swung wide, and she ran out on to the lawn. The Baba-Yaga seized from the wall one of the skulls with burning eyes and flung it after her. "There," she howled, "is the fire for thy stepmother's daughters. Take it. That is what they sent thee here for, and may they have joy of it!"

Wassilissa put the skull on the end of a stick and darted away through the forest, running as fast as she could, finding her path by the skull's glowing eyes which went out only when morning came.

Whether she ran a long way or a short way, and whether the road was smooth or rough, toward evening of the next day, when the eyes in the skull were beginning to glimmer, she came out of the dark, wild forest to her stepmother's house.

When she came near to the gate, she thought, "Surely, by this time they will have found some fire," and threw the skull into the hedge; but it spoke to her, and said: "Do not throw me away, beautiful Wassilissa; bring me to thy stepmother." So, looking at the house and seeing no spark of light in any of the windows, she took up the skull again and carried it with her.

Now since Wassilissa had gone, the stepmother and her two daughters had had neither fire nor light in all the house. When they struck flint and steel the tinder would not catch, and the fire they brought from the neighbors would go out immediately as soon as they carried it over the threshold, so that they had been unable to light or warm themselves or to cook food to eat. Therefore now, for the first time in her life, Wassilissa found herself welcomed. They opened the door to her and the merchant's wife was greatly rejoiced to find that the light in the skull did not go out as soon as it was brought in. "Maybe the witch's fire will stay," she said, and took the skull into the best room, set it on a candlestick and called her two daughters to admire it.

But the eyes of the skull suddenly began to glimmer and to glow like red coals, and wherever the three turned or ran the eyes followed them, growing larger and brighter till they flamed like two furnaces, and hotter and hotter till the merchant's wife and her two wicked daughters took fire and were burned to ashes. Only Wassilissa the Beautiful was not touched.

In the morning Wassilissa dug a deep hole in the ground and buried the skull. Then she locked the house and set out to the village, where she went to live with an old woman who was poor and childless, and so she remained for many days, waiting for her father's return from the far-distant kingdom.

But, sitting lonely, time soon began to hang heavy on her hands. One day she said to the old woman: "It is dull for me, Grandmother, to sit idly hour by hour. My hands want work to do. Go, therefore, and buy me some flax, the best and finest to be found anywhere, and at least I can spin."

The old woman hastened and bought some flax of the best sort and Wassilissa sat down to work. So well did she spin that the thread came out as even and fine as a hair, and presently there was enough to begin to weave. But so fine was the thread that no frame could be found to weave it upon, nor would any weaver undertake to make one.

Then Wassilissa went into her closet, took the little doll from her pocket, set food and drink before it and asked its help. And after it had eaten a little and drunk a little, the doll became alive and said:

"Bring me an old frame and an old basket and some hairs from a horse's mane, and I will arrange everything for thee."

Wassilissa hastened to fetch all the doll had asked for and when evening came, said her prayers, went to sleep, and in the morning she found ready a frame, perfectly made, to weave her fine thread upon.

She wove one month, she wove two months—all the winter Wassilissa sat weaving, weaving her fine thread, till the whole piece of linen was done, of a texture so fine that it could be passed, like thread, through the eye of a needle. When the spring came she bleached it, so white that no snow could be compared with it. Then she said to the old woman: "Take thou the linen to the market, Grandmother, and sell it, and the money shall suffice to pay for my food and lodging." When the old woman examined the linen, however, she said: "Never will I sell such cloth in the market place; no one should wear it except it be the Tzar himself, and tomorrow I shall carry it to the Palace."

Next day, accordingly, the old woman went to the Tzar's splendid Palace and fell to walking up and down before the windows. The servants came to ask her her errand, but she answered them nothing, and kept walking up and down. At length the Tzar opened his window, and asked: "What dost thou want, old woman, that thou walkest here?"

"O Tzar's Majesty!" the old woman answered, "I have with me a marvelous piece of linen stuff, so wondrously woven that I will show it to none but thee."

The Tzar bade them bring her before him and when he saw the linen he was struck with astonishment at its fineness and beauty. "What wilt thou take for it, old woman?" he asked.

"There is no price that can buy it, Little Father Tzar," she answered; "but I have brought it to thee as a gift." The Tzar could not thank the old woman enough. He took the linen and sent her to her house with many rich presents.

Seamstresses were called to make shirts for him out of the cloth; but when it had been cut up, so fine was it that no one of them was deft and skillful enough to sew it. The best seamstresses in all the Tzardom were summoned, but none dared undertake it. So at last the Tzar sent for the old woman and said: "If thou didst know how to spin such thread and weave such linen, thou must also know how to sew me shirts from it."

And the old woman answered: "O Tzar's Majesty, it was not I who wove the linen; it is the work of my adopted daughter."

"Take it then," the Tzar said, "and bid her do it for me."

The old woman brought the linen home and told Wassilissa the Tzar's command: "Well I knew that the work would needs be done by my own hands," said Wassilissa, and, locking herself in her own room, began to make the shirts. So fast and well did she work that soon a dozen were ready. Then the old woman carried them to the Tzar, while Wassilissa washed her face, dressed her hair, put on her best gown and sat down at the window to see what would happen. And presently a servant in the livery of the Palace came to the house and entering, said: "The Tzar, our lord, desires himself to see the clever needlewoman who has made his shirts and to reward her with his own hands."

Wassilissa rose and went at once to the Palace, and as soon as the Tzar saw her, he fell in love with her with all his soul. He took her by her white hand and made her sit beside him. "Beautiful maiden," he said, "never will I part from thee and thou shalt be my wife."

So the Tzar and Wassilissa the Beautiful were married, and her father returned from the far-distant kingdom, and he and the old woman lived always with her in the splendid Palace, in all joy and contentment. And as for the little wooden doll, she carried it about with her in her pocket all her life long.

Tales From India

—

WHY THE FISH LAUGHED

By JOSEPH JACOBS

Illustrations by JOHN D. BATTEN

AS a certain fisherwoman passed by a palace crying her fish, the Queen appeared at one of the windows and beckoned her to come near and show what she had. At that moment a very big fish jumped about in the bottom of the basket.

"Is it a he or a she?" inquired the Queen. "I wish to purchase a she-fish."

On hearing this the fish laughed aloud.

"It's a he," replied the fisherwoman, and proceeded on her rounds.

The Queen returned to her room in a great rage; and on coming to see her in the evening, the King noticed that something had disturbed her.

"Are you indisposed?" he said.

"No; but I am very much annoyed at the strange behavior of a fish. A woman brought me one today, and on my inquiring whether it was a male or female, the fish laughed most rudely."

"A fish laugh! Impossible! You must be dreaming."

"I am not a fool. I speak of what I have seen with my own eyes and have heard with my own ears."

"Passing strange! Be it so. I will inquire concerning it."

On the morrow the King repeated to his vizier what his wife had told him, and bade him investigate the matter, and be ready with a satisfactory answer within six months, on pain of death. The vizier promised to do his best, though he felt almost certain of failure. For five months he labored indefatigably to find a reason for the laughter of the fish. He sought everywhere and from everyone. The wise and learned, and they who were skilled in magic and in all manner of trickery, were consulted. Nobody, however, could explain the matter; and so he returned broken-hearted to his house, and began to arrange his affairs in prospect of certain death, for he had had sufficient experience of the King to know that his Majesty would not go back from his threat. Amongst other things, he advised his son to travel for a time, until the King's anger should have somewhat cooled.

The young fellow, who was both clever and handsome, started off whithersoever Kismet might lead him. He had been gone some days, when he fell in with an old farmer, who also was on a journey to a certain village. Finding the old man very pleasant, he asked him if he might accompany him, professing to be on a visit to the same place. The old farmer agreed, and they walked along together. The day was hot, and the way was long and weary.

"Don't you think it would be pleasanter if you and I sometimes gave each other a lift?" said the youth.

"What a fool the man is!" thought the old farmer.

Presently they passed through a field of corn ready for the sickle, and looking like a sea of gold as it waved to and fro in the breeze.

"Is this eaten or not?" said the young man.

Not understanding his meaning, the old man replied, "I don't know."

After a little while the two travelers arrived at a big village, where the young man gave his companion a clasp knife, and said, "Take this, friend, and get two horses with it; but mind and bring it back for it is very precious."

The old man, looking half amused and half angry, pushed back the knife, muttering something to the effect that his friend was either a fool himself or else trying to play the fool with him. The young man pretended not to notice his reply, and remained almost silent till they reached the city, a short distance outside which was the old farmer's house. They walked about the bazaar and went to the mosque, but nobody saluted them or invited them to come in and rest.

"What a large cemetery!" exclaimed the young man.

"What does the man mean," thought the old farmer, "calling this largely populated city a cemetery?"

On leaving the city their way led through a cemetery where a few people were praying beside a grave and distributing chapatis and kulchas to passers-by, in the name of their beloved dead. They beckoned to the two travelers and gave them as much as they would.

"What a splendid city this is!" said the young man.

"Now, the man must surely be demented!" thought the old farmer. "I wonder what he will do next? He will be calling the land water, and the water land; and be speaking of light where there is darkness, and of darkness when it is light." However, he kept his thoughts to himself.

Presently they had to wade through a stream that ran along the edge of the cemetery.

The water was rather deep, so the old farmer took off his shoes and pajamas and crossed over; but the young man waded through it with his shoes and pajamas on.

"Well! I never did see such a perfect fool, both in word and in deed," said the old man to himself.

However, he liked the fellow; and thinking that he would amuse his wife and daughter, he invited him to come and stay at his house as long as he had occasion to remain in the village.

"Thank you very much," the young man replied: "but let me first inquire, if you please, whether the beam of your house is strong."

The old farmer left him in despair, and entered his house laughing.

"There is a man in yonder field," he said, after returning their greetings. "He has come the greater part of the way with me, and I wanted him to put up here as long as he had to stay in this village. But the fellow is such a fool that I cannot make anything out of him. He wants to know if the beam of this house is all right. The man must be mad!" and saying this, he burst into a fit of laughter.

"Father," said the farmer's daughter, who was a very sharp and wise girl, "this man, whosoever he is, is no fool, as you deem him. He only wishes to know if you can afford to entertain him."

"Oh! of course," replied the farmer. "I see. Well, perhaps you can help me to solve some of his other mysteries. While we were walking together he asked whether he should carry me or I should carry him, as he thought that would be a pleasanter mode of proceeding."

"Most assuredly," said the girl. "He meant that one of you should tell a story to beguile the time."

"Oh, yes. Well, we were passing through a cornfield, when he asked me whether it was eaten or not."

"And didn't you know the meaning of this, father? He simply wished to know if the man was in debt or not; because, if the owner of the field was in debt, then the produce of the field was as good as eaten to him; that is, it would have to go to his creditors."

"Yes, yes, yes, of course! Then, on entering a certain village, he bade me take his clasp knife and get two horses with it, and bring back the knife again to him."

"Are not two stout sticks as good as two horses for helping one along on the road? He only asked you to cut a couple of sticks and be careful not to lose his knife."

"I see," said the farmer. "While we were walking over the city we did not see anybody that we knew, and not a soul gave us a scrap of anything to eat, till we were passing the cemetery; but there some people called to us and put into our hands some chapatis and kulchas; so my companion called the city a cemetery, and the cemetery a city."

"This also is to be understood, father, if one thinks of the city as the place where everything is to be obtained, and of inhospitable people as worse than the dead. The city, though crowded with people, was as if dead, as far as you were concerned; while, in the cemetery, which is crowded with the dead, you were saluted by kind friends and provided with bread."

"True, true!" said the astonished farmer. "Then, just now, when we were crossing the stream, he waded through it without taking off his shoes and pajamas."

"I admire his wisdom," replied the girl. "I have often thought how stupid people were to venture into that swiftly flowing stream and over those sharp stones with bare feet. The slightest stumble and they would fall, and be wetted from head to foot. This friend of yours is a most wise man. I should like to see him and speak to him."

"Very well," said the farmer; "I will go and find him, and bring him in."

"Tell him, father, that our beams are strong enough, and then he will come in. I'll send on ahead a present to the man, to show him that we can afford to have him for our guest."

Accordingly she called a servant and sent him to the young man with a present of a basin of ghee, twelve chapatis, and a jar of milk, and the following message: "O friend, the moon is full; twelve months make a year, and the sea is overflowing with water."

Halfway the bearer of this present and message met his little son, who, seeing what was in the basket, begged his father to give him some of the food. His father foolishly complied. Presently he saw the young man, and gave him the rest of the present and the message.

"Give your mistress my salaam," he replied, "and tell her that the moon is new, and that I can only find eleven months in the year, and the sea is by no means full."

Not understanding the meaning of these words, the servant repeated them word for word, as he had heard them, to his mistress; and thus his theft was discovered, and he was severely punished.

After a little while the young man appeared with the old farmer. Great attention was shown to him and he was treated in every way as if he were the son of a great man, although his humble host knew nothing of his origin. At length he told them everything— about the laughing of the fish, his father's threatened execution, and his own banishment—and asked their advice as to what he should do.

"The laughing of the fish," said the girl, "which seems to have been the cause of all this trouble, indicates that there is a man in the palace who is plotting against the King's life."

"Joy, joy!" exclaimed the vizier's son. "There is yet time for me to return and save my father from an ignominious and unjust death, and the King from danger."

The following day he hastened back to his own country, taking with him the farmer's daughter. Immediately on arrival he ran to the palace and informed his father of what he had heard. The poor vizier, now almost dead from the expectation of death, was at once carried to the King, to whom he repeated the news that his son had just brought.

"Never!" said the King.

"But it must be so, your Majesty," replied the vizier; "and in order to prove the truth of what I have heard, I pray you to call together all the maids in your palace, and order them to jump over a pit, which must be dug. We'll soon find out whether there is any man there."

The King had the pit dug, and commanded all the maids belonging to the palace to try to jump it. All of them tried, but only one succeeded. That one was found to be a man! !

Thus was the Queen satisfied, and the faithful old vizier saved.

Afterwards, as soon as could be, the vizier's son married the old farmer's daughter; and a most happy marriage it was.

THE FARMER AND THE MONEY LENDER

By JOSEPH JACOBS

Illustration by JOHN D. BATTEN

THERE was once a farmer who suffered much at the hands of a money lender. Good harvests or bad, the farmer was always poor, the money lender rich. At the last, when he hadn't a farthing left, the farmer went to the money lender's house, and said, "You can't squeeze water from a stone, and as you have nothing to get by me now, you might tell me the secret of becoming rich."

"My friend," returned the money lender, piously, "riches come from Ram—ask *him.*"

"Thank you, I will!" replied the simple farmer; so he prepared three girdlecakes [griddle-cakes] to last him on the journey, and set out to find Ram.

First he met a Brahman, and to him he gave a cake, asking him to point out the road to Ram; but the Brahman only took the cake and went on his way without a word. Next the farmer met a Jogi or devotee, and to him he gave a cake, without receiving any help in return. At last, he came upon a poor man sitting under a tree, and finding out he was hungry, the kindly farmer gave him his last cake, and sitting down to rest beside him, entered into conversation.

"And where are you going?" asked the poor man, at length.

"Oh, I have a long journey before me, for I am going to find Ram!" replied the farmer. "Could you tell me which way to go?"

"Perhaps I can," said the poor man, smiling, "for *I* am Ram! What do you want of me?"

Then the farmer told the whole story, and Ram, taking pity on him, gave him a conch shell, and showed him how to blow it in a particular way, saying: "Remember! whatever you wish for, you have only to blow the conch that way and your wish will be ful-

filled. Only have a care of that money lender, for even magic is not proof against their wiles!"

The farmer went back to his village rejoicing. In fact the money lender noticed his high spirits at once, and said to himself, "Some good fortune must have befallen the stupid fellow, to make him hold his head so jauntily." Therefore he went over to the simple farmer's house, and congratulated him on his good fortune, in such cunning words, pretending to have heard all about it, that before long the farmer found himself telling the whole story—all except the secret of blowing the conch, for, with all his simplicity, the farmer was not quite such a fool as to tell that.

Nevertheless, the money lender determined to have the conch by hook or by crook, and as he was villain enough not to stick at trifles, he waited for a favorable opportunity and stole the conch.

But, after nearly bursting himself with blowing the conch in every conceivable way, he was obliged to give up the secret as a bad job. However, being determined to succeed, he went back to the farmer and said, cooly: "Look here; I've got your conch, but I can't use it; you haven't got it, so it's clear you can't use it either. Business is at a standstill unless we make a bargain. Now, I promise to give you back your conch, and never to interfere with your using it, on one condition—whatever you get from it, I am to get double."

"Never!" cried the farmer; "that would be the old business all over again!"

"Not at all!" replied the wily money lender; "you will have your share! Now, don't be a dog in the manger, for if *you* get all you want, what can it matter to you if *I* am rich or poor?"

At last, though it went sorely against the grain to be of any benefit to a money lender, the farmer was forced to yield, and from that time, no matter what he gained by the power of the conch, the money lender gained double. And the knowledge that this was so preyed upon the farmer's mind day and night, so that he had no satisfaction out of anything.

At last, there came a very dry season—so dry that the farmer's crops withered for want of rain. Then he blew his conch, and wished for a well to water them, and lo! there was the well, *but the money lender had two!*—two beautiful new wells! This was too much for any farmer to stand; and our friend brooded over it, and brooded over it, till at last a bright idea came into his head. He seized the conch, blew it loudly, and cried out, "Oh, Ram! I wish to be blind of one eye!" And so he was, in a twinkling, but the money lender of course was blind of both, and in trying to steer his way between the two new wells, he fell into one, and was drowned.

Now this true story shows that a farmer once got the better of a money lender—but only by losing one of his eyes.

THE ASS IN THE LION'S SKIN

By JOSEPH JACOBS

Illustration by JOHN D. BATTEN

AT the same time when Brahamadatta was reigning in
Benares, the future Buddha was born one of a peasant
family; and when he grew up, he gained his living by tilling the
ground.

At that time a hawker used to go from place to place, trafficking

in goods carried by an ass. Now at each place he came to, when
he took the pack down from the ass's back, he used to clothe him
in a lion's skin, and turn him loose in the rice and barley fields. And
when the watchmen in the fields saw the ass, they dared not go near
him, taking him for a lion.

So one day the hawker stopped in a village; and whilst he was getting his own breakfast cooked, he dressed the ass in a lion's skin, and turned him loose in a barley field. The watchmen in the field dared not go up to him; but going home, they published the news. Then all the villagers came out with weapons in their hands; and, blowing chanks, and beating drums, they went near the field and shouted. Terrified with the fear of death, the ass uttered a cry—the bray of an ass!

And when he knew him then to be an ass, the future Buddha pronounced the first verse:

> "This is not a lion's roaring,
>   Nor a tiger's, nor a panther's;
>   Dressed in a lion's skin,
>   'Tis a wretched ass that roars!"

But when the villagers knew the creature to be an ass, they beat him till his bones broke; and, carrying off the lion's skin, went away. Then the hawker came; and seeing the ass fallen into so bad a plight, pronounced the second verse:

> "Long might the ass,
>   Clad in a lion's skin,
>   Have fed on the barley green.
>   But he brayed!
>   And that moment he came to ruin."

And even whilst he was yet speaking the ass died on the spot!

THE GOLD-GIVING SERPENT

By JOSEPH JACOBS

Illustration by JOHN D. BATTEN

NOW in a certain place there lived a Brahman named Hari-datta. He was a farmer, but poor was the return his labor brought him. One day, at the end of the hot hours, the Brahman, overcome by the heat, lay down under the shadow of a tree to have a doze. Suddenly he saw a great hooded snake creeping out of an ant hill near at hand. So he thought to himself: "Surely this is the

guardian deity of the field, and I have not ever worshipped it. That's why my farming is in vain. I will at once go and pay my respects to it."

When he had made up his mind, he got some milk, poured it into a bowl, and went to the ant hill, and said aloud: "O Guardian of this Field! All this while I did not know that you dwelt here. That is why I have not yet paid my respects to you; pray forgive me." And he laid the milk down and went to his house. Next morning he came and looked, and he saw a gold denar in the bowl, and from that time onward every day the same thing occurred: he gave milk to the serpent and found a gold denar.

One day the Brahman had to go to the village, and so he ordered his son to take the milk to the ant hill. The son brought the milk, put it down, and went back home. Next day he went again and found a denar, so he thought to himself: "This ant hill is surely full of golden denars; I'll kill the serpent, and take them all for myself." So next day, while he was giving the milk to the serpent, the Brahman's son struck it on the head with a cudgel. But the serpent escaped death by the will of fate, and in a rage bit the Brahman's son with its sharp fangs, and he fell down dead at once. His people raised him a funeral pyre not far from the field and burnt him to ashes.

Two days afterwards his father came back, and when he learnt his son's fate he grieved and mourned. But after a time, he took the bowl of milk, went to the ant hill, and praised the serpent with a loud voice. After a long, long time the serpent appeared, but only with its head out of the opening of the ant hill, and spoke to the Brahman:

" 'Tis greed that brings you here, and makes you even forget the loss of your son. From this time forward, friendship between us is impossible. Your son struck me in youthful ignorance, and I have bitten him to death. How can I forget the blow with the cudgel? And how can you forget the pain and grief at the loss of your son?" So speaking, it gave the Brahman a costly pearl and disappeared. But before it went away it said: "Come back no more." The Brahman took the pearl, and went back home, cursing the folly of his son.

THE LAMBIKIN

By *FLORA ANNIE STEEL*

ONCE upon a time there was a wee wee Lambikin, who frolicked about on his little tottery legs, and enjoyed himself amazingly.

Now one day he set off to visit his Granny, and was jumping with joy to think of all the good things he should get from her, when whom should he meet but a Jackal, who looked at the tender young morsel and said—"Lambikin! Lambikin! I'll EAT YOU!"

But lambikin only gave a little frisk, and said—

> "To Granny's house I go,
> Where I shall fatter grow,
> Then you can eat me so."

The Jackal thought this reasonable, and let Lambikin pass.

By and by he met a Vulture, and the Vulture, looking hungrily at the tender morsel before him said—"Lambikin! Lambikin! I'll EAT YOU!"

But Lambikin only gave a little frisk, and said—

> "To Granny's house I go,
> Where I shall fatter grow,
> Then you can eat me so."

The Vulture thought this reasonable, and let Lambikin pass.

And by and by he met a Tiger, and then a Wolf, and a Dog, and an Eagle, and all these, when they saw the tender little morsel said—"Lambikin! Lambikin! I'll EAT YOU!"

But to all of them Lambikin replied, with a little frisk—

> "To Granny's house I go,
> Where I shall fatter grow,
> Then you can eat me so."

At last he reached his Granny's house, and said, all in a great hurry, "Granny, dear, I've promised to get very fat; so, as people ought to keep their promises, please put me into the corn-bin *at once*."

So his Granny said he was a good boy, and put him into the corn-bin, and there the greedy little Lambikin stayed for seven days, and ate, and ate, and ate, until he could scarcely waddle, and his Granny said he was fat enough for anything, and must go home. But cunning little Lambikin said that would never do, for some animal would be sure to eat him on the way back, he was so plump and tender.

"I'll tell you what you must do," said Master Lambikin, "you must make a little drumikin out of the skin of my little brother who died, and then I can sit inside and trundle along nicely, for I'm as tight as a drum myself."

So his Granny made a nice little drumikin out of his brother's skin, with the wool inside, and Lambikin curled himself up snug and warm in the middle, and trundled away gayly. Soon he met with the Eagle who called out—

> "Drumikin! Drumikin!
> Have you seen Lambikin?"

And Mr. Lambikin, curled up in his soft warm nest, replied—

> "Lost in the forest, and so are you,
> On, little Drumikin! Tum-pa, tum-too"

"How very annoying!" sighed the Eagle, thinking regretfully of the tender morsel he had let slip.

Meanwhile Lambikin trundled along, laughing to himself, and singing—

> "Tum-pa, tum-too;
> Tum-pa, tum-too!"

Every animal and bird he met asked him the same question—

> "Drumikin! Drumikin!
> Have you seen Lambikin?"

And to each of them the little sly-boots replied—

> "Lost in the forest, and so are you,
>   On, little Drumikin! Tum-pa, tum-too;
>   Tum-pa, tum-too; Tum-pa, tum-too!"

Then they all sighed to think of the tender little morsel they had let slip.

At last the Jackal came limping along, for all his sorry looks as sharp as a needle, and he, too, called out—

> "Drumikin! Drumikin!
>   Have you seen Lambikin?"

And Lambikin, curled up in his snug little nest, replied gayly—

> "Lost in the forest, and so are you,
>   On, little Drumikin! Tum-pa——"

But he never got any further, for the Jackal recognized his voice at once, and cried, "Hullo! You've turned yourself inside out, have you? Just you come out of that!"

Whereupon he tore open Drumikin and gobbled up Lambikin.

THE RAT'S WEDDING

By FLORA ANNIE STEEL

Illustrations by LOCKWOOD KIPLING

ONCE upon a time a fat sleek Rat was caught in a shower of
rain, and being far from shelter he set to work and soon dug
a nice hole in the ground, in which he sat as dry as a bone while
the raindrops splashed outside, making little puddles on the road.

Now in the course of his digging he came upon a fine bit of root,
quite dry and fit for fuel, which he set aside carefully—for the Rat
is an economical creature—in order to take it home with him. So
when the shower was over, he set off with the dry root in his mouth.
As he went along, daintily picking his way through the puddles,
he saw a poor man vainly trying to light a fire, while a little circle
of children stood by, and cried piteously.

"Goodness gracious!" exclaimed the Rat, who was both soft-
hearted and curious, "what a dreadful noise to make! What *is* the
matter?"

"The bairns are hungry," answered the man; "they are crying for
their breakfast, but the sticks are damp, the fire won't burn, and so
I can't bake the cakes."

"If that is all your trouble, perhaps I can help you," said the good-
natured Rat; "you are welcome to this dry root, and I'll warrant it
will soon make a fine blaze."

The poor man, with a thousand thanks, took the dry root, and in
his turn presented the Rat with a morsel of dough, as a reward for
his kindness and generosity.

"What a remarkably lucky fellow I am!" thought the Rat, as he
trotted off gayly with his prize. "And clever, too! Fancy making
a bargain like that—food enough to last me five days in return for
a rotten old stick! *Wah! wah! wah!* what it is to have brains!"

Going along, hugging his good fortune in this way, he came
presently to a potter's yard, where the potter, leaving his wheel to

spin round by itself, was trying to pacify his three little children, who were screaming and crying as if they would burst.

"My gracious!" cried the Rat, stopping his ears. "What a noise! —do tell me what it is all about."

"I suppose they are hungry," replied the potter ruefully; "their mother has gone to get flour in the bazaar, for there is none in the house. In the meantime I can neither work nor rest because of them."

"Is that all!" answered the officious Rat. "Then I can help you. Take this dough, cook it quickly, and stop their mouths with food."

The potter overwhelmed the Rat with thanks for his obliging kindness, and choosing out a nice well-burnt pipkin, insisted on his accepting it as a remembrance.

Went away gingerly, his tail over his arm.

The Rat was delighted at the exchange and though the pipkin was just a trifle awkward for him to manage, he succeeded after infinite trouble in balancing it on his head, and went away gingerly, *tink-a-tink, tink-a-tink,* down the road, with his tail over his arm for fear he should trip on it. And all the time he kept saying to himself, "What a lucky fellow I am! And clever, too! Such a hand at a bargain!"

By and by he came to where some neatherds were herding their cattle. One of them was milking a buffalo, and, having no pail, he used his shoes instead.

"Oh, fie! oh, fie!" cried the cleanly Rat, quite shocked at the sight. "What a nasty, dirty trick!—Why don't you use a pail?"

"For the best of all reasons—we haven't got one!" growled the neatherd, who did not see why the Rat should put his finger in the pie.

"If that is all," replied the dainty Rat, "oblige me by using this pipkin, for I cannot bear dirt!"

The neatherd, nothing loath, took the pipkin, and milked away until it was brimming over; then turning to the Rat, who stood looking on said, "Here, little fellow, you may have a drink, in payment."

But if the Rat was good-natured he was also shrewd. "No, no my friend," said he, "that will not do! As if I could drink the worth of my pipkin at a draught! My dear sir, *I couldn't hold it!* Besides, I never make a bad bargain, so I expect you at least to give me the buffalo that gave the milk."

"Nonsense!" cried the neatherd. "A buffalo for a pipkin! Who ever heard of such a price? And what on earth could *you* do with a buffalo when you got it? Why, the pipkin was about as much as you could manage."

At this the Rat drew himself up with dignity, for he did not like allusions to his size. "That is my affair, not yours," he retorted; "your business is to hand over the buffalo."

So just for the fun of the thing, and to amuse themselves at the Rat's expense, the neatherds loosed the buffalo's halter and began to tie it to the little animal's tail.

"No! no!" he called, in a great hurry. "If the beast pulled, the skin of my tail would come off, and then where should I be? Tie it round my neck, if you please."

So with much laughter the neatherds tied the halter round the Rat's neck, and he, after a polite leave-taking, set off gayly toward home with his prize; that is to say, he set off with the *rope,* for no sooner did he come to the end of the tether than he was brought up with a round turn; the buffalo, nose down, grazing away, would not budge until it had finished its tuft of grass, and then seeing another in a different direction marched off toward it, while the Rat, to avoid being dragged, had to trot humbly behind, willy-nilly.

He was too proud to confess the truth, of course, and, nodding his head knowingly to the neatherds, said, "Ta-ta, good people! I am going home this way. It's a little longer, but much shadier."

And when the neatherds roared with laughter he took no notice, but trotted on, looking as dignified as possible.

"After all," he reasoned to himself, "when one keeps a buffalo one has to look after its grazing. A beast must get a good bellyful of grass if it is to give any milk, and I have plenty of time."

So all day long he trotted about after the buffalo, making believe; but by evening he was dead tired, and felt truly thankful when the great big beast, having eaten enough, lay down under a tree to chew the cud.

Just then a bridal party came by. The bridegroom and his friends had evidently gone on to the next village, leaving the bride's palanquin to follow; so the palanquin bearers, being lazy fellows and seeing a nice shady tree, put down their burden, and began to cook some food.

"What detestable meanness!" grumbled one. "A grand wedding, and nothing but plain rice pottage to eat! Not a scrap of meat in it, neither sweet nor salt! It would serve the skinflints right if we upset the bride into a ditch!"

"Dear me!" cried the Rat at once, seeing a way out of his difficulty. "That *is* a shame! I sympathize with your feelings so entirely that if you will allow me I'll give you my buffalo. You can kill it, and cook it."

"*Your* buffalo!" returned the discontented bearers. "What rubbish! Whoever heard of a rat owning a buffalo?"

"Not often, I admit," replied the Rat with conscious pride; "but look for yourselves. Can you not see that I am leading the beast by a string?"

"Oh, never mind the string!" cried a great big hungry bearer. "Master or no master, I mean to have meat to my dinner!"

Whereupon they killed the buffalo, and, cooking its flesh, ate their dinner with relish; then offering the remains to the Rat, said carelessly, "Here, little Rat-skin, that is for you!"

"Now look here!" cried the Rat hotly; "I'll have none of your pottage, nor your sauce either. You don't suppose I am going to give my best buffalo, that gave quarts and quarts of milk—the buffalo I have been feeding all day—for a wee bit of rice? No!—I got a loaf for a bit of stick; I got a pipkin for a little loaf; I got a buffalo for a pipkin; and now I'll have the bride for my buffalo—the bride, and nothing else!"

By this time the servants, having satisfied their hunger, began to reflect on what they had done, and becoming alarmed at the consequences, arrived at the conclusion it would be wisest to make their escape whilst they could. So, leaving the bride in her palanquin, they took to their heels in various directions.

The Rat, being as it were left in possession, advanced to the palanquin, and drawing aside the curtain, with the sweetest of voices and best of bows begged the bride to descend. She hardly knew whether to laugh or to cry, but as any company, even a Rat's, was better than being quite alone in the wilderness, she did as she was bidden, and followed the lead of her guide, who set off as fast as he could for his hole.

The rat begged the bride to desend.

As he trotted along beside the lovely young bride, who, by her rich dress and glittering jewels, seemed to be some king's daughter, he kept saying to himself, "How clever I am! What bargains I do make, to be sure!"

When they arrived at his hole, the Rat stepped forward with the greatest politeness, and said, "Welcome, madam, to my humble abode! Pray step in, or if you will allow me, and as the passage is somewhat dark, I will show you the way."

Whereupon he ran in first, but after a time, finding the bride did not follow, he put his nose out again, saying testily, "Well, madam, why don't you follow? Don't you know it's rude to keep your husband waiting?"

"My good sir," laughed the handsome young bride, "I can't squeeze into that little hole!"

The Rat coughed; then after a moment's thought he replied, "There is some truth in your remark—you *are* overgrown, and I suppose I shall have to build you a thatch somewhere. For tonight you can rest under that wild plum tree."

"But I am so hungry!" said the bride ruefully.

"Dear, dear! Everybody seems hungry today!" returned the Rat pettishly. "However, that's easily settled—I'll fetch you some supper in a trice."

So he ran into his hole, returning immediately with an ear of millet and a dry pea.

"There!" said he, triumphantly. "Isn't that a fine meal?"

"I can't eat that!" whimpered the bride. "It isn't a mouthful; and I want rice pottage, and cakes, and sweet eggs, and sugar-drops. I shall die if I don't get them!"

"Oh, dear me!" cried the Rat in a rage. "What a nuisance a bride is, to be sure! Why don't you eat the wild plums?"

"I can't live on wild plums!" retorted the weeping bride. "Nobody could; besides, they are only half ripe, and I can't reach them."

"Rubbish!" cried the Rat. "Ripe or unripe, they must do you for tonight, and tomorrow you can gather a basketful, sell them in the city, and buy sugar-drops and sweet eggs to your heart's content!"

So the next morning the Rat climbed up into the plum tree and nibbled away at the stalks till the fruit fell down into the bride's veil. Then unripe as they were, she carried them into the city, calling out through the streets—

> "Green plums I sell! green plums I sell!
> Princess am I, Rat's bride as well!"

As she passed by the palace, her mother the Queen heard her voice, and, running out, recognized her daughter. Great were the rejoicings, for everyone thought the poor bride had been eaten by wild beasts. In the midst of the feasting and merriment, the Rat, who had followed the Princess at a distance, and had become alarmed at her long absence, arrived at the door, against which he beat with a big knobby stick, calling out fiercely, "Give me my wife! give me my wife! She is mine by fair bargain. I gave a stick and I got a loaf; I gave a loaf and I got a pipkin; I gave a pipkin and I got a buffalo; I gave a buffalo and I got a bride. Give me my wife! give me my wife!"

"La! son-in-law! What a fuss you do make!" said the wily old Queen, through the door, "And all about nothing! Who wants to run away with your wife? On the contrary, we are proud to see you, and I only keep you waiting at the door till we can spread the carpets, and receive you in style."

Hearing this, the Rat was mollified, and waited patiently outside whilst the cunning old Queen prepared for his reception, which she did by cutting a hole in the very middle of a stool, putting a red-hot stone underneath, covering it over with a stewpan lid, and then spreading a beautiful embroidered cloth over all.

Then she went to the door, and receiving the Rat with the greatest of respect, led him to the stool, praying him to be seated.

"Dear! dear! How clever I am! What bargains I do make, to be sure!" said he to himself as he climbed on to the stool. "Here I am, son-in-law to a real live Queen! What will the neighbors say?"

At first he sat down on the edge of the stool, but even there it was warm, and after a while he began to fidget, saying, "Dear me, Mother-in-Law! How hot your house is! Everything I touch seems burning!"

"You are out of the wind there, my son," replied the cunning old Queen; "sit more in the middle of the stool, and then you will feel the breeze and get cooler."

But he didn't! For the stewpan lid by this time had become so hot that the Rat fairly frizzled when he sat down on it; and it was not until he had left all his tail, half his hair, and a large piece of his skin behind him, that he managed to escape, howling with pain, and vowing that never, never, never again would he make a bargain!

THE TIGER, THE BRAHMAN AND THE JACKAL

By FLORA ANNIE STEEL

ONCE upon a time a tiger was caught in a trap. He tried in vain to get out through the bars, and rolled and bit with rage and grief when he failed.

By chance a poor Brahman came by. "Let me out of this cage, O pious one!" cried the tiger.

"Nay, my friend," replied the Brahman mildly, "you would probably eat me if I did."

"Not at all!" swore the tiger with many oaths. "On the contrary, I should be forever grateful, and serve you as a slave!"

Now when the tiger sobbed and sighed and wept and swore, the pious Brahman's heart softened, and at last he consented to open the door of the cage. Out popped the tiger, and, seizing the poor man, cried, "What a fool you are! What is to prevent my eating you now, for after being cooped up so long I am just terribly hungry!"

In vain the Brahman pleaded for his life; the most he could gain was a promise to abide by the decision of the first three things he chose to question as to the justice of the tiger's action.

So the Brahman first asked a pipal tree what it thought of the matter, but the pipal tree replied coldly: "What have you to complain about? Don't I give shade and shelter to everyone who passes by, and don't they in return tear down my branches to feed their cattle? Don't whimper—be a man!"

Then the Brahman, sad at heart, went farther afield till he saw a buffalo turning a well-wheel; but he fared no better from it, for it answered, "You are a fool to expect gratitude! Look at me! While I gave milk they fed me on cotton-seed and oil cake; but now I am dry they yoke me here, and give me refuse as fodder!"

The Brahman, still more sad, asked the road its opinion.

"My dear sir," said the road, "how foolish you are to expect any-thing else! Here am I, useful to everybody, yet all, rich and poor, great and small, trample on me as they go past, giving me nothing but the ashes of their pipes and the husks of their grain!"

On this the Brahman turned back sorrowfully, and on the way he met a jackal, who called out, "Why, what's the matter, Mr. Brahman? You look as miserable as a fish out of water!"

Then the Brahman told him all that had occurred. "How very confusing!" said the jackal, when the recital was ended. "Would you mind telling me over again? For everything seems so mixed up!"

The Brahman told it all over again, but the jackal shook his head in a distracted sort of way, and still could not understand.

"It's very odd," he said sadly, "but it all seems to go in at one ear and out at the other! I will go to the place where it all hap-pened, and then perhaps I shall be able to give a judgment."

So they returned to the cage, by which the tiger was waiting for the Brahman, and sharpening his teeth and claws.

"You've been away a long time!" growled the savage beast. "But now let us begin our dinner."

"*Our* dinner!" thought the wretched Brahman, as his knees knocked together with fright. "What a remarkably delicate way of putting it!"

"Give me five minutes, my lord!" he pleaded. "In order that I may explain matters to the jackal here, who is somewhat slow in his wits."

The tiger consented, and the Brahman began the whole story over again, not missing a single detail, and spinning as long a yarn as possible.

"Oh, my poor brain! Oh, my poor brain!" cried the jackal, wringing his paws. "Let me see! how did it all begin? You were in the cage, and the tiger came walking by—"

"Pooh!" interrupted the tiger. "What a fool you are! *I* was in the cage."

"Of course!" cried the jackal, pretending to tremble with fright. "Yes! I was in the cage—no, I wasn't—dear! dear! where are my wits? Let me see—the tiger was in the Brahman, and the cage came walking by——no, that's not it either! Well, don't mind me, but begin your dinner, for I shall never understand!"

"Yes, you shall!" returned the tiger, in a rage at the jackal's stupidity. "I'll *make* you understand! Look here—I am the tiger——"

"Yes, my lord!"

"And that is the Brahman——"

"Yes, my lord!"

"And that is the cage——"

"Yes, my lord!"

"And I was in the cage—do you understand?"

"Yes—no— Please, my lord——"

"Well?" cried the tiger, impatiently.

"Please, my lord!—how did you get in?"

"How!—Why, in the usual way, of course!"

"Oh, dear me!—my head is beginning to whirl again! Please don't be angry, my lord, but what is the usual way?"

At this the tiger lost patience, and, jumping into the cage, cried, "This way! Now do you understand how it was?"

"Perfectly!" grinned the jackal, as he dexterously shut the door. "And if you will permit me to say so, I think matters will remain as they were!"

LITTLE ANKLEBONE

By FLORA ANNIE STEEL

Illustration by LOCKWOOD KIPLING

ONCE upon a time there was a little boy who lost his parents; so he went to live with his auntie, and she set him to herd sheep. All day long the little fellow wandered barefoot through the pathless plain, tending his flock, and playing his tiny shepherd's pipe from morn till eve.

But one day came a great big wolf, and looked hungrily at the small shepherd and his fat sheep, saying, "Little boy! shall I eat you or your sheep?"

Then the little boy answered politely, "I don't know, Mr. Wolf; I must ask my auntie."

So all day long he piped away on his tiny pipe, and in the evening, when he brought the flock home, he went to his auntie and said, "Auntie dear, a great big wolf asked me today if he should eat me or your sheep. Which shall it be?"

Then his auntie looked at the wee little shepherd, and at the fat flock, and said sharply, "Which shall it be?"—why, *you*, of course!"

So next morning the little boy drove his flock out into the pathless plain, and blew away cheerfully on his shepherd's pipe until the great big wolf appeared. Then he laid aside his pipe, and, going up to the savage beast, said, "Oh, if you please, Mr. Wolf, I asked my auntie, and she says you are to eat *me*."

Now the wolf, savage as wolves always are, could not help having just a spark of pity for the tiny barefoot shepherd who played his pipe so sweetly; therefore he said kindly, "Could I do anything for you, little boy, after I've eaten you?"

"Thank you!" returned the tiny shepherd. "If you would be so kind, after you've picked the bones, as to thread my anklebone on a string and hang it on the tree that weeps over the pond yonder, I shall be much obliged."

So the wolf ate the little shepherd, picked the bones, and afterwards hung the anklebone by a string to the branches of the tree.

Now, one day, three robbers, who had just robbed a palace, happening to pass that way, sat down under the tree and began to divide the spoil. Just as they had arranged all the golden dishes and precious jewels and costly stuffs into three heaps, a jackal howled. Now you must know that thieves always use the jackal's cry as a note of warning, so that when at the very same moment Little Anklebone's thread snapped, and he fell plump on the head of the chief robber, the man imagined someone had thrown a pebble at him, and, shouting "Run! run!—we are discovered!" he bolted away as hard as he could, followed by his companions, leaving all the treasure behind them.

"Now," said Little Anklebone to himself, "I shall lead a fine life!"

Piped away on his shepherd's pipe.

So he gathered the treasure together, and sat under the tree that drooped over the pond, and played so sweetly on a new shepherd's pipe, that all the beasts of the forest, and the birds of the air, and the fishes of the pond came to listen to him. Then Little Anklebone put marble basins round the pond for the animals to drink out of, and in the evening the does, and the tigresses, and the she-wolves gathered round him to be milked, and when he had drunk his fill he milked the rest into the pond, till at last it became a pond of milk. And Little Anklebone sat by the milken pond and piped away on his shepherd's pipe.

Now, one day, an old woman, passing by with her jar for water, heard the sweet strains of Little Anklebone's pipe, and following the sound, came upon the pond of milk, and saw the animals, and the birds, and the fishes, listening to the music. She was wonder-struck, especially when Little Anklebone, from his seat under the tree, called out, "Fill your jar, mother! All drink who come hither!"

Then the old woman filled her jar with milk, and went on her way rejoicing at her good fortune. But as she journeyed she met with the king of the country, who, having been a-hunting, had lost his way in the pathless plain.

"Give me a drink of water, good mother," he cried, seeing the jar; "I am half dead with thirst!"

"It is milk, my son," replied the old woman; "I got it yonder from a milken pond." Then she told the king of the wonders she had seen, so that he resolved to have a peep at them himself. And when he saw the milken pond, and all the animals and birds and fishes gathered round, while Little Anklebone played ever so sweetly on his shepherd's pipe, he said, "I must have the tiny piper, if I die for it!"

No sooner did Little Anklebone hear these words than he set off at a run, and the king after him. Never was there such a chase before or since, for Little Anklebone hid himself amid the thickest briars and thorns, and the king was so determined to have the tiny piper that he did not care for scratches. At last the king was success-ful, but no sooner did he take hold of Little Anklebone than the clouds above began to thunder and lighten horribly, and from below came the lowing of many does, and louder than all came the voice of the little piper himself singing these words—

> "O clouds! Why should you storm and flare?
> Poor Anklebone is forced to roam.
> O does! Why wait the milker's care?
> Poor Anklebone must leave his home."

And he sang so piercingly sweet that pity filled the king's heart, especially when he saw it was nothing but a bone after all. So he let it go again, and the little piper went back to his seat under the tree by the pond; and there he sits still, and plays his shepherd's pipe, while all the beasts of the forest, and birds of the air, and fishes of the pond, gather round and listen to his music. And sometimes, people wandering through the pathless plain hear the pipe, and then they say,

"That is Little Anklebone, who was eaten by a wolf ages ago!"

Fables From Aesop

Illustrations by RICHARD HEIGHWAY

THE MAN, THE BOY, AND THE DONKEY

A MAN and his son were once going with their Donkey to market. As they were walking along by its side a country-man passed them and said: "You fools, what is a Donkey for but to ride upon?"

So the Man put the Boy on the Donkey and they went on their way. But soon they passed a group of men, one of whom said: "See that lazy youngster, he lets his father walk while he rides."

So the Man ordered his Boy to get off, and got on himself. But they hadn't gone far when they passed two women, one of whom said to the other: "Shame on that lazy lout to let his poor little son trudge along."

Well, the Man didn't know what to do, but at last he took his

Boy up before him on the Donkey. By this time they had come to the town, and the passers-by began to jeer and point to them. The Man stopped and asked what they were scoffing at. The men said: "Aren't you ashamed of yourself for overloading that poor Donkey of yours—you and your hulking son?"

The Man and Boy got off and tried to think what to do. They thought and they thought, till at last they cut down a pole, tied the Donkey's feet to it, raised the pole and the Donkey to their shoulders. They went along amid the laughter of all who met them till they came to Market Bridge, when the Donkey, getting one of his feet loose, kicked out and caused the Boy to drop his end of the pole. In the struggle the Donkey fell over the bridge, and his forefeet being tied together he was drowned.

"That will teach.you," said an old man who had followed them:

"PLEASE ALL, AND YOU WILL PLEASE NONE."

THE DOG AND THE SHADOW

IT happened that a Dog had got a piece of meat and was carrying it home in his mouth to eat it in peace. Now on his way home he had to cross a plank lying across a running brook. As he crossed, he looked down and saw his own shadow reflected in the water beneath. Thinking it was another dog with another piece of meat, he made up his mind to have that also. So he made a snap at the shadow in the water, but as he opened his mouth the piece of meat fell out, dropped into the water and was never seen more.

"BEWARE LEST YOU LOSE THE SUBSTANCE
BY GRASPING AT THE SHADOW."

THE FOX AND THE STORK

AT one time the Fox and the Stork were on visiting terms and seemed very good friends. So the Fox invited the Stork to dinner, and for a joke put nothing before her but some soup in a very shallow dish. This the Fox could easily lap up, but the Stork could only wet the end of her long bill in it, and left the meal as hungry as when she began.

"I am sorry," said the Fox, "the soup is not to your liking."

"Pray do not apologize," said the Stork. "I hope you will return this visit, and come and dine with me soon."

So a day was appointed when the Fox should visit the Stork; but when they were seated at table all that was for their dinner was contained in a very long-necked jar with a narrow mouth, in which the Fox could not insert his snout, so all he could manage to do was to lick the outside of the jar.

"I will not apologize for the dinner," said the Stork:

"ONE BAD TURN DESERVES ANOTHER."

THE CROW AND THE PITCHER

A crow, half dead with thirst.

A CROW, half dead with thirst, came upon a Pitcher which had once been full of water; but when the Crow put its beak into the mouth of the Pitcher he found that only very little water was left in it, and that he could not reach far enough down to get at it.

He tried, and he tried, but at last had to give up in despair. Then a thought came to him, and he took a pebble and dropped it into the Pitcher. Then he took another pebble and dropped it into the Pitcher. Then he took another pebble and dropped that into the Pitcher. Then he took another pebble and dropped that into the Pitcher. Then he took another pebble and dropped that into the Pitcher. Then he took another pebble and dropped that into the Pitcher.

At last, at last, he saw the water mount up near him; and after casting in a few more pebbles he was able to quench his thirst and save his life.

"LITTLE BY LITTLE DOES THE TRICK."

THE FOX AND THE CAT

A FOX was boasting to a Cat of its clever devices for escaping its enemies. "I have a whole bag of tricks," he said, "which contains a hundred ways of escaping my enemies."

"I have only one," said the Cat; "but I can generally manage with that." Just at that moment they heard the cry of a pack of hounds coming toward them, and the Cat immediately scampered up a tree and hid herself in the boughs. "This is my plan," said the Cat. "What are you going to do?" The Fox thought first of one way, then of another, and while he was debating the hounds came nearer and nearer, and at last the Fox in his confusion was caught up by the hounds and soon killed by the huntsmen. Miss Puss, who had been looking on, said:

"BETTER ONE SAFE WAY THAN A HUNDRED ON WHICH YOU CANNOT RECKON."

THE LION AND THE MOUSE

ONCE when a Lion was asleep a little Mouse began running up and down upon him; this soon wakened the Lion, who placed his huge paw upon him, and opened his big jaws to swallow him. "Pardon, O King," cried the little Mouse; "forgive me this time, I shall never forget it: who knows but what I may be able to do you a turn some of these days?" The Lion was so tickled at the idea of the Mouse being able to help him, that he lifted up his paw and let him go. Some time after the Lion was caught in a trap, and the hunters, who desired to carry him alive to the King, tied him to a tree while they went in search of a wagon to carry him on. Just

then the little Mouse happened to pass by, and seeing the sad plight in which the Lion was, went up to him and soon gnawed away the ropes that bound the King of Beasts. "Was I not right?" said the little Mouse.

"LITTLE FRIENDS MAY PROVE GREAT FRIENDS."

THE FOX AND THE CROW

A FOX once saw a Crow fly off with a piece of cheese in its beak and settle on a branch of a tree. "That's for me, as I am a Fox," said Master Reynard, and he walked up to the foot of the tree. "Good day, Mistress Crow," he cried. "How well you are looking today; how glossy your feathers; how bright your eye. I feel sure your voice must surpass that of other birds, just as your figure does; let me hear but one song from you that I may greet you as the Queen of birds."

The Crow lifted up her head and began to caw her best, but the moment she opened her mouth the piece of cheese fell to the ground, only to be snapped up by Master Fox.

"That will do," said he. "That was all I wanted. In exchange for your cheese I will give you a piece of advice for the future—

'DO NOT TRUST FLATTERERS'."

THE COCK AND THE PEARL

A COCK was once strutting up and down the farmyard among the hens when suddenly he espied something shining amid the straw. "Ho! ho!" quoth he, "that's for me," and soon rooted it out from beneath the straw. What did it turn out to be but a Pearl that by some chance had been lost in the yard? "You may be a treasure," quoth Master Cock, "to men that prize you, but for me I would rather have a single barley corn than a peck of pearls."

"PRECIOUS THINGS ARE FOR THOSE THAT CAN PRIZE THEM."

THE FOX AND THE GRAPES

ON A HOT summer's day a Fox was strolling through an orchard till he came to a bunch of Grapes just ripening on a vine which had been trained over a lofty branch. "Just the thing to quench my thirst," quoth he. Drawing back a few paces, he took a run and a jump, and just missed the bunch. Turning round again with a One, Two, Three, he jumped up, but with no greater success. Again and again he tried after the tempting morsel, but at last had to give up, and walked away with his nose in the air, saying: "I am sure they are sour."

"IT IS EASY TO DESPISE WHAT YOU CANNOT GET."

HERCULES AND THE WAGONER

A WAGONER was once driving a heavy load along a very muddy way. At last he came to a part of the road where the wheels sank halfway into the mire, and the more the horses pulled, the deeper sank the wheels. So the Wagoner threw down his whip, and knelt down and prayed to Hercules the Strong. "O Hercules, help me in this my hour of distress," quoth he. But Hercules appeared to him, and said:

"Tut, man, don't sprawl there. Get up and put your shoulder to the wheel."

"THE GODS HELP THEM THAT HELP THEMSELVES."

THE DOG IN THE MANGER

A DOG looking out for its afternoon nap jumped into the Manger of an Ox and lay there cosily upon the straw. But

soon the Ox, returning from its afternoon work, came up to the Manger and wanted to eat some of the straw. The Dog in rage, being awakened from its slumber, stood up and barked at the Ox, and whenever it came near attempted to bite it. At last the Ox had to give up the hope of getting at the straw, and went away muttering:

"AH, PEOPLE OFTEN GRUDGE OTHERS WHAT THEY
CANNOT ENJOY THEMSELVES."

THE JAY AND THE PEACOCK

A JAY venturing into a yard where Peacocks used to walk, found there a number of feathers which had fallen from the Peacocks when they were moulting. He tied them all to his tail and strutted down toward the Peacocks. When he came near them they soon discovered the cheat, and striding up to him pecked at him and plucked away his borrowed plumes. So the Jay could do no better than go back to the other Jays, who had watched his behavior from a distance; but they were equally annoyed with him, and told him

"IT IS NOT ONLY FINE FEATHERS THAT MAKE FINE BIRDS."

THE WOLF AND THE LAMB

ONCE upon a time a Wolf was lapping at a spring on a hillside, when, looking up, what should he see but a Lamb just beginning to drink a little lower down. "There's my supper," thought he, "if only I can find some excuse to seize it." Then he called out to the Lamb. "How dare you muddle the water from which I am drinking?"

"Nay, master, nay," said Lambikin; "if the water be muddy up there, I cannot be the cause of it, for it runs down from you to me."

"Well, then," said the Wolf, "why did you call me bad names this time last year?"

"That cannot be," said the Lamb; "I am only six months old."

"I don't care," snarled the Wolf; "if it was not you it was your father"; and with that he rushed upon the poor little Lamb and—

WARRA WARRA WARRA WARRA WARRA—

ate her all up. But before she died she gasped out—

"ANY EXCUSE WILL SERVE A TYRANT."

————

THE WOODMAN AND THE SERPENT

ONE wintry day a Woodman was tramping home from his work when he saw something black lying on the snow. When he came closer, he saw it was a Serpent to all appearance dead. But he took it up and put it in his bosom to warm while he hurried home. As soon as he got indoors he put the Serpent down on the hearth before the fire. The children watched it and saw it slowly come to life again. Then one of them stooped down to stroke it, but the Serpent raised its head and put out its fangs and was about to sting the child to death. So the Woodman seized his ax, and with one stroke cut the Serpent in two. "Ah," said he,

"NO GRATITUDE FROM THE WICKED."

SOURCES OF STORIES IN VOLUME I

The Story of the Three Little Pigs: The Story of the Three Bears, from The Golden Goose Book, by L. Leslie Brooke, Frederick Warne & Company, Ltd.

The Old Woman and Her Pig: Tom Tit Tot: Mr. Miacca: Jack and the Beanstalk: Mr. Vinegar: Teeny-Tiny: The History of Tom Thumb: Cap o' Rushes: Molly Whuppie, from English Fairy Tales, by Joseph Jacobs. G. P. Putnam's Sons.

The Three Wishes: The King o' the Cats: The Hobyahs: Hereafterthis: The Black Bull of Norroway, from More English Fairy Tales, by Joseph Jacobs. G. P. Putnam's Sons.

The Field of Boliauns: Hudden and Dudden and Donald O'Neary: Andrew Coffey, from Celtic Fairy Tales, by Joseph Jacobs. G. P. Putnam's Sons.

Conal and Donal and Taig: The Old Hag's Long Leather Bag: Manis the Miller, from Donegal Fairy Stories, by Seumas MacManus. Doubleday, Doran & Company, Inc.

Billy Beg and the Bull, from In Chimney Corners, by Seumas MacManus. Doubleday, Doran & Company, Inc.

The Wolf and the Seven Little Goats: The Elves and the Shoemaker: Hansel and Grethel: The Frog Prince: Cat and Mouse in Partnership: The Golden Goose: Rapunzel: The Goose Girl: The Bremen Town Musicians: The Fisherman and His Wife, from Household Stories from Grimm, translated by Lucy Crane. The Macmillan Company.

Little One Eye, Little Two Eyes, Little Three Eyes: The Nose, from The Children's Book, by Horace E. Scudder. Houghton Mifflin Company.

Snow-White and Rose-Red, Junior Classics. P. F. Collier & Son Corporation.

The Golden Bird: The Princess Whom Nobody Could Silence: The Doll in the Grass: Gudbrand on the Hillside: The Squire's Bride, from Fairy Tales from the Far North, by P. C. Asbjörnsen. A. L. Burt Company, Inc.

The Cat on the Dovrefell: The Husband Who Was to Mind the House: Why The Bear is Stumpy-tailed: The Lad Who Went to the North Wind: Boots Who Made the Princess Say "That's a Story," from East o' the Sun and West o' the Moon, by Sir George W. Dasent. G. P. Putnam's Sons.

Little Red Riding-Hood, from The Children's Book, by Horace E. Scudder. Houghton Mifflin Company.

Puss in Boots: Cinderella: The Sleeping Beauty in the Wood: Beauty and the Beast, from The Fairy Book, by Dinah Maria Mulock Craik. The Macmillan Company.

Blue Beard, adapted from The Fairy Tales of Charles Perrault. George A. Harrap & Company, Ltd.

Budulinek: Zlatovlaska the Golden-haired, from The Shoemaker's Apron, by Parker Fillmore. Harcourt, Brace & Company.

357

Longshanks, Girth and Keen, from Czechoslovak Fairy Tales, by Parker Fillmore. Harcourt, Brace & Company, Inc.

The Bun: Mr. Samson Cat, from Picture Tales from the Russian, by Valery Carrick. Frederick A. Stokes Company.

The Little Humpbacked Horse: Wassilissa the Beautiful, from Russian Wonder Tales, by Post Wheeler. The Century Company.

Why the Fish Laughed: The Farmer and the Money Lender: The Ass in the Lion's Skin: The Gold-Giving Serpent, from Indian Fairy Tales, by Joseph Jacobs. G. P. Putnam's Sons.

The Lambikin: The Rat's Wedding: The Tiger, the Brahman, and the Jackal: Little Anklebone, from Tales of the Punjab, by Flora Annie Steel. The Macmillan Company.

Fables from Aesop, from The Fables of Aesop, edited by Joseph Jacobs. The Macmillan Company.